Men Wear Stilettos Better Part 3

Ruby's Story

P W Matthews

First Edition 2015

First Edition Ltd Cover 2020 Front cover:

Leland Bobbe @ Pintrest and Pixaby

Other books from the stiletto trilogy
Men Wear Stilettos Better – Part 1
Men Wear Stilettos Better – Part 2

'I am but a cocoon in this vessel I share,
and it is only when I transgend,
do I become the butterfly that I was meant to become.'

© P W Matthews 2012

Introduction

Ruby always knew that she was different, and not the boy she was supposed to be. Born Anthony Ruebens, she hated everything about her name to the body she occupied. She never shared the same feelings about being a boy, like her brother did, as she always felt she had the characteristics and personality of a girl and always felt trapped and confused in her body.

It was not until puberty began in her early teens that her problems really came into account. Ruby always wanted to be a girl and could not understand why she had the body of a boy, her complete opposite.

Later in life, she knew that being gay, straight or lesbian was always a choice; but feeling as she did about herself, she knew she never had a choice, because her birth genes had got everything wrong. She felt that she was trapped, and did not know where she could turn to, or ask for help without being judged as a freak, or attention seeker as people had declared her to be.

Ruby was everything female; and felt that she had been cheated on at birth; and could not do anything about it. She played alongside the idea of being gay, in her early life, as she did have a sexual attraction to men; however, looking in the mirror she never saw a man, she always saw a girl. She would try not to let anyone touch her, on that hidcous thing she had dangling between her legs, and often she contemplated in cutting it off, as maybe this would show people just how much she hated the body in which she possessed.

Ruby also had days of guilt where she would believe that she was a gay man, so partook in the guilt's of the flesh, to try and quench the ideals of becoming some part of a community that may indeed understand her.

It was not until many suicides attempts later, that her doctor finally listened to her; where he put her in touch with a psychiatrist who worked in this field. All those years of fighting against her identity, she now felt she had someone to listen to her.

Follow her story as she comes to terms with who she is, and how she becomes successful as a cabaret artiste, making friends along the way. How she began living her dream when she met her partner, and finally making her dream of transition reality.

Follow her story of sex, drag, and living life as a woman; in a world of bitchy gay men and drag queens. And now in this gay world, how she put her dream on hold, and started to live in her partner's world. But even this became too much for Ruby, as she had to be true to herself; and live her life as she had always dreamt of.

Follow her through her attempt to be accepted, not just by her family and friends; but by all who did not understand the world of transgender.

Ruby's Story

Just Look at the view I have, sand sea and a gorgeous house on the edge of town, with a husband who treats me as a wife should be treated. It has taken me a lifetime to get here, to get to this point in my life, but it was all worth it in the end, as I look back at the road I had taken, from that very first day I knew that I was different to any other boy.

I had a tough life growing up, but now I can proudly say, that my life has turned out just as I had hoped it would. I always felt that I belonged to the other sex, the other sex of that of my birth sex; and as long as I can remember, I always wanted to be a girl. I never liked what I saw in front of me, when standing in front of a mirror naked, that is why I never looked that often at myself naked. The male sex organs that I had, were so alien to me; and I often told myself, that they were disgusting deformities of being born onto the wrong body. I knew that for me, to be who I truly wanted to be, would mean that somewhere down the line of my adult life, surgery was going to be my only option.

I hated those first few months of sessions with the psychiatrist, as he really knew how to mess with my head, especially when he made reference to me being homosexual; and that I was dressing as a woman just as means to deny that I was really gay. When he mentioned, what would be the situation once corrective surgery had been performed; and that I no longer would represent a male, but now would represent that of a female, would this new woman still be homosexual?

I never ever classed myself as homosexual, a gay man, as I always classed myself as a woman; and in classing myself as such, I was therefore a heterosexual woman, who wanted a relationship with a man, because as a woman I had no sexual feelings towards another woman.

If reason and common sense were applied, then the respective patient should be treated as an individual and not a rubber stamp for medical assessments, as such wordings can be seen as confusing and degrading.

I strongly felt that such labels ignore the individual's persona sense of gender identity, taking precedence over biological sex, rather than the other way around.

If you are a male to female transsexual; and you have a relationship with a male, then you are labelled a gay man, seeking escape from stigma.

If you have a relationship with a woman, you are labelled a gay man who identifies himself as a lesbian.

I am neither. I am a woman born into the wrong body; and my sexuality has no reasoning or judgement for my gender or wanting to transition.

Then there were the people in my life, those who I thought made a difference and accepted me for who I really was.

In a strange way I missed Johnny's affection, because he too would have an issue with my identity. I tried living a gay life; and on a few occasions, letting him touch me in a way that gay men touch each other. However, this made me cringe; and it was not long after, that I put a stop to my genital area being touched; and gave him a chance to find a gay man, so that he could live his life as intended. In the end it was not meant to be, as he did not want another guy, and his loyalty to me was second to none, as he stayed by my side. I often felt guilty, because we never had anything sexual going on; and I think a lot of that was due to the fact he did not understand the ways, or the desires of a transsexual woman. He liked cock and tits; and would not entertain the fact that I was not a cock in a frock; and that someday that hideous male sex organ would go…

Sure, I lived the gay lifestyle, but it was not what I was comfortable with, as I was not being truthful to myself. I needed to be me; and if people think me cruel for my actions towards him, then that is their concern and not mine. For unless someone can walk in my shoes, their concerns will not interfere with my own beliefs; and then if they did, it would still not have any effect on how I lived my life.

And then there was Roxy, Well, let me tell you a few things about that queen. Poor poor Roxy, the queen who had it all and then lost it in the blink of an eye. Walking in the room, showing off her many diamonds; and revelling in her celebrity status, living a life of pretence, a life of a woman, when she was nothing more than a gay man in a dress. Staring down at you with unsympathetic views, as she argued about the equality of the LGBT community; and then runs and hides instead of facing the public to account for her actions, acting all innocent just to get another holiday till the dust settles.

As for her boy's, what's that all about? Swanning around playing the doting wife to her partner Danni; when truth be known she was getting laid by her so called boy's; and then hushing it up as though I did not know what she was up to. Oh yes, from the outside, she certainly put on her Aire's and graces, parading around like it was woah is me, yet underneath all that falseness she sold her wares like a common whore.

She never understood me, or even anyone else who was like me, battling with society as well as my own demons, as I continuously fought to be accepted for who I truly was. She never walked the road of a transsexual; and had no clue what we go through on a daily basis. She is nothing but a drama queen, a gay man, a dizzy bitch, a fuckin cock in a frock.

Roxy was each and every one of those characters, where I was true to myself, a transsexual, a woman trapped in the wrong body. I had one life and one aim in life; and I never had multiple characters, so she would never understand the road I walked.

So yes, I had it tough; but I can now live my life as I was intended too.

Where it all began

I was a very quiet child growing up, but I always knew
that I was different to all the other boys in the street.
I had two sisters and a younger brother, but as a child I
was much closer to my brother, as my sisters were much
older than I was and therefore were not around much.
We would very much do the brotherly things together,
and when I was going out with him to play, I often
looked upon him as being his sister, rather than his older
brother. Even at a very young age I was very girly, and
he was very my opposite of being the boisterous lad.
We would do the usual boyish things like climbing trees,
even though I was not much of a climber; and we would
put plastic spiders in my sister's bed; and my brother one
day decided to play a real naughty joke, as he changed
the sugar bowl for salt.
My god did we get into trouble from mother, as she had
one of her lady meetings going on at the time.
As I got a little older, I was caught trying on my sister's
clothes, much to my mother horror, as she went
absolutely mad at me.

*"Get out of those clothes now you filthy boy, I knew you
should have been born a girl. Never ever let me catch
you up here again, you bloody pervert."* She screamed,
as she hit me around the ear.

I took no notice of her, because whenever I was at home
alone, I would go into my sister's room and play with

her makeup and clothes, as I looked at myself in her bedroom mirror.

As I started comprehensive school, things were becoming very hard for me. I became the subject of bullying from boys who could not see past the feminine side of who I was, as well as have them call me names which at times was very harsh and hurtful.

I was bullied, because I would not take part in the roughness of their boyish games; and the pranks they played on girls whenever they felt fit, as well as singling out specific people they thought were weaker than they were; and to coin a phrase, 'to beat the crap out of them'. This went on for a considerable amount of time, which made me go into my shell most times I was at school, and if I saw them coming, I tried desperately to hide from them to avoid contact.

I was about fourteen years old when I was befriended by this other boy at school, who came and stopped what could have been the worst beating up that I could have ever imagined, as he came to my rescue.

He stopped this group of boys beating me up, as I often was the first who came to be the centre of the school bullies' fist… boys as well as girls sometimes.

I did not really have many friends at school, except for some of the girls who lived in my street. These girls I kept as my real friends; and stayed in their company as long as I could, avoiding these boys as much as possible. So, it was a complete shock to me, that whilst it seemed as though I was going to get a beating, this lad who was much taller than I was, pulled the boys off me.

"Fuckin leave him alone you bastards, does it take all of you to fight?" He said, as he pulled one lad off me by the scruff of his neck.

Then the ringleader looked up, and as he stared at him, he said.

"Oh, don't worry, its Felicia the faggot, do you want a bit of this too?" as he raised his fist to him.
"If you think you are man enough to do it, you fuckin retard." He replied, as he lunged at the ringleader
"Oh suck my fuckin dick, you queer." The ringleader said, now placing his hand over his groin.
"Don't make me laugh, you pathetic fucker. I would need a dick to suck; and I have seen you in the shower. You are no bigger than my little finger, and an excuse of a boy. My baby brother has a bigger dick than you do, and he is only five." He said, now making fun of him as he placed his little finger in the air and waved it about.

Just then the one who was beating me up went to go for Felicia, so he got him by the neck and with his other fist knocked him to the ground.

"Now fuck off you retarded wanker, if you mess with him again you mess with me; and that goes for you and all your fucking dimwits." He said, as he held the boy down, still with his fist in his face.

They scarpered, as the main boy ended up with a bloody nose that was oozing over his shirt. He then came up to me and introduced himself.

"Hi, my name is Michal, but everyone calls me Felicia as you have just heard. What's your name?"

"Hi, my name is Tony Rueben's, and why do they call you Felicia?" I replied, as we shook hands.

"I got the name from a bully I beat up a few years ago, as I could not stand it anymore; and as it seemed I was beginning to grow and tower over him, my hormones were all over the place and I had a burst of extra testosterone dearie. He never came near me again bless him, especially after I told his gang we had been boyfriends for the past few years; and then told them all about the size of his dick and of course the little birthmark on his ass, which he gave up to me on many occasions. Words are mightier than the fist at times Tony, especially if you back it up with the truth. And by the way, my last name is Feliciano, half Italian and half English; and I quite liked the name, as it kind of stuck. Besides being a girly-queen, you need a camp girly name." Felicia said, as she began to smile at me.

"So how did these boys get to know that you were gay? And is it right what that other boy said about you; you know about sucking his dick? Was he your boyfriend?" I replied, forgetting what Felicia had said, as I was caught up in the moment.

"No, he was not my boyfriend, that was the guy who has since left school. He was older than I was, but I kinda grew up quicker than he did. This was all new, but by now my reputation proceeded me. I sort of had an encounter one day behind the bike shed as I was sucking this guy's dick, he later on began to badger me all the time; and then began to bully me, because I would not suck his dick when he wanted me too. It was then after a

12

long time of being bullied, that I had had enough again of guys who want you to suck them off, then call you all the names they can, when it was them who started it all in the first place. So, I hit out and busted his nose, not before telling his gang I sucked his dick more than once; and even fucked him. They never bothered me again, but the name Felicia kind of stuck. The guy who was having a go, was one of the younger gang members now the leader; and as for his dick... HELL YES, I had seen it; and he aint got much. I don't think they will be bothering you again Tony." He said, as he asked me to follow him to the top playing field past the playground.

"*Thanks Michal, I thought I was going to go home black and blue today.*" I replied, thankful that he came to my rescue.

"*Please love, call me Felicia, after all I am more used to that now.*" He told me.

We ended up chatting on the playing fields, and he asked me to tell him more about myself. I started off slowly by saying I thought I was different to other boys; and although I have girlfriends at school, I was not interested in them sexually. He suggested to me that maybe I was gay, after all there was nothing wrong in wanting a bit of cock, whether gay or straight. That at the end of the day, cock is cock, and if you like it, then what's the problem? I told him that I was not sure, that I had not had any, and that I thought it was much more than that, in which I did not know how to explain, pondering over what he had just told me. It was then we spoke a little longer, and then the bell sounded for end of dinner time.

"Do you fancy playing hooky?" Felicia said, as we got up off the grass.

"Hooky!" I replied.

"Yeah, you fancy skipping school and going for a walk? I do it all the time, and it beats just sitting in boring lessons looking into space." He replied.

"I have never done it before Felicia, but sure I am up for it." I replied, now with my heart racing.

We walked around the edge of the playing field until we were sheltered by the bushes and the bike shed, where we then made our way out of the far gates into a small lane that headed to the woods. We quickly ran into the woods and found a quiet spot near the disused railway line, where we sat down and again chatted.

The more we spoke to each other, the more I felt comfortable with Felicia; and I ended up telling him about how I felt.

I told him about the time I dressed as a girl; and how I had always longed to be a girl instead of a boy; and how comfortable and free I felt when I had my sister's clothes on. I also told him how I hated being Tony; and how I felt trapped inside this body I had. He then came back to me and told me that he had dressed too, but not so much like a girl but more outrageous than that.

"I have a good friend who is a drag queen; and I was so lucky to find her, because it was her who taught me how to do makeup. I am too young to go to the bars, but every now and then she lets me in when she knows it is going to be a little quiet; and she refers to me as her little brother. I often go around her house and we have a

*natter, and just chat. She is such a lovely guy, and I
know that it will be something I will end up doing as I
get older; maybe even have my own club one day.*"
Felicia said, which got me so intrigued.
"*Wow Felicia, that sounds great, and why do you refer
to him as a she?*" I asked.
"*It's just a gay code love, drag queens are called dear,
or love, but are mainly referred to as she; and by the
way please never refer to me as my male name and never
ever call me he or him.*" She said, as she explained in
full.
"*Ok Felicia, so if I call you she… that is ok?*" I replied.
"*Yes love, that is perfect. And whilst we are on the
subject,t we need to get you a name.*" She replied.

We sat there and we were going through all the names
connected with Tony, and then names I may look like,
even to the silliest things like my mother and sister's
name.

"*I know how about Ruby, as a shorter version of your
surname.*" She suggested, as I pondered over the name.
"*I think that is a great idea, and I think it will make me
passionate about my chosen road.*" I replied, rather
excited that I had someone who would listen; and
someone who was now helping me.
"*Brilliant, Ruby Passion it is. See two heads are just as
good as one. Well Ruby today you are reborn, and you
have your female name which will be with you for your
life as a girl.*" She said, as she looked as proud as punch.
I did tell Felicia, that whilst at school I did not want to be
called Ruby, at least not whilst others could hear.

I had no problem with it when we were alone, but I was still slightly scared. We spent many days bunking off school and going into those woods to chat, to see how I were getting on, as we chatted and chatted until it was time to go back home.

Felicia invited me to come and visit her friend Kitty, who would also teach me makeup and how to style myself clothes wise. I was over the moon; and thought that my long desire of being a girl was finally coming true, which gave me butterflies, as I was excited about the whole idea.

As we sat there on the grass, Felicia got up to take a pee, and she did not just take her cock out of her trousers, she dropped them to the floor revealing her ass. Startled, yet excited about seeing a man's cock for the first time, other than my own, which I never described it as such, Felicia asked me if I had ever sucked a guy's dick before, as she looked behind her and peed over the grass. I was gobsmacked at what she had said, as I told her right away that I had never seen a guy's dick, let alone sucked one, now feeling rather nervously at her remark. She then asked me if I would like to try; and get it over and done with, because that way it would see if I liked it or not, as she gave me a glimpse of her dick. Still shocked but yet feeling strange inside, I hummed and erred, as I told her I did not know, as I shook a little.

After a little bit more of a debate, I plucked up the courage to try, as she ordered me to get on my knees; and as I did, she turned around and placed her cock in my mouth. She told me what to do with it, and how I should suck it; and it was not long before I got the hang of it, and found she was very pleased.

"*I bet you have been dying to do that for ages love, there is nothing better than a guy or girly guy sucking a man's dick Ruby. Girls are rubbish at it, and I believe men know how to do it better.*" She said, as she waved her dick at me, gyrating and thrusting her hips.

"*I have wanted to try but have been too nervous, as I have never had any idea of who to ask or indeed where to go.*" I replied, still feeling excited and nervous.

"*Well until you find yourself a man there is nothing wrong in you sucking my dick love, maybe even try other things later if you wish.*" She said, now with a sparkle in her eye

"*Other things, like what Felicia?*" I asked.

Just then Felicia took off her shirt to reveal her nice slim tender chest, with just a bit of red hair starting to come through it. She already had the soft hair around her dick, which was not bushy as she said she trimmed that area all the time, as it was much nicer. She then stepped out of her trousers until she was completely naked; and did not flinch as she stood before me. I could see now that she was not a small guy, as she was very thick and about seven or eight inches; and as it was a very hot day, the sun shone on her, as she looked like Adonis, or in her case Aphrodite.

She then asked me to take off my clothes, as she wanted to see the wonders that lay behind my school uniform, as she kicked hers out of the way. I was scared at first, as I hated my body; and things were now beginning to change, change in a way that I hated my body even more. Again, she asked me to get naked, as she told me not to be shy or nervous. I did as she asked, and before long we

were both stark naked on the grass, near the woods and disused railway tracks and sidings.
Felicia then looked at me and just said.

"Oh, a late developer, you are just starting puberty love. It will not be long before you fully develop."

It was true, I had only just started to change. I had a small amount of pubic hair growing; and my dick was no longer tiny, as now it had filled out and grew quite a bit. I still never liked it, and it seemed to have a life of its own as it got hard for no apparent reason. Felicia asked me if I wanted her to suck my cock, as I did hers; but I was so very confused. She had begun to put things into my head over the last few months, and I did not know if I was a gay man, a drag queen, or what the hell I was. She then looked at me and told me to relax as she then started to suck my cock. I thought I was going to shoot my load there and then, as it was so intense, as I began to have a very strange feeling ripple through my loins. I did not know if I liked it or hated it, as I did have a thing about not liking my cock at all; and would have much preferred to have had a vagina, however, the feeling I had was both intense and sexual as the feeling began to blow my mind. It was not long before I felt my body shaking; and then I could not control myself as I shot my load. Felicia did not mind at all as she took me down her throat and swallowed all I had, holding onto me so she did not spill a drop. I apologised to her for shooting so quick, and that she had to stop as I was now feeling very sensitive down there. She told me not to apologise, as cumming early was just a natural thing; and it could have been the fact that it was just my nerves, what with it being my first time. Then telling me on her first time, she shot her load in less than two minutes, but now can control those urges. She then asked me if I would like to try something else; and that she promised to be nice and gentle, as she now stood up leaving me to wipe the last drops of my juices on my hand. I asked her what she had in mind, because surely there was nothing else to do. She then asked me if I trusted her. Well, the answer to that was definitely yes, as over the months we had got so close, that I trusted her with my own life. Felicia was not one to show malice, but instead looked after her friends. I told her that I trusted her, then asking her why she asked such a question. She picked up her socks; and told me to leave everything else on the grass. Then she took me into a shady area and bent me over this thick tree branch, tying my hands so I could not move. It was not that I was scared as I knew she would not harm me; it was more that I was concerned about people passing by and seeing us, even though I knew this was an area that hardly had people passing by. Felicia saw this concern on my face and soon told me, that no one ever walked this side of the woods anymore; as she had been coming here for years; and thinks she saw one person walk their dog, but they were the other side of the railway, but the woods obscured their view. She then asked me to open my legs, which I did without question, when I then felt a sharp stabbing pain by my ass.

"Jesus fucking Christ Felicia, what on earth is that?" I asked, now looking behind me at her.

19

"*Just relax love, I will not hurt you. I will be gentle and ease myself into you. If it is too painful let me know and I will stop.*" She said, feeling her dick inside me.

I felt every inch of her go inside me; and yes, it did hurt but strangely, I was also enjoying it. I felt her withdraw her cock and then heard her spit on it as she thrust it back inside me. Eventually I took all of Felicia's cock as she penetrated me harder and harder, her breathing getting heavier and heavier as she held onto my waist, thrusting herself deeper into me. I felt her tight grip, as she could thrust no more, but screamed as she shot her load deep inside my ass as she thrust so hard, I thought the branch was going to break underneath me. Holding me there for a second as she just kissed me on the back of the neck as one last thrust made me shoot my load again. She then untied me, and we lay on the grass holding each other, as she thanked me and told me that I had a lovely cock; and a lovely tight ass.

We would spend many a day in our favourite place, as she taught me other things to do sexually, all the time wishing that I could be made love to like a woman.

I learnt how to suck a dick properly; and I was taught how to swallow without it making me gag, God, she even taught me how to rim a guy's ass. As I didn't like to fuck with my dick, because of believing that I was a woman trapped in this body, she told me that I did not have to penetrate a guy. That there were other things you could do without penetration, and there were even roles that one could adapt as in being dominant or passive. Over yet more time with Felicia, she eventually introduced me to a strap on dildo, and told me as I did not like to use my dick, I could put this on and fuck a guy with it. She even let me rim her and fuck her with the strap on; and as I had already swallowed her juice.

"Although you don't fuck anyone at the moment love, you should try. Make the most of what you have got while you have it." She said, again making me question myself.

"I am not sure Felicia; I find my dick hideous and it doesn't feel right on my body. I have so longed for a flat panty line instead of a bulge." I replied, confirming my belief in what I wanted for myself.

"You need to make the most of what you have Ruby, try a little bit at a time, and if you want to, you can try on me. I would let you fuck me first to see how you feel if you wanted too; and then if you really do not like it then you are going to have to use the strap on. You will get some guys whether gay or straight, who love girly cock; and not just sucking it but being fucked by a girly boy too. Trust me; try all of your options first Ruby before you finally say no." She said, as she placed her hand on my cock and kissed me on the lips

"I will try Felicia, but at the moment I am so fuckin confused. This thing sticks up whenever it feels like it and I cannot control it. My head tells me one thing; and my heart tells me another Felicia. So, if I do contemplate on trying to fuck a guy with my cock, did you really mean it when you said I could fuck your ass?" I replied, babbling with no proper reason.

"You sure can Ruby, and you are going to I can promise you that." She said with a big grin.

My head was buzzing, as not only had I just had my first encounter with Felicia penetrating me, I actually began enjoying it, and could not wait to try it again. As she entered me, I did not feel like Tony, but felt every bit like Ruby, even though it hurt like crazy, but I did enjoy everything I had taken. I even enjoyed being tied up, although I would not want it to be like that every time.

I eventually visited Kitty with Felicia and I was allowed to play with makeup and at dress up, which I was in my element with all her gowns and jewellery.

As I got to my late teens and about ready to leave school, I visited Kitty and Felicia all the time, spending weekends with them. Kitty often let me dress up when I wanted as she saw me progress from a very pretty boy to a simply gorgeous drag queen… in her words.

I was fifteen when I went to my first gay bar; and as I was with Kitty no one asked any questions, as she had already told them I was her seamstress.

Kitty owned a little back street gay bar called Kit Kat Lounge; and she was known to many as Madam Kitty, inside the club as well as with business like gentlemen. She had lots of drag acts performing throughout the week, in which I was introduced to most of them, as well as having a few guys after me.

This was still pretty new to me; and having a guy actually like me as Ruby and not as my male self was amazing. I was getting to understand and feel better with whom I was becoming, as I still had crap days where I questioned myself, which often put me into a downward depressive slump.

I was easily influenced by the likes of Felicia and Kitty, as well as fight my own feelings about who I really am, however, I was beginning to feel comfortable in a strange way to the new world I had been introduced too. Because of my age, Kitty would not allow me to have any contact sexually with her clients; and I did understand as she could have easily lost her bar licence, but I thought if only she knew what Felicia and I had been up to; it would surprise her. She did though say what I did outside of her club was up to me, but whilst I was there, I had to abide by strict orders, but this still did not stop some of the men grabbing hold of me; and sliding their hands up my skirt when we were out of sight in a dark corner somewhere. The number of times I was asked to give them a blowjob, as they got their dicks out and you had to feel because of the subtle lighting. You were ok if you were in the cabaret room, but as soon as you wandered through the corridors, it soon began to get a bit darker in certain rooms, but I had to grin and bare it, as I helped by collecting glasses and cleaning the tables.

There was one section of the club I was not allowed in; and this was heavily guarded by doormen. I was later told by Felicia, that it was the knocking shop side of the club, where Kitty's clients would be entertained by her girly boys for sexual favours; and it was heavily guarded because of the high profile of her guests, being that of Judges, MP's and even Royalty at some point or other. Felicia did make me laugh, but she told it as it was and did not paint it up fancy. She told me because she knew I could keep a secret; and she knew in time Kitty would trust me enough to take extra work by cleaning the bedrooms, as apparently Kitty had taken a shine to me.

My father was very high up in the world of employment, as he was a barrister. A few times a week he would have his work colleagues come to the house to see him; and often I was there when father let them in. I am not sure if they knew that I was different from other boy's, but they did seem to visit when I was home alone; and they seemed to time it very well.

Mother worked in government and I hardly saw her; and my sisters were now married and had left home.

My younger brother was still at school; and never bunked off like I did, which gave me time to dress at home and be myself without interruption. I had collected a few clothes from Kitty and Felicia, where I kept them safe and sound in a box in my bedroom, with my shoes and makeup, which mother never ever did find.

This one day the doorbell rang, it was Mr Bellows.

I always called him Mr Bellows, as that is how I knew him, however, he was in fact a Judge and father's very best friend. As I opened the door, I was a little taken back, as he seen me with my make up on and a dressing gown wrapped around me. He just looked at me with his mouth open; and I do not know who was more shocked, him or me.

"Close your mouth dear, before your tongue rolls over the carpet. Would you like to come in Mr Bellows?" I asked.

"Yes, Tony that would be really nice of you Thank you very much. Is your father home Tony?" He asked me, now walking into the hallway.

"No Mr Bellows, he is at the office, would you like me to give him a call? Can I get you a cup of tea or something?" I said to him.

"Or something would be nice, forget the tea; and no, I will phone your father later." He replied with a strange grin on his face.

"Mr Bellows, what do you mean?" I asked, being a little naive about what he had said.

He then tapped me on the ass and told me to get dressed; and that he would make a cup of tea, knowing that I was in the house all alone. I do not know what made me do the next thing, because I just thought whilst I was still in make-up I may as well go all the way. As I got upstairs, I quickly put on my stockings, and I had been given a vintage corset from Kitty so put that on and attached the suspenders. Just as I was putting on my pencil dress and making sure I was as perfect as I could possibly be, I heard Mr Bellows at the bottom of the stairs calling to me.

"Tony, are you sure your parents will not be home."

I finished making alterations to my appearance; and as I got to the top of the stairs, I looked at him and said.

"Mr Bellows you are a naughty boy my name is Ruby, never ever forget that. And both mother and father will be out for the day, so please do not worry."
"Yes, Miss Ruby, I do apologise for getting your name wrong. Maybe one should have asked first, before

assuming you would not have changed it." He replied, now quite apologetic.

"*Yes, one should have asked first, it is after all polite to ask a lady's name, but not polite to ask her age.*" I said, with a cheeky grin

"*Yes, Miss Ruby you are correct, I assure you that it will never happen again.*" He replied, as he knew that I was totally in control.

"*Right off with you to the lounge, as I need to finish getting ready; and take my cup of tea into the lounge with you please Mr Bellows.*" I told him.

"*Yes, Miss Ruby.*" He replied.

I then made my way back into the bedroom to finish off, by just putting on another pair of shoes. They were a little higher, than the ones he had seen me in; and they also made me a little taller. I then just brushed my hair and sprayed it lightly, as I was now ready to make my first entrance to someone other than Felicia and Kitty. I was very scared because I thought what if he told my father, then again, he should have known better not to come in here as I am only fifteen years old. I made my way into the lounge, and as I went to sit down, he actually stood up until I was seated, which I knew was because of his generation, as they were so well mannered people and did things properly. For a judge he was very young, I think he was about the same age as my father which was thirty five.

"*You look simply divine Miss Ruby, so much like your mother.*" He said, as he waited for me to sit down.

26

"*Thank you Mr Bellows, I will take that as a compliment.*" I replied, now feeling good about myself.
"*Oh, please Miss Ruby, call me David.*" He said, now asking to drop all formalities.
"*Do you think I should, after all this is the first meet you will have had with Ruby, is that not a bit too informal at this moment in time?*" I replied.
"*I insist Miss Ruby, one as pretty as you cannot keep calling me Mr Bellows. Besides you are not the other person I knew, you are someone else now.*" He said, which a cheeky grin.
"*In that case Mr Bellows I will call you David, but I am still Miss Ruby.*" I replied.
"*Yes Miss Ruby.*" He answered.

We sat there for a while drinking tea; and chatting to one another very formal and proper from such a dignitary. Each time we looked at each other, I would go a little red and then drop my head. It was then I noticed he had something stirring in his trousers; and thinking to myself I have got to do this; I then placed my hand on his knee. Well, Christ did he make me jump. I thought he was going to have a heart attack, as he took a deep intake of breath, nearly spilled his mug of tea, when he then looked at me he said.

"*Oh my lord, I did not expect that.*"
"*I am so sorry David; would you prefer me to take my hand away?*" I replied, thinking I had fucked things up; and got the wrong signals from him.

"Not in the least my pretty thing, but you took me by surprise and I nearly shot my load." He said, as he calmed me down.

"MR BELLOWS! How rude of you." I said, rather sharply with a lustful look.

*"I a*m so sorry Miss Ruby; I really am not used to all of this." He replied

"Then I think we must get you used to it, had we not David?" I told him.

"Oh yes please Miss Ruby, I must get used to having a young lady be flirty towards me." He answered.

I stood up and looked at him, when I ordered him to stand up. I then told him that he was going to kiss me, and then he was going to hold me in his arms.

He did just that, kissing me softly on the neck as he then moved his lips to my mouth, holding me close to him as I felt his hard bulge press against my tummy.

He was a very tall man standing at around six foot two with dark hair and cleanly shaved; and he was quite muscular but not athletic in build, however he was all man and stood tall against me, even in my stiletto's.

I then started to undo his shirt to find a mass of thick black hair, in which I just stroked as he gazed into my eyes that were trying to seduce him.

After removing his shirt, I slowly undone his belt and unzipped his trousers, dropping them to the floor for him to step out of them. Being orderly and proper, I picked them up and laid them over the chair, as I then ordered him to step out of his trousers, as I caught a glimpse of the mass of hair he had. His thick chest hair thinned out as it went down his tummy; and he had that distinctive black line going from his tummy all the way down inside his briefs towards his manhood, which I had seen so many times in the magazines that Kitty and Felicia had. I could see now that he had a rather large bulge, so I once again pressed my body into his, as I placed my hand over the swelling in his briefs. He then unzipped my dress and let it drop to the floor, revealing my corset and stockings.

"Oh my goodness Miss Ruby, you look so ravishingly beautiful." He said, as he savoured every minute looking at me.
"Thank you David, you are very much a handsome man yourself." I replied.

I placed my hand inside his briefs, where I felt his wet sticky thick cock, so I began gently playing with the tip of his cock between my fingers, as I got my other hand inside his briefs around the back playing with his ass. He then placed his hands in the back of my panties; and started to finger my ass crease. He did attempt to touch me around the front, but I soon told him that it was out of bounds; and he respected this and just caressed and fingered my hole. Shortly afterwards I removed his briefs and got on my knees, where I looked him in the eye and told him I am going to take him in my mouth. I looked at his cock and it was not massive, it was around six inches but very thick, with once again a mass of beautiful black hair. I slowly licked the tip of his cock sending him into convulsions of pleasure, as my tongue slid over his slit, and around the head and then my mouth encased his thick wet cock; firmly taking him all the way in my hot warm mouth.

Before long I felt him holding onto my head as he started to push his cock further into my mouth, as he started to moan with intense pleasure.

I on the other hand, was only semi hard, as even with Felicia I rarely got a full erection; and I was slightly nervous as he was my dad's best friend. However, I was very wet myself and dripping, so I started to wipe the moistness onto my fingers and spread it around my ass. I then sat David on the couch where he looked up at me like a little boy spoilt, as I then straddled him. He placed his hands on my little boobs as he waited for what was in store, as he savoured every moment that I took hold of him. I got my hand behind me as I gently positioned his cock into place, with it now touching my hole ready for him to take me.

"Now gentle David, take me very slowly and be very gentle with me." I told him.
"Yes, Miss Ruby, I promise." He replied.

It took a bit of persuasion at first because his cock was so thick, but once I got the tip of him inside me, the rest of him followed. It also helped that he was oozing precum, which as he withdrew, lubed my ass and made it easier for him to penetrate me. I was now riding him hard and fast, as I felt his breathing becoming heavier and heavier with the indulgence of his desires towards me. Just then he must have hit my g-spot, as all of a sudden I shot all over his tummy, as my girly cock had slipped out of the corner of my panties. This really turned him on and as he was rubbing my juices into his tummy with his fingers, as he then told me that he too was ready to shoot.

"That's a good boy, fuck that virgin ass David; now take your Miss Ruby." I told him, as I felt him penetrate my tight ass.
"Oh goodness yes Miss Ruby, I am afraid I am going to shoot my load real soon." He replied.

He held onto my waist as he thrust deeper inside me, so I just grabbed hold of his nipples and gently squeezed them. That did it, because he fucked me faster as he enjoyed me tweaking his nipples; and then he just thrust a few more times until he began emptying himself inside my ass. He then held me so gentle as he told me that what we just did was absolutely wonderful; and that he had not had sex like this that in a good ten years or more, now regaining normality to his breathing. I then suggested to him, that I thought we should do something about it, then asking for his approval. Well, he jumped at the offer, now looking at me like a boy who had just been given a new toy. He told me that he would like that very much indeed, then calling me a very sexy young lady. One in which, he cannot wait to pursue further liaisons, even though he knew I was underage, but to be frank, I could not give a fuck. He was a lovely man; and he knew how to make love to you.
I waited for his cock to go soft before getting off him; and then kissed him again on the lips. It was then that I told him he had best go upstairs to the bathroom to remove all the lipstick that had got onto his face, as I knew he had to go back to work. He picked up his

clothes and made his way upstairs to the bathroom, as I got myself dressed again and powdered my face and applied more lipstick as I did not want to look like a clown. Once David came back downstairs, he told me that he had best go, otherwise he would surely be missed; and he did not know of an excuse he could give as his thoughts would most definitely still be on me.

He had since gotten dressed; and I was so sad to see that horny man cover up such a lovely body. I did not want him to go as I really had enjoyed myself; and this was my first bit of intimacy since Felicia, plus he was a family friend and I had always had a crush on him from such an early age.

"I would like to see you again Miss Ruby, if that would be to your liking?" He said, as he placed his hands onto my shoulders and looked me in the eyes.

"Yes, sure I would like that too David. I am free most afternoons, as I am afraid I do skip lessons." I replied, now looking at him like a naughty schoolgirl.

"Naughty girl, but how about we say Thursday, as it is only three days away? And Miss Ruby, do you think you would like to take my virgin ass one day?" He asked.

"Not with this hideous thing I have between my legs no, I cannot ever think I will get used to it." I replied

"Then do not worry about that, I may have something for you to try if you wanted to, as I would love you to take me next time Miss Ruby, take my virgin ass and use me as you see fit. It all takes time, and we need to feel comfortable and confident when doing something we have not really done before. My first experience with a guy was very nerve wracking, so much so that I shot my

load in just under a minute because it was so intense and scary. Then when he asked me to fuck him, I simply could not get it fully hard. It took a lot of patience, and a lot of trying so I can wait for the real thing." He said, as I felt he needed to explain to make me feel better. "*Then if you want me to take your ass, you buy the things for me to do it. But you are not getting this hideous dick up your ass David, not yet anyway.*" I replied, now thinking about what Felicia had told me.

He then looked at me, and still holding onto my shoulders, he asked me how much I owed him. That threw me off my game, because I had no idea what he was on about. I just explained to him that I did not know, because I had never been given anything before, as he was my first, then telling him that if I took money, I thought that it would make me a prostitute. Being very understanding, he was so sweet as he told me that it did not apply to such indeed. That I was a different sort of girl; and a very classy one at that, then asking me again how much he owed me. Then I had a great idea, as I told him not to let any money pass between our hands, as I did have morals. That in the hallway, there was a wooden box, my box that I put trinkets in from time to time. That he could put something in there, which would be a nice surprise for me later. He agreed, then asking if we should meet on the Thursday? I told him that we could meet, but now he must go before he gets me into trouble. Then telling him not to let my father know I was at home as I put my finger to my lips

"Oh and Miss Ruby, if you are interested I do know a few more people who would be interested in spending some time with you." He replied.
"It sounds so much fun, let's see how we get on then David." I replied, excited but scared at what he had just said.
"I will put something in the girly fund, as that way it sounds better." He said, smiling at me and then giving me a kiss on my cheek.
"Thank you David." I replied, now wanting him to leave, as I needed to get changed.

He kissed me again, but this time on the neck; and told me that he wished he could stay a little longer, when he then put something in my jewellery box; and then looked around towards me and blew me a kiss.
He then shut the door behind him.
For a moment I just stood there in amazement, that I had just had sex with my dad's best friend. I was fifteen years old and just had my first paid encounter, which made me feel a little dirty. I firstly thought of it as having a bit of sexual fun; and they just helped me with my girly fund, as that way I handled it much better.
I did wonder how much he had put into the jewellery box mind you, as I was still buzzing but still very scared. I was nervous to look, but also now very excited, so as I opened my jewellery box, he had put in forty pounds, which I could just not believe. I was lucky to get one pound for pocket money; and here I am with four ten pound notes; and I had never seen so much money in my life, let alone have it all to myself.

Father always believed we should save; and I did have a bank account with the TSB, so I thought on Friday I will skip the afternoon from school and bank it, as I knew my parents never ever looked at my bank book. I then made my way back upstairs and took the money to put into my bank book, as I then got out of my makeup and clothes and dressed again as Tony.

My ass was still slightly sore from being fucked raw; and I thought I had best get some cream for the next time we should both meet up. As I sat on the bed, I just couldn't believe what I had done; and I so wanted to tell everyone. I thought I had best tell Felicia first as she was my best friend, but she will have to wait until Saturday when I see her again. I then had thoughts about David coming over on Thursday; and I got quite excited again as I wondered what would be in store for me.

Finally, Thursday had arrived, and at around 11am the doorbell rang. Upon opening the door, I was this time dressed en-femme and saw David was standing there will his briefcase.

"Good morning Miss Ruby, may I please come in?" He asked, very much like the city gentleman with all the proper mannerisms that came with it.
"Yes, you may David; please go straight into the lounge for me." I replied.

He came inside as I closed the door behind him; and made his way down the hall to the lounge. He was just standing there waiting for me, when I was beginning to wonder what he was up to.

35

"*What on earth are you doing David? Why are you still standing up?*" I asked, with a puzzled look, which must have shown my inexperience in such matters.
"*Because Miss Ruby, you only ordered me to make my way into the lounge. I am your obedient servant; and will only do as you command me to do.*" He replied, standing there ready for my next order, like that of an army drill sergeant.

Well, this was new to me as I had no fuckin clue what he was on about, or indeed what I should say to him.
I could only think of the times my mother ordered me about; and thought that I would have to improvise.
After all I couldn't really ask him to do the dishes, or make the beds could I? I then told him that in future when he arrived here, he would give me a kiss on the cheek and then make his way to the room I had instructed him to go into. There he would strip for me until he was left just in his briefs, or something tighter, as I hated men in loose underwear because it reminded me of my father, as many times I had to iron his boxers when I helped mother out. He agreed with this, and as I was standing next to him, I just asked him to strip.
Once he was standing in front of me naked, I began to inspect him. I remember having to do this at school, as we were often inspected to make sure we were in the correct uniform, however, we were not naked thank goodness; and I thought it was a good place to start.
I thought about tying him up, just like Felicia did to me that day I had my first encounter with her, so, looking at his bag I asked him what was in it. He explained that there were a few items in the bag, in which he thought

36

would have been of interest; and should I see fit, then I could use them on him. I then opened his briefcase, and apart from a little bit of paperwork, he had a carrier bag with some rather strange things inside.

"If Miss Ruby cares to open the bag, I think she will be surprised at her servant. You may use them on me at your own leisure Miss Ruby." He said, with a very childish smile, which did nothing for me, because you are either a child or an adult I thought.

"How dare you tell me what I can and cannot use on you David, you are mine to do with as I wish." I said sternly.
*"Yes, Miss Ruby, Sorry Miss R*uby." He replied, now with his head facing the floor
"Now get on your hands and knees David, I am not having you order me about." I told him.
"Yes, Miss Ruby, sorry Miss Ruby." He again replied.

David then got onto all fours, as I looked inside the carrier bag. Inside the bag were a few dildos' and a vibrator, plus a strap on and a leather horse riding crop. I got hold of the crop and brought it down onto his ass, which made quite a mark. This was not really to my liking as I found it a little too severe, so as I looked at his trousers and noticed he had a leather belt, so I removed his belt and folded it in half. I then began to spank his ass with the belt, but not that hard as I was just getting used to the idea; and I did not want to mark him.
Each time I spanked him he would flinch; and I think moan in pleasure. I spanked him a few times leaving a nice red patch on both of his cheeks; and after each

spanking I would gently rub his ass to sooth him.
Having now emptied the carrier bag onto the couch, I
asked him what the small clamps were, to which he told
me they were nipple clamps. Dropping my guard, I
asked him how to use them, in which knowing I was
nervous, he asked my permission to show me what to do.
I agreed with this, as I knew I was still learning.
Once he had placed them on his nipples, there was a lead
that you attached, and then the penny dropped. I could
now guide him around the room with these on all fours,
just like a pet on a leash. I then ordered him to stand up
and to bend over mother's dining room table. Thinking
again at my first sexual encounter with Felicia, I asked
him to spread his legs for me; and to spread them wide.
He got up and spread his legs, holding onto the sides of
the table; as I too had come prepared and had brought
down a bottle of baby oil from mother's side of the
bathroom cupboard, in which I gently rubbed into his ass
and into his hole. I began gently fingering his ass as he
took what I gave him, inserting one finger then two until
I managed to get all four fingers up his tight ass. I was
pulling on his balls and cock, and noticed he was oozing
precum, so I rubbed it over the head of his cock as I
closed my hands tight. He asked me to slow down,
because he was close to climax. I listened to him and
slowed down, as I didn't want him shooting his load just
yet. But I also reminded him that he had no rights to ask
me to slow down, as it was completely my choice. I also
knew that if he were to cum too soon, then he would be
useless too me.
As we had a very strong sturdy table, I ordered David
now to lie on top of it, as he did so I managed to work

out how this strap on worked, and as I fastened it to me, I found it looked rather strange me having a strap on when I had a dick; but thought that this was much better. I oiled up the strap on and gently placed it in position of his now open wet hole, and as I held his legs in the air, I gently penetrated him. Slowly at first, as I was having a little bit of trouble, this was because he was so tight; but after a little bit of persuasion; he managed to take the entire monster dildo I had in my hand; taking about eight inches of thick black rubber as I gently pushed it further inside him.

"Oh my goodness Miss Ruby, that is so good. You are the first to fuck my virgin ass, oh Miss Ruby this is simply divine." He said, now looking at me as he looked down to see the dildo in his ass.

I held onto his legs tighter as I pushed myself into him, fucking his ass harder and faster. Deeper he was breathing as he was holding onto the table for dear life, asking me to fuck him harder.

"Please Miss Ruby; I will not be far off shooting my load, my dear. Will you please allow me to jerk off, as you fuck me?" He asked.
"Not just yet David, I will tell you when." I replied, as I could not believe that a mere fifteen year old, had this hunky man on the table to do with as I pleased.
"Thank you Miss Ruby, thank you." He said, trying to hold back from early ejaculation.

I continued to penetrate him a little more with the strap on, and then reaching over I got hold of a smaller dildo. Now with that in my hand I just stayed where I was and greased it up, slowly inserting it into his ass till he had both dildos in his very wet ass. I could hear him moan in a little bit of pain, but knew he was thoroughly enjoying every minute of what I was doing, as I also saw the look on his face showing me that he was indeed in need of exploding. His cock was incredibly rock hard and very blue in colour, so I then ordered him to start playing with himself as I fucked him harder, where it was not long before he shot all over his tummy and chest.

We just lay there a while as he gained his composure, then as I removed myself from him, I asked him to kneel down on the floor, as he pleased me by doing as I asked of him without question.

Standing in front of him in just my corset stockings and heels, I turned around and told him to eat my pussy.

He went to go for my dick, but I just told him off saying that was not my pussy, as I then pointed to my ass. He parted my ass cheeks as he slid his tongue deep inside me which tickled at first, but then felt so good. I could also feel my own cock beginning to get soaked as I oozed my juices. With me bent over and holding onto my heels, I told David to place his hand out as I wiped my juices on his hand; and then told him to taste what I had on offer for him. He was in heaven and told me that I tasted so sweet; and how he wished he could take it in his mouth. As I was bent over, I noticed he had got rock hard again, so I got him to sit on the dining chair, with my back towards him I sat on his lap, now guiding his cock deep into me.

I do not know what come over me, but I allowed him to touch my cock, in which he managed to get me just as hard as he was, and for some strange reason I did not mind, as I was feeling so horny now.

He was the first one to get me fully erect, and as he held me in his hand, he started to play with me as he pulled down my foreskin jerking me off as he fucked me.

Lying back onto him and feeling his chest hair next to my back was so nice, as was feeling him actually playing with my cock as I felt begin to shake. I was really enjoying this; and rode his cock faster and harder.

"Careful Miss Ruby I am very close again, and goodness you are tight. What a lovely tight hole you have my dear Miss Ruby." He said, holding onto my waist as he helped me ride him.

"If you continue doing what you are doing David, I am afraid I am going to lose control too and shoot all my juices." I replied.

"Oh yes Miss Ruby, I would like that. Do you want to cum in my mouth?" He asked, as I had since forgot roles and just got into the moment or ecstasy and orgasm.

"Yes, I would like that, but stop for now and fuck me till you fill me up." I answered.

David took hold of my waist; and pulled me down onto his throbbing wet cock; until he screamed in delight as he shot his load deep inside me. He thrust harder and harder until I had drained every last drop from him, and then he lifted me up off him as he turned me around.

He took my cock into his mouth, and this was the first time he had seen me now, fully erect and dripping pre cum.

"My God Ruby, you do have such a fantastic big thick cock, for such a young girly boy. I am going to look forward to you fucking my ass and filling me up one day." He told me, now working the head and shaft of my wet dick, waiting in anticipation for the moment I shoot down his throat.
"We will see David, and don't forget it is Miss Ruby at all times." I replied.

He again apologised as he took my hard cock again, and I think I stood about seven inches with a nice foreskin. He took me in his mouth until my legs started to shake, as I was now beginning to cum as my legs started to go into spasms, as David just held my cock there in his mouth as he slid his tongue over the head of my cock. Then it happened, I just screamed in delight as I shot my load down his throat. He swallowed every last drop; and tried to get more from me, but I was so sensitive that I had to withdraw from him as I pulled away, just like I did that day with Felicia. He then kissed me on the lips as he held me tight, and then proceeded to ask me if I would be his girlfriend.

"I do not know about that David; after all I have never gone steady with anyone; as surely a bit of fun is much better?" I replied, now dumfounded at his question.

"You could still be my special girlfriend, couldn't you? I could bring my other friends to come and see you; where before long you will have your girly fund." He replied.
"But if I am your girlfriend and you bring others here, then that makes me feel like you are pimping me out; *and I don't like that idea."* I said, not quite understanding what he meant.
"Not at all Miss Ruby you can still be my girlfriend; and do a few extra favours for shall we say, people with money who is willing to have such a beautiful person, as you to teach them what they need to know. You know Miss Ruby, you being their mistress. They will pay handsomely for your favours." He replied, now putting a bigger thought into my already over imaginative mind.

I told him that as the girlfriend goes, we would keep it on hold for the time being, as I would like to get to know him better, but that he does hold a special place in my heart; and I would keep him there. He then told me that he understood, and he would like to see me on a regular basis; and it would all have to be kept a secret because of his position and status. I gave him full discretion that my lips were sealed; and he would get no trouble from me, as I also told him that he could never tell my parents for I would certainly be in trouble as would he for having such encounters with me.
It was arranged that he would bring a colleague next time, and we would see what happened then. I then told him that I was not able to do next week due to my parents being home, but I would be available the following week for three weeks. My parents were taking my younger brother on holiday, and I had decided to stay

at home as I needed to revise for my exams. My aunty would come in once a day, on her way to work to see if things were ok, plus I did have the home phone in which he could check if the coast was clear. He again kissed me as he placed some money in the box, and then left the house as he told me thank you.

All that week my head was buzzing; and I just about managed to tell Felicia what had happened, as I had not seen her for a while with her being busy herself. She went crazy at me; and said that if these people have money, I had undersold myself; and that next time I should tell them the price has gone up. She told me that they could afford it; and the higher up the ladder they are love, the more you ask for. Never ever under sell yourself as you have something that they want, and if they want it that bad, they will pay for it for sure, besides I had a good bargaining chip, as well as letting them know that I was after all underage, now speaking to me like a head teacher. I went silent, then told her that I thought that it was prostitution; and if I used the underage weapon, then that would make it blackmail.

"Fuck no; it is not like you are on the streets selling yourself for a quick fix, is it love? And you have said that you are not getting payment in your hand, so you are more like an escort and a fuckin high class one at that. All you need to think about, is it is just sex; and it is money for your… what did you call it?" She asked.
"Girly fund." I replied.
"Yes, your girly fund. If you just think of it as your girly fund, then it will not sound as bad as you make it out to be. Nothing in life is free Ruby, and you must take what

44

you can without looking too cheap. Most girls on the block would charge a fiver for a fuck, and here you are with a week's wages, which just goes to show that you are high class; and people will pay good money for that. It will not be long before you get yourself a nice pair of tits and a vagina either. I guess the underage card was a bit cutting, but at the end of the day my love, they know that it is dangerous anyway; and that with them having sex with me, meant a jail sentence if they got caught, so it is them playing a dangerous game and not you." She told me, as she gave me a few figures that I should charge, according to what service I provided.

I did feel better after we had a little chat; and told her that I felt guilty that I had gone against my wishes, as I let him have my dick. She just told me that these things happen, and it does not mean I still do not want to become a woman. She told me that I have to use all I have, to get to where I really want to be; and I will have to do things that I really do not want to, like use my dick or fuck a guy to get more towards my goal. She also said that I may even have to fuck a few fatties and ugly fuckers for extra cash, as not all men were as fit and handsome as David. Then as per usual, she took me by the arms and kissed me, where we too ended up in bed as she fucked me till she shot her load; and I sucked her until I swallowed all she had.

"*Well, I aint paying you one shilling Ruby, I am after all your tutor and will teach you a lot more.*" She laughed. "*Yes Felicia; and I wouldn't charge you anyway.*" I replied, as I winked at her.

"That's good then and I have to admit even though you don't like it, you do have a fuckin lovely dick and ass. But I still need to teach you a few more things, as guys will love being told what to do, especially if you tie them up and spank them as hard as they can take or ask; and humiliate them a little bit." She said, as once again I became the pupil.

"I am a willing learner Felicia; and I do trust you so you will have to practice on me." I replied.

"Oh trust me I will, and it is not practice honey as I know what I am doing. It will not be long until I have enough cash to open my own club, I can tell you, as we girls need a place where we can be free and have special men friends. If you got any spare punters pass them my way, as I could do with a few high rollers." She told me, as she began to laugh.

I just looked at her and then knew she was actually like me; and that she herself must have been doing this for ages, because no wonder she went mad at me and advised me about what to charge.

I spent that week wondering what I should ask David or indeed his friends for, as I did feel guilty, as I had conflicting questions in my head, but I stayed true to myself and told myself that once I had enough money, that I would give all this activity up. I just needed to make sure I had enough to at least get me by; and to enable me to start a new life, as I had less than a year left at school. I had already been to see the doctor and told him how I felt, who eventually sent me to see a psychiatrist as he thought this was a phase I was going through. This was not such a common thing back then and I was often persecuted by my doctor, who had a few lashes of my tongue I can tell you, which did not help, as I seemed to lose my temper a lot, only because I knew what I wanted. The doctor told me I was too young to be put on such medication; and he would first have to consult my parents, as well as it not being that simple to change your sex, as you would change the curtains in your lounge; and that he felt I had an unbalanced amount of testosterone in my body which made me feel the urge to want to become a woman.

I was against him notifying my parents, but it did not matter because mother was going to get a phone call; and I just thought the nasty fucking bastard, whatever happened to patient confidentiality?

I thought to myself that I was not having any of this, so I told him that if he told my parents about what I had told him, I would deny it and tell them he had been touching me in places he should not touch a boy. The doctor was fuming and told me to get out of his office; and that he would be letting my father know about my nasty behaviour and slur against him, which could get him into a lot of trouble, as well as to ruin his reputation.

This put me into another depressive slump, as I was rather frightened about the doctor contacting my mother, but another part of me was pleased as now finally maybe she will understand me.

All that week I was quiet, wondering when the doctor would phone and ask to see my mother. I contemplated suicide, as then I would be nobody's problem and I would not need to answer to anyone. I thought about running away, maybe go to Felicia's, as mother did not know where she lived. I even contemplated cutting my dick off; and then maybe they would have to let me be a girl, after all I would no longer have that fucking awful thing that I was born with which distinguishes me so different to how I had imagined my body to be.

I have always dreamed about being made love to like a woman; and not have to always take it up the ass which I found very uncomfortable, but that was not the whole reason, I always knew I was in the wrong body; and no matter what doctors said or thought they knew about me, that part of me being true to myself never changed.

Listening to Felicia's words I thought that it was not fair, that I had to do things that I did not want to, but I also understood and that I am still only fifteen; and apart from living at home under my parent's rule, as well as not have a proper fund yet, I just had to grin and bare it, so what made it easier is I knew I could not be too picky when coming to having clients, but one day it would be me who made the rules.

I just thought that life really sucks; and I cannot wait until I leave home, where I can be who I really want to be, but for now I had to concentrate on my studies as I was nearing my final exams.

A week later I was over at Kitty's, as she had to go out briefly and asked Felicia if she would dog sit. She had the cutest King Charles Spaniels you could dream of; and they were no trouble as they both lay on their royal cushions pampered with the finest of foods and treats. Once Kitty had nipped into town, I began messing around with makeup and I then decided to begin my transformation into Ruby. I noticed Felicia look over at me; and although she was not dressed in girly mode, she told me how beautiful and fuckable I was as a girl.

48

It was then that Felicia came over to me and placed her hand on my knee.

"You look so beautiful Ruby, what with your slim figure. Your dick and ass are simply to die for; and remember what I said before about fucking me?" She said, reminding me of our last conversation.
"Yes I remember." I replied.
"Well, I am going to take your dick today." She said, in a way that I knew I could not deny her.

We then started to fool around; and I had got so used to Felicia now, that I soon got aroused and was standing to attention. She stood me up, where she slowly undressed me until I was down to my black corset by Miss Mary of Sweden, which defined my body even more. Then as she started to play with my cock, she kissed me on the lips as we entwined in male lesbian passion. I called us lesbians as we were both girly guys; and it seemed like we were very much girls, even though Felicia was today dressed as a guy and had not become her female self.
Getting me to sit on the couch, Felicia straddled me and placed my cock between her legs. I was so nervous, that I began going soft as well as going bright red. Felicia told me to relax, because if I did then it would rid me of my nervous disposition; and then everything would be fine, speaking softly softly to me to make me feel calmer. I apologised, as I told her I really did want to try her sucking my cock, but I was bricking it, as she told me I was over thinking things. She then shifted the idea; and told me not to think of her as a friend or sister, but to think of me as a punter, when I laughed and asked her

what I should charge her. That seemed to do the trick, as I relaxed, with Felicia called me a cheeky bitch, as she then told me that I was going to get my ass filled with her dick soon.

After a while of going up and down like a yoyo, I finally managed to get pretty hard again. Felicia had already lubed her ass up ready to take me; and she then took charge as she gently guided me into her. I could not believe it, as I pushed into her and felt the tight warmth of her ass, which squeezed against my cock and it nursed me, as she took me deeper into her. I thought I was going to shoot my load there and then as she was so tight, which I could not understand as she had regular clients in and out of her home. Slowly I thrust into her; and then withdrew as I seen my cock now all silky with the lubricant. It was so intense; and the tightness of her ass against my cock was mind blowing.

"Fucking hell Ruby, you may not be solid, but fuck me you are big. Take my tight ass Ruby, fuck me with that thick girly dick." She said, as she kept putting me back inside her, when I fell out of her ass.

Somehow that made me hornier and relaxed, as I felt my cock swell even harder, now giving Felicia my full erect cock as she took me all the way inside her.

"Just shut the fuck up, you filthy bitch." I replied, as I pushed deeper into her.
"Yes Miss Ruby." She replied.

We then started to talk dirty to each other, which got us both off quicker. Felicia was now solid as a rock with pre cum oozing from her cock as she rode me harder.

"Right Felicia, get by the table and bend over it for me. You are going to break my fuckin legs bouncing up like that." I told her.

She moved to the small dining table in the corner of the room; and there she bent over it spread eagle, as I began pounding her ass, feeling my balls slapping against hers. For once I was not thinking of Tony the boy, or Ruby the girl, but more of Ruby with a girly cock which seemed to work for me, as I tried not to think too much.
Felicia was rubbing her cock vigorously as I thrust deeper inside her, until I could hold on no more. I told her I was ready to shoot my load, in which she told me to empty my load into her hot wet ass. She then began talking dirty to me again as I could no longer hold on; and as I held onto her waist, I thrust myself in to her one last time, as I exploded and shot deep inside her.

"Fuckin hell Ruby you are good, if this is what you are like when you fuck someone they will be in for a treat." She said, as she felt each thrust that I made, as her body hit the side of the table.
"Thank you Felicia, but now I feel awful. I am a strange cow, so I do apologise." I replied, now beginning to feel bad at what I had done.
"Don't be love, we all get guilt complexes, it's now Ruby the girl who is feeling wrong about what you did because of you thinking about your dick. Just think of it as Ruby

with a girly dick and you will start to feel better. Anyway, you did say you wouldn't do this all the time, so think of it as another side of you, after all it is just sex Ruby."
She said, making me feel a little better.
"Ok Felicia, I know I have a lot to learn. I cannot help that I am repulsed with my boy's body, but I also liked what I did." I replied
"Then for God's sake shut the fuck up and bend over, as now it is my turn." She said, as I did exactly what she asked of me.

I then was pushed over the table, where Felicia then took control and penetrated me till completion. That would not be the last time I would be intimate with Felicia, but it was rare that it was I who took her tight ass.
The three weeks that my parents were away, David visited me every few days bringing a colleague with him. When he asked me if I could help his friend, I told him that I could; and I then asked him what position he held on the social table. Once he told me that, I knew this would vary on what I would ask them to put into the girly fund, though I never told them an actual figure, I just reminded them the higher the position, the more for the fund I expected. This was relayed by David to his friends; and nothing was ever mentioned again; as they all knew where they stood; and as I did not like to be handed any sort of money directly into my hands.
David also relayed this to them, as he told them I had a cash box in the hallway for them to discreetly place their fees; and I think it was David who actually gave his colleagues the figure in which to pay for my services.
I trusted David; and therefore, had no reason to question

his judgement as I knew he would look out for me.
It was also not just the daytimes, that David would come around to see me, as on this one specific night I had been Ruby all day; and I was just about to get ready for bed when the doorbell rang.

"Good Evening Miss Ruby, how are you?" David asked, as he stood on the front porch.
"I am fine thank-you David; a little late isn't it for a social visit, as I was just off to bed?" I replied, now wrapping the dressing gown around me because of the night air, that was a little chilly.
"I am so sorry Miss Ruby, but I thought I would introduce you to a very special friend." He said, as his friend smiled at me.
"Well in that case, you had best come off the cold step and come into the warm." I replied.

They both walked into the lounge, where I went into father's drinks cabinet and offered them both a scotch.
I did not worry about the bottle emptying as I could get another one from Kitty when it had gone; and then father would not have known the difference.

"This is Percy Miss Ruby… Lord Percival." He said, as I could not believe that I was being introduced to someone from the peerage class.
"Lord Ermm, my Lord, nice to meet you." I replied.
"The pleasure is all mine Miss Ruby; and please do call me Percy." He replied, in that upper snobbish sort of way.

"*Percy, it is very nice to meet you.*" I said, as I held out my hand waiting for him to kiss it.

We sat there for a few minutes chatting, as both David and Percy kept staring at my legs through my mother's negligee, which I quickly put on before answering the door; and relieved that it was not my aunty. I asked them if everything was ok, because I could not begin to wonder what they were staring at, when David told me that it was my legs, that they were incredibly beautiful; and they looked so attractive through the tempting nightwear I had on. I could not believe they were staring at my legs, when I had taken an age to perfect my make-up, and they did not compliment me on that aspect of beauty. Looking at them both, I told them that I did not have any nightwear of my own yet, and what I was wearing, belonged to my mother, when Percy mentioned that he would have to change that, as you cannot have a beautiful young lady with no lingerie of her own, that it was a cardinal sin. When I then became brave but rather cheeky, as I told them that I agreed; and that they should not visit me again if they do not bare gifts. David then suggested to me, if I could help Percy; and that it would be truly wise to consider this as he winked at me. I took them into my parent's bedroom, as they had a four-poster bed, which was better than mine, as mother had done it out all boyish, with blue wallpaper and bedding. I told David to strip off and stand in the corner, where I then looked at Percy and told him I was going to inspect him. I looked him over even though he was taller than I, then ordered him onto his knees. When he did this for me, I told him that I thought that it was much better, as a servant should not stand taller than their mistress.

"*No Miss Ruby, that is correct.*" Percy replied.

I removed his shirt to see a man that for once was not as fit as the others, as he had a little bit of padding on his belly, but because of his height it did not make him look at all fat. He had the slightest of chest hair but not that much that it was noticeable, but it was such a delight to see. I then ordered him to stand up so that I could remove his trousers, as he was now beginning to get rather excited about the whole thing. Once I had done that, I noticed unlike some guys he did not wear briefs, but instead had on a nice shiny white pair of trunks. Being curious, I asked what he was wearing, because I thought they were beach wear, when he told me they were boxer trunks; and that he got them whilst he was in America visiting his family. I thought they were really nice and sexy, and I relayed this too him as I told him I approved, as I looked at David and told him that this was how a man should dress; and in future I would expect him to dress in the same manner, as I was sure the fine menswear shops would also sell them. He smiled at me; and told me that he would have a look in the city, next time he is working, in which he could have a look when he takes his lunch.
I then slowly removed Percy's boxer shorts, to see a wonderful well-trimmed cock and balls. It was not too bushy, as you could see that he spent time grooming himself; and as for his cock it was not big at all which was such a relief to me, as big cocks were my pet hate.

He had a six inch cock when erect; and it made for a pleasant surprise, as when it was flaccid you would never have thought it would have grown as much.

I was so relieved, as I did not really like large cocks penetrating my ass, as it took some time to get used to them, so seeing someone with a normal size cock really did please me a lot. Looking at him directly in the eyes, I told him that what I saw was very nice, very nice indeed, as I quickly placed my hand underneath his balls.

"Thank you Miss Ruby, I am so pleased that you like what I have to offer to you." He replied.

Now that I had both men naked before me, I got Percy to kneel doggy on the bed; and with David I got him to stand by the side of the bed as I tied him to the posts so that he could watch what I was doing to Percy.

I went into my bedroom and pulled out my little bag of tricks, and then made my way back into my parent's room; firstly, getting the paddle out, as I then began gently slapping Percy's ass, as he flinched excitingly as David overlooked in an erotic sort of jealousy.

I then noticed that David was not as restrained as he could be, so I went back over to him and spread his legs wide; and tied them to the bottom of the bed posts. I also placed a pair of nipple clamps onto him, and just left him there as I returned back to Percy.

As I was greasing his hole, I slowly and gently slipped a dildo inside him, as I again began to use the paddle on his ass.

"Oh Yes Miss Ruby. That is so wonderful, thank you." Percy said to me, now taking the dildo deep inside him,

as I then asked him if he had ever tasted cock before. Going a little shy, which was funny to see, as I had this grown man on all fours, with a dildo up his ass; and he told me he had never tasted cock before, which I think was a little white lie. I then told him that tonight he is going to try; and I would not take no for an answer.

"I do not know Miss Ruby; one has never done anything like this before." He again said, looking a little nervous.

Getting into my role, I told him that I did not care if he had not tried, that tonight he is going to take a man's cock, as he then gave in and told me he would do whatever I desired, as he looked back at me.
I ordered him to change his position; and told him to place his mouth over David's cock. He did not question me; and did as I asked of him, as knelt on the bed with his head by David's cock, where he slowly started to take him in his mouth.
It was so sexy seeing two grown men make out with each other, especially as I was, I guess, the instigator, but it was just horny seeing them suck each others cocks. Percy was doing his best, being cautious at first, when I then told him that if he does not suck David's cock properly, then he would be punished.

"Yes Miss Ruby, one is trying too." He replied, taking David further into his mouth.
"Try harder, once you have it down your throat you will know how far to take it, then you will know how far to stretch your limits." I said, as I placed my hand on his head forcing him onto David's cock.

"Yes Miss Ruby." He replied.

As he was sucking David's cock, I stood up and just looked at them, as I could not believe I had two men in which I could control. I must admit seeing two guys and being in control of them was totally amazing. For once it was I who gave the orders and not them; and I savoured every moment that we were in the bedroom.

I then slipped into the strap on that David had left for me on his last visit, and then looked at Percy and told him that I want him on his back, as I wanted him to take David's cock right down his throat as Miss Ruby does something to him.

"Yes Miss Ruby." He replied.

As he lay on his back, he positioned himself so that David's cock was able to go down his throat better than it did on his knees. I then stood behind him as I removed the dildo, and then got another one and asked him to start fucking David's ass with it. Gently I eased myself inside him, inch by inch until he had the full strap on inside his now stretched ass. This was so intense, as never before had I seen a guy sucking a guy's cock and fucking his ass with a dildo, as I was fucking him. Percy's cock was now rock hard and very moist, and every time I thrust a bit deeper; I am sure I hit his g-spot as he oozed precum from his now tempting glistening cock.

There were a few times, that I had to tell Percy off, as he went for his own cock, he tried to rub it hard whilst telling me that he was close to shooting his load.

I then removed myself from Percy; and slid another

dildo inside him; moving around the bed I went to where David was, and removed the dildo from him as I then began to fuck him.

"Oh God Miss Ruby yes, that is so good." He said, as he felt me hold onto his waist; and penetrate him deeper.

I then noticed Percy's head beginning to stare at me from under David's legs, where I just looked at him and stared. He told me that it looked so good, when he then said that I was so hot.
After a few minutes I untied David, and then told Percy to stay where he was on the bed. I then told them that before they got to play with me, with their Miss Ruby, they had to do something for me; and that was for them to penetrate each other. In unison, they both agreed, as they waited for my instruction. David went to the end of the bed, as Percy was still on his back, he raised his legs over his shoulders, as started to penetrate his ass, as Percy started licking my ass, and stroking my buttocks. David lay on his back and let Percy take his tight ass, as he also licked my ass and balls, as I even let David take my now erect cock down his throat.
It now was my turn, and as I sat on top of Percy, feeling him deep inside my wet ass; David straddled Percy's face who by now had taken David down his throat. David and I started kissing as I heard Percy moaning in complete ecstasy as he was about to cum.

"That's it Percy, fuck me; and fuck that nice tight ass." I told him, as I took him deep inside me, clenching a few times as I rode his cock.

"Yes Miss Ruby, one cannot hold back for much longer my dear; for I fear I am going to cum very soon." He replied, as his body began to shake, and his breathing became erratic.

"Good boy Percy; cum for your Miss Ruby." I told him.

"Yes Miss Ruby I am almost there my dear." He replied, now holding onto my waist as he thrust upwards, giving me all that he had.

Shortly after saying that, he grabbed hold of my waist as he thrust hard into me, breathing and shouting heavy as he emptied himself into me.

"Oh My God Ruby; oh fuckin Jesus Christ that is so good." He shouted, now not so much in a posh voice.

I then just got off him, as I told him to stay lying down as I would straddle him in a sixty nine position.

He stayed lying down for me as I lay over him, my cock now halfway down his throat, as I raised his legs and held then up towards me, as I gripped them with my arms so that I could rim his ass and lick his balls. I then ordered David to come behind me; and told him to fuck me until he shot his load. David then got behind me and started penetrating my ass with his very wet cock, and I then sat up and took my cock out of Percy's mouth and asked him if he had ever tasted cum, which was a stupid question, because he had never tasted cock until tonight, or so I was led to believe. Anyway, I did give him the benefit of the doubt as he told me he had never tasted cum, not even his own, after the many times he had jerked off. I told him that if he carried on sucking my

cock like he was doing, that he would soon get a
mouthful; and to be very gentle sucking me, because one
day my cock will become my vagina, as he was a little
eager with his playful biting.

Again, I went back to Percy's ass where I slid my tongue
deep inside him, as he took my cock further down his
throat. It was too much as I could not hold back any
longer, and I shot my load down his throat, withdrawing
it which also spilled cum on his chin. David saw this,
when he too could no longer hold back and fucked me
until he shot deep inside me; at this point I noticed Percy
was hard again.

Once I had been filled by David, I then ordered Percy to
fuck him until he shot deep inside him, which was a
struggle for him the second time, but he did manage it
after a lot of persuasion. The pure struggle of it I thought
would have given him a heart attack, as he grunted and
panted hard, that I thought his chest would explode.

When we all finished, we cleaned up and then proceeded
to go downstairs. Again, I poured them both another
scotch each, as we sat and chatted and arranged another
meet. When they were ready to go, they took something
out of their pocket and placed it in the girly fund box.

I said goodnight to them both; and proceeded upstairs to
have a nice bath before going to bed.

I did not worry too much about the neighbours, as we
lived on a private road, in a Victorian house that was set
back from the road. The nearest neighbour was about
two hundred yards away, and they too had a house set
back from the road and sheltered by trees, so we were
very secluded, and free from prying eyes.

I had arranged with David that we should have a party,

and as it would be a few people they should also bring a bottle, as I would not raid father's drinks cabinet every visit. It was arranged for the following Friday night to have a big get together in which I would lay on some food. I told him that I did not mind if they were male admirers or gay men, so long as I was respected; and that they made sure the house was not trashed, as well as informing them, that there would be a fee to pay as nothing was ever free.

David just looked at me and told me he understood.

I also knew if I was going to have a few more people in the house, I was not going to chance leaving my girly fund on the radiator shelf as I did not know them all.

I had decided that I would keep it in the drawer of the telephone cupboard, until I let them out.

That night in bed I just thought about the night's events with a smile on my face, as it slowly sent me to sleep.

I never even thought to look inside the girly fund to see what was there; but as I was on my own, I knew there was no need to remove it until the morning, where I could place it in my bank book when I went into town.

Over the next few weeks, I started writing down the names of people who visited; and put them in my secret little black book. So as not to give away their names, should anyone find my book; I used what was only known to me. Lord Percy became LP; whilst Judge David Bellows became JDB; and so, the list went on.

I was at this point, getting quite a clientele from a few ordinary people who were friends of father, to the ones who were in a much higher position. I was not a nasty person; but thought this would come in handy once I left school and I needed any help. I also had a code of conduct, and that was you never snitch on money, because once you do it is not just that which stops, but the rest of your income. By keeping quiet you gained respect by the piers; and you were well rewarded accordingly for your discretion.

I now could boast that I had judges, police officials, even members of the government as some of my highly respected clients; and had got a name for myself that was one of complete trust and discretion.

I had decided that I would be leaving school on my sixteenth birthday, having stayed on an extra year to take business studies, as well as my A levels in maths, English, Spanish, not quite knowing what I wanted to do when I left school for good.

I had already accumulated a couple of grand, which I had saved up and had banked; and made sure I kept my bank book well out of the way of my parents.

As well as sitting my exams I took a part time job in a department store in the city; and Kitty let me help out in her bar in the evening, giving me a bit more spending money. I used to collect glasses, and I was her wardrobe assistant, which was a start, and in which it put me within the safety of my own kind, without worry of being bullied or beaten up.

The party that I hosted for David went well, which ended up with everyone getting naked and having sex. I had invited Felicia along, as I did not want to be in a house with a dozen men all alone. Felicia made a killing that night by seducing many of them, and having her way with all of them, making me feel at ease by having company. This really did not bother me, as I was given respect; and did not have to perform a sexual act on everyone, as I had taken it in my stride to becoming that of the hostess, so for Felicia to fuck the brains out of them was such a relief. I did however make a fortune in hosting that party; and other than my fee, Felicia got a good payoff too. David and I did get it on, but it was not in an environment where I dominated the situation, as it was more the nicer thing about sex in which I liked, just two consenting people.

At first, some of my clients were a little cautious about Felicia, but when I told her that she was a trusting person; and that their identities would remain a secret, they warmed to her. And that was only because I told them, that she would be a fool to lose good money, as everyone then saw the funny side.

A few days later my parents came home with my brother, who had told me that they had all had a wonderful holiday; and it was a shame that I decided to stay at home to revise. They reminded me that I had missed quite a lot of things, in which I smiled as I thought so had they; then as mother opened her mail, she looked at me and asked what I had been saying to the doctor as he wanted to see us both.

My world started to collapse, and I just thought that I was now in for it. I was dreading the next few days, as I could not think of anything to say to mother when she asked me; and even my brother could tell I was not with it as I lost interest in playing with him; and so many times I thought should I just tell the truth?

I just wanted to get it all out of the way, and had to bite my tongue, and hope for the best.

It was then the day of the appointment, and mother marched me into the surgery where the doctor asked her to sit down. He looked at me; and then told me to remain silent, because he would have no words spoken like the last time I was in his office. He then explained to her what I had said about wanting to change my body; and how depressed I was, then telling her about my attempt to blackmail him.

Mother was so shocked, then looking at me she said, in that headmistress voice.

"You dirty little pervert, you have been hanging around with those bloody queer's, again haven't you? They have got you thinking all sorts of rubbish, so that you become like them. You are a boy Tony, not a bloody girl; and I forbid you to have any dealing with that sort from now on."

She then asked the doctor what he suggested, as she was not having any of this; and that father would go absolutely mental if he found out.

Lots of things were discussed, and the doctor suggested electric shock treatment, as maybe that would help sort out my mental state. She agreed, when the doctor told her, that he would arrange for me to see a specialist who dealt with Electro Convulsive Therapy, also known as ECT. I screamed at my mother, telling her no I do not need that sort of thing, when she slapped me across the face and told me to be still. I was bricking it and wondered what the hell I was going to do, as I did not want my brain frazzled. I knew about ECT, because in the older days, of the days gone by, patients who were in mental asylum's had that sort of treatment; and it did not cure them, they just became living zombies.

I kept quiet for a few days, just going into my own world where I would not speak to anyone. I began to feel more depressed, and really did not know who to turn to.

That day as I went to school, I never turned up, I just ran to Felicia's home, with who I told her everything that had happened. She was fuming that I had a mother who would do this to me, as it was not a matter of shock treatment that would help; but more an understanding of who I was. She told me to keep quiet and tell her it was a mistake, and that I no longer feel like that anymore.

"Blag it Ruby, you cannot have anyone mess with your brain, it is so fuckin barbaric. You only have another six months at school, so keep your head down until you can finally leave home." She said, begging me to try and get out of what my mother had planned.

"But Felicia!" I cried.

"But Felicia crap. It is going to be damn hard Ruby, but you have to do this for yourself. Just remember we sometimes have to do things that we do not like, just so we can make it better for us in the future. When the time comes when you have to see the specialist, tell your mother that it is all ok now. AGREE with what she wants to hear, but do not for Christ's sake let them give you shock treatment at any cost. Also remember, in six months time, you can leave home, put your concentration into that; and if you leave home you can either come and stay with me, or stay with Kitty, because she will fuck anyone up who tries to mess with her girls." She begged

66

me, now becoming very worried at the prospects of what my mother had agreed to do.

I promised her that I would try, and told her I will try my best to hide who I was, but it was so unfair after how far I had come. I had accepted that I was a gay girly boy, but also accepted that I wanted to become a woman, so I was already confused; and I knew trying to say I was ok, would only hurt me in the long run. However, I knew where she was coming from; and I hated my mother from that day.

After a few days it was too much for me, and I went into the bathroom cabinet and took a drugs overdose. It was my mother who had found me, as she thought I had been in the bath too long.

"*You stupid little boy, what on earth possessed you to do such a thing.*" She screamed, as she rushed downstairs to call an ambulance.

I was rushed straight to hospital where I had my stomach pumped, but as I had been sick in bathroom there was not much to pump out. The few days I was in hospital I had lots of doctor's visit me, who were not very nice to me at all; and the nurses just left me alone; and as they passed me, they gave me dirty looks and passing rude comments which made me feel worse. Then the psychiatrists visited me, who tried to get to the bottom of why I had done what I did. Mother had mentioned the fact I wanted to become a girl; and that I had been listening to too many puffs and perverts who she thought had influenced me.

I just totally ignored them not letting on about Ruby, or even feeling that I was trapped in the body I had.
They just put it down to me wanting attention; and for them to keep an eye on me.
Three days later I was released and went back home.
I never ever told anyone else about my gender until I moved out of my parent's home. Those last days in the hospital, I denied myself. I told the doctors and the psychiatrists, that I had got into a group of undesirable people, people who liked their own sex; and people who dressed up in ladies' clothes; and wore make up; and it was not of my Christian belief, which was just like that of Sodom & Gomorrah, which pleased my mother, being such a brown-nosed Christian, who had her head so far up the clergy's assholes it was unforgivable.

Three Years Later

I was now eighteen years old; and I decided to move out of the family home and make a life for myself, without the prying eyes of my parents. I had since had a big argument with them a few weeks before, and thought it was all I could do. I decided that I would not move out, those days of my mother wanting to take me to have ECT, but instead concentrate on my studies. Those three years I kept a low profile; and I kept my secret life well hidden. I still saw Kitty and Felicia; and I used an excuse that I was working a few hours over-time, just so I could get to see my friends. When my parents went on holiday, this time it was fine with me not going, because I was now in the class of working; and a contributer to my mother's household. But alas, when they went away, I made the most of it; and threw those parties every other day. I did not want leave at all, and I hated the fact that I left my brother behind; but the argument was too much for me to cope with, and I thought I would explain to my brother once he got older; and old enough to understand. My parents would not even let me say goodbye to him, as they told me to leave there and then knowing I was going to move out anyway.

I did not go to university as my parents wanted, so they gave me a small inheritance payment, as they did my sisters, and then told me never to darken their doorstep again until I had sorted myself out.

Not letting them know I had money, I took this small inheritance and put a deposit on a small apartment in the vicinity of London Bridge. It was a four storey building, and I had one of the one bedroom flats; with mine being the basement flat with small garden. I continued to still have the parties at my parent's house when they went away, as they always asked me to look after the house for them. I also now had to let my clients know, that I could no longer put on such lavish parties due to having a small flat; as I could only entertain a few people at a time, which they understood as they kindly brought all of the drink with them, as well as still give me a fee for hosting the parties.

I was now no longer a wardrobe assistant for Kitty or Felicia, but now a fledgling drag queen. It was not long after that, where I would hand my notice in at work, as my cabaret bookings were filling up my diary.

Kitty helped me become a member of equity; and whilst a lot of my venues were in London, I was still able to work at the Kit Kat Lounge.

Felicia was saving as hard as she could, as down the road from the Kit Kat, was premises she was looking at to make into a club. She had also retained a small group of clients like me; and swore once she had enough for her bar/club she was going to give the clients up.

I still however would keep some of my client's as they visited me through the week; and by now I had a really big healthy bank account.

I never did become David's girl but instead we became very good friends, and friends with benefits.

David soon settled down with a male companion, even though he was also married; and we still would have our little meets but nothing like we used to. It was whilst I was eighteen David brought another of his friends over, with whom he introduced me too.

"I think this guy will be very beneficial to you my dear Miss Ruby; and you will need him on your side if you are still thinking about your old thoughts?" He said, as he gave me a wink of his eye.

"Old thoughts David?" I replied.

"Yes Ruby old thoughts, your Ruby thoughts." He said, as he made a sign of a pair of scissors.

"Oh right I am with you now; and why would he be useful to me?" I asked him.

"Because he is a doctor Ruby; and one I think would be good to keep in with." He replied, as I told him I hoped he was not a fuckin psychiatrist.

I just looked at this guy and gave him the nod, as David introduced us.

70

"Brian I would like to introduce you to a very special young lady. Brian this is Miss Ruby, Miss Ruby this is Brian."
"Hello Ruby, it is very nice to meet you." He said, as he took my hand and kissed it.
"And nice to meet you too Brian, and next time please call me Miss Ruby." I whispered.

We started chatting as I offered them both a drink, when David told me he had to go back to the office and asked me if I would be ok on my own. I told him that I would and that he must call in again, which then left me alone with Brian. I was not sure if he was trying to analyse me, or if he was actually listening to me and taking things in. I told him about my old doctor not being able to help me, in which he understood as I was under-age. He then told me that he did not know who my present doctor was, but that he would give me his card, so that he or she could refer me to him. I thanked him, not really sure what he meant, now looking at his card.

"That is if you still would like to go down that path you have often dreamed about?" He asked.

Looking at his card I noticed he was in my area, so as I had a big smile on my face, I looked at him and said.

"Or Dr Brian, I could change surgeries and be a patient of yours."

He then asked me who my doctor was, in which I then told him, that since moving I had changed; and I now had a female doctor. Once I had given him the surgery and her name, he just looked at me with; and with a cheeky smile he just said.

"Oh I know your doctor as we were at medical school together, so if you see her ask her to refer you to me. She has referred a few girls to me, and she knows the protocol."

I was over the moon, and the next thing I remember is I just threw my arms around him and kissed him. Next thing I knew we ended up going to bed, where he just quickly removed his clothes and then started to rip mine off me. I had never had sex like this before, as it was so passionate and wild that Miss Ruby did not even get a chance to tell him what to do. This time he called the shots and Miss Ruby was happy to oblige; and it was nice actually having a man tell me what to do for once. Once he had ripped all my clothes off me, leaving me just in my lingerie and shoes, he started to kiss my neck. He was a little rough as he started to bite my neck, in which I flinched. I have never been given a love bite before, so I just looked at him and told him, that he would have to do it below my neck due to work.
Now as naked as the day we were born, he pushed me on my knees where he thrust his cock inside my mouth, telling me to take all of it.
Well, I nearly gagged with the force he was using, but before long I knew how to relax a little more as fighting him only turned him on that much more. He was quite an aggressive lover, but I was not complaining, as he told me that he had no interest in my cock; and he could not

wait until I started on my hormones as he wanted to be able to grab hold of my tits properly instead of grabbing a girly boy chest.

He then got me back on to my feet; and as we were by my dressing table, he just pushed me down onto it and ripped off my panties, where he then just rammed his cock deep inside me as I screamed, as he was not a small guy. He was very large and very thick, but no matter how much I screamed he just carried on fucking me. With him still inside me he lifted me up and walked me to the bed where again he thrust inside me as he placed me on all fours.

It was there that I finally received all of his ten inches and damn did I feel it.

After about thirty minutes of making love, he started to quiver, and he kept telling me that he was going to cum. Once he shot his load inside me, he fell onto me as he just lay there; holding me tightly as he started to get his breath back. I then told him thank you but next time if he wants to visit again, he is going to have to do it my way.

"So you didn't like me taking control then Miss Ruby, did you not like what we have done." He asked.

"Sure I liked it Brian, but there is no need to be that rough. It almost felt like I was being violated, even though there was some excitement there." I replied.

"I am so sorry Miss Ruby; I thought this is what you really wanted?" He said, sounding surprised

"Brian, NOT all women want a man to simply rip off their clothes and butt fuck them into insanity. There has to be some sort of foreplay, and definitely some intimacy. I think you have been going to the wrong bars, as some

girls need respect Brian. Next time you visit you will give me just that or you can fuck off, as I am not being violated for the sake of getting special treatment and a course of fucking hormones." I said, now rather livid.
"I am sorry Miss Ruby; the other girls didn't seem to mind." He replied as I interrupted him.
"Other girls? OTHER FUCKIN GIRLS Brian? Just remember I am not other girls; and you will not have it that way again where I am concerned. I am a woman and will be respected as one, as I am not your seedy little backroom whore." I said, rather annoyed at his response.

He apologised again and told me it wouldn't happen like that again, as he would now let me take the lead.
He also said that what had happened would not have any effect on me seeing him professionally, and I was never his whore as I was too classy; and no one had ever spoke up towards him. He slowly gained my favour back and he kept to his word; as over the next few meets, he had become quite the submissive guy, even to the fact after a while he did used to suck my cock a few times.
When I next had a day off, I decided to visit my doctor, in which I sat down and spoke about my gender issue and about gender reassignment. We had a very long discussion, and before she suggested what to do next, I gave her the name of Brian and her eyes lit up.

"Oh Tony you have thought this through haven't you? And I know Brian very well as we went to medical school together. So how do you know Brian, or is it a secret?"
She asked.

"I met him through a friend of my father's; and have known him now for several months. He knows I have had transgender issues from an early age, and of hearing it from an old family friend. He just told me that if I was serious about this, to come and see you and ask you to refer me to him." I replied, now rather excited that I was finally being listened too.
"Well, I can certainly do that, but please don't expect to be started on treatment right away, as there is quite a wait I believe; I am not totally sure, as this will be my first transgender case in a very long time." She replied.

She also told me, that although Brian was a surgeon who specialised in the transgender field, I would still have to be referred to a psychiatrist for evaluation; and it was a very long slow winding road. I finished my appointment with her; and had thought that I had taken my first big step; in finally becoming the woman I truly believed I was. I was scared at first but was so glad I had gone to see her to discuss this, as she did have time for me; and she explained things to me which made things seem clearer. I never heard anything from my doctor or Brian, for around three months or so, then one morning I had a letter on the floor which was my referral letter.
I was now very excited; and could not wait to start my new journey. I had already begun to get rid of some of my male clothes, as I had started living as Ruby a little bit more from around my eighteenth birthday.
As I now had a steady career in cabaret; and had a few television appearances, as well as a diary that was fully booked throughout the year, that I decided to move out of my little flat and look for something bigger.

The penthouse flat had become available and I put an offer in for it which I won, so I decided to let out my other apartment out as I did not need to sell due to having good finances put in place a while back.

I know I had used some of my girly fund, but I knew I would get this back as I did further work; and of course held a few more parties. This was also ideal, as I had now moved to a three bedroomed apartment; which I could easily cater for more guests.

I made plans to see Brian at his practice; and picked out just a normal everyday business suit. He was very pleased to see me, and again we had a lengthy talk.

I told him that I had a referral letter to see a psychiatrist; and he just told me that it was formality. He told me that he had heard about this from my doctor, and he accepted this appointment with him just to see if I was truly sure about this journey; just because he was a friend of my doctors. He also told me that he could not do anything as everything had to go through the right departments, but he wanted me to make appointments with him as that was his way of getting to see me on a one to one without anyone knowing.

This first meet was just to make sure he got all the details down so he could make assessments and get it on file, but I also knew it was for another reason as I also caught him altering his dressage a little; and could see he was aroused. I placed my hand on his knee and told him thank you for doing this for me, and I would never forget his kindness. As I did this, he rose to the attention even more, and as I looked behind me to make sure the door was locked, I undone his zip and placed my hand inside.

"If we had more time Brian, we could have done something about this, but I understand you need to make reports so please let me just say thank you to you in my own way." I told him.

"This is an unofficial consultation Ruby, and yes that would be great Ruby, but please have no worries no one will be in as I have strict orders not to be disturbed on a consultation." He replied.

"That's good, but I also know I only have an hour and thirty minutes have already gone." I replied, because I was warming to this doctor; and he was certainly top of the list when it came to good looks.

"Well next time then, as I will need to give you a full medical examination, so you will have to be naked in front of me. Best make sure we are not disturbed then." He said, as he raised his eyebrows.

I then moved over towards him where I removed his cock from his trousers; and started to gently rub it. He was now fully hard and moist and enjoying the moment which was a mixture of excitement and fear as he kept looking over his shoulder. Luckily for us we were on the first floor so no one could look in, but he was still full of adrenalin just wondering what if someone did come in. About fifteen minutes later, I felt him thrust himself towards me as his thighs began to tremble. I placed my mouth over his cock and let him cum deep into my throat.

As he stood up, he held my head, where his trousers fell to the floor. With my hand under his balls, I pulled down on them as he thrust his cock further into my throat, making me swallow all of what he had for me.

Once we had finished, I took out my handkerchief and wiped his cock for him, then gently wiped my mouth before putting the handkerchief back into my bag.

"This is off the record and I am asking you for complete discretion." He told me, as he began to get dressed.
"You know you have that already Brian, and I am a woman of my word." I replied.
"Well, congratulations Ruby, I am really pleased for you, pleased that you have decided to stay on the road you have so longed for. Right shall we say we make an appointment to see you in four weeks' time, as I will need to take a few more details from you and then assess you medically? Just remember this is only a medical assessment, I can do nothing without the correct information or go ahead without seeing your psychiatric assessment. I cannot give you hormones; it will come from his or her evaluation. I am only seeing you because I have really missed you, and would like to see you more often, and away from the parties." He said, smiling and I would imagine, anticipating our next meeting.
"Sure that's fine, but Brian you have seen me naked, or is this just a plot to get me undressed in your office and fuck me stupid?" I laughed.
"Oh Miss Ruby, you know me so well." He replied.

I left his office and made my way home, where I just crashed on the sofa in relief. There was a message on my phone to say I could pick up the keys for my penthouse apartment any time after Thursday, in which I was very excited. So that evening I decided to go and see Felicia and Kitty, where I gave them the good news.

78

I now became even more busier with my shows, and my
notoriety had got around London like the plague; so
much so, that I had people call me or my agent to see if I
would compare a show for them or design a set, as I was
beginning to be known in the world of runway for set
design. One such person was a lady by the name of Suzie
Wong, as she was big in the fashion world, and I was
told that she wanted someone like me, who would not be
afraid to tell a few people what I thought.

It was a further two months before I got a letter from the
psychiatrist to go and see him, so being all nervous I got
myself ready to attend. I did not know if I should go as
Ruby or as Tony, as I had no clue how or who I should
react and be.

Those first few meetings were awful, as he started asking
me if I was gay, did I have gay sex; and did I hate
women, in which I attacked him now with an acid
tongue I had got through my live shows. I gave him a
right mouthful, calling him all the names under the sun.
It made me utterly frustrated, and depressed as I tried to
take my mind off things by throwing myself into my
work; and by now I had become very close to Suzie;
with whom I was preparing to compare a fashion show
she was holding. I went over to see Suzie, but as a man
as it was only for chatting about what she wanted, and
what I was supposed to do for her. She then noticed that
I was not really with it; and asked me what the problem
was. I confided in her and told her all about my meetings
with the psychiatrist; and how it had left me feeling
depressed and angry, which was the reason for how I

was feeling today. She then looked at me and began telling me a story.

"My dear Ruby, there is something you need to know about me. I am a post-op male to female transsexual. Yes, I was born in a man's body; and I did everything I could to fit into society, even ended up getting married. But this was never enough for me; and having spoken to my wife I decided to fulfil my dreams."

Well, I was in total shock, as I always thought Suzie was a real woman from birth. She then looked at me, and then again went on to say.

"Transsexual really is a misleading word, as I feel it should be transgender. Transsexual seems to feed people the wrong image as it states sexual, where transgender states gender. You can be transgender and still like to be intimate with girls, or transgender where you like to be intimate with men. Transgender is not about whom you are attracted too, but more who you identify yourself to be. I have known transgender guys fuck girls and guys, where some of us do not like to use that part of our anatomy; and we adopt the role of the one who takes it up the arse until they decide to transgend. Some stay with their wives, whilst some separate and go with men. Some do not want to be with either a girl or a guy so sexually they become attracted to a pre-op transgender, giving them the best of both worlds; as they feel they want to be with a man, but also feel they need to be with a woman. I knew who I was; and I wanted to stay with my wife; but I will be honest with you Ruby. Before

80

surgery I did sleep with a lot of men, until I could save
enough money to fully transgend. I have kissed a lot of
ugly frogs to get to where I am now; and I would not
change a single thing. I fought my corner to be who I am,
and to live my life as I felt it was intended. As for the
psychos, they are testing you my dear, they have to make
sure that this is truly the right thing, so expect those little
blows where they say no; and just try and stay strong.
Sadly, my dear Ruby, I have known friends who thought
they wanted to transcend, as they too believed they
wanted to become the other sex, when it was all too
much for them; and later down the road, they committed
suicide. So, you need to look deeply within; and there
find your own answers about transcending to become a
woman."

Having heard what Suzie said, seemed to make sense;
but it was still not going to be an easy road. I did have to
stay strong, I had to take the rough with the smooth, but I
did not know how long I could keep up this facade.
Suzie was born in the late twenties, where she left her
home of wales at the age of 14, to discover the bright
lights of London. She first of all became a high class call
girl, unknown to her aunt with whom she lived; and a
few years later was accepted at RADA, where she then
became a successful male actor and transgirl model;
where she took Hollywood by storm. However, she
always yearned for the lights of London; and therefore,
she moved back to start her own business.
Suzie had a colourful lifestyle, dating four Hollywood
directors, one Senator; and a numerous string of men
from the law industry. I also heard that she married

briefly, to a well-known Hollywood actress by the name of Lien Hua Wong, until her transgender reassignment in the middle of the Sixties. I put this to Suzie, who corrected some of the information, as I was informed that she was still married to Lien Hua Wong.

"My dear, Felicia has it all the wrong way in context. I was married to the beautiful Lien Hua, but we divorced when it was known about the issue of my gender reassignment. We are still friends today; and we still stay in touch. She offered me money to set myself up in business, however, I had enough of my own and therefore, I did not need her to help me out like some tabloids had exposed. I then met George on set as Suzie, as he was directing a documentary about my life; and we just hit it off. And I must say, it has been twenty years or so that we have been together; and we're still going strong. Poor Felicia, she has been taking too much Charlie whizz my dear." She informed me.

I then asked her what Charlie whizz was, as this was unknown to me.

"Charlie whizz dear, you know… coke, cocaine." She explained to a baffled Ruby.
"I never knew Suzie." I replied.
"Oh yes dear, she was rather fond of sniffing a few white lines, instead of working for me as she should have. I caught her one afternoon, as I was having a launch party for a new line of clothing; and I caught her in the bedroom with one of my ex's, stark naked I ask you. Stark naked as she spread the lines over my ex's chest;

and then rode him like she was on fucking heat, like an alley cat." She continued to say.

I just thought that I wouldn't have known, where on earth to look, if it had been me walking in on her. But then again, I know Felicia; and I have seen her in action, for it has been be that she had been fuckin.

"*You could not help but see my dear, as she straddled him, whilst he was obviously inside her ass fucking her, all oiled up and glistening. I could not look at a silk bed throw again, without thinking about the dirty bitches; and on my new bedding too.*" She said, as she gave out a little posh totty laugh.
"*Good job it was not rubber bedding, or the pair of them might have slid out of the window. Now that would have been a sight.*" I laughed
"*Oh you are a card my dear, that I would have loved to have seen. I can see we are going to get on very well together.*" She told me.

Suzie then told me that my reputation had proceeded me; and for a minute I thought she had caught wind of my early years with my parties, when she put me at ease with my reputation being that of a set designer.
She told me that she was making plans for her new line of clothing; and she wanted me to design the set for me, as she had seen some of the work I had done for another person, as well as that of working alongside the big names of Thames Television and ATV. So, I agreed, as Suzie and I became the best of friends, with her even asking me to be a model in her show, which I declined as

I was not one for the fashion world, because I excelled better on the cabaret circuit for which I was known; and knew I was not a fledgling model. She also told me with regards transcending, if I did not want to go all the way, then this would not be a problem, for she had lots of friends who were women with cocks, as that is what they preferred. Tits and cock, arouses so many men, whether gay or straight.

I went through hell and back over the next two years, ending up in hospital with just under thirty suicide attempts. Then this one day out of the blue, a letter had dropped through my letterbox. Upon opening it, it was not an appointment for the usual psychiatrist I had been seeing, but now one who wanted to see me at the gender reassignment clinic at Charing Cross Hospital. I had feelings of happiness and of sadness, and again I never had an idea what I should do. I finally picked enough courage to find out what to wear, and I just thought that out of respect I wanted to make a good impression; so, I had best go as Tony. I made my way to the hospital, where eventually I got to see the psychiatrist. When it was my turn to be seen, he came out of his room and called me over. Looking at me, he looked a little bewildered at first, and then we began to speak.

"So Ruby is it?" He asked, as he put his glasses onto the rim of his nose.
"Yes doctor, it is." I replied.
"Ok then tell me why you feel you want to change your body." He asked, scribbling a few notes as we further chatted.

"*I have always felt like this since I can remember, however, I kept it to myself. I then took the courage to tell my doctor when I was fifteen, who in turn told my mother; and they both suggested electric shock treatment.*" I told him, as the memories came flooding back.

"*That is barbaric, and we do not take that type of actions today.*" He replied, making me feel at ease.

"*Well, he fuckin wanted to.*" I shouted, as I still was not certain about psychiatrists, no matter how cute they were.

"*And do you think Electro Convulsive Therapy would have helped you?*" he asked

"*No I do not. No amount of bloody torture would have taken away how a person really feels about themselves inside doctor.*" I replied, putting up my guard.

"*And how do you feel now then.*" He asked me.

"*I feel people have always judged me as being gay, or a cock in a frock; just so I can sleep with men who like that sort of thing. You know have something extra in their panties.*" I told him, as he perked up.

"*And do you think you are gay then.*" He replied.

"*No I do not. I have never classed myself as being gay; as I have always been a girl in my mind and my soul. It is just this fuckin body which I strongly feel is so wrong. I have the wrong body for what my mind tells me I should have.*" I said sarcastically

"*So what about sex, do you have sex with men or women?*" He asked.

"*I am sorry doctor, but you are beginning to fuckin piss me off. Sex has nothing to do with wanting to change your body. Sex has nothing to do with the feeling, that you are trapped inside something that is foreign to you.*

And sex does not make you a man or a woman, sex is fuckin sex for Christ's sake." I screamed.

He then told me to calm down, otherwise I would burst a blood vessel, as he then questioned me about my last statement. He said that if I say that I was trapped in a male body; and that I felt I wanted to be a woman, because that is what was in my mind. Then why had I come to visit him today, dressed as a man. Again, I saw red, as I told him that I visited him as a man out of respect, respect towards him, as that is what I was taught from my mother, to respect others; and as I did respect him, then the decent thing he could do would be to respect me.

Now being a little calmer, the doctor told me that I first of all have to respect myself, before you get respect from others, which made me realise how true he was. He then told me that he would take on my case; and that he would not be starting me on hormone treatment right away. He expected me to live my life as a woman, living as Ruby for a minimum of two years. That he would contact his colleague in the clinic, where he would put my case too him, and he would see me again in about three months' time. I told him that I was prepared to do all what he had suggested, when I then asked him to let me finish what I had going on in my mind. I told him that if people like him were not so full of shit in the first place, then people like me would have a clearer insight to how things were. Well, once again I had struck a nerve, but I had to be honest and say how it was.

"*Full of shit, Ruby. You think I am full of shit, when I have* already agreed to take on your case. I could have easily." He replied as I then interrupted him.
"*Yes, full of shit. And I know you were going to say, that you could have easily refused my application; and if you had done, I would have complained to the fact of discrimination. Full of shit, I meant as in you lightly used sex as trying to deter if I was a cock in a frock, wanting sex with guys. Full of shit, as in thinking ECT could cure something that is not a disease. Please forgive me doctor, but I am transgender, not a common disease, and it is for that reason I said you were full of shit. If it offended you, then I apologise for my way with words, but not for my explanation of who I am.*" I told a not so silent doctor.

I left that appointment totally drained; but felt I had put across a strong argument; an argument I thought that no doctor had reason to question, let alone think I was positively diseased. As far as I was concerned, he should have listened to my feelings, and saw that I was passionate about my identity; and it was not conjured up on a childish whim. I also understood that certain questions needed to be asked; it was just that he pissed me off, when it was I who knew my own mind, and he thought he knew better. The next time I had an appointment with him, I went as Ruby; as did I with every other appointment.
Over the next two years, I concentrated on my shows and television appearances; and working alongside Suzie, who was an immense sort of help as she listened to me. I had got my penthouse to my liking and had a regular

weekly party and before long, I had got all my money back into the bank. I was finally given hormone replacement treatment, after two years of appointments with the doctor, who over time had got to know me well; and got to know that I did indeed have a fiery temper, in which I often corrected him by telling him not to mistake fiery for passionate.

I still had my ups and downs with them, which made me moody, as well as having my happy times, but the nicest thing was I was now developing a nice pair of breasts. My own GP had been given permission to give me the prescription, and I still have a quarterly meeting with Brian at his office; and got to see him regular at my parties. I was not a gay man, but had to embrace the gay scene, even with their bigotry and hate towards my kind, with their rude and quite often bitchy remarks.

Transgender was in its infancy on the gay scene, as it was dominated by gay men and lesbians; and at that precise moment, we transgender people had no other place to go.

Because I had nowhere else to go, I had to adopt a somewhat gay lifestyle by becoming a drag queen, because I could not frequent the many straight bars around London as a woman, even though I had now got used to shopping as Ruby. It was easier for me to hide within the gay community as a drag queen, until the time was right for me to come out as a transgender woman, because I knew that it would not always be that way; and that one day I would be accepted for the woman I am and not the drag queen I once was.

Felicia had now made a success with her club which she called Diamonds, in which I too was a regular act there.

It was there that I met this very young handsome guy, who I knew was going to change my life forever.

I had noticed he had been looking at me, on more than one occasion, as I had also seen him at a few of the other venues that I worked at. I did nothing to encourage him, because most guys I got to meet were just the ones who wanted to fuck a tranny; and then go back to their wives of boyfriends, but the more I tried to avoid him, the more he became persistent. He would first of all raise his glass, then when I showed him no attention, there would be a glass of vodka, brought up to me from the barman.

Many times, I said on the mic, that I had a secret admirer; and that first glass brought lots more to follow; which I ended up having to tell them to stop, for fear of me being a drunken old tart. So, this night that he was there, as usual he raised his glass towards me; and then leant onto the bar as I got on with my show, as he constantly kept looking at me with eyes transfixed, in a rather sexy but scary manner.

When I had finished my show, I made my way back to the dressing room; and there I got changed into a beautiful sequin gown, where I then made my way to the bar. Just as I was about to get my complimentary drink; yes, complimentary, as it was a code of respect that you got one free drink from management. Well… just as I was about to get my drink, this guy butted in and said he would pay for it. I looked at him and laughed, as I told him it was a free one, but he can get the next one.

I then sat on the barstool at the end of the bar, when this guy turned around and then introduced himself to me.

"Good evening Ruby, very good show tonight." This tall guy said.

"Thank you dear, I am glad you liked it." I replied, as I looked him up and down.

"I have seen you a few times; and you always surprise me with your ever flowing new material, some drag queens use the same old crap all the time." He said, as he handed me my glass of wine.

"That's why I prefer to go live, as it is an unwritten script." I told him.

We then started to get into conversation, and he told me that his parents owned a bar in Bethnal Green; and that he was in finance, as well as putting his hand into a bit of building renovation on the side. He then told me that he hoped to own his own bar one day, but for now he was quite happy doing what he is doing, as we engaged in light conversation. I just thought that was that not the whole point of it. To do what you enjoy doing, as it was no good being in a job that you do not like, sounding a little bit sarcastic, which was not meant to come off that way. He agreed with me, as he then introduced himself to me.

"By the way my name is John, but people call me Johnny." He said, as he held out his hand.

"So nice to meet you Johnny. So tell me, are you gay or straight? As I am a little confused, because you have been staring at my tits for the last twenty minutes or so." I asked him.

"Oh, you noticed, so are they real or is it just a bra? Or is this a drag secret?" He said, marvelling at my chest.

"*Oh they are definitely real dear, as I have been on hormones for a while now.*" I replied.

"*Is that for your cabaret career then Ruby? And yes I am gay.*" He told me.

"*No dear, I do not class myself as gay, even though I do drag. I am transgender and feel that I am a woman trapped inside a man's body; and have always felt that way, this is just the beginning of my transformation. I am transgender and cannot wait to be fully me; and be true to myself. Until then I will continue doing my shows; and living life on the drag scene until I feel the time is right for me.*" I replied, now preening myself as he too looked me over.

We then started chatting some more, about if I liked men or women, as well as business, which made for a welcome change, from the guys just trying to fuck a drag queen, as I thought he simply was not interested in that part of me, as he used no chat up lines. I think he just liked me and what I was about; and never once had he overstepped the mark of being rude and crude, like so many guys I had come in contact with.

Having an acid tongue was also quite fortunate, as I was lucky that I could put them back in their rightful place, as still no one got the better of Ruby Passion.

Early that morning he made sure that I got back home ok, as he saw me to my door, where he then he turned around and I guess made his own way home.

He was a very handsome guy standing at around six foot and a bit, with nice dark black hair; and I noticed through his open shirt that he had some chest hair, but not a lot so that it protruded out from his neck.

He was very much a gentleman and never ever pushed himself onto me, but then again it was the 70's; and most men were gentlemen back in those days. We then exchanged phone numbers after a little light conversation; and made arrangements to meet the next day for lunch. This went on for around six months, as we got closer and closer, where Johnny still made no attempts to force himself upon me.

The thing is, I too was an old fashioned kind of girl; and I know I had history when I was in my teens. It was what helped me raise money, to put aside for that special day in which I would transform. I promised myself, that if I ever met the right guy; and he would be the one I would settle down with, then I would let him know about my past. I think it was also pretty obvious, that I was not your typical, everyday sort of city girl. I was born with a dick for heaven's sake, but I am a girl none the less, despite what folk may think.

I always believed in love and romance, as well as chivalry; and I always felt an element of pride in being that way, because I was and still am an old fashioned romantic person. I have my father to thank for that, as he always showered mother with gifts and flowers; and showed me that love was still alive, no matter what your age. I also felt, that as we had now approached the next generation… the 1970's; and the generation of Glam Rock, that it will be a world that will become modern with the acceptance to music and culture, as people struggle to have their identities acknowledged.

There were times that I felt it was still hard to believe in true love; and waiting for the right person to come along in fear of being left on the shelf, because women are beginning to stand up for themselves now; and are now ready to be recognised for their own independent reasons. I felt that the days of the swinging sixties; and the time of the hippies and free love was coming to an end, as women no longer wanted to be the sole object of a man's way of thinking. And I think it was a sort of anarchy towards men, because you often heard guys in the bars or clubs talking about their latest conquests, their one night stands, as they talk about sex so positively, as they rated how good the sex was; which I think was now beginning to piss women off.

It is very hard for a woman to try and enter into a relationship, when men are so immature these days by not wanting to commit; and I have nothing against casual sex, I have done it myself, however, that was purely for business.

As for my soulmate, casual sex and hook ups are really not for me, because I do not want my first encounter waking up to a man that I am in love with, to have happened after a drunken night out, that I feel I would end up regretting it. I would want it to be with someone I truly cared for, that I felt I could spend the rest of my life with him, because it is not about sex, it is more about love; and about the love that we have for one another.

I would also hope that the man in question would feel the same way as I do, as we would smile at one another when we awake. To spend the day with him, and to miss him when he is not around; and the thoughts of him that make you smile inside and out.

Cheesy, I know, I know some would think of that statement as such, but old fashioned I would say.

Some may say or think that I am a fruit loop, to want to

spend the rest of my life with someone, but I think it is romantic; and it shows commitment.

What is wrong with that?

I also think that like my father, he too should wine and dine me; and open doors for me, as well as buy me flowers for no reason at all, but because he is old fashioned. All I really want is to be able to spend the rest of my life, with a man who wants me for me. Who can walk with me on my journey; and embrace the changes that I will make to become the butterfly that I was truly meant to be.

Because Johnny has made no effort to force himself onto me sexually, tells me that I think he could be that man in which I could spend the rest of my life with.

By the end of 1970 I finally plucked up the courage to invite Johnny inside my home, where I made him a scotch as I poured myself a vodka and coke. We sat there until the early hours of the morning chatting when I started to fall asleep, so I invited him to stay over with me, as I thought it was pointless him going back to his own home, with it now being so late.

Through our courtship, Johnny had been like my father and brought me flowers and chocolates. We had cosy nights in and out, but he never stopped over that often, as he always told me that he too was old fashioned; and that he wanted to take it slow. This evening however, Johnny agreed to stay over with me; and so we then made our way upstairs to the bedroom, taking our drinks with us. Johnny stripped off in front of me and climbed into bed, where he had such a lovely fit body with just the right amount of chest hair, as I hated hairy men; and around a seven-inch thick cock to top off a beautiful manly body. He was not very bushy down below, but at the same time he was not shaved or trimmed like some of the gay guys I knew. He was truly an all-round natural good looking guy, who only needed to prune himself on his facial features, as sometimes he sported the five o'clock shadowing to his young face.

That evening in bed was somewhat slightly awkward, as I did not want to come across to him as the Miss I had been with my clients. I wanted to be different and wanted to be the real Ruby away from the parties and drag circuit, as that is how he made me feel.

He lay on top of me as he kissed me on the lips; and moved his lips over my body, removing my panties as he reached for my cock. I am not sure if it was the hormones or my nerves, but for once I could not get an erection, so I just placed my hand over my dick and said.

"Please Johnny not that hideous thing, I do not like it to be touched there at all. I pray for the day it will be removed."
"I thought you didn't mind being touched there, as our conversations had mentioned earlier?" He replied.
"Well eventually I want it removing, so it must be nerves Johnny, no one has ever been this loving and gentle with me so please be patient. I am not promising you anything, but I also thought you liked me just like I am, and not for that hideous thing you call a dick." I told him, now feeling rather confused.

He never touched my dick all that night, as he just slid his tongue down my groin and under my balls, until he raised my ass in the air and he saw my hole. He lifted my legs up and slid his tongue deep inside me, making me moan with every inch he touched with his tongue. Before long he had my legs over his shoulders, where he rammed his cock deep inside me, as he pulled me towards him and then thrust himself deeper into my ass. He soon began panting heavily, as he told me that he loved me, when he then just grabbed hold of my waist.

"Oh God Ruby, I am going to cum." He began saying, as his legs started to shake
"Come on dear, shoot into my ass, you know you want to. Come on my horny stud fill your Ruby up." I replied, now coaxing him to hurry up, as I was tired and just wanted it to end.

As he pulled me harder onto him, he just let go and thrust one last time and emptied himself inside me, reaching down as he kissed me on the neck, pushing that last bit of him into my hot moist ass, as I felt his breath on my neck. That morning he asked me if I would be his girl, in which I replied I would; and we spent the next few days with each other, making love and getting to know each other better. When he came to see me from work, I would be showered with flowers and perfume; and he would say that we would eat out rather than stay in, even though he was an excellent cook.

In the New Year of 1971, I asked Johnny to move in with me. He accepted my offer, where over the next few weeks he had moved out of his parent's bar, as we started our life together as a couple.

He became very good friends with Felicia, giving her advice financially about her business in which she was grateful for. For once in my life, I felt like the real woman I wanted to be, I had a home and a husband with a very good job, and money in the bank. I never ever thought about being that boy I used to be as I had now got used to my life as Ruby.

Johnny tried a few times to touch my dick when we made love, but it was only when I reminded him that it was out of bounds, did he realise. He did used to ask sometimes why I referred to my male organ as a dick; and yet I called his male organ a cock. I told him if I called mine a cock, then I accepted that I was a man, but calling it a dick made no reference in my eyes as being that of a man, as I told him I said strange things at times, but it was my way of coping

I did not know why he stayed with me after all he was a gay man and loved cock; and I was transgender and hated what I was given. But still he got to play with my tits and fuck my ass, so I guess he did not feel the need to complain. We were certainly not the usual gay relationship people mistook us for; and I had no intentions of turning him straight like so many people thought I would, as I heard the gossip of the scene when walking through the door to a gay bar. I liked my life as it was; and Johnny was the perfect partner any woman could ever wish for.

Over the next two years, we had got very close together; and we became inseparable. I truly believed that Johnny embraced my gender issues, as he slowly understood who I was. I did a few times tell him to go with a nice pretty gay boy, just so he can experience sucking a guy off, but then it was always whilst I was under the influence of vodka.

Whilst visiting Madam Kitty, I noticed the bar around the corner was for sale, so I phoned Johnny at his workplace. I could sense by the tone of his voice that he was thrilled; and once I had given him the contact number, he told me that he would phone them straight away, as he was busy at that moment sorting someone's finances out, but he did phone then that day.

The next few weeks were intense, as he waited by the phone for a call, as well as waiting by the door to see if the agents or postman had posted anything through. Then out of the blue he got a phone call offering him a viewing, in which he could have snapped the agents hand off. He put in an offer, which was soon accepted; and as he had contacts in the building trade, he soon got them in to refurb the place. He was now the proud owner of his own bar; and you could see he was like a little boy with a new toy. He had decided to change the name from The Boars Head to The Rainbow; and had it fitted out very nicely indeed, making sure that there was also a stage for me to perform; and a royal box for me to entertain when I was not on the stage. He had a few more projects to do as the upstairs was a very large flat in which he was going to make into the dressing rooms; and downstairs was the kitchen in which was going to be the stock rooms.

It was 1973; and it was in this year when his name went above the door; and you could see how proud he was of it too. Both of us standing outside, admiring the name plate that was being put up over the doorway as it then sunk in that it was indeed Johnny's bar. Felicia had popped the champagne that Kitty had given her; as the four of us toasted Johnny's ownership; and our new venture together.

"Well, Mr Johnny Delaney, you are now the proud owner of your first bar." I told him as I gave a smile. *"You are indeed right, my dear Ruby; and you have your very own stage, so now you can deal with the cabaret bookings. Together Ruby, we are both going to make this such a success."* He replied, as you could see how happy he was, again we toasted our new venture together.

I told Johnny about the parties I used to host; and how now they are not sexual due to being with him. I also mentioned to him that once a week I will still have a few people round, however, I suggested once he has completed the upstairs dressing rooms then we should host the parties at the Rainbow. I only felt the need to tell Johnny about the parties, as I could trust him. Besides it was not as though he did not have a shady past, as he was not all innocent and light. He had a few encounters with men, who were looking for sex in the park, as they cruised single men around the pond and the woods, as well as a brief time of going to the toilets on the hunt for some fun. Cottaging it was called, which I thought was a strange name to call something so horrid, as looking for sex in a toilet.

"Oh, and why is that Ruby, surely we would get into trouble with the law?" He asked, as I again told him of my parties.

"Not with my contacts Johnny; and it would bring in extra revenue of anything up to five grand a party; depending on who would attend." I replied.
"But that would be a lockdown; and you know how the police patrol this area to catch people out." He said, now rather concerned.
"Yes, they do Johnny, but not if one of your guests is the chief superintendent dear. So, with your building skills I would suggest you hurry up and finish the upstairs; and then it will be a little more cash in the till, as there are only limited supplies, I can bring up here. Most either drank whiskey or champagne anyway, so you can get it cheaper from the suppliers." I replied.

He then told me that he would get on with it as soon as he could, as he thought he could maybe call in a few mates from his dad's bar to help. I thought that he was so sweet, as I told him I would let my clients know, that there will be a new venue for them in the coming months. Now smiling, as I told him of the income it would produce.
Giving me a certain look, he smiled as he said '*clients*!' which sounded very seedy. Asking me if I was sure that it was not sex; and was it for those people who wished not to be seen in a gay bar in normal hours, mainly because of their job that they were most concerned about.

"Yes Johnny, I did tell you that before seeing you, that it was based on sex, hence the money for my girly fund. I do not need that now as I am not that sexual since taking the hormones, so would much prefer to be a hostess. Besides one of the judges himself likes to dress up, so

what better place to do it than here." I told him, as I reassured him.

I then began to get questioned by Johnny, as he asked me about the judge's intentions; and if he wanted sex, would I arrange it? I began to get tired of his questioning, because at the end of the day it was money, and no businessman runs away from money.

"There is a lot of what if's here Johnny, what I say is if there was someone who wanted to participate then I would make sure they had privacy, besides five grand and above for a party in your till is not bad at all, so don't knock it. And you will be legit as we have not just judges, and barristers here, but also the police. If you are referring to him wanting sex with me, then the answer is no, you are all I need and want Johnny; and this is just extra business" I said to him sarcastically.
"Ok I will try it, but I am not completely100% happy with it Ruby. The money would sure come in handy to pay off the bar too, but what about your cut?" He asked, trying to seem interested.
"Oh, don't worry about that, they will pay for the drinks at your price even if you charge more; and I will get my own fee for hosting the party. They all know the score Johnny; and this is big money so please don't worry about anything, because I have it covered. I do not want parties at home anymore, as I want to keep that just for us, our private time together, without thinking of all or sundry popping their heads in, in all manner of dress or undress." I replied, now showing him my business knowledge.

So, I had sorted out the future of my parties; and I told Johnny they would go ahead and happen, as it was nicer having them in the bar, where they could be looked after better; and could disappear through the back door without our residents twitching their net curtains.

Johnny was a lovely man; and I knew he loved me, but what I said did eventually go, besides I was doing him a favour too with business. I even changed my name through the courts to Ruby Delaney; and kept Ruby Passion just as a stage name, even though I was hoping that one day Johnny would propose to me.

I now felt very girly, with having a proper name and not a stage name to use, which were eventually put on my bank books, accounts and cheque book etc.

Though we did have sex, I was not overly keen as I knew the hormones gave me mood swings. I did not always like it being shoved up my ass anyway; and I prayed for the day that I would have my dick made into a vagina, so I could be the woman I was meant to be. Johnny still tried touching me there from time to time, which I am sure he knew wound me up, even more so when we cuddled and he fell asleep with his arms around me, as I would get his warm breath on my neck; and his hand placed over that alien of a dick that I had to wear. It was only on a few odd occasions it would get hard, but it never stayed hard for long, much to Johnny's disappointment as he thought I had shown him interest.

Well yet another morning came along; and today was my appointment with the doctor. I only saw him now every six months at his office, even though I saw him as a regular customer at my parties. Johnny had previous left at six am, as he was renovating the upstairs, which was nearly finished, so it left me all alone to get ready.

I showered that morning, putting on my best lingerie and perfume as I picked out the minimalist of dresses.

It was a nice flowing fifties style dress, so easily accessible I thought, as I knew something would happen as it has been so long. Underneath I just had a bra and panties with a suspender belt; and my boobs really did fill out my bra giving me such a lovely cleavage.

Being on the hormones certainly thickened my hair; and prevented my beard from coming through, so I was very lucky that I never had to shave, as I never had much of facial hair anyway which was a godsend.

I used my own hair which was a rich chestnut brown, and it was only in the shows where I would put on a wig. Now that I was all ready to leave, I then checked myself in the mirror to see if I passed. I never went anywhere if my makeup was too much or not right, or if a hair was out of place. I had to look very feminine otherwise I would not walk out the door; and I had to completely change into an everyday woman; and not the one he was so used to see at my previous parties.

The dominant side of Ruby was now phasing out, as I was becoming that woman I had always dreamed about. It was only when in the bedroom did the real Ruby Passion come out; and on a one to one basis. I then left the apartment, and made my way to the underground garages. Having placed my bag and coat in the car, I made my way to the doctors, having the sunroof down at the same time.

I loved my little red Triumph convertible; and it was a

very girly car for me, as I just loved going for a drive as I felt the wind rush through my hair, but not messing it up as I had my scarf securely tied around my head. Having got to Brian's office I announced that I was there and what time my appointment was, in which the receptionist asked me to sit down. I had not sat down that long and was just about to pick up a magazine, when Brian came out of his office. He called me over; and then went over to the receptionist to tell her that under no circumstance must he be disturbed, as he was in a medical examination. That confirmed to me that he had something planned, as by now my heart was racing.

As strange as it seemed, I loved my Johnny; and he was the sweetest kindest man you could have as a partner, yet there was something different about Brian, as he had that effect on me that it became forbidden fruit. We walked around the corridors and up one flight of stairs to his office; and then once inside he put a sign on the door saying examination in progress where he then locked the door behind him. He asked me if I would like a drink, in which I asked for a cup of tea. Once all the formalities were over, he asked me how I had been, how the business and cabaret was doing in which I let him know things were fine.

His office faced the back and being on the first floor was not over looked, so we had a beautiful view of the lawns and a small pond which has already enticed a few ducks. As it was not overlooked there was no need to draw the blinds, which were a change from the first visit when his office was downstairs, although not overlooked you had to be careful just in case the gardeners were out.

The sun also shone in the room which made it feel warm

and cosy; and not long after being in his room I was asked to take off my jacket.

Although the door was locked, Brian had also pulled the changing screen in front of the door as a precaution.

He then asked me to sit on the couch so he could take my blood pressure, and with his stethoscope check my breathing. Once he placed the stethoscope on my back, I jumped slightly and then said.

"Brian, you could have warmed that up as its cold."
"I am sorry Ruby, but at least I can see you're your reflexes are fine." He laughed.

I then felt his warm breath on my neck as he then began to unzip my dress, which then fell off me and dropped to my waist revealing my breasts in my bra. Again, he used the stethoscope checking my back, and then he came around to my front where he placed it on my chest. Once this had been done, he put his stethoscope away, and then proceeded to undo my bra and let my breasts fall naturally. Usually for a transgender girl you would not have a very large breast, as he then told me that my sisters and mother must be largely formed, because I seemed to be following them.

As my breasts were now on show he placed them in his hands and had a good feel; and I was so thankful that his hands were warm. As he continued to do this, I looked up at him and there it was… that little sparkle that made my heart race. By this time, although not erect I had myself began to stir; and I could see by now that Brian was fully erect. I kept thinking to myself do I touch him, or shall I wait? Is he ready or am I being too forward?

I just thought that it would be best if I let him play with my breasts a little longer; and if he wanted to take it further, then maybe I should wait for him to make his move. He then once again moved behind me and again I felt his warm breath on my neck, as he again brought his hands around me and cupped them under my breasts. Now he had his fingers gently squeezing my nipples, which sent me stirring passionately. I placed my hand onto his and asked him to stop, as I was going out of control. He then kissed my neck as I lay my head to one side, as he again stroked and played with my breasts and nipples. It was then that he asked me to stand up; and as I did my dress just slipped to the floor, when he then placed his hands on my hips; and there he gently removed my panties as he slid his tongue deep inside my hole, grabbing onto my waist as he pulled me towards him. As he held me there tightly, with his hands parting my ass cheeks he then told me to spread my legs and lean towards the couch. This I did; and in doing so he parted my ass a little more as he slid his tongue deep inside me. Much to my surprise and horror, I was by now fully erect as I felt him sliding his tongue deeper into me. This was so good, in which I told him not to stop, as the heat was beginning to stimulate the whole of my body. As I looked down, I could see him on his knees; and as I felt him tongue fucking my ass, his own cock was simply bulging and I knew I wanted to get on my own knees and suck his thick hard cock. He then surprised me, as he brought one of his hands under my legs and reached for my wet hard cock, placing it in his hand and gently rubbing it until my senses sent me into a frenzy. I just shook with nerves and excitement, as I then told him to stop as I was not sure if I wanted him touching me there.

"So, you like your doctor playing with your girly cock do you Ruby?" He replied, with the biggest grin you could imagine.
"Oh yes doctor I do now, you can do anything you want to me, I am all yours." I told him, as I strangely liked him sucking and playing with my cock.
"But I thought it was you who liked me to be submissive Ruby, not the other way around." He replied.
"Brian today I don't give a damn who is or who is not submissive, just make love to me please." I begged.

I could not understand why I didn't like Johnny touching me there, yet I had just got so aroused with Brian, that I so wanted him to touch me on my girly cock, now surprising myself as I referred it to such a name.
Having then put that to one side, I just looked at him and threw my arms around him, he then stood me up and turned me around, where he placed his lips on mine.
He kissed me passionately, thrusting his tongue down my throat and playing with my tongue, so I then started to undress him by removing his shirt and tie first, then by undoing his trousers. Before long we were both naked in his office, and as I held his hard cock, he had his hands around mine.

"This has been far too long Ruby; I cannot go six months again. I will need to see you more often if you will see me? And for some unknown reason, I really want to taste

your girly cock" He said, as I could feel that he had indeed waited for such a long time to savour me.
"Oh, and what about the other so called girls Brian?" I replied, knowing that there were others.
"Since meeting you I only now see them on a doctor patient scenario, I only want to be intimate with you Ruby. I told you even though I am top, I will only ever be your sub guy; and I am just waiting for you to accept me." He said, as I now believed him.
"Wow Brian, you would do all that for me?" I asked.
"Yes Ruby, and more. And I cannot believe I have actually got hold of your cock, as it never really was my thing." He replied
"More Brian, what do you mean?" I said rather confused.
"I would like you to be the first girl who fucks me, because I have often wondered what it was like; and I would like you to be the first one to take my virgin ass Ruby. I know you want to because look at you as hard a rock downstairs." He said, as he held onto my hardness a while longer.
"God do I Brian, I have been waiting years for this." I replied.

He kissed me again, as he held me in his arms; and he then dropped to his knees and took me deep inside his mouth, slowly fingering my ass as he took all of me down his throat. As he was kneeling there, looking down at him I noticed he was oozing precum, as the end of his cock just glistened at it nestled there just like a bird in its nest.

"Slow down Brian or you will make me cum, and unlike you I cannot perform twice just like that." I said, as I was trying hard to force myself not to shoot my load.

Brian stopped and then he sat on the couch as he called me towards him, with his legs wide open I placed myself between him and started taking his thick hard cock down my throat. For a moment I forgot how big he was, so I had to do it in stages, slowly easing more of him into me. I then asked him to lie on his back; and as he brought himself to the end of the couch, I raised his legs as I slid my own tongue deep inside his ass, now making it moist, ready for him to be taken by his Ruby. Gently I rimmed his ass as I fingered him, and I could see him playing with his own cock.

"Now don't you get shooting that load too soon Brian, I want you to save some for me." I told him, as I smiled at him.
"It is all yours Ruby, just let me know when you want it; and I will give it to you." He replied.
"So, are you ready for Ruby's cock Brian?" I asked.
"I sure am Ruby, and please be gentle." He replied.

I placed some gel onto my fingers and wiped it over his hole, placing the rest over my cock. I then positioned myself nervously by him placing my hard wet cock by his hole and gently pushed into him.
"Oh God Ruby, that's great. I have so wanted this; and thank you for being my first." He said, as he waited impatiently for me to penetrate him.

"Good, now just relax so I can get deep inside you." I said, as I placed my girly cock by his ass.
"Yes, Miss Ruby, whatever you say." He replied.

He did finally relax, and I got all of my thick cock inside him. I had never been so hard or thick like this before; and this was definitely my first fuck without a strap on, in so many years. I think I only ever managed it once, however, I was not completely sure now.

Harder I pushed myself into him as I could see his face enjoying every moment, as I pulled his legs towards me as they lay against my breasts. My cock now deep inside him as I placed my hand over his; and with my finger I spread his pre cum over the tip. Brian was just lying there with his legs resting on my shoulders, as I held onto him and thrust myself into his ass, as he rubbed his rock hard ten-inch cock that was still oozing pre-cum. He too told me to stop otherwise he would shoot his load too, and he was saving all of this for me. It was not long before I felt my body shake vigorously, as my legs began to spasm, as I was now on the borderline of shooting my load. I could not hold on any longer, and as my legs began to quiver, I told Brian that I was going to shoot my load. He then told me that I was a good girl; and that I should fill him, I should fill my doctor's ass up with my creamy girly cum. I just held his cock tight, as I thrust a few more times shooting deep inside him. I kept thrusting until I could thrust no more; and until he had drained me of all my juices, still holding onto my hips as he pulled me towards him, looking at me and thanking me for a beautiful moment, telling me that he had to stop playing with his cock for fear of shooting at the same

110

time I emptied myself into him. I then withdrew my cock from his ass; and lay over him; where he then asked me to go into the same position as I had put him into. He wanted to see me in my full glory; and how horny it was to see my tits; and drained girly cock, as he then wanted to penetrate my tight ass. I lay on the end of the couch, as he placed his cock by my hole. My legs now thrown over his shoulders, as he guided himself inside me. Once I had got all of his massive cock inside me, he grabbed hold of my breasts and played with them as he fucked me. Harder he penetrated me as he took my breasts and squeezed my nipples, getting himself worked up more and more as he began talking dirty to me.

"Oh God Ruby, this is fantastic. I have waited so long for this I can tell you. Just seeing you there with your tits and girly cock is divine, fucking your tight ass is heaven." He said, now making sure I have every inch of his erect cock.
"That's good Brian, even if you are a big boy and it fuckin hurts. Just fuck me dear; and fuck me good and proper." I replied, as I pulled him towards me so that I could give him a kiss on the lips.
"It is no good Ruby, I need to suck on your tits, so I am going to have to sit down and get you to straddle me." He said, now lusting over me as he licked his lips.

He moved me towards him; and still with his cock deep inside me, he carried me to his chair. There he sat down as I sat on top of him, with my legs straddling his waist. My breasts were now in full view of his face as he took

each one in turn, where he kissed and sucked them.
As he held my waist, he guided me up and down onto his
cock, with my breasts slapping him in the face.

*"God Ruby, I am going to cum soon. Let me fill your
tight with my creamy cum."* He said, as his breathing
became harder and more intense.
"Yes Brain, fill your Ruby up." I replied.

He again held onto my waist as he thrust deep inside my
ass, as I held my breasts out and placed them in his face.
My hands now holding the back of his chair, as his face
was buried in my breasts. I heard his whimpering moans
as I felt him thrust faster into my ass, and his mouth
suckling my breasts just like a baby.

"Oh God Miss Ruby, fuckin hell I am cumming." He said,
becoming more erotic as he kissed my breasts.

He now laid his head back and pushed me hard down
onto him as he fucked me one last time, sending him into
a wild frenzy, as he shot his load deep inside me.
I just sat there and waited until he went soft, before
getting up and removing his cock from inside me. I then
bent over and kissed him on the mouth, as I again let him
kiss my breasts, before going to the wash basin to clean
up before leaving.
As I was cleaning up, I noticed I only needed to touch up
my lipstick. I did not wear foundation as my complexion
was fine without it; and as I had no beard cover it was
just a matter of a tinted moisturiser. I again applied my
lipstick and brushed through my hair, when Brian came

behind me, as again he had started to get rock hard whilst I was making sure I looked fine.

As I held onto the sink, he came behind me and with his knee he slowly parted my legs where he began fucking me again. With my breasts hanging he held them in his hands squeezing them and playing with them until again he shot deep inside me. I too had again got a little hard, but I knew I would not be able to cum as I knew it would be a struggle. Still Brian tried, as he manoeuvred his hands from my breasts to my cock, trying to get me off again as he became hornier with each thrust in my ass. Eventually he gave up, as he once again emptied his load inside me. We then got dressed and he told me to make a further appointment for a month's time. He then told me that he would still come to my parties; and he would love for us to be as intimate as today, should we find ourselves alone. I thought that I could allow that, as it was not as though Johnny would be interested in joining us, when Brian then asked me if he may ask a question, as he was at the wash basin cleaning himself. To my surprise, he asked me if we could see each other on a regular basis, as he then asked if I would be his girl. I told him that he knew I was with Johnny, as I then reminded him that he too was married, so we could only see each other as we do now. He knew I was with Johnny; and that he has a wife, but that he would really love to be with me, as he no longer loved his wife. He asked me if I would consider leaving Johnny; and would I be his full-time girlfriend.

"I am gobsmacked dear, I never thought you had such feelings for me. And what happens when I end up having

my girly cock chopped off, will you like me then?" I
replied.
*"Oh, Christ yes, even more Ruby. Don't get me wrong I
do enjoy your cock from time to time, but as a woman
you would be my dream girl."* He said, as again he asked
if it could be possible.

I did not know what to do, I mean I am with Johnny; and
though sex is not great, I really do love him because he
looks after me. I told him that I was not promising him
anything, and we should play it by ear. I let him know
that apart from my Johnny, he was the only other man I
actually sleep with. He told me that he was fine with that,
as he no longer sleeps with his wife that much anyway,
well sexually that is; and he was prepared to give himself
to me fully. I explained that for some reason I cannot
give Johnny my cock, like I have just given him. He was
very pleased about that and told me to keep it that way.
He told me that he did not mind sharing me with Johnny;
and he did not mind Johnny taking my ass, but to let him
have just the one thing I would let no one else have from
time to time; and that was for him to have his Miss Ruby
take his virgin ass; and for her not to fuck another guy.
Then he told me that he was not gay, but he would love
to have my girly cock every now and then; and knowing
that Johnny never got it was a big turn on for him.
I gave him a kiss on the lips, checked my make-up was
as it was, then I walked into his office walking on air,
where I then made my way to the reception to make
another appointment. After leaving his office I still could
not believe what I was hearing, Brian asking me to be his
girl. Not only do I have a partner, but I now have a lover

and it felt so exciting and put me in a zone which I was buzzing.

Over the next few weeks, things were fine with the parties and with the bar. I had made sure I booked acts a month in advance, with a few forthcoming attractions that pleased the lesbians as well as the straights in the bar. Johnny had completed two dressing rooms upstairs; and was finalising the third one; and I started taking all my costumes from home, where I started putting them in my dressing room which gave me so much more room at home to place my now everyday women's clothes.

I saw Brian most weeks when he came to the party; and there I spent a while in his company, without letting on to Johnny and the others of our affair.

I had secured a good evening with not just Brian, but also with the Judge and of course with my special copper, Paul… the Chief Superintendent, as well as with a few more from the law industry. They approached me a while back, when they asked if I would close the bar for them so they could have a private party. I put the matter too Johnny; and told him that it would increase takings as they are of money; and like before things would be above board having Paul on board, as well as London's most famous Judge. I say famous, because he was notorious of not having the wool pulled over his eyes or indeed, falling for a sad story. He was ruthless; and he passed a stiffer sentence to those in his court, than that of his colleagues who were easily swayed too lesser the sentence, but he still fell within the guidelines of the sentencing charter. Judge Bellows was old school; and he believed that National Service should be brought back as a deterrent, rather than put young offenders into

Borstal type prisons. He thought that this was the right thing to do, as not only would it get them off the streets from committing further crimes, it would also give them a trade for after their service; and of course show them the respect that they needed to give that had to be earned. I knew people in the bar were talking, as you just sensed that third eye looking at you; and it was those naughty girl stares they gave you when you walked past them.

I could not understand that really, as these guys were cheating on their wives, so we were all in the same boat, however, I still never let on and kept this a secret between Brian and myself.

The following few weeks I went to see Felicia, in which I asked for some advice. I explained to her that I was serious about going all the way with my feelings to becoming a woman, but I was very confused.

I had not really given Johnny the benefit of the doubt with regards our relationship, and now I had become a mistress and taken on a lover.

"*Fuckin hell Ruby, you work fast love.*" She said, now in shock at what I had told her

"*Surely Felicia, what I am doing with the doctor, I should be doing with Johnny?*" I asked.

"*Well yes you should Ruby, but we girls do need a bit of spice from time to time. I mean unless you are going to be faithful to one man only, why not share what you have with another guy. Besides the doctor sees you as a woman, and Johnny sees you as a guy dressed as a woman, there is a slight if not big difference between gay men and straight men darling and it can be pretty confusing*." She replied, not helping me in the matter, as I was more confused than when I started.

"*Yes, the doctor sees me and treats me like a woman, but now I have feelings for him in my girly cock; and I get very hard for him. Johnny has always wanted this side of me, but I have always denied it him, and rarely get stirred by him if he goes there.*" I said, feeling rather guilty of what I was doing.

"*What you have to ask yourself Ruby is this, are you transsexual or are you a gay man who likes to dress as a woman. Then and only then will you find your answer love.*" She told me.

"*I have always considered myself a transgender Felicia, yet my partner is a gay man. I have not yet found a straight man who wants a pre-op transsexual as a partner, well not until now.*" I replied.

"*Then you have a lot to think about don't you? Do you finish it with Johnny and go with your doctor friend full time? Do you live life as a gay man who dresses as a woman and live together as a gay couple? Or do you have the operation now and think about a partner later?*" She said, now making me rethink things.

"*I don't know Felicia, because in a way I do really love my Johnny. He is the sweetest man I have ever known, and I know he loves me as there is nothing, nothing at all that he would not do for me.*" I told her.

"*And!*" She replied.

"*And I do have strong feelings for my doctor, the way he makes love to me, the way I get turned on makes me feel every part a woman. How he loves my breasts, where Johnny ignores them. The fact he encourages me to be Ruby, and revels in the day I fully transgend.*" I replied.

117

"But you haven't given Johnny a chance yet Ruby, so let me think. When is it you were thinking of having? Ah the elusive snip?" She asked, rather argumentative.

"Not for a good few years yet, as I am wanting bigger breasts first and then will go for the snip. It will give me plenty of time to save, and only when I know I am ready will I go through it." I replied.

"Also, cheaper if you have them both together, I will give you my friend's number as she is a post op transsexual and is now a fashion designer and is very well known too in the industry. You may have heard of her in Carnaby Street and on the grapevine? Her name is Suzie Wong." She told me, still in a mood which was becoming lame.

"Oh yes, I have heard of her; and I have spoken to her a few times. When I met her, I thought she was a real woman." I replied, knowing that I wanted to be just like her, in all which I found to be beautiful.

Felicia then told me Suzie had her operation in the mid-sixties, just as it was becoming known. She had then in her early years got together with a wealthy man in the film industry who gave her the break she needed; and she hasn't looked back since. She never needed his money as once she became Suzie, her business just rocketed. She also went on to say that she was once married to a well-known actress; and played the loyal husband. When her wife was on location filming, the real Suzie would come out and have a party. Suzie and her wife kept it all a secret from the newspapers; and kept it a secret for many years; and although Suzie still sees her man friend from time to time, she is still with her wife as a married couple.

I just thought I had heard Suzie's story from her own lips; and I did not want to let on to Felicia, as I did not tell everyone everything that I knew so I continued to listen to her, all the time thinking how her story was so very wrong; and that if it was true about her snorting Charlie-whizz, then it had indeed mushed up her brains.

She then suggested, that as my plans to change were not going to be for a few years, then why not give Johnny a little bit of what I was giving my doctor. That she thought it may help me with my relationship with him, as she thought I was being unfair to him. Afterall I was shagging the doctor, and giving my partner jack all, and I guess she did have a point. She then told me that being transsexual was not a label you can erase, as you would always be transsexual. That I should just try and live in his world a little bit more than I do, besides I did love cock; and I did now loved mine being played with, so I guess it was a good reason to give him a chance.

"Of course you are right Felicia, and I will try my best as he has been there for me from when we first met. It is just I much prefer Brian to have my girly cock now and then, with Johnny only having access to my ass." I replied.

"I am sure you are due a holiday, so why not take one and see how you go. It is always better to start these things away from home and see if there is still that spark, besides Ruby you never know; you may even like it, and if you feel that you are still uncomfortable, there is nothing wrong in staying as you are now, but do not just pass it off as a no. Johnny should be more important to

you than the doctor, as he should be just your lover."
She said, which I knew made sense.

I gave her a kiss and thanked her for the chat, as well as having a bit of a play in which she did not overstep my boundaries by making me cum. I then got dressed, where I made my way home. After getting home and sorting something out to wear in the evening Johnny walked in.

"*Hi sweetie, how has your day been?*" He asked.
"*Not too bad dear, been to see Felicia and then wondered about booking a holiday. What do you think?*" I asked.
"*That would be great sweetie, we haven't been on holiday for such a long time. Had you anywhere in mind, or would it be a late booking?*" He asked.
"*I will go to the travel agent's tomorrow and pick up a few brochures, but I am picking the holiday Johnny; as last time we went on a package deal and it was full of screaming kids and drunken dads.*" I replied, rather sternly.
"*Ok sweetie; I know I am no good at those things so will leave it all up to you.*" He replied.

I then looked at him as I smiled, I then went up to him and told him that he knew it was a true fact, a fact that men are useless without a good woman, as all they can think about is beer and sport. Johnny called me a cheeky cow, as he then told me he was better than that, as at least he can also think of dining out and sort out the finer restaurants rather than the cheap nasty ones.
I agreed with him and then went up to him and gave him

a kiss on the lips, as I put my arms around him. I then told him that I do love him; and that I had let certain things get the better of me lately. He told me that I should visit Felicia more often, as it had been ages since I was in the mood that I was in now. He then put his arms around me; and told me that he would always be there for me, to listen to what I have to say; and what is on my mind; and that he would always support me in whatever I do. It was then that I realised, I had been a nasty bitch to him; and yes, it should be him that I put first; and Brian should be classed as my lover. I then held him tight, as I slowly slid my hand onto his ass. He looked at me and gave me a kiss on the lips, gently sliding his tongue into my mouth.

Moving my hands around to his front I placed them on his chest, as I gently stoked him as he kissed me passionately. I felt the bit of chest hair he had as I moved my hand down towards his tummy, until I had reached his cock which by now was rock hard. Placing my hand over his trousers, I undone the buttons and let them drop to the floor, as he had made it much easier for me as he had gone commando, so my hands were able to take hold of his cock straight away. He then undone my dress and let it drop to the floor, revealing my silk matching lingerie; as he then kissed me on the neck as he held me tightly towards him, still with me holding onto his cock.

"You smell gorgeous Ruby, and I have not seen the real Ruby for such a long time. I think we have both been side-tracked with things sweetie." He said, as I agreed, we had got lost, which I knew was my fault.

"Yes dear, I think we have, and it is nice to see your cock has missed me too; I have really missed us being like this." I replied, thinking now that I should not keep evaluating matters, but to put Johnny first.

"Ruby why don't you slip into bed as I need to take a quick shower, I will not be long I promise you." He said, removing his clothes, and almost falling over when his trousers hit his ankles.

I took him to the bedroom where we had an en-suite; and lay on the bed as he quickly showered. It was so horny watching him lather up, as his ass cheeks hit the glass, and as he turned around giving me a quick glimpse of his loins as hard as usual. I couldn't bare it anymore, so I went over to the shower and walked right in, startling him at first. He wrapped his arms around me as he kissed me, my breasts pressing firmly against his chest.

I started to kiss him as my lips moved from his mouth to his chest, kissing and nibbling on his nipples before moving down to his tummy. I was now on my knees as I slowly took him into my mouth, Johnny just holding my head there as he couldn't believe what was happening.

"Oh, fuck me Ruby; that is so good." He said, as he held my head in place, slowly thrusting his cock into my mouth and gyrating his hips.

"If you want me to make love to you I will Johnny, I just want us to be a proper couple again." I replied, now feeling that I would like to try, after all I had let Brian do things to me, that Johnny never did.

"Wow Ruby, you would really do that for me?" He said in disbelief.

"Yes Johnny, I will try anything once to see if I am going to like it; and I think we should start over again." I replied.

I then went back towards his bulging cock; and there I proceeded to take him back into my mouth where by now I had got him all inside me. I looked down, and for the first time in a very long time I noticed that I was beginning to get aroused by him, I was getting aroused for my Johnny, which made me wonder if all the worry of previous times were the hormones fault. I then stood up and looked at Johnny, with my hand firmly over his cock I asked him to take me to bed, because I wanted him to make love to me. Johnny looked at me in amazement, as he switched off the shower and put a towel around me. He then quickly dried himself as he picked me up and placed me on the bed and in doing so my towel had opened revealing to him my thick erect cock. He could not believe it as he told me that he had never seen me so horny, using some cursing words in the process. Wondering if the doctor had given me something else, other than the hormones I was taking, now lapping up what I had asked him to do.

I told him that I had had a lot on my mind; and that now, I had decided to put off the operation for a while. I wanted to see if fully transcending was what I truly wanted; and I want to try other things before dismissing all I have dreaded.

"I cannot believe it Ruby, you are just like the woman I met all those years ago; and God you are still so very incredibly gorgeous. I think this is the first time I have seen you fully erect sweetie, and you know what I would

123

like to do?" He said, looking as happy as a boy with a handful of candy.

"*Johnny enough of the talking just suck it for Christ's sake, before it goes limp.*" I said, offering him my cock.

Johnny did just that as he laid me back on the bed, he then knelt on the floor as he took my hard wet cock inside him. I had only just begun to put my cock into his mouth when I yet again freaked out, so I told him to stop, and that I could not go ahead with it as I cried uncontrollably and began pulling away from him. Johnny comforted me telling me that everything would be alright, as he stopped and just looked at me. He then suggested that I have a drink to try to relax me, so he went to the lounge to get me a glass of vodka and coke. As he did, I rushed into the bathroom and locked the door behind me. Sitting on the toilet I kept going over things; and kept thinking what Felicia and Suzie had told me. I knew that I was over thinking things, and then decided that if I treated him as a client; just like I did with Brian things should be fine. Johnny came back into the bedroom then knocked on the bathroom door to see if I was ok. I just told him that I would be out in a short while as I was drying my eyes. Shortly afterwards I came out of the bathroom, where I made my way over to the bed to where Johnny was. I sat on the bed; and I had a mouthful of vodka and coke as I tried to relax, thinking all the time that he was a punter, when Johnny then suggested we do a sixty-nine, so I moved around so that my head over hung the edge of the bed and that Johnny could slip his throbbing cock down my throat. I now had my legs pulled up to my chin, as Johnny moved from my cock to my ass and back again, all the time gently fucking my mouth at my pace. I could feel him getting harder and wetter, as he slid his cock down my throat leaving little traces of his warm sweet precum. With a finger inside my ass, and his other hand pulling down on my balls, he placed his mouth again over my cock. I felt him once again take me deep into his throat, as I felt his stubble around my shaved pubic area and felt myself hit the back of his warm mouth. He would tease the end of my cock with his tongue, as he again sucked me until he had just the head of my cock in his mouth, again thrusting his wet mouth all the way down my shaft.

By now he had three fingers inside my ass, as he was taking me deep inside him; and I felt that it would not be long before I would cum. I was taking him inside my mouth, as well as licking his balls and nice hairy ass. I then told Johnny that I could not hold on anymore, and that I was cumming. With his fingers deep inside my ass he sucked me harder and faster, I removed my head from his cock as I too started to finger his ass, as I told him now not to stop as I was almost there. I quivered as I felt my balls start to empty my juices down his throat, where he just held his mouth over my cock and let me thrust it deep inside him. Once he had drained me, he got up and looked at me, where he then said.

"Fucking hell Ruby, that was beautiful. You taste just as sweet as you look; and fuck me I want to do it again."
"Now it's your turn dear, Ruby wants to feel you deep inside her." I said, now realising that I had missed him so much.

"I will not be long Ruby; fuck knows how I just didn't shoot my own load tasting all of yours." He replied.

He got me into the doggy position and pulled me towards him, where he rammed his cock deep inside my ass. Holding on to my hips, he held me there as he rammed his way home, making sure I took all of his cock. I heard him breathing very quickly and heavy, as I placed my hands underneath my balls and ass and pulled on his balls.

"Oh God Yes Ruby, pull on those balls; it will not be long now sweetie, and I am going to fill your horny hot ass with my juices." He said, panting heavily, as he held onto tightly, in a bid not to let me go.

I pulled harder on his balls as he penetrated me, again breathing heavy and faster, as he started shouting that he was cumming, as he began groaning in sheer pleasure. With each thrust he shouted oh god yes, as I felt him thrust himself deeper inside me. My breasts and cock were now swinging freely, as he thrust again and again until he just stopped.

"That was fantastic sweetie, what on earth did I do to deserve that?" He asked.
"I just thought it was about time we rekindled what we used to have, and I wanted to see if I liked being touched before just saying no." I replied.
"And did you Ruby, did you like me touching you?" He asked.

I never answered, as by now I had begun to feel guilty, as I remember that I had promised Brian I would never let Johnny touch me there; and I had broken the promise in which we had made. We then just lay on the bed in each other's arms, as he then asked me if I would like to go out for dinner, maybe have a nice meal out, then go to the bar before coming back home and making love once again. I smiled at him, as I looked towards his crotch, when I told him I was not sure he could wait that long, as he seemed pretty hard once again. He giggled, but in a manly giggle, as he told me that he wanted what the doctor had prescribed me, as he had never been so aroused like that in such a long time. I explained to him that the doctor prescribed me nothing, that it was Felicia who suggested that I try different things, before deciding whether to fully transcend or not. And to be honest I did enjoy it, and seeing him happy had also made me happy, so I was prepared to wait, that's if I have surgery in the end. Johnny could not believe what I was saying, as he asked me if I would do that for him, then confusing me by saying what about wanting to become a woman.
I know deep down I wanted to become a woman; and that I was slightly confused, because I now enjoyed my cock being played with. I really enjoyed seeing him swallow all of me; and feeling him take me in his mouth. I knew I should try the gay life, because again, if it were not right then I did not have to do it; and my name was Ruby Passion; and if I don't like anything, I am brash enough to tell you so.

"Well, I am not going to complain Ruby; I enjoyed making love to my partner and her making love to me,

and not just about fucking you either. You have made me the happiest man alive." He said, now in such a happy mood, that I could not burst his bubble through my insecurities

"*Then let's leave it at that; and get ready to go out and eat. Finish the night off with a few drinks at the bar, and then let's come back home.*" I replied.

"You got it Ruby, I just need to find a decent suit to wear." He told me, sorting through the many he had hanging up.

Johnny then went to the wardrobe and picked out one of his nice suits, as I chose a nice green velvet snuggly fitted dress and a bolero jacket. We made our way into Soho, where we both had decided to have Italian.
We ended up having a lovely evening; and one we hadn't had for such a long time as we sat there like it was our very first date. I kept thinking to myself, was I really such a fussy bitch the months before, as all we seemed to do was work and sleep. If there was any sex, it was mainly Johnny just fucking me and me sucking him, but since meeting Brian I had a different aspect towards sex; and what I had started to like more since a certain part of my body became more aroused.
Having that talk with Felicia also helped; and I could not stop wondering whether all along I have just been a gay man who loves to dress, so for now I put it to the back of my mind. I still kept taking my hormones as I loved my breasts, but I never again thought about having my girly cock made into a vagina. I was living the life that Johnny was happy with; and in some respect a life I was getting used to, so I left it like that for the time being.

128

We finished our meal and caught a cab to the Rainbow, where I went to the royal box with a nice bottle of bubbly to end celebrating what seemed like my new life. Johnny made sure that the bar was running in order, before he came and sat next to me. With his arms around me he told me that he loved me very much; and we just sat there chatting and acknowledging the customers as they came in, giving a nod or raising a glass in gesture. Once time had been called, Johnny put the takings in the safe and then let everyone out. He locked up and again hailed a cab, where we then went home; and we made love with each other all night.

I had never had so much sex in one night, with Johnny emptying his load three times into me throughout the four hours, as well as him getting me hard twice.

Over the coming weeks, we made love at least three times a week, it would have been more; but I had bookings that I had to do; and by the time I got back home I was very tired, so I just quickly showered and got myself ready for bed.

By now the third and final dressing room had been completed, as Johnny had almost got the place looking the way he wanted. All he needed to do now was to build a staircase from the dressing room corridor, to come direct to the stage without running down a flight of stairs to get into position.

We had our usual cabaret on the board such as Felicia, Totty and a few spots from Kitty, as well as the up and coming new acts. London had a thriving drag scene, and many of them at some point were booked into the now famous Rainbow. I had also pushed myself more into my cabaret life having bookings most weekends, in which

Felicia and Totty would take it in turns to compare for me, where I did the same for them when they had venues; by going to Diamonds to compare.

We were a small circle of drag queens, but we were very close; and we certainly looked out for each other, where some may say we were clicky, but I say we were close. We were not like the small groups who snubbed others, as we were not afraid to let others into our circle in time, we just made sure we sifted from the waifs and strays; and that of the bitchy arrogant queens who thought themselves better than us. Sometimes it felt that it was more work and no play; and Johnny and I often spoke about going on holiday just to get away from the circuit, the bar and of course the whole scenario of life at the Rainbow.

As my schedules were very busy, I had to book another appointment to see my agent just to get time off for a holiday; and I made sure that Johnny and I booked one after our first new love session together. I decided to book a villa, as I did not like the package deals being packed with all or sundry. This was slightly more expensive I know, but it was not as though we were both short of money, so we paid that little bit extra for a bit of special time together, without the noise of kids and drunken dads; and mothers going a little wayward with their loud yells and skimpy tops, which was brazen and tarty looking. I informed my agent the dates I could not work, which were noted; and it gave Johnny and I two special weeks together, where we had to think of nothing and no-one, as we just relaxed by the pool; and hired a car to explore should we wish too. This would also be our first holiday for a long time; and it was in a lovely little romantic village, on the island of Corfu, as we were getting fed up now of going to Spain, as these days it seemed like you were leaving the UK, only to find an influx of Brits who had brought property over there, so in truth we felt we were not getting away from the noisy British holiday layabouts.

A few weeks later we were on our way on our long awaited holiday; and it was very exciting. The weeks before I had spent many times at the market; and of course, Oxford Street, looking for suitable clothes for us both. Also, from our experience with Spain, I decided to pack a small case with just a few provisions, as you could not beat a bit of proper Danish bacon; and of course English tea and marmalade. I had never been to Corfu before, so I was just taking precaution by packing what we liked.

When we were on the plane, Johnny let me sit by the window so that I could see where we were; and he was happy sitting in the middle, which also lucky for us the plane was under booked, so no one else sat next to us. I did have a few inflight nerves, but this was soon remedied with a nice bottle of champagne. Once we arrived in Corfu, it was through customs before getting our luggage. I had a few stares as I had my male picture in my passport, as well as my picture of Ruby. It was still not recognised to be a woman, if you were born of that of a male; and so eyebrows were raised, although I found customs in Europe a lot more understanding than that of our own customs officials.

As we did not have to wait for excursions and hotel coaches, we just made our way to the hire rental office, where Johnny decided to upgrade the car we were allocated, to a nice luxury saloon car. He knew I liked my luxury; and I would not be happy with what they first gave us, as the Fiat 850D did not even have room for my make-up bag, let alone two large suitcases and a small one. So once getting our route details and car we upgraded to a 1970's Iso Rivolta, we headed out of the airport and made our way to the villa.

Once we got our bearings as we drove around the town for a little while, whilst Johnny got used to both the car and the road, then it was a matter of dropping off our bags in the villa to have a look around, in which we were very pleased with both the town and the villa.

The villa had a beautiful view across the town to the sea; and had its own large pool free of neighbours. Once we had taken in the spectacular views, we decided to go to the local store for provisions; and of course that important commodity… alcohol.

As we had planned to eat out, we made sure we got just enough for breakfast; and something for supper should we feel peckish, as well as the important wine and spirits. I was pleased that I had packed the Danish, because unless you went into the main town, there was not a lot of British food in the local supermarket.

That fortnight was the best two weeks of my life, where we toured the island and ate out in almost every restaurant there was in each town.

Although Corfu town was the place to be for Brits, as well as Kavos, which was becoming ever increasingly popular, we decided to keep out of the mainstream Brits holiday spots; and hired a beautiful villa just out of Corfu town in Dasia, which was in between Ipsos and Gouvia. We still encountered some fellow Brits when visiting old town in Corfu, but at least we did not have to suffer them for the entirety of our holiday.

We had the usual Italian and Chinese, as well as the local Greek cuisine; with the many bars offering food and their famous breakfasts, which seemed to look very nice in the menu's that had pictures, but very dodgy when you saw people eating them, as they looked well cooked and very greasy. We did not want to go to the bars, as we had got away from all that, so we just chilled by eating out and then going back to the villa where we made love all night long.

Yes, Johnny was very horny over those two weeks in Corfu, with us making love in the villa, in the pool, on the lounge area as we soaked up the sun; in fact, there wasn't any place we missed. We even stopped the car one evening as we saw the view of Dasia from the mountains, as we had decided to go inland, where Johnny held my hand as we decided to look further towards the distant views, as we took in its breath-taking sights. There he stripped off as he got me over the bonnet of the car; and fucked me senseless.

It was scary and exiting at the same time, wondering if we would get caught, but knowing that there were not many cars in our vicinity. Johnny even drove home naked a few times which was nice, especially as I started playing with his cock as he tried to concentrate on the driving. I made him cum a few times as well, much to his delight as romance seemed to blossom once more. We were both like teenagers again, making love for the first time, but he got no complaints from me.

The scariest moment we encountered on the holiday, was when we were coming back from a meal; five days

before we were due to go home, when Johnny decided to pull over. We had found this quaint little family run Greek restaurant off road in the Karakinos mountain range, next door to the Paloma Blanca Hotel, in which first caught my eye in the brochure. We both sat on the bonnet of the car as we looked over towards Dasia Beach, with all of its bright lights shining like a firework display. Johnny had stripped off as usual, when he undone my dress and pulled me towards him; and with my back facing him, he removed my panties and sat me on his cock, as he slid his cock between my legs.
He then stood up and got me to lean on the bonnet, when he just said.

"I think we are being watched, there is someone on the other side of the road."
"Where Johnny, I can't see?" I replied, now with my heart beating so fast, I thought I was going to have a heart attack.

Although it was dark, the moon was shining lighting us both up for anyone to see. It was then that this figure came over to us; and I nearly died there and then, as it was a traffic cop who walked towards us. As he came over to us, I noticed he had an erection and his zip was undone, he had obviously been playing with himself as he looked over at us. He then looked at us, as Johnny stood there with his cock still deep inside my ass, and as I stood up trying to cover my breasts as he caught a glimpse of my cock.

"*Good evening, I see you are having much fun.*" He said, as his hand was clearly placed over his groin.
"*Sorry officer, we will get dressed and go home as we only live down the road.*" Johnny told him, sounding rather calm.
"*You both like man cock I see.*" He replied as he pointed to mine.
"*Yes, we do, why do you want a piece of this ass too?*" Johnny said, rather sharpish.
"*Johnny please be quiet, or you will get us both arrested; and then what will we do?*" I replied, now rather scared.
"*I don't think so Ruby, he is as solid as a rock and look at him touching it. He is enjoying this; and I bet he wants you to suck him as I fuck you.*" Johnny said.
"*Johnny be quiet, I am scared. He has a fucking gun for Christ's sake; and we are in the middle of nowhere and he could easily bump us off.*" I whispered.

Johnny then removed his cock from my ass; and decided to call the police officer over. The police officer looked at me; and now with his cock removed from his pants he said to me.

"*You want police cock; you want to suck this thick police cock lady?*" He said, as he waved it about
I then looked at Johnny, who just told me to think of the parties I held.

"*Oh yes I do for sure, come here and let me suck your nice big thick cock.*" I replied, still shaking at the thought of him having a gun just a few inches from my face.

135

He then came over to me and sat on the bonnet of the car, where he removed his trousers revealing a very nice thick seven inch cock. He was covered in hair, which was beautiful to see, although not my cup of tea.
As he removed his shirt, I could see he had a mass of black hair going all the way from his chest towards his cock; and he was that hairy, I thought he was wearing a fur coat. He then placed his hand over my cock, as he placed his head into my chest and kissed my breasts.

"Very beautiful lady; and a very beautiful lady cock."

Looking at Johnny, he told him to fuck me again, as he made me eat his cock. This really got Johnny worked up as he saw the police officer fuck me harder than he had before, as he saw me sucking on this now, naked police officer's thick cock.
Shortly afterwards the police officer placed me on the bonnet where I was laying on my back, with my legs in the air as he again began fucking me.

"I like that, do you like being fucked both ends pretty lady?" The police officer said.
"Yes sir I do; and what about you? Would you like to be in this position and get fucked by my Johnny?" I replied.
"Oh yes missy, I would like to be man fucked." He said.

Johnny lifted me off the car bonnet; and told the officer to lie down, in which he did right away. He was a beautiful tall handsome man, and he easily managed to lie over the car where he was able to spread his legs wide, in which to let Johnny get between his legs so that he could fuck him. The officer then got me to fuck his mouth with my cock, as he started to play with his now very wet hard cock. I do not know if it was nerves or what, but I felt like I was going to shoot my load there and then. I withdrew my cock from his mouth and told him no more, as I was going to cum. He understood everything I said, as he told me to put my cock back, and cum into his mouth.

"*And what about Johnny what if he is ready to cum, where do you want that?*" I replied.
"*Mr Johnny, man fuck my ass and fill me with your man seed.*" He said, as he sucked my cock, and withdrew as he wanted to speak.

Again, I placed my cock into the officer's mouth, where he fingered my ass as he took me deeper inside his mouth. I could feel his tongue swishing all around my wet cock, tantalising me as I was ready to shoot, as I looked at Johnny and told him I was ready. Johnny withdrew from the officer; and told me to lie on the floor as he placed his jacket, then he told the officer to lay over me pointing to a sixty-nine position. The police officer placed my cock into his mouth, as I took him in mine as he was on all fours, whilst Johnny got behind him and again penetrated his horny hot ass.

"*Come on Ruby, fuck that horny cop's mouth and fill him with your juices. Come on sweetie do it for your Johnny, I want to see you enjoy yourself as you empty yourself in his mouth.*" Johnny said, now very horny as he rode that police officer like it was his first time; and speaking as though he was a porn star.

I could not hold back as I emptied my load into his mouth, pulling out to show Johnny as I dribbled over the officer's lips and then thrust back inside him. Johnny then followed suit, seeing him take all of my cock and cum, as he too could not hold back as he pushed himself harder into this policeman, thrusting into him as he knocked his head under my balls, as the officer was still fingering my ass whilst Johnny fucked him harder, as the officer was now groaning more with pleasure.

"You are big Mr Johnny; fuck me Mr, fuck me till you cum inside me." He told him, now finishing licking the drips from my cock.

I pulled away from the officer; and told Johnny to quickly get him on his back. As he did, I placed my breasts into his face, with his hands now squeezing my breasts he kept groaning for Johnny to give him more. Johnny was almost there as he saw me being pleased by the police officer, and then he himself groaned as he filled up this officer's very tight ass.
"Yes dear, fuck him hard. This officer needs a bit of man cock, as I don't think he has been fucked for ages." I told Johnny, as the police officer looked towards me and smiled.
"I don't think he has ever been fucked at all Ruby; he is so fucking tight I can't help it; I am still cumming." He said, giving this cop his entire load.

The next thing I knew was the police officer had ordered Johnny onto the car, as he told me to hold his arms, stretching him over the bonnet of the car. There he placed his cock by Johnny ass and began fucking him, as he asked me to fuck Johnny's mouth. I was not hard, but I still placed myself into Johnny's mouth, as Johnny took all of my now soft wet cock inside him as he still tasted my juices. I just couldn't believe what was happening, we had been making out all week at this spot and never saw anyone; and then the next thing we knew, was we had a police officer join in with our moonlight nuptials. It could have been very different as we could have been arrested, if not shot.

Twenty minutes had gone by and the police officer was still fucking my Johnny, and he was getting nowhere. He asked me to sit on the bonnet with my legs wrapped around his waist, as he then began to fuck me. I looked at Johnny and told him to get behind the officer, when I then told him to start fucking him again.

So again, positions were changed, and Johnny slid his cock inside the officer, as the officer then slid his cock deep inside my ass; when it was not long before the police officer began shaking as he began moaning in pleasure as he filled up my moist ass.

As soon as the officer shot his load inside my now very wet ass, I heard Johnny moaning again as he again shot inside the officer's ass. As quickly as the officer arrived, he again got dressed and told us he would escort us back to the villa. We never bothered getting dressed, as we just got into the car and with a police escort drove back down the long winding road back towards the safety of the villa. Once we arrived back at the villa, we said our goodbyes as again the police officer had become hard; and he gave us both a kiss and told us to enjoy the evening. We then went inside where we quickly locked up, and both took showers, then decided to have a drink as the adrenalin was still pumping.

Whilst we sat out by the pool, we chatted about what had just happened in disbelief. We both thought that was the end of it, but we were very much mistaken.

Two days later we were having a light lunch by the pool both naked as we heard the doorbell ring, so Johnny put a pair of shorts on and went to the door. To my surprise he came back to the pool with the same police officer that we had met a couple of nights before. He looked different now as he was not in uniform, but he was still very sexy. He looked at me and smiled as he saw me at the table naked, with me just looking towards him with a look of shock. He came to tell us, that he enjoyed that sexy night that we all had encountered, explaining that when he saw us by the car naked, he could not help but look at us both, and that it turned him on to see a man lady being penetrated by a nice big man. Again, I thought him sweet, as I told him that I was glad he had enjoyed himself, knowing it could have easily gone wrong, as another cop could have easily arrested us for being indecent.

"I sorry, but you no worry to, most police have seen this before and have helped to be sexy." He said, in a way that we still understood him.

Joking, I asked him that we were pleased, as I then told him that I was relieved that there would be no handcuffs and police cells for our actions. In a nice rather broken English voice, which was so sexy to listen to, he told us that with him there would be no handcuffs, just nice man fuck. I then invited him to come and sit with us, even though I was as naked as a new born; and he was in uniform with a now rather hard bulge in his trousers. I asked him to chill out with us; and to grab himself a bite to eat should he wish too.

"Thank you miss I will, I no stopping long, I have to go take wife shopping. I see you both later for some more man fun please? I visit you here." He asked.
"Sure, that will be ok with us, but remember we do not have many days left here before we go back to England." Johnny said, standing in front of him in all of his glory.
"Ok will come to visit ten thirty tonight, before I go work. Leave open gate I will drive bike inside. You want me undressing." He replied, as his hand was placed over his erection, which I think was because of embarrassment, due to the fact he needed to go back to work, and he did not have time to relieve himself.
"Why not leave your uniform on, that way Miss Ruby can take it off for you." Johnny said.
"Ok see you tonight Miss Ruby and Mr Johnny, ten thirty and Miss Ruby strip me naked as Mr Johnny kiss me and fuck me sexy from behind. I am my name Helios; Helios Antonopoulos, but you call me Helios, yes?" He replied.
"Careful because you are getting even harder again; and yes we will call you Helios." I said, as I placed my hand over his cock.
"I sorry Miss Ruby I go now. I see you tonight both of you." He said as he quickly left.

He then left, as we looked at each other and thought that his broken English was quite charming. That a European accent, was so sexy, spoken from the right person; and Helios was everything that a man could be. Tall, hairy, masculine voice, and of course, a nice thick cock with a bush that I thought needed a bit of a trim.

Johnny then came back to the table and finished his lunch, where we then just lay by the pool and chatted. Once again Johnny stripped off as he jumped into the pool, and then threw water over me in which I slowly got up and began to throw water over him. Johnny then grabbed hold of my hand as he pulled me into the pool; and then we began playing around for a while like little children, which was really nice to be able to just let go and have a bit of fun without prying eyes. Again, in the evening we drove to a local restaurant, where we ordered some local food and drink before heading back home.

We then showered and once we had finished, I got dressed into a 1950's panty-girdle and stockings, as Johnny put on a t-shirt and shorts. We poured ourselves a drink as we waited for our police officer, as we began to get excited but still quite scared.

This was the first time we had ever had a threesome together, and it was quite thrilling, but also quite scary, as it could have easily gone pear shaped.

Ten thirty arrived and no police officer, so we thought he must be running late. We poured ourselves another drink; and put on some soft music as we left the patio doors open. Then it was eleven pm and we just looked at each other and thought he may not be coming, especially as now it was quarter to twelve, so we decided to go to bed and just call it a night. It was not until twelve thirty that we were woken by a noise outside, as we heard what could only be describes as a motorcycle with a bit of engine trouble. Johnny got up to see what the noise was, where he then saw the police officer at the gate; in which Johnny had forgotten to lock. The police officer got off his bike and closed the gate behind him, then came towards the door. Johnny then called me to get dressed, as the officer was now here, and so I got dressed and got up. I put on a side lamp and sat on the sofa, as I waited for Johnny to let him in.

"I sorry I so late, I have busy night with drunken tourists and needing help. I hope I not get you out of bed."
"That's ok Helios; we were in bed as we both wondered what had happened. So, would you like a soft drink, or would you prefer a hot one?" I asked him.
"I would not mind a cup of coffee, if is ok to ask. I best think I not have alcohol, for it is my job I could lose if I go drunk." He told me, as I made my way to the kitchen to make him a coffee.

We just stood there for a moment in the kitchen, as I had put a jacket on as it had got slightly nippy that morning. I did feel the cold unlike Johnny and this police officer, who was standing waiting for me to undress him.
I could see by now he again had an erection, and his hand kept rubbing his cock as he looked at me, so I went over to him and placed my lips on his mouth as I kissed him and slowly undone his tie. I then had undone his shirt removing it and letting it drop to the floor, before undoing his trousers and dropping both them and his

pants to his knees. I got on my knees, I undone his boots and removed them, as he stepped out of his trousers and pants. We now had him standing in the kitchen completely naked and hard, as he pointed his cock towards me to take into my mouth. I took him by the hand and walked him into the lounge, where I sat him down on the end of the couch. As it was open plan it was easier to do all sort of naughty things, as there was no wall you could walk around the low backed couch.

There I sat on my knees between his legs as I started to take his cock into my mouth, and Johnny stood before him so that he could take Johnny's hard cock into his mouth. I got up from between his legs and straddled him, as he played with my breasts and he pushed his bulging cock into my ass. Then after a short while, he could not hold on as he licked my breasts, holding onto my waist and pushed that last time, flooding my ass with his juices. Johnny then told me to come behind the couch, so that he could go where I had stood.

He told the police officer to get to his knees and reach over for Ruby's cock, as he then inserted his very thick wet throbbing cock into his hairy ass.

The police officer kept muttering words in Greek, but we had a feeling we knew what he was talking about, as again he became erect; as Johnny fucked him to completion, as he also took my cock and sucked me until I had nothing left to give. Shortly afterwards I stood up and took him again by the hand, where I led him into the bedroom. He just stood there by the bed, as I got on my knees and again took his cock into my mouth, as Johnny got on his knees and started to rim his hot hairy ass. After I started sucking his now wet hard cock, he placed

144

his hands on my shoulders as to lift me up. He told me to kneel on the bed, and as doing so he came behind me where he then began fucking my ass. Holding onto my waist as he pushed deeper inside me and with Johnny still rimming his ass, he was moaning in pure delight. Again, it was not long before he was ready to shoot inside me, as I heard Johnny tell him to open his legs wider as he rimmed him deeper. Now with his legs astride of me I could hear his balls slapping against my ass cheeks, as he thrust deeper inside me moaning as he pushed himself further into me.

As I was on my knees, I could see Johnny still rimming this guy's ass, as I could see Johnny's cock shining with all the precum that had oozed out. Helios just groaned as he was ready for completion, as he thrust deep inside me filling me up with his hot cum. Johnny was still rimming and fingering his ass, as he emptied himself into me.

He then just rested himself there, as I then removed myself from him and sat on the bed as my breasts were now on show as he bent down to kiss them. I looked at Helios; and told him to get onto the bed, and to get onto his knees. I then started to fuck his now wet ass, that Johnny had already worked on; making it much easier for me to penetrate him.

I told Johnny to go to the front of him and make him take his moist hard cock. I could hear the officer gagging, but he did not stop as he took Johnny all the way down his throat, and as this got me rather hot and horny, I looked at Johnny and told him I that I was about to cum myself.

"Yeah sweetie, fuck his wet ass; fill this cop with your thick creamy juices sweetie." He told me.

As soon as he said that I could not retain myself and I started pushing deeper inside him, as my breathing got heavier and faster. I heard him gagging on Johnny's cock, and I just told Johnny that I was cumming.
As soon as I let go and filled Helios's ass, I heard Johnny moaned with pleasure, as Helios was still gagging on Johnny's cock. Johnny could hold himself better than I could, he waited until I had finished; and removed myself from this cop's ass. Then he told me to go to the front of him and let the officer play with my breasts, as Johnny now got behind him and entered his very wet hairy ass, filling him to the brim as his balls slapped against the cop's own balls.
The cop then started kissing my breasts, and with one hand under my legs began fingering my ass as he jerked his cock with the other hand. Just as Johnny heard this cop moan and begin to breathe heavier, he shot into his ass as the cop shot over my tummy.
We just held ourselves there for a moment before withdrawing, and then I reached for our coffee's which by now was cold. Helios then began playing with my breasts again, as he started to kiss them and nibble on my nipples which again started to get some kind of life back in his cock. I started playing with Johnny's cock, which soon became rock solid as it usually was.
We spent a further thirty minutes playing with each other, going from one to the other as we kissed and sucked each other's cock's; just as Johnny sat on the bed and pulled the officer towards him. I just looked at him and

said I was going to get a glass of wine and that they both should have a little play whilst I was away.

This they did, and upon returning I found that they had just come out of a sixty-nine position, when I saw Johnny moving off him as he sat on the bed. He called Helios over and told him to sit on his now well-oiled cock, in which the officer stood up and then moved in between Johnny's legs, as he began sitting on his cock. It was much easier now for him especially as he had already been fucked earlier, so there was not much pain received. He just sat down on his cock and took him deep inside him, with Johnny now laying down on the bed as he cupped his hands over the officer's buttocks as he thrust into him. Helios called me over to him, but first I took a mouthful of champagne and got on my knees as I placed the cop's cock inside my mouth. This was a new revelation to the Helios, as I think it blew his mind as he shouted 'oh fuck me. I can only assume, that this was the first time he had experienced such an act. I began sucking his cock swishing the champagne around until I took my mouth off his cock, and then placed my mouth over his and started kissing him, exchanging the champagne from my mouth to his.

He then pulled me away as he gently lowered me onto his very wet thick cock again taking it in my mouth. Shortly afterwards I told Johnny I would have to get up as I was beginning to get cramp in my legs, so I removed myself from the cop's cock.

As I stood up, he got off Johnny's cock and then moved me to the dressing table where he bend me over and again started fucking me. Johnny got behind him, and started fucking him, as they both moved in and out on

147

one another. I was quite lucky as I only needed to be bent over as I let them do all the work, as by now my own cock was lifeless. Helios then told me he was going to cum, and he held onto me tightly as he played with my breasts. Again, he groaned in ecstasy as he rammed his hard cock home, taking Johnny's deeper inside him. Johnny then began breathing heavy as he said that he was ready to cum yet again, when just then I felt Helios tremble at the knees as he groaned and filled my ass up again. Just as he was cumming inside me, Johnny also climaxed and as he thrust deeper inside the police officer, he must have had an extra boost of energy as he again thrust deep inside me, telling me he was still cumming; and that I was so hot.

I could see from the wardrobe mirror both my boys fucking each other which again made me moist, and as the officer came into my ass and then tensed up slightly, he made it that extra sensitive for Johnny who in turn held onto him as he thrust deep inside his ass sending his hot creamy cum flooding into him filling him up.

When they had both finished, they stood up, and Johnny removed himself from the officer, as he then removed himself from me. As I turned round, they could see that I was again a little hard and wet, so they lay me on the bed and then they lay next to me. There they both started sucking my cock as they kissed each other, and with their hands under my ass they both finger my hole.

With both of them now sliding their mouths up and down my shaft, as they gripped my cock between their mouths; kissing each other and sliding up and down my cock, where it was not long after that I start to raise my body, as I was in heaven and very close at letting go of juices that were ready to explode from my cock.

"*Johnny I am going to cum.*" I told him, barely able to hold on anymore.

He then looked at Helios and told him I am ready; and that he should get ready to taste me again and to get my cock harder between their mouths, so that I had no choice but to forcibly cum quickly. They both did this, and the pressure of their mouths and their tongues around my shaft; and Johnny's finger spreading my precum over the head of my cock, sent me in to a frenzy. Both of them now finger fucking my ass faster and harder, as they moved up and down my cock; as I then screamed as I began to reach climax, my body shaking as all of a sudden, I could no longer help myself. I was about to cum, when I saw Johnny look at Helios; and then he pointed to my cock. Helios all of a sudden placed his mouth over my cock sucking just the head of it, as Johnny now got on his knees and started fingering me even more. I began getting very sensitive as I felt the officer's mouth just licking the head of my cock, and then I just shot. As I did, I heard the officer make a small groaning noise, as I must have hit the back of his throat, so then he sucked my cock harder as he then took me deep down his throat as he swallowed all that I had, draining me completely of my juicy load, he licked me dry. I then just lay there as I told them no more please, it is fat too much. I am far too sensitive, to allow them to carry on, as I needed him to stop. We all finished off and then got dressed, and Johnny saw the police officer to the door where again they hugged each other and kissed each other goodbye.

We never saw that police officer again; and spent the last couple of days just chilling out by the pool, then going into the town for a meal before coming back to the villa to crash, but Helios was always at the back of our minds when we drove down that winding mountain road.

That was certainly a holiday to remember, and one I will never forget. I never told anyone about that experience, but often Johnny and I would look at each other and as we chatted, we would have a laugh and get quite horny. That was the first; and would be the only time we would ever be involved in a threesome.

Once we flew back home, we again got back into our usual work routines. I had started to make a friendship with Suzie Wong; and ended up doing a few fashion shows for her as her compare. But when she told me that she had a lot more work for me from other designers she knew, I declined as I already had a workload to contend with and could not commit to her deadlines.

I know she was looking for a girly boy model; and she was herself looking for a little star, which I felt that it was not me. She couldn't do it herself as she was now a renowned designer; and it was so sweet of her to think of me I thought. I just told her that one day she would find her starlet, but until then she will have to dream.

For the next few years, I again got back into my cabaret and a few television performances, plus, the odd Christmas play at the theatre. I had played an ugly sister, widow-twanky, as well as an evil witch. All of this was fine as it kept me busy, but deep down inside Ruby was still hurting and I was again becoming very lonely.

The year was now 1978; and I was given my first booking down on the sunny south; and although I had done most of the UK, I had never worked in Brighton. So being excited about working in Brighton, I thought I would do an old show as they had not seen any of my shows before. I got to the bar in good time; and once I put my things into the dressing room, I made my way to see the cabaret manager, when all of a sudden, I was greeted by this very young queen. Well, in all honesty I wouldn't have called him a queen, as he didn't come across as camp or bitchy as one, he came across as just a very nice pretty boy; and my god was he pretty.

He introduced himself to me as Bobby; and he was such a lovely host, asking me if there was anything, he could get me, as most people who greet the cabaret just leave you to it. I told him that I was going to see the cabaret manager, as I needed to give him my signed copy of the contract. Fees were not exchanged, as all monies went directly to my agent, who in turn, paid me upon the monies being cleared in his bank account.

Once I finished the show, I went over to him and thanked him for his hospitality; and I then got into my car and drove back home to London. I knew that my encounter with that lovely boy, would not be the last one, as I had been given another date from the bar I had just performed at. I also knew that I would have stayed the night, but most of the gay hotels, were filled with sex starved gay men, looking for sex with anyone; and I did not like that side of staying in a gay hotel.

That week I hit a slump, as Ruby had begun to resurface even more. I was beginning to get withdrawal symptoms and was now going off sex again. I no longer wanted to live a life of sex and parties, as now I wanted to relax more and become Ruby as I so wanted too so many years previous. The next day I went to see Felicia; and I told her how I had begun feeling again, as I knew she would listen without judging; and she would tell it as it is. I told her I have lived Johnny's life for so long, but I felt it was not my life. I needed to be Ruby; and could no longer live a gay lifestyle. She knew where I was coming from, when she then told me that at least I had given it a try; and in doing so, I had found out it was not for me.

"It is obvious Ruby that the gay world is not your world, so therefore I think you need to slowly change your path. But do not rush, as you also need to speak to Johnny and let him know how you are feeling love." She told me.
*"I know dear, and as much as I love Johnny, I am so fucking miserable. I really do need to be Ruby, and I cannot put it off any*more." I replied.
"Then don't put it off Ruby; as you will always have the knowing that you never failed, because you tried it Johnny's way; and it was not for you. There comes a time Ruby, when you have to count your losses; and start living your life as you intended. I am always here for you Ruby, please always remember that." She said, as she seemed to make sense, and helped to convince me, that I was on the right path all along.

I then went home where I waited for Johnny, wondering what I was going to say, and how it would come out. As Johnny walked through the door, he noticed I had been crying. He asked me what was wrong, when crying,

I told him I cannot do this anymore. That I cannot live this life I had been living. That I had been living in his world for so long, that I had lost my own world in the process. That I cannot live a life of pretence; and live a gay life just to make him happy. Now sobbing profusely, I told him that I needed to live my own life, in my own world. This knocked him back, as he got a little annoyed, telling me that he thought I was happy with the life that had been mapped out for us. That he thought I was happy being gay.

"*I never said I was GAY Johnny; I have always said I was transgender.*" I shouted, absolutely furious at his comment.
"*But you knew I was gay; and you stayed with me, if you had any inkling that you were going to change when we were together, then you should not have led me on Ruby.*" He replied, now making me so infuriated
"*WHAT! What did you fucking say Johnny? How dare you say I led you on, I have been living your life and not my own. You knew from the very first day you met me that I was not gay, how dare you say that to me. If you are not happy, then there's the door fucking use it.*" I cursed.
That really hurt Johnny, as he told me that he could not leave, because he loved me so much; and that I knew just how much he loved me, which to be honest, I did. He had always been there for me; and I could not question his loyalty. He then got my goat up again, when he told me that we have a home and business together as well.

"Wrong Johnny it is my house, and your business. I am eventually going to be a woman; and you need to understand that. I am going to end up becoming a woman." I said, as Johnny interrupted me.

"You… you, selfish bitch Ruby, after all what I have done for you; and what we have done together." He shouted, swearing and calling me names.

"I am going to save harder to get the surgery I want, so that I can be Ruby all the time; and feel like Ruby inside as well as on the outside. You are either with me or without me Johnny, it is your choice. Now you can call me a fucking bitch, and you can get out of my fucking house." I told him, furious at how low he had sunk to get his nasty words across, to make me feel like crap about myself.

Johnny then stormed out of the apartment slamming the door behind him, as I picked up the phone and called Felicia. She eventually calmed me down and told me that things would settle down, that I had to let blow off steam and let him get used to the idea now. Ruby told me, that if he loved me, he would come crawling back with his tail between his legs; and most likely bringing chocolates and flowers, as most men do. I just put the phone down and had a shower, before going to bed. I thought fuck the bar I am not going out tonight; and I am certainly not changing my mind.

All my life I have done things for others; and have ended up putting my plans on hold. I knew I should have started all this when I began seeing the doctor, but I also wanted a business and a home that it had to wait.

I kept thinking that I should never have got involved

with a gay man, as at the end of the day they are only interested in cock and ass. I was beginning to well up and feel guilty about the argument, but I knew I could not live a lie anymore. I then went to the fridge and got myself a bottle of vodka and took it to bed, where after a few glasses I soon fell asleep.

That morning I noticed Johnny had not come home, and he was not in the spare room. I just kept thinking he was like a spoilt child who had thrown his rattle out of his pram and he wanted someone to give him the attention. I then just shouted '*no fuck him, I am not backing down.*' Though no one was there to hear me, it did feel good getting all the negativity out of my system, or at least a good part of it, which seemed to calm me down slightly. For three days, I stayed in my apartment crying my eyes out, wondering where the hell Johnny was.

I called the Rainbow a few times, only for Johnny to tell me he was busy in which he put the phone down on me, not wanting to listen to me or indeed speak to me.

I had now had enough; and having drunk all the vodka I reached for the wine where I ended up drinking about two bottles. With my eyes flooding in tears wondering if I was doing the right thing, I could not cope anymore. I then went to the medicine cabinet and took out a bottle of pills, in which were prescribed to me a while back when I could not sleep. Without even thinking twice I emptied the pills in my hand; and one by one I started to take them, as I rinsed them down with yet more white wine. Before I knew it I had emptied the bottle; and I then made my way to bed, being in a state I wished it would end there and that I would not wake up.

I must have got up during the night, as I remember being

really poorly. I had then fallen asleep in the bathroom, and upon waking noticed that most of the digested pills had come back up in an acid form, whilst my head felt like I had been hit with a baseball bat, and my tummy was in bits. I still felt very sick and very tired, so again I decided that the best place for me, would be to go back to bed and try and sleep it all off.

I spent the next four days in bed, just sleeping and not answering the phone to anyone.

It was not until this one morning, the fourth morning, that as I was grabbing a glass of water, that once again the phone rang so I answered it.

"Ruby its Felicia, I have been trying to get hold of you for the past four days. Are you ok as I haven't heard anything from you since you visited?" She asked.

"I am ok Felicia, just very tired." I replied, not wanting to let her know how stupid I had been.

"You don't sound ok Ruby, what's' wrong?" She asked.

"Nothing dear, I just need to be left alone, now goodbye." I snapped.

"You haven't done anything silly have you Ruby, you wouldn't do that would you… Ruby… Ruby are you there, have you done something silly?" She called out.

I just snapped and replied.

"Yes, I did four days ago, now leave me alone. GOODBYE." I cried, as I slammed the phone down.

I then again went back to bed, after I had slammed the phone down on Felicia; and had managed to get back onto the bed as I was still drowsy, where I soon fell asleep once more. I do not know how long I had dropped off, but all of a sudden, I felt someone shaking me and calling my name.

"Ruby, Ruby wake up, its Johnny. Are you ok Ruby?" Johnny said, as I heard him faintly.

I then woke up, looked at him as I asked him what he was doing; and why was he in my apartment. He told me that Felicia had called him at the bar; and had told him that she expected that I had done something silly. I looked him square in the eyes, with a face that could have looked like I was possessed, when I asked him what he thought I had done. Then after shaking me again, which was where I told him to fuck off, as I was not a fuckin ragdoll. He then told me that he expected that I had taken some pills; and why in god's name would I do something like that?
I told him to leave me alone; and that I just want to sleep, as I turned back round.

"Ruby look at me please, what have you taken and how many?" He asked, sounding rather frantic and worried.
"I don't fuckin know Johnny; I just emptied the bottle. Now leave me alone Johnny, you haven't wanted to know me for the last week, so why bother now? Just go back to where you came from." I cried.

Johnny then went into the lounge, where I heard him talking to someone, so I guess he had picked up the phone. After about ten minutes or so he came back into the bedroom with a coffee for me. He told me that he had phoned the doctor; and had explained to him, what I had done, telling me that the doctor had said, for the fact that I was still alive, proved that I couldn't have taken that many pills. That I had best make sure I had to drink plenty of fluids as the pills would have really got into my system; and if I had taken the whole bottle, I would have been dead.

"Thank God you are not Ruby; why oh why did you feel you needed to do this sweetie?" He asked.
"I have lived the life you wanted me to live Johnny; and I could see you were very happy. Inside I was hurting and dying; and I felt that I was living a lie, but I could not bare to take away your happiness. I listened to Suzie, Felicia and Kitty, as well as my doctor and it was too much for me to cope with. I wanted them to listen to me, to listen how I was feeling; and as they didn't, I felt as I was slowly dying so I thought I may as well end it and end my misery." I cried, trying to get him to listen to me.
"You wait until I see those three, I will give them a piece of my mind." He said angrily.
*"Don't you dare Johnny; and don't you dare have a go at Felicia. It was Felicia who told me to try your world for a while, as I may actually like it. So, I did just that and it was really not me, so don't have a go at her for suggesting I try and live your life Johnny; she has been the only one who has listened to me; and stayed by my sid*e." I told him, telling him that there would be trouble if he had a go at my friends.

"Ok, but nothing is worth this Ruby. Nothing is worth taking your life for, as we can always sort things out." He replied, as he sat on the bed holding my hand.

"So, what do we do now Johnny, what about you? I do really need to go down the road that I had made for myself a long time ago, but first I need to sleep all of this off." I told him, now feeling drained at the whole episode, but pleased that Johnny was there to listen

"I will try my best Ruby, but please understand I do not mind the pre-op version of Ruby, because I do love your cock. I am not sure I could deal with the full woman Ruby; after all I am a gay man. Give me time to get used to it, but if it doesn't work, I am sure we can always be friends." He replied.

"After all we have gone through, you would if you couldn't handle it, only be my friend." I said, as I questioned him.

He then explained to me, that I too needed to understand that he was gay; and he liked cock and ass. If I become a woman totally then I would have something which does not interest him. That I keep saying that I need to do this for me; and not do it because of what I like that I should get it into my head that he is gay; and that I am a transsexual. That it is a strange mixture indeed, but nothing was stopping us from being friends.

"I guess so Johnny, but I do love you." I cried.

"Yes, I know you do but you cannot have it all your own way Ruby; I will also promise you that as soon as you become your true self, I will still act as though nothing has changed and we are still together. This is between you and me and has nothing to do with anyone else, so I

*will still make it look as though we are a couple. That's
the least I can do Ruby; and remember this too will hurt
me but I will still stand by you. Now drink your coffee
and get a little bit more rest, as I need to tidy up.*" He
said, now comforting me.
"*Oh, and by the way Johnny, I didn't take the full bottle
of pills. I must have taken about twenty five, but my
tummy couldn't handle them; and in the night I was very
poorly. I think I had brought a lot of them back up, as I
spent the early hours of the morning with my head in the
toilet. I am sorry Johnny, but I just wanted to die.*" I
cried again, now just wanting him to hold me, and for
him to tell me that it will all be ok.

He then gave me a kiss on the forehead as he pulled the
covers up to my chin, then went back into the lounge;
where it was not long before again, I had dropped off.
A few days later I was back on form, though not eating
properly, but I still made sure I had a regular amount of
water going into my system so as not to dehydrate.
My eating slowly got back too normal; and I apologised
to my agent for cancelled bookings, even though I had
told him I had a bad stomach bug.
Within a few weeks I was back on track, as Johnny and I
seemed to understand each other a little bit more.
Felicia was a true friend; and took control over the
comparing at the Rainbow, which helped Johnny out a
lot; and to my surprise he did not say anything to Felicia.
There was never any pressure anymore, we would go out
and have a meal, go to the bar and then trot off home.
Once we got to bed, he would put his arms around me;
and we would both just fall asleep.

160

Sex became a distant thing as we only seemed to be intimate when I made the first move, much to Johnny's delight even though he did stay clear of my cock on the hope that I would offer it to him. Yes, things had certainly changed and for the better, I loved this new look on our relationship.

I did love Johnny; and I suggested to him a few times that he should hook up with one of the bar staff, just to get rid of his sexual tension, but he was not interested. I had listened to him, and I understood that he was a gay man, so I often asked him to date someone else because I knew he would not be fully satisfied with me. I had a cock and tits; and I knew he wanted to play around with my cock, but I just could not let him. I hated that part of me with a vengeance; and I often had to tell him that he would have to get used to it, because there would come a day where it would finally be removed.

I had since had a few more bookings in Brighton, where again I bumped into Bobby. On my last show I decided to have a few drinks with him first; and when it was ready to leave, I asked Bobby if he knew of any hotels I could stay in for when I came down to work in the near future, as that way it would not matter about drinking. I remember that I asked him the last time, but things seemed to slip my memory, so then Bobby suggested I stay with him which I thought was really sweet of him. Bobby and I became very good friends; and he was like a younger sister to me; and I say sister because he was a pretty boy and not a macho butch guy.

I stayed in touch with Bobby calling him regular through the week, or more if I was not working. I then invited him up to London as I knew he was not happy where he was; and I just thought to myself that the break may do him good.

In the beginning of 1980 Bobby came to London, where he stayed with me and Johnny. The first time Johnny laid his eyes on Bobby, they seemed to get on very well; and the three of us grew closer together. I also saw Johnny's face light up a few times, when Bobby was around; and I am sure if I had not been around, that something possible could have happened, as I also saw Bobby's face light up whenever my Johnny came into the room, or in the bar come to think of it.

Bobby used to help Johnny out in the bar, whilst I was on stage; and he would just stand next to him as he watched me like a hawk doing my routine. Despite me thinking, that both Bobby and Johnny may be better suited than that of Johnny and myself, I used to love Bobby coming up to visit, as it took the pressure off me wondering if Johnny would get frisky, where we would end up arguing in front of him. I also knew that Johnny was of the old school; and he was not a guy who would cheat behind your back. I may not have been all that he wanted, because of my transgender issues, but I give Johnny credit, he always stuck by me.

Yes, those first few months that Bobby came to see us was a big relief; and it enabled me to go about my business without concern about sex.

The latter part of 1980, I asked Bobby to come up and stay with us, as I got to hear her story about some of the queens of Brighton giving her a hard time, in which I thought the move up to London, would give her a deeper insight to things; and would take away the hurtful remarks and isolation, she had received from those Brighton queens.

By now, Johnny had got himself a new friend; and he introduced me to him on one of the nights that he came into the Rainbow. He was a lovely young man, with a really nice European accent, as Johnny told me that his name was Danni Svenningsen. He knew Johnny through business, as his business partner Steve helped with the renovation of the bar, but Danni was too shy to come in on his own. It was whilst they had a prior business engagement with each other, that Johnny told him to come into the bar, where he could sit at the end of the bar with him. I was so glad that Johnny had a buddy, as again it took pressure off me once again; and like a gentleman Johnny never let on to anyone about the little issues we had together.

To put Danni's mind at ease, I would sometimes ask him to come up to the dressing room; and help me to change in and out of my costumes, which again he did as he was out of the public view; and away from my barmen's prying eyes, always undressing him when he walked in the bar. Poor little thing, there was not a night go by where he was not propositioned by one of the bar staff, or indeed from some of the customers, but he never took anyone up on their offers.

One night whilst getting ready, Danni brought me up a bottle of Vodka; and a bottle of coke, as he knew that was my preferred poison. He then sat down next to me, as I told him that my costumes were all in order; and all he needed to do was unzip, hang up, and re zip the costumes.

"This is the order Danni, so you will not get lost or confused. Remember once you unzip me out of one, do not throw my gown of the floor like many stupid queens, place them neatly over my sofa; and then once I have the next dress on you zip me back up. Then when I go back out, you hang the gown up, and get the next one ready."
"Yes Ruby, I have got all that." He replied, though I was sure he did not want to be surrounded by all this glitter and make-up. I was sure he would have preferred to be standing next to Johnny.
"It is Miss Ruby, Danni. Always call me Miss Ruby, as I would not want people to think you are more special than they are." I told him.
"Yes Ruby, I mean Miss Ruby." He replied nervously, as I then asked him why he was not with anyone, as he has had such a lot of interest.

He told me that he was not ready to be involved yet; and that he would know when the time was right to think about such things; and for the moment he would rather stay single, as he was contented with his life. Trying to pry a little further, I asked him if he had a certain type, as looking at him he looked like a clone, in which I thought that would be his type. Or did he like pretty boys, butch guys, drag queens etc. he again told me that he did not have a type. That he would like to find a guy who has a personality rather than an image. It is what that person feels like inside; and how they converse with you that he liked. That you do not have to have money, as that would not impress him; and you do not have to be posh, as sometimes it can come across as becoming quite snobbish. That just a nice everyday regular guy, would

164

be all that he could ever hope for and wish for, he explained, in that beautiful and sexy Scandinavian accent that he had.

"Well, Danni; the bar staff here are really nice, and you turned down them in the blink of an eye." I told him.
"Yes, Miss Ruby they are nice, but one is a little too camp for me, the other looked at my crotch whilst talking to me, instead of looking at my face, so that was just sex as far as I was concerned. And the two guys in the bar were old enough to be my father. I have a feeling I will know when the right guy comes along Miss Ruby." He replied.
"You are a sweet boy dear, and yes you will find a guy when the time is right." I told him, as I got a bit more of an insight to this handsome young man. A man who had hit on my senses, as I imagined that we could be the perfect couple, as I had a liking to this young man.

I then told him to go back to the bar to see Johnny; and when he heard the DJ announce that I will be on stage shortly, to return back to the dressing room.
"Yes Miss Ruby, I understand." He replied.

It was not that I was not interested in him, I just wanted to be on my own as I got ready. I was not interested in Danni sexually, as he was a gay man; however, sexually he did tick my boxes because he gave me a strange feeling inside, in which I had to try and cancel out, because I needed a man, and not a pretty boy. I also liked him because he was a friend, because he respected me, because I had nothing he was interested in, so I knew I was completely safe being in his company.

I often wished Johnny was like that, but he would test me sometimes. All I could offer Johnny was my ass, but I so wanted to be made love to, like a proper woman; instead of taking it up the ass all the time.

Right on cue, the DJ announced ten minutes to show time; and there was a knock on my door a minute later. Danni never ever just walked in, but always knocked and announced that he was there. I told him to come in, where he sat down as I just got a passing aroma of his cologne. It was sweet and masculine, and now just taking a look at Danni, I could now really appreciate just how well-groomed he was. He never had a hair out of place, and he always dressed impeccably.

He also never had five o'clock shadow, but instead a well-groomed goatee with a very smooth face, showing no more hair but that on his head and around his mouth. I mostly caught him with a suit on, so it was nice to see he also had a casual side to his wardrobe.

If he wore jeans, he was still immaculate in appearance; and it was for that reason I could truly understand why he was prepared to wait; and it was not because he showed off his big package either, which I knew was why the boys were after him. He did not want a guy who was scruffy, who reeked of alcohol; but more one that was on his level, who looked after themselves on the outside as well as the inside.

We had our fair share of rent boys and chavs, as well as those who thought it was hip to wear jogging bottoms and dirty jeans; and of course, there was the older cliental, whom I preferred as they were well behaved.

I can truly say we had a mixed bag at the Rainbow, but

still our Danni kept himself to the shadows, as time and time again he would decline the offers from the pretty boy's in the bar. I then got myself ready to go out on stage, and just before walking down the stairs, I gave Danni a kiss on the cheeks much to his shocked look.

"It is only a drag kiss dear; there is nothing in it like a hidden agenda." I told him, as he began to go red.
"A drag kiss, Miss Ruby?" He asked
"Yes dear, it means thank you, see you later, take care, missed you, etc. No real meaning; and no hidden agenda. It is a drag queens code dear." I explained.
"I see, well thank you for explaining Miss Ruby, enjoy the show and go get them." He replied.

I then walk out on stage as my intro was being played, and then began my performance. I had a few people heckling as you always do when you have a show.
But they did not get the best of me, as I soon put them in their place. Forty minutes later; and around five changes, my show was finally over. I got back into the dressing room, where I asked Danni to pass me the long red sequin gown, then told him to go back to the bar.
He told me how frightened he would be if he were in the audience, as I had something of an acid tongue.
I just laughed and told him that it was part of the act; and if you let anyone from the audience get the better of you, then your reputation will be tarnished. Danni then made his way to see Johnny, as I relaxed for a few minutes before getting changed.
Upon returning back to the bar, I had the regulars who came up to me and congratulated me; and some who you

could see kept out of my way. Johnny kissed me on the
lips as he told me well done, offering me a vodka, as
Danni then gave me a drag kiss.

I stayed with the boys for a few minutes, before going
around everyone and collecting a few glasses, as I gave
the bar staff a look of dread. Then I made my way to the
DJ box, with a list of next week's cabaret and asked him
to announce them. After all that, I made my way back to
the boys, where I then excused myself and made my way
to the royal box; where I invited one or two of my
regular lesbians to sit with me.

Once we had turfed everyone out, we had a few drinks
with the bar staff, with Johnny and Danni serving them,
as it was now their turn to chill out before locking up and
going home. Danni asked us if we wanted to go for a
meal that following day, in which we agreed. He bid us
goodnight; giving me a drag kiss and Johnny a man hug.

I was so pleased to get home, as my legs were killing me;
and I was very tired as it had been a very long day, as
well as my feet blistering because of trying to break in a
pair of shoes.

The next day, I did my usual Saturday morning shopping
at Old Spitalfields Market; and just like me I looked for
a few bargains on the way, before making my way to
Covent Gardens to the flower market, so that I could
redress the tables in the bar, as I thought plastic flowers
to be tacky, so I used fresh flowers just for the daytimes.
I could never be happy with one bag, as you could
guarantee I would come back with my hands totally full.
It was definitely a taxi job whenever I went shopping, so
made sure I had some extra cash in my purse. I had also
picked up a lovely 1970's white and mint green flared

skirt and jacket, for the meal we were going to go to with Danni that evening. I was very excited as this would be the first time in nearly a year that we were going out to eat, and even more excited to be accompanied by two men. When I got back home, Johnny laughed and asked if I had left anything for anyone else to buy, as he then came up to me and helped me with all of my bags. Johnny placed all the meat into the freezer; and put the rest of the food into the fridge. I trimmed the flowers, as Johnny said he would rush to the bar as Ellie was going to look after it for us until we got there; and she would arrange the flowers on the tables putting attention to detail for the royal box posy. I just chilled out before taking a shower, as Johnny went to the bar to cover the morning shift; and to wait for Ellie to take over around 2pm, so that he could get back home and start to get himself spruced up and looking like a million dollars. We had arranged for Danni to come to ours at 5 o'clock, where we would then head off for dinner. Danni told us not to book a cab, as he had asked Marcus to take us there, Marcus being the chauffer for his father's company, as well as giving Danni a helping hand every now and then. Johnny arrived home from working the morning shift; and just sat down and relaxed, as I made a pot of tea. I went into the bedroom and brought out my suit, in which Johnny told me it was gorgeous. I told him I was fed up with wearing black, and needed a bit of colour in my life; to which he laughed again.

It was now 4pm, and Johnny made his way to the bathroom, as I had already showered, I just went to the bedroom and steadily got my make-up sorted before making myself look a little bit more presentable.

169

My make-up was a little heavy, as he liked girls like that, but no way did I look like a drag queen as that would be so embarrassing, as I did not want to come across as a cock in a frock, or as Johnny often said a bag in drag.
I did not have the face to be able to wear just a little bit of make-up; and as I modelled myself on Sue Ellen from Dallas, that seemed to be the look that was very much in the now. This was not to point the finger at me, even though I knew what he was talking about, as some drag queens looked horrendous, I just wanted to look more natural than I did on stage, so instead of over emphasizing my face, I did tone it down slightly still keeping the dynasty look.
Johnny had finished in the shower, and then before coming to the bedroom, where he did his usual routine by cleaning and tidying up after himself. He then walked through as he picked out his suit, which was a dark blue one with a dark blue and pink tie.
I have to admit he always scrubbed up well; and he never ever put me to shame. Just then the doorbell rang; and Johnny answered it as I then heard Danni's voice as he walked in. Johnny poured Danni a bourbon, as he made himself a scotch, pouring a glass of wine out for me. As I made my way out of the bedroom, I could see that Danni's eyes nearly popped out.

"You look gorgeous Miss Ruby." He said, eyeing me up from head to toe.
"You do Ruby; you look totally amazing." Johnny also said.
"Thank you boys, as you can see I do not always look like a drag queen. Drag is best kept on the stage where it

170

belongs; and not brought out for public engagements." I replied, as I felt I had passed inspection.

I finished my glass of wine, as Danni then announced that Marcus was waiting for us downstairs. I reached for my keys; and once out of the apartment Johnny locked up. Danni made his way to the elevator and called the lift, as he and Johnny both gave way for me to walk in first like proper gentlemen. I could not believe it when I got to the foyer doors; and standing to attention I saw Marcus in his black uniform and cap, standing by the car as he waited for us by the black limousine… I felt like royalty.

"OMG, you have a limo just for us Danni." I asked
"Only the best for my family." Danni replied.
"How on earth am I going to top this one Danni?
Ruby will want this kind of treatment more and more,
now she has got the taste of it." Johnny replied.
"It is the only way to travel Johnny; and if you are lucky
enough to have use of it, then you may as well use it and
not waste it." He said, but not in a condescending manner.

Marcus then held the door open, as we all got inside, when Danni told him to take us to the Dorchester, as we had a six thirty booking.

"Right away sir, we will be there in roughly ten minutes
depending on traffic." Marcus replied.

Danni then opened the drinks cabinet; and asked me and Johnny what we would like to drink. So as usual it was a scotch for Johnny, vodka and coke for me, and bourbon on the rocks for Danni.

I really could get used to this I thought, as well as thinking how articulate this young man is; and how real and down to earth he is, as I thought I wish he were straight. I hated false people, as well as those who were arrogant, but knowing he was born to money, Danni never once threw it in your face. He was one of us; and a guy who worked very hard for what he had, even though he did not have to work if it pleased him.

Upon arriving at the Dorchester, I was about to get out of the car, when Danni put his hand on mine. He told me that I should wait, as it is formality to wait until Marcus opens the door for us, in which I apologised, as I was not used to such extravagance, as I then told him that when we were not in the bar or in company of the drag circuit, that he should just call me Ruby, and not Miss Ruby call me Ruby. He totally understood, telling me that he would try not to get things mixed up.

Marcus held the door open as Danni got out first, who then took my hand as I climbed out the car, even politely grabbing hold of Johnny's hand as he gave him a cheeky wink and a smile. He then informed Marcus to come and pick us up around 8pm; and that if there were any delay's he would phone him first.

"*Yes sir.*" Marcus replied.

We walked up the stairs to the Dorchester; and yet again another door opened as we were welcomed, in which I thought that this is definitely the life I could really get used to. I was having a ball, but all the time grateful for the evening that Danni had carefully thought out for us; and who impressed us because it was nicer than what we were used to. We got to know Danni a little bit more that evening, as he told us that he was born in a small village in Norway, near Drammen, but a little further north near the capitol of Oslo.

He went on to say, that after only four years being in Norway, his mother who was an American, had not settled in Europe and wanted to go back to New York, so they had to up and leave to go back to America to please his mother. Then he told us of the arguments that his parents used to have, eventually it ended with them splitting up, which was very hard for him as he loved his father so much.

As fate would have it; and with a twist of luck, his mother, who by now was money orientated, had since sold his father the parental rights to him for one million dollars; and as soon as the deal was struck, he was sent to go and live with his father. He told us of the awful childhood he had with his mother, who never really wanted him, as she only ever wanted money and to be free to go out with other men when she had the chance too; and how he felt he was a hindrance to her lifestyle. He was very happy when his father gave her the money, as he never had to see her that often again.

He went on to say, that his parents did try and rekindle things, but it never worked out which in a not so nice way he was pleased it didn't. Unfortunately, she became pregnant again by his father and had twins, a boy and girl. Again, they split up and he went to live with his father; and he only saw his mother when he was able to see his brother and sister; and then he would be grilled about what his father was up to; and of course, how much money he had coming in.

He told us that he had missed out on seeing them grow up, but it was arranged that once a month his father would have the twins for a week, in which a nanny was hired to look after them; and those times he had with them were the best he had ever encountered. They would ask him questions about why he did not live at home with them, but he would never tell them the real reason as he thought them too young to understand, so he just said that he helps their father in his business and is getting ready to go to university. That the nanny who looked after them, was the wife of Marcus; and both Marcus and his wife became a special part of their family. When Danni and his father moved from America to London on business, he told us that he decided to stay in London, so Marcus moved here too with his wife to make sure he was not alone; and his mother who was now infuriated at the thought she no longer had a nanny, threatened his father with the '*you're not going to see your children card*.' So, to keep the peace he made sure he found her another nanny, who was of equal standing. We just thought what a sad story, but with a nice happy ending because he could have easily been placed into care. At least he had some form of family life, and one with a parent. Johnny thought that his mother sounding like a very nasty woman, a woman who was out to get what she wanted, with no concern for others.

"Nasty Johnny, I think that is an understatement? She is a cold-hearted bitch, with an appetite for money. She is a gold digger who only thinks of herself. I am lucky that my father is a billionaire, because without him paying her off for parental rights, I could have been so unlucky like a lot of children; and put straight into the care system. I am very privileged to have had a very good upbringing, even if it was only with my father, I could have not wished for a better parent." He replied, as he told us all about the kindness his father had.

"What about your mother now?" I asked him, now being a little bit nosey.

"I do not see my mother that often, especially now that I am in England. When I go over to New York, I only see her briefly as I really only go to see Jake and Sophie; and catch up on what they have been up to. We do however, occasionally all sit down together for Christmas Dinner, but that is for the children's sake not hers. She still asks my father for money; and like a fool he gives it her. But I cannot really question my father, as I have been lucky to have been schooled in the best private ones in New York. I have also been privileged in receiving a good education by studying hard; and I have been fortunate to follow my father in business. I work hard Ruby, and I am grateful for what I have. It is for that reason I am cautious, because I would hate to get involved with a guy, who ended up being like my mother. I can wait, and I will know when I have found the right person." He replied, as we both listened and warmed to him.

It was then we fully understood him, understood why he says he will wait with regards a partner. He was very astute; and looks at his past to right his future. Of course, you do not want anyone to know you have money, for they will see you just for what they can eventually try and take from you; and it is going to take a special person to look beyond that.

We had a very nice evening that night, with Danni buying me the best of champagne, whilst he had a bottle of scotch put on the table for Johnny and a bottle of bourbon for himself. I could not fault the dinner service, with having a wonderful five course meal, which afterwards I could have eaten again as it was out of this world. Then as Danni asked for the bill, Johnny got his wallet out and went to reach for some money, when Danni told him not to dare reach for any money, that this was his special treat for his two special friends. Johnny still wanted to oblige, as he asked him to at least let him pay for something, when again Danni told him that this was his treat; and if he wanted to contribute, then he could buy the next meal, with a cheeky smile on his face. Johnny struck a deal with him, shaking his hand, as he told him that I would not be as fancy as what we had just had, as he was sure you would need a second mortgage to eat there. Danni then told us that he did not always eat there, as there were so many fine restaurants around London, but that we must do this again, as it made a nice change from buying take outs, or dining with people that you wish you could be miles away from, because of their arrogance and ignorance. I then told him that it would be fine; and like Johnny had mentioned it would be our treat, agreeing with him about the ignorance of some people.

Just because they are born of money, or have come into money, they feel they have the right to judge others, before even looking at themselves, which I fear they feel they are simply perfect in every way.

Danni then suggested that we go to the bar, before we have one last drink in the Rainbow. We got out of our seats, as both Johnny and Danni pulled my seat away and escorted me to the bar. The waiter then asked if everything was fine with the service, in which I told him it was beautiful. Danni then slipped a fifty pound note into his hand, and thanked him for the enjoyable evening, that he had had.

We spent a further thirty minutes in the lounge bar, before an usher came in to and told us that our car was waiting. We then made our way over to the Rainbow, as I could not believe the evening I had just had.

When we arrived, Ellie asked if we had a good night, and I pulled her over and whispered in her ear that it was a night fit for a queen. She was so pleased, as she told me the bar had been dead all night; and only now was it beginning to fill up. She also told me that the cabaret was going to be thirty minutes late, as they were stuck on the M1. That gave me enough time to sober up, as I was a little tipsy; and thought I had best not do a full show. Johnny asked what I would like to drink, and I just told him I would make a pot of tea in my dressing room.

With his arm over Danni, he got their drinks as they just chatted, and kept an eye on things in the bar with Ellie. You would have thought they were partners rather than buddies, as Johnny always had his arm over him as they spoke to each other.

But I knew it was just good buddies bonding.

Over the next few weeks, we would all go out on a Friday or Saturday evening for dinner. Johnny kept to his word and paid for the next meal, and again we had a lovely evening with laughter and business. I then mentioned in conversation, that I had always wanted to try French food, so Danni told us he would take us to one of his favourite French restaurants the following Friday.

Through the week I spent most my time going around to see Felicia, who by now had got everything finally sorted in her club. She had a year's bookings of cabaret acts, and still asked me to compare on the nights that she was out working, as she needed to still do a bit of private work herself just to help with the business.

I had also been to see Kitty, who had now had a change of direction, as she had turned her club into a fetish club, where I was introduced to Madam Zandra, who was a real woman and a fetish mistress.

I was also introduced too Mistress Sasha, who took the role of headmistress and policewoman, as well as a few more newcomers who were in training in her care.

I found it was a little scary at first seeing all of the ropes and whips and Christ knows what, but I soon got used to it as that was something that was not my cup of tea.

That Saturday, I wore a black trouser suit, with white edging around the pockets of the trousers and jacket. Johnny again wore a suit, as he would take over from Ellie when we got to the bar. Danni was his usual self in designer wear, and not a hair out of place. He came in as he just waited for me to get my purse, and Marcus drove us to Mayfair where we went to a gorgeous French restaurant. Danni told us that this was one of his favourite restaurants, as he often visited this restaurant with his father, when he was in London. I thought it looked a bit posh but was not out of place when it came to Danni and his attire. He was so suited to all this fine dining, where I was quite happy with fish and chips, or even a kebab if I was slumming it. I then told him that he has to stop spoiling us like he did, because I could so get used to it. Then thinking how I wished I was with Danni instead of Johnny, because he had grown on me so much, but also realised that I was not his cup of tea. He was a young queen, and wanted to find a young pretty boy, which I could understand, as a guy like him did not want to be with an ageing drag queen like myself.

As we walked in, we stood at the entrance waiting for the booking clerk to come and see us; where we were then escorted to our table which was in the far corner, as the waiter pulled out our chairs for us.

Well, I had died and gone to heaven, the place was simply stunning, and I did feel like I was a movie star. You could tell that this was a suit and tie kind of place, as there was no one who was at all who was in an untidy attire; and shortly after us all sitting down, a young man came over to our table and offered us the menu.

Yes, it was expensive, and we did not really complain as Danni looked after us, as we did him. He rarely paid for his drinks when he came into the bar, as it was our way of saying thank you. I then asked Danni, if he could nudge the barman, to which he responded.

"He is the Maître De; Ruby."
"The what?" I replied

"*The Maître De, the person who looks after the service of the restaurant.*" He replied, with a cute smile that melted me like a knife through butter.
"*I feel such a fool now.*" I told him, feeling rather flushed.
"*Don't worry Ruby, I had no idea either.*" Replied Johnny.

Danni asked if we were ready to order drinks, in which we were. And as Danni made a slight movement to his hand, it got the attention of the guy who gave us the menu's in which he then came over.

"*Bonjour* Madame, Bonjour Monsieur. Etes-vous pret a commander?"
"*Bonjour, Je voudrais commander une bouteille do Moet, un double scotch sur les rocher, et un double bourbon sur les rochers. S'il vous plait Monsieur.*" Danni replied, with little effort to struggle with a language.

I looked at Johnny, and with my mouth open in shock Johnny looked at Danni and said to him that he did not know that he could speak French.

"*Oh yes, sorry I thought I had mentioned it before when we were last out.*" He replied
"*No not at all Danni, but whatever you said it sounded so sexy.*" I told him, now rather impressed with this young man.

"I have just ordered a bottle of champagne for the lady, a double scotch on the rocks for Johnny, and my usual double bourbon." Danni replied.

I then asked him how many languages he could speak, in which he told me that he majored in French, German, Italian, and American English of course, as well as speaking his native Norwegian. And as they have had dealings with Japan, he can speak a little of that language to get by, just so he does not look or sound stupid. I told him he knocks the socks of me, because I can only speak English and Spanish.

"What about you Johnny?" Danni asked
"I speak English, Italian and a little Spanish." He replied, telling him that he was not as fluent as he was.

He then explained that he had to learn those languages, as they were an important necessity to his father's company. That he also majored in Business and Economics, unlike people thinking because his father owns the business, that he was offered it by my birth right; and not had to graft hard and study hard. That being the boss' son was difficult at times, as some thought I had certain privileges. I told him that unfortunately people are like that; and I say forget them as they are not worth it, as my father used to say.

"This is a very nice place Danni, how did you come across it again?" Johnny asked.

"My father brought me here as a boy when we visited England, and Ruby; some nights you do get movie stars here. As a boy I saw a few in my time in London, with the likes of Cary Grant, Ursula Andress; and of course, Sean Connery who posed for a photograph with me. Quite often it is also used by government officials, the rich and famous, bureaucrats and the odd spy." He said, as he winked his eye.

"So, are you a spy then Danni?" I asked jokingly

"I am afraid I cannot divulge that information Ruby, without otherwise having to kill you." Danni said, with a smile.

Well laugh, I nearly piddled myself, but I still remained ladylike by keeping my composure. Danni went on to tell us that the restaurant we were in called Le Gauroche. That the brothers Albert and Michel Roux helped lay the foundations of London's world class dining scene; with the opening of this fine restaurant in Mayfair in the year 1967. We got to appreciate his educated mind and the world he came from; and we began to give him the respect that he thoroughly deserved.

He again ordered all of our food in French, before we thought about leaving around 9pm. I had no worries that evening as Felicia was doing me a good turn; by taking over the comparing. Once we got to the bar, I moved to the royal box, and just enjoyed the rest of the evening as I watched the hilarious Felicia, as well as the mad but funny Totty.

It was now December of 1980, and I had asked Bobby in the November of that year, to come and move in with us in London. We spoke about the cabaret scene; and how she wished she could do it, but felt it was far above her as she was a nervous little thing. I gave her the opportunity to try it out; and when she agreed, we spent all month rehearsing for a new show. I had by now chosen a name for her, and after a few days going through what I could think of, I just used her own name in the same way as Felicia had chosen mine.

I called her over and told her that she looked like a Roxy; so, after going through lots of names which were rejected, we finally found one that was suitable, as she would be called 'Roxy Garcia' which was really her own name so to speak.

Over the next few weeks, I noticed that Danni was coming into the bar more regular, taking a lunch break here and there as he watched the pair of us rehearse, but if truth had it, he was really there looking at Roxy as he was engrossed with her, which I thought may have been because of her slim figure, and her lovely boyish looks. Still chatting with Johnny, he looked back at the pair of us, making contact with us as he would raise his glass. It did not dawn on me until the last week of rehearsals, that I thought he really did have a thing for my Roxy, as he seemed transfixed towards her when she was rehearsing. I never got to introduce Roxy to Danni during rehearsals, because as we finished, he seemed to have already left the bar. It was not until the night of the show, where I would try and put my plan in force, as I went downstairs and called Danni over. I asked him if he would help my new sister in cabaret; and would he like to be her new wardrobe assistant. He agreed and told me that he would love to, so I got his hand and took him upstairs to the dressing rooms, where I then introduced him to Roxy.

"Roxy this is Danni; Danni this is Roxy."
"Miss Roxy, I am your designated wardrobe assistant."
He replied, with a little twinkle in his eye, which we both noticed, as Roxy then looked at me in shock, with her mouth open.
"Close your mouth dear, there's a swarm of flies outside looking for a new home." I said, rather sarcastically.

She then looked at Danni again, and looked at me as she mimed the words 'he is gorgeous.' So, I just said.

"Well, you did not expect to dress yourself now, did you? Danni is your wardrobe assistant, and whatever else you need him for. You know like drinks, and other things."

I then went back to my dressing room to finish off getting ready, before giving the crowd a glimpse of my new partner in crime, as I thought it best that I let them introduce themselves to each other.
When the show had finished, I just looked at Roxy and told her that she was a natural. She told me that she was really nervous and nearly piddled herself, but as soon as she put her foot on that stage it was as though she had been doing it for years.
I stayed on stage for a little while just to give a few more announcements, before going to see Johnny and get a much deserved drink. I asked Johnny if he had put the flowers in Roxy's dressing room, in which he told me that he had done; so, I decided to go up and see her.

As I got to the door it never dawned on me to knock, so I just opened the door and walked in. It was then that I literally screamed, because as I opened the door, I saw Danni with his jeans down by his ankles, and Roxy laying on the chaise lounge. Danni was reaching over towards Roxy, his dick just dangling as it was touching her trannie asshole, giving me flashbacks of the encounter that Johnny and I had with that lovely police officer.

"Oh… I am sorry dear; I didn't realise you were fucking the help. Ooppps I mean I didn't realise he was fucking you, well at least you kept your heels on like a good drag queen." I said, with a little glint in my eye.

Danni just stood up, as I heard Roxy shout, 'Fuck, get me up, I can't breathe.' Danni then ran out of the dressing room, as he had now pulled his jeans up.

"Shut that door before the draft chaffs my lips." Roxy said hysterically.

I did not look behind me to see if Danni had closed the door, instead I went over to help Roxy up off the floor until she said.
"Ruby shut the door please and give me a hand, make sure the door is shut as I don't want to be accused of being a trannie fucker."

I just looked at her with daggers as I told her that wouldn't happen, so I then continued to help her up, so she composed herself. I again told her how well she had done, and that I was very pleased of her.

"Well... this is a first Roxy, who would have thought that I would have been helping a drag queen up off the floor, with her cock and ass in full view. You know I love you, dearie, but I would have settled for a vodka and coke. Well, fancy being fucked by the help dear; and on your debut night too." I said, as I then had a smile on my face.
"I was not being fucked Ruby, we were fooling around yes, but I was not being fucked. I simply lost my balance." Roxy replied all apologetic.
"Well, it didn't look like you had fallen from where I was standing dear; you are quite a big girl for a drag queen; so now wonder Danni was turned on. Mind you he has fancied you for the past three to four weeks, ever since we started rehearsals together... you lucky bitch. All the pretty queens are after him, and he chooses a drag queen. You are going to break some hearts tonight dearie, but I do give you my blessing." I told her.
"Ruby we are not together; it was an honest accident. Danni and I are not seeing each other." She replied, feeling rather embarrassed at the whole scenario that had unfolded.
"No Roxy you are not together; you were just fucking each other. But anyway, give it time, because I know he fancies you and I somehow know that you two will end up together; as I see the way he looks at you when you come to rehearsals." I said, as I had since helped her up off the floor.

Just then Danni came back into the room, where he asked if it was safe to do so and where he apologised to us both, as I told him I did not recognise him with his jeans on, which made him give me a strange but cute smile. I then looked at Roxy and told her that her audience awaits her; and not to keep them waiting.

I then went back downstairs as Johnny's sister was in the house and it was her birthday. I just thought I would make two killings with one spotlight. I left Roxy and Danni to it, as I made my way downstairs. I got to Johnny and told him what I had just seen; and he couldn't stop laughing. Johnny told me that he wished he had seen it, as he thought it would make a good story on stage. It was then that I definitely thought I am going to use this, as I know it will tickle a few people.

I finished my drink and decided to see the DJ to see if he had the record set up that I wanted to use, and as he did, I went backstage ready to make another appearance.

I picked out a special dress given to me by Suzie, it was absolutely stunning. It was a long purple evening dress, encrusted with diamante on the shoulders and neckline fading out as it followed the dress to the floor.

I sang a few songs, and then slated a heckler who was really pissing me off.

"*My god what a gob you have on you, if I could afford the wood, I would have it boarded up for you.*" I told him, much to the delight of my audience.

Well as usual for the crowd, they roared with laughter.

"There is no bigger bitch than this bitch on the stage, so think before you mess with Ruby Passion." I said, looking him right between the eyes.

He again started to say a few things, and I had now had enough, so I ripped into him; my last comment froze him in his tracks with his mouth wide open.

"Close your fuckin mouth dear, the number 48 will be passing by soon, and he will think you're a parking space." I said, again much to the delight of the crowd.

Again, the crowd roared and applauded, as the guy now sat down red faced. I then went on to mention the first part of the show; and how well Roxy had worked and that it was her debut show. The crowd whistled; and jeered as Roxy then appeared from behind the curtain with Danni. She sat down where I could see she was holding Danni very close to her. I looked over and gave her a wink, as I then thought I had to do it, I simply had to say what I saw.

"Well… what can I say Ladies and Gentlemen? Our Roxy has been a very hard worker this evening ladies and gentlemen, but she was not satisfied with one performance as she ended up doing a private one."
I then saw Roxy pick up her champagne glass and take a mouthful, choking on it when I said.

"Swallow dear, how many times do I have to tell you that drag queens swallow dear, they do not spit?"

I then saw her mine the words you bitch to me, so again I looked at her and winked as I looked at the audience.

"Not only was she not satisfied with her debut show, I decided to go backstage only to find her laid over the chaise lounge with her legs in the air, giving a performance for the wardrobe assistant. I ask you ladies and gentlemen; there she was being fucked by the help. And staff so hard to find these days, bless her."

Everyone laughed and applauded Roxy, as Roxy then went and hid behind Danni. It was then that I called Ellie on stage, and like a scared rabbit, she came up to me; not knowing what I had in store for her. I got everyone together and asked them to sing happy birthday, and when it was over the cake came out and I looked at her and told her that I was going to get a church candle, as it would have been cheaper; but thought against it as I know she would need a lot of puff to blow out twenty-one candles; and there are a lot of puffs in here who will help her. I then asked her to help me with a number before she left the stage, and like a trooper she helped me out. I have never seen her go so red, or the crowd piddle themselves with laughter when I got her to do 'tits and ass' with me from the musical 'A Chorus Line.' Finally using a pair of really big false boobs, and a fake ass; she looked hilariously funny but carried it off. Once we had finished, I showed my appreciation by applauding her, then did another number before leaving the stage. I went over to Johnny where I gave him a hug, and then joined my family.

"You cow Ruby; I didn't know where to look." Roxy said, still blushing at the fact I had told the crowd about her mishap with Danni.

"I just had too dear. I couldn't miss my opportunity. You should have seen the boys behind the bar, they were so jealous." I replied.

We then just held each other and giggled like schoolgirls, as we went to the royal box.
When we had cleared the bar, I asked everyone if they wanted to go around to the club as Totty was performing her new show. So, with that we gathered our things and went around to Diamonds to watch Totty. I introduced Roxy to Felicia and Kitty, where I then made my excuses as I wanted to go and have a word with Totty.

"Roxy come with me; I would like to introduce you to Totty." I told her.

Roxy then followed me as we went backstage, to the dressing room door. Standing there I just knock and said it was royalty.

"Come on in dear that must be you Ruby." Was spoken.

We walked into the dressing room, as Roxy could not believe all the costumes Totty had; with feathers sticking out everywhere. I then introduced Totty to Roxy.

"I have heard all about you Roxy, and it is finally nice to put a face to a name." Totty said.

Roxy was still amazed by her costumes, but acknowledged Totty's remark, as Totty looked at me and spoke.

"You will have to excuse me for being in drab mode, usually I have my slap done by now, but it has been a horrendous journey getting here."

She then gave us both a drag kiss, as she started dishing all the gossip. She went on to explain that she was only in London for one night, as she was flying off to Spain to work a six-month contract in one of the bars there.
I was intrigued as I asked her to tell me more.

"It is an up and coming resort in Gran Canaria, and it is going to be a big resort one of these days. It is already showing promise with the gay community, and the bar is in Playa del Ingles. You both must come and visit." She told us.
"That would be lovely Totty, and it sounds very exciting for you." I replied
"When I get back, we will catch up properly, you must come over to Kensington and stay with us a few days." She continued to say.
She then told us that she had to get ready and she needed her privacy. We all left and made our way back to the Rainbow crowd, as we waited for the show to start.
Her show went down a storm, and once again Roxy was fixated by her many gowns of sequin and feather, as you saw the cogs go running at ten to the dozen.
When it was time to leave the club, as expected Danni asked if he could take Roxy home with him. Roxy was a

little hesitant as she had no male clothes with her, but Danni soon came up with an answer, and a cheeky look. Johnny did however say that they were welcome to come home with us and have a night cap, as well as staying over if they wished, but I thought he looked just a little uncomfortable with our offer. I knew he wanted to spend a little private time with her, and I could not blame him, as they seemed to be getting on so well together.

"Or Miss Ruby, with your permission Miss Roxy could come with me in a cab and stay over. We are about the same size so she would have no worries about drab clothing." He said, as I saw that glint in his eye, which told me that he really did have a thing for my little starlet. *"Oh… I don't know about the size issue, you are certainly a big boy."* I replied, now beginning to tease him.

This made him go very red, as well as Roxy.
I told Danni not to keep her up all night because of rehearsals the next day, so Danni agreed as they went off on their way as I went home with Johnny and Ellie.
"I know I embarrassed her at the bar, but I simply had to do it." I told him, now glad that I did, because I think it brought them together that little bit more.
"You should have seen her face; I have never seen her go so red like that before. You really did get her unawares sweetie." He replied, telling me that it was funny, but was it necessary?
"Well… it was a funny situation, and even if nothing had happened; I cannot fathom out why Danni had his jeans

*around his ankles. She was being a little rude I would
imagine, but a quick worker.*" I said as I giggled.
"*I do so wish I had been there; it did sound so funny.*"
He replied.

I then went on again to say that I hoped they got on, as
they did seem very suited together. And yes, I was
jealous, because this guy had only just come into our
lives; and I felt that Roxy was going to take him away
from me. I knew Danni had a soft spot for Roxy; and
now after just a month or so of being here in London,
she had already secured a date with our dearest friend
Danni. I knew she was safe, as well as knowing Danni
would be fine; and I was just crossing my fingers that
everything would go well for them both. But I so wished
it was me that Danni was taking on a date; and maybe
Roxy could have got off with Johnny.
On the way home we were talking about how lovely they
both looked together; and how you could see that they
were engrossed with each other's company, without
being trashy by being over each other like a rash.
I commended Danni for not straying, or testing the water
before Roxy came along, as I knew there was going to be
something good about these two, because I could see a
proper romance blossoming.
I still wondered though why Danni was not attracted to
my other pretty boys, as in guy mode Roxy was just that,
a pretty boy. I then thought that maybe it was the fact
she did not throw herself at him or was it because he
liked the feminine side of her because of her act.
Either way it was nice to see the pair together, despite
my jealousy; and I knew she was not after his money,

because otherwise I would not have introduced them to each other.

"She looked absolutely stunning tonight Johnny, and both Roxy and Danni reminded me of a younger us." I told Johnny.
"Hey sweetie, yes they did. However, don't pass us off yet as we are not all that old, there is still some life in this one, and as always you looked beautiful." Johnny replied.

I looked at Johnny and smiled, as I then placed my hand onto his and told him thank you. By now Ellie had fallen asleep, too much excitement and alcohol I would have guessed. It did also surprise me as Ellie was not much of a drinker, but then again too much champagne always does the trick. It still gets me from time to time, but I was a bit of a lush anyway when it came to champers and wine.
We finally got home where Johnny held onto Ellie, as she was well and truly bladdered. I opened the security doors and made my way to the elevator, as I stood there I grabbed hold of Ellie's bag and goodies as Johnny had to carry her as she had now lost her legs.

"Ah, what it is like to be 21 again Johnny, I don't think I was ever like that was I?" I asked.
"No, you were quite the lady Ruby, handled your drink well and then when we got home you seduced me." He replied.

"*I never did anything of the sort Johnny; you took advantage of a merry twenty one year old; and decided that you would make love to her.*" I said, putting up my defences.

"*And I never heard you complain sweetie, and if I can recall we did it twice and you still wanted more.*" He replied with a laugh.

I looked at him with a girly look, as I went a little red but still giving him the flirtatious eye. Once in our apartment Johnny took Ellie straight to her bedroom as he picked her up because of the fact she could not walk, where he left the side light on for her just in case she needed to get up in the night. He was not concerned about her needing the bathroom, as she had an en suite; however, he did slightly wake her and let her know what room she was in and where she was just in case she wandered.

I had since gone into the kitchen and put the kettle on, as I needed a cup of tea before going to bed.

It was routine and essential, as I could not really drop off without a cuppa and it did seem to help me.

So, having made myself one, Johnny decided to finish the night off with a scotch as he just collapsed on the sofa. We then started to chat about the evening again, and of course the now new Danni and Roxy.

We giggled about the incident when I caught them in a rather uncompromising position, and then seen how they were very well suited together. Shortly afterwards we heard moving in Ellie's room, so Johnny went to check on her as I made my way to bed. I was being kind of seductive that evening; and as I undressed, I quickly climbed out of my corset and climbed into a nice red

negligee with matching panties. I was not trying to lead
Johnny on, but thought if anything happened then I
would be ready to wow him. I really was not too
concerned, as I was once again going through a stage
where I wanted intimacy with him; and on the other hand,
I couldn't give a damn.

Again, my thoughts of wanting to be Ruby; outweighed
the thoughts of wanting to be sexual as a guy. I did not
want to be touched at the front, yet another part of me
still enjoyed that, so I was having pretty much of a bad
confusing time.

I was quite lucky that evening, as by the time Johnny had
come into the bedroom, we were both slightly whacked,
Johnny needed to be up early to sort out stock, giving me
plenty of time to relax before going to rehearsals. Johnny
then jumped into bed noticing I was the lady in red; and
simply said 'Divine', then placing his arm around me he
kissed me on the neck as he snuggled up to me before
dropping off to sleep. It was not long before I did the
same, and although this time I would not have minded a
little bit of fun, I was also relieved that we both just had
enough and were whacked, that we just dropped off.

The next morning, I was woken to breakfast in bed,
which Johnny would do on a Sunday as he was always
the first one up, as Sunday's were the only day in which
I spoilt myself by having a lie in. He bid me a good
morning; and hoped I had slept well, as I bid him the
same, in a still rather tired voice. He then told me that
there was no need to get up; and that he had checked on
Ellie, who was doing fine, as she is still sleeping off her
late night drunken stupor; and that he was going to go to
the bar to get things sorted.

"Ok dear, by the way what is the time?" I asked.

"It is 9.45am sweetie, so you have a couple of hours so you can go back to sleep if you like?" He replied.

"No dear, I shall have to get up soon as I will need to shower and get changed. I have told Roxy it is rehearsals today, but instead I am going to take her to meet Suzie." I told him, as I wiped my eyes and gave an almighty stretch.

"Ok Ruby; and maybe tonight if you are up for it, we could go out for a meal instead of you cooking. Then get to the bar a little later, as Ellie will be fine, I am sure to cover." He asked.

I told him to maybe see how Ellie was first; and if she was fine, then yes it would be a nice treat, but if not that I would cook us all something. He looked at me and whispered ok, as he then told me that he was going to pop off for a few hours; and that he would see me when I get to the bar for rehearsals, then telling me to be good, which I knew would be a fine thing, as I had nothing else planned for the day anyway.

"Be good in deed, as if I am ever naughty you cheeky thing. Go on off with you, so I can eat my breakfast in peace". I replied, at the very thought of me being good.

So off Johnny went, after he gave me a kiss on the forehead and left me to finish off breakfast. I heard him call in to Ellie to see if she was ok, and I then just heard her slightly stir. Once I had finished breakfast, I had my shower and started to get myself ready; and then I made my way into the lounge, only to find Ellie had already got the coffee on; and was looking much better than I assumed she would.

"You look brighter this morning dear, had a good night did we?" I asked.
"Yes thank you Ruby, mind you my head is a bit thick this morning, but nothing a few more cups of coffee will not fix." She replied.
"It must have been the champers dear; it does get to you like that; especially if you are not a drinker." I told her, knowing that she could not handle her alcohol intake.
"Yes, I think you are right, as I am usually half a lager girl." She said with a smile.

We then caught up with the night's events; and how she laughed about being on stage even though she was very nervous. She knew I would never harm her or bitch her intentionally; and by all accounts she did tell me that she did have a good time. We also spoke about Danni and Roxy; and she agreed with me how lovely they both looked together, where we both hoped this would develop into something special.
We had a little bit of a bond with both of them, in their own individual selves as we had all warmed to them; and the bar had really taken Roxy under their wing.
Not everyone to walk through the door of the Rainbow is embraced by the punters so quickly, but there was something about Roxy in which she captured everyone feelings, as she had time to say help to each person individually and on a personal level. After finishing off a walk down memory lane, I asked Ellie if she was ok and had she sobered up, as she looked fine and told me so.

I then grabbed my bag, where I then proceeded to give her a kiss on the cheek as I made my way to the bar.

I was slightly early, which I didn't mind as I had a few things myself to sort out. However, not long after I got there, as regular as clockwork Roxy walked in. Her face was a picture as it just beamed, and I knew everything was fine. She then proceeded to tell me about her evening with the handsome Danni; and how he did not take advantage of her, instead letting her sleep in one of the spare rooms, even though she knew he wanted to spend the evening with her.

She did make me laugh though when she told me she couldn't sleep, and Danni made her jump as he crept into the kitchen. But it was also romantic to find they both ended up in bed, and all that Danni had in mind was to hold his dear sweet Roxy closely. It almost brought a tear to my eye, just to see this special friend of mine be happy. I had also listened to her stories from her childhood which broke my heart; and seeing how she did not have such a great time of it in Brighton, I was so proud to have met her and have her join my special circle and family.

I also knew wherever a person is in the likes of clicky groups, that it is hard to adjust and fit in, and I was so glad that we clicked as I felt that I had found myself a very close sister and friend.

Having now been fortunate to hear both stories from Danni and Roxy; I had this feeling that they were meant to be together. Roxy, like Danni never used the fact she had money; and kept it to herself as she never thought she was above anyone else.

Like Danni, she too was just a regular guy.

I told Roxy that I had taken Danni to one side, where I told him that he had to remain a gentleman. I also stated that if he got up to any funny business, then he would have me to deal with.

"You did not say that did you Ruby?" She asked
"I sure did dear, but I knew he was ok." I replied.

Johnny then brought us both over a second orange juice as we finished chatting, where I told Roxy it was not rehearsals today as I was going to take her to see a dear friend of mine. She was a little taken back when I told her we were going out, as she said she was not dressed to go visiting, but as usual Roxy was too modest and humble to think highly of herself, even though no matter what she wore she looked absolutely stunning.
She wore a pair of Danni's jeans, which were turned up at the ends; and being the queen she was, she also had a pair of stilettos on. Roxy would dress femme even if she had no make-up on; and as it was the eighties, it really did not matter as such a pretty boy like Roxy simply got away with it.
By the time we had got to Suzie's, Roxy was like a little schoolgirl on a day out, as the look in her eyes as we drove past shoe shop after shoe shop, as well as the high street fashion shops simply had her marvel at the displays. It was only when we got to Suzie's that her face fell to the floor, as I could see that she was in shoe heaven, as before her sat hundreds of designer shoes from seasons back which were still very collectable and desirable.
I introduced her to Suzie; and straight away she took a

shine to her. Suzie and I then decided to have a chat whilst we left Roxy to look in ore over the number of shoes that were there; and in which Suzie had said she could try any on. I then saw all the machinery in Suzie's head working overtime, and then it dawned on me. Roxy, Suzie, fashion show….

'*OMG she is looking her up to be her Tran's model.*'

As we were on the balcony, Suzie then asked Roxy if she would do a catwalk for her. Roxy had no hesitation and grabbed hold of a pair of shoes…

"*She is a natural Ruby, where on earth did you find such a gem?*" She asked, in awe of how Roxy portrayed herself, with that natural feel about herself.
"*Yes, she is Suzie; and it looks like you may have found yourself a star.*" I replied.
"*It certainly does Ruby, but you got to tell me where you have been hiding this girl.*" She asked.
"*Suzie! Roxy is actually a guy; she is not a real girl. I met her in Brighton when I did a few gigs there, she was so very nice and kind to me which is unusual for some queens; and we really just hit it off.*" I replied.
"*Never Ruby, she is all woman surely?*" She asked, as I interrupted her.
"*Trust me she is a guy, and she will tell you that herself if you ask.*" I told her, now knowing that Roxy did have a certain air about herself.
"*You have really shocked me Ruby, I would never have guessed, because she has such great bone structure and a clear complexion. Now wonder you hit it off as I can*

*see in her presence how lovely she is. I know she has
jeans and a t-shirt on, but I really thought she was a girl.
Yes, she actually does have that presence and
personality about her Ruby; now wonder you have kept
her to yourself.*" She replied.
"*You should see her in make-up, she looks even more
beautiful; and she looks like a very young Sophia Loren,
no one would know the difference.*" I told her, feeling
proud I had met her; and made her what she was today
"*I want her Ruby; she simply has to do my show for me if
you will ask her.*" Suzie replied.

We continued to chat, and Suzie asked how things were
going with me. I told her I have my ups and downs, my
good days and my bad days. How Johnny seems to want
more when it comes to sex, and then other times just
leaves me alone.

"*You have to expect that dear, Johnny is a gay man; and
although he is seeing you transform, he is losing a part
of you each day. I think he is frightened that once you
transgend he will have lost you for good, as you will not
let anyone near your ass then, as you have the right
vessel to be made love to with. Just give him time.*" She
said, letting me know what I already knew in my heart.
"*It is just he keeps asking me if he can have my dick,
sometimes it is ok, but mostly I cannot be bothered with
it all.*" I replied
"*That's only natural Ruby, you are kind of going through
your second puberty, but in your eyes, it is your first, as
you are now feeling puberty because of the hormones.
Before it was as Tony, now it is as your true self Ruby.*

Part of you is going to feel guilty because you are with Johnny; and you want to make him happy, as the other part of you, your Ruby side says that you need to be you and therefore your happiness comes first." She explained.

I really enjoyed talking to Suzie; and I soon got off the subject because I did not want Roxy to see me becoming upset and confused. I often looked at Roxy and thought what a beautiful woman she was; and if she committed herself to going all the way with surgery, then I thought she could become an even more beautiful woman. Roxy however was happy at being a gay man who dressed as a woman, where I on the other hand was a woman who hated being a gay man; and leading a gay life just for the happiness of my partner. I wanted Ruby to develop more as a woman; and was beginning to despise anything that was gay, even by questioning my own relationship. I was very unhappy; and often when I went to bed, I would just place my arm around Johnny, where we would just end up going to sleep. It was hurting me how I felt, but I could not help it, I was living a lie and not being true to who I truly was.
It felt cold some nights, as I am sure Johnny could sense that something was wrong, as he too would often turn towards me and place his arm over me, where he would gently stroke my face and then my tummy, but I would just lie there without feeling in my body. I would not give him any inkling that I wanted it to go further, instead I was like a stone cold heartless bitch.
He would gently place his head on my chest, and then whisper to me that he loved me, only for me to say that I loved him too.

Often, he would hold me with his hand gently caressing me as he moved lower down my body towards my dick, I would just pretend that I was falling asleep. He would then say goodnight to me, as I turned around and placed my lips on his and gently kissed him. Again, he would turn around as I felt his arm over my waist. He would tell me that he loved me, but it fell on deaf ears as I tried to switch off and forget what he had said. I would just lay there hoping he would no longer pursue touching me, and wanting me to engage in intimacy with him, as I lay there in silence as I tried to go to sleep.

My thoughts of suicide kept creeping back into my head, as I was becoming more lost and lonelier. Here I was, still kind of living a gay life with a wonderful man, that anyone would have been happy with, yet I felt I had betrayed myself, as I was not the person everyone wanted me to be. I so longed to be made love to as a woman, and not the quick touch and then penetration of my ass. I wanted to be held as I felt my husband's breath on my neck, as he held me close to him, kissing me softly all over my body as he cupped his hand under my back and arched it, so that he made contact with my navel as he gently pressed his mouth over my tummy. With his warm breath making me tingle as he moved his tongue around my navel, and his other hand gently stroking my thighs. To be able to have my husband part my legs as he positioned himself in between me, as he gently placed his throbbing manhood inside me as I felt him taking me slowly and lovingly. All the time his eyes fixed upon mine, as he whispered softly to me pushing further into my moist vagina. I hated this man cock that I had; and every time I dreamed about being made love to properly, it only made me more determined to want to become Ruby completely.

I know Johnny loved me, but I no longer loved him like I used too. I felt we were now just like companions and business partners. I had lost the love I had for Johnny a long time ago, but I did not have the heart to tell him. We had a lot of history together; and I did not want to break his heart. I just took it out of myself, and I blamed myself for the position I was in, as I now knew that I should never have got involved with anyone until I had finally had surgery, but it was too late for that now as I had since put my life on a back burner; and got kind of lost in the whole situation of things.

But still this did not defuse from the fact that I had to become Ruby, and it was now a matter of time and I would have to deal with the consequences then. I could no longer bare the life I was living, and I had no one I could truly confide in, not even Roxy.

I did want to fully open up to Roxy, but I was afraid she would only talk to me on the level of a gay man who dressed as a woman; and she would not understand who I really was. She had strong feelings for both Johnny and me, and I knew it was wrong to involve her into a situation where she may have ended up having to choose between those she cared about.

Each day I saw Roxy and Danni, I saw how close they grew together, yet for Ruby and Johnny, we seemed to be drifting apart more and more. The love I once had for Johnny, was not so much different to the way Roxy loved Danni; and it really hurt me seeing the two people I had grown to love, get closer and closer and develop something that I had always wanted. Yet no matter how much I thought about the situation, I knew I had to be true to myself and eventually let go of the past.

I knew eventually I would have to say goodbye to Johnny as well as to Roxy and Danni, as they were a constant reminder of the life I was living, and the life I so detested.

This was my battle; and I had to try and sort it out myself, but no matter how I tried I just got myself deeper into trouble, and further into a world of loneliness.

There was one thing I was proud of, and that was the fact Johnny and I never aired our dirty laundry in public.

We were two very private people who put on a brave face when meeting our public, it was how we always were and that would never change.

Once we had finished with Suzie, we made our way back to the Rainbow, as I told Roxy how impressed Suzie was; and how Suzie wanted her to be a part of her fashion show in a few months' time. I told her how she looked like a little girl in a sweet shop with all the shoes that were on show; and how I was going to go shopping with her more and more, as she had good taste in shoes and clothes.

Time was now getting on; and Roxy announced that she was going out for dinner with Danni.

"Oh, get you dear, dinner already and it's only your second date." I said, seeing how things were developing nicely between the two of them.

"I am so excited but nervous too Ruby, I have never been to dinner before on a date." She replied.

I assured her that she would be ok, just as Johnny did; and with that Danni came over to her, as I went into the office to sort out some paperwork for the drag shows. By the time I had got down to the bar, Danni and Roxy had left, but Johnny did pass on the message that they had both asked him to say goodnight to me.

We finished up at the bar and then went home, where Johnny got a little frisky. We did start to kiss and play around, but it soon fizzled out as Johnny could see I was in no mood. He then got up, where I heard him banging around in the kitchen. I could only assume that was because we did not go out for a meal, as he had asked me to earlier; and also, nothing happened in the bedroom department which showed with his clinking and clanking in the kitchen. Sometimes he was just like a perpetual young boy, not getting his way, so he kind of threw a tantrum but in an adult childish manner.

I just switched off and fell asleep.

A few weeks had passed now, and Danni and Roxy had got very close, much to the annoyance of the boys in the bar, as they thought it would never last; and I believe they had all put bets on how long before Danni swayed and went with a guy who was mostly a clone of himself. Johnny and I went quiet towards each other when at home, but now I was beginning to come out of my depressive slump, which I was grateful for as I hated being miserable. Johnny and I however had made love a few times in those few weeks; and for once he never asked me for my dick which was a massive relief. It was easier for him, as I was not in the mood to shoot my load, so he really only needed to look after himself; and it surprised me how he still managed to go two or three

times in one night, as he was like a rabbit at times
Yes, our Danni and Roxy were getting very close now, and we were very happy for them. As usual when they came into the bar, Roxy would come up to the dressing room to see how I was doing, whilst Johnny would be chatting with Danni at the end of the bar.

Roxy and I had another show that evening, in which we had rehearsed all month. When she came on stage, I could not believe my eyes, as all her make-up had changed. She had gone from drag make-up to looking like a very feminine and beautiful woman. I told her how gorgeous she looked, as I still could not get over her appearance and how she carried herself.

I have to admit, I had to take a second look.

When we finished our show, I told her that I would be down shortly as I had a few things to do. Well to my surprise next thing I heard was banging and bumping on the walls, as Roxy screamed as well as making what seemed like sexual noises. I could not believe it, there I was trying to catch with an episode of 'Corrie' that I had since recorded; and all I could hear was those two making out in the very next room, which left nothing to the imagination with their moaning and groaning. I need thicker walls I thought to myself, whilst a part of me was actually getting turned on.

After a little while I could not take anymore, I was getting very hot and could not let Johnny see me like this. So, I stood up, and then I continued to bang on the wall, as I then shouted.

"Get a fuckin room next time, you dirty bitches. I was watching corrie and it was off putting."

It then went silent, as I am sure I heard them laugh after they shouted sorry back. I then made my way back downstairs, as I went to the bar. Johnny was coming up to me, as he then put his arms around me and told me what a great show we put on, as he kissed me on the lips telling me that I looked so beautiful. I do not know what come over me, but I placed my hand on his ass and gave his ass cheeks a squeeze. I then told him thank you, as I placed a kiss on his lips, still squeezing his ass.

He pulled me towards him as I was now looking at him face to face, as I then stroked his chest through his shirt, I kissed him again on his lips as my hands gently stroked his ass.

"You ok sweetie, you seem a bit fresh tonight?" He asked.
"Yes, I am ok dear; can a girl not give a bit of attention to her man?" I replied, as my hand now reached towards his cock

"I will give you thirty minutes to stop Ruby." He said, with a glint in his eye.

Well with that I had to stop, as Roxy and Danni had just walked in. I then went over to them and gave them a kiss on the cheek, as I whispered in Roxy's ear.

"You need to get yourself a room dear; I thought I was listening to a porn movie."

I then gave her hand a squeeze; and told her that I was happy for her. After closing the bar and when everyone had left, we had our little get together as usual with the

staff, where Johnny and I noticed Ellie was holding onto the pair of them for her dear life.
Johnny then looked at Ellie and spoke.

"What's wrong baby girl you can tell Johnny?"

She looked at him and was about to say something, when a flood of tears came rushing to her face. She then got up and walked over to Johnny, where she threw her arms around him and then began sobbing her heart out.

"I am sorry Johnny; I am a disappointment." She cried, as she ran out of the bar, when Johnny then looked at Roxy and shrugged his shoulders as to say what the hell is going on? Johnny then said.

"Women's trouble?"
"No." Roxy said
"Fuck she isn't pregnant, is she?" He asked, looking rather worried.
"No Johnny, think about it." Roxy said, as she looked at us both then eyeballed a pretty young girl in the corner
"Oh God, she isn't upset because she is gay is she?" He replied.
"Finally, the penny drops, Ruby. I am sure it is the men who are the weaker sex." Roxy said laughing at us.

Then we all went on a hunt to see where Ellie was.
After a lot of searching, we finally found her in Roxy's dressing room with some coats over her. Johnny told her that things would be ok, and we all went back downstairs.

Shortly afterwards and somewhere around 2am; Danni and Roxy said goodbye as we stayed in the bar talking. Once we had finished drinking and had decided that it was time to lock up, we made our way home in which we were glad that another night was over, as it seemed like all work and no play.

Hearing Danni and Roxy make out, really did get me worked up earlier; and then having the dilemma with Ellie I could not wait to go home. I was still very horny, which was unusual but had to make the most of it.

I could see Johnny in the kitchen as I crept up next to him making him jump, when I put my arms around him.

"Hiya sweetie, you ok?" He asked

"Yes Johnny, just glad to be home. What a night tonight with all the drama. Hope Ellie is ok." I replied.

"Got to keep it in the family sweetie, I knew she was gay a long time ago, and I know she will feel alright once it all sinks in." He replied.

I placed my hands over his crotch, as I kissed him on the neck. Just standing there, he placed his hands on the worktop where he just let out a little moan. I then placed my hand by his zip and undone it, also undoing his belt as I let his trousers drop to the floor. He then turned around and grabbed me, as we began to kiss passionately, with Johnny now removing my dress.

I stepped out of my dress, and as I was reaching down to pick my dress up, I was now in full front of Johnny's rather big bulge. With my lips I kissed his cock through his boxers, as I moved my dress out of the way.

Johnny was holding onto my head as I was pressed

211

against his crotch, so I slowly removed them as I let his cock spring out, hitting me on the nose. The smell of his shower gel and deodorant hitting me like the scent of a bouquet of flowers, with the enticing look and feel of a fully aroused cock, as again he held me on the head, so I took him by the hands and held them firmly on the work top, as I took him slowly into my mouth taking full control of the situation.

"Oh God Ruby, that's wonderful." He said, enjoying everything that I was doing to him.

I continued playing with his cock, as I took him down my throat, still getting an aroma of his cologne as shower gel as well as the sweet taste of his pre cum. Now rock hard, as my own cock was full in my panties, Johnny lifted me up and led me into the lounge.
As we made our way into the lounge, he picked me up as we kept on kissing; just coming up for air now and then. He then just put me down as he turned me around making me hold onto the edge of the couch. There he pulled down my panties, allowing me to step out of them, as he then held me down and caressed my back as he slid his very wet cock into my ass.

"You are so sexy Ruby; God you are so sexy." He said.

Then as I had him deep inside me, he thrust slowly, moving quicker as his breathing began to change. Still holding onto my waist, he kept pushing deep into me as I could hear him getting very close; then he just started to tremble as he let out a yell as he filled my ass to completion. He stayed there until I had every drop from his cock, pulling out of me and pushing back into me, dripping some of his juices over my ass and balls. Then he just stood up and said.

"God that was so good sweetie, you really are one sexy lady."

I then turned around, and before he could even look at my dick, I went behind him and told him it was his turn. He was shocked but did not say anything, so as he was bent right over the couch, I spread his legs wide; and then I began poking his hole with my wet throbbing girly cock. As I began slowly entering him a little bit each time, he enjoyed every bit of my girly cock inside him. I put my hand in between us as I pulled on his balls, when he began pulling on his nipples and then just like Johnny he was moaning with pleasure.

A further ten minutes went by as I thrust harder into him, finally screaming as I began to lose control and shoot inside him, withdrawing as my cock slid between his ass cheeks shooting my seed up his crack as well as inside his ass. I proceeded to get off him, and just went to the couch where I sat down and collapsed. Johnny came and sat down next to me where we ended up kissing before going to bed where again Johnny made love to me.

The next day it was back to the bar, just like my routine had been for the past few years. I needed to sort a few contracts out for the cabaret over the next few weeks anyway. Thinking about the shows that Roxy and I performed, I reminded myself that I had lovely friends in our Roxy and Danni; and often thought that we were all blessed to be so close with each other.

Roxy used to help out at the bar; and I did offer her full time with benefits of time off for her shows, but she always told me that she did not need the money, as she had her own, as well as from the cabaret and television. She worked at the bar without pay; and it was then that I knew Roxy was special. It was then that I came to realise, that both Danni and Roxy were meant for each other, as she never once asked for or needed any extra money.

She used her own; and was not one for hand-outs as she too paid for a round of drinks, even in the presence of Danni which I know annoyed him at times, as he wanted to be the man and look after her, as deep down inside I had the feeling he knew that she liked him for him; and not for anything she could get out of him.

I also think that Roxy wanted to look after Danni, as she was that way inclined with the big heart she had.

Thing is Roxy was free spirited; and she always said she would never be in anyone's debt by having them pay for her drinks all night, or even pay for her full stop.

We always made sure she was looked after, by giving her a bottle of champagne, flowers and paid her bar tab when she ever had one at the Rainbow.

Roxy had just started to rehearse for Suzie's show, and this one day Danni came into the bar looking for Johnny. That day Johnny had just gone out to the wholesalers, when he came over to me and greeted me with a hug.

I was on my own that morning, so I just sat Danni down and we started to chat. My morning barman was not due on until midday, so I was happy just being landlady of the Rainbow and sitting on the end of the bar with my coffee and paperwork in front of me.

"*I really do have to apologise Miss Ruby about the other night, I do not know what came over me in Roxy's dressing room. We were both being a little naughty by flirting, as she made me feel so comfortable; and I should point out that I am the one to blame really and not Miss Roxy. I just thought why not, it is only a bit of harmless fun. I was not making love to her I promise, she really did fall down off her dressing chair. I am not a tart, but I would have loved to have gone a little further with her, because she brings the best out in me for sure Miss Ruby.*" He explained.

"*I know Danni; I was only teasing you. You are a sweet man, and I know you have good judgement. But Danni can I ask, is she really the one?*" I asked him, hoping he would say no; and that it was me that he truly fancied.

"*I do believe she is Miss Ruby, don't ask me how I know, I just have that feeling. I get excited being in her company and my heart skips a beat; and when I am not with her, I feel lost and alone. For that reason alone, I know she is the one.*" He replied, now standing tall; and so very happy that love should fall at his feet.

"*So why Roxy, what has she got that the other boys are missing?*" I asked, still trying to persuade him otherwise, which was my jealousy that was taking over.

"*She makes me laugh and she is very beautiful, both on the inside and on the outside. She speaks to me on the same wavelength that I am on; and does not speak as if she is someone she is not. She does not talk about money or sex, and she even paid for a meal on one of the times we were out, much to my annoyance, which shows me that she is not after my money. I took her to my father's apartment, and she was like a little girl in wonderland looking at everything, without putting a price on them by asking how much those certain things were worth in value. Roxy listens to what I have to say, and picks things up like languages just to be polite in saying thank you when we are out, which also impressed me.*

That shows me that she has a lot of respect towards others, as well as for the company she is in. Roxy makes me feel like me; and makes me feel so alive. Miss Ruby, I want to spend the rest of my life with her; and I do know that she really is the one." He said, as he gave me an in-depth synopsis or her.

"*That is so lovely dear, and it looks as though you have really fallen for her. But you still have not told me why she is different to the other pretty boys in the bar; and will you be taking her to your home then*? I asked, as I began to dig a little deeper for an answer from this love struck guy.

"*I think I have well and truly fallen for her; it is just something about her Miss Ruby. And yes, I am going to take her to my apartment, because I can honestly say that I whole heartedly trust him... her. See I am flustering already about her. I do not want to keep anything away from her. As for the other pretty boys, well they just look at me like I am a piece of meat. I have even heard them say I have money, so get in there. I will not play their games Miss Ruby, because I have seen it all of my life with my mother and father. Roxy has never once asked me for money, or to pay for something. She has herself paid for what she wanted; and has often told me that she will not be a kept man/woman. It is because she is independent and wants me for me, that has made me fall in love with her even more. And she is not and will never be one of those pretty boys, just out for what they can get.*" He replied, as you could see just how much this young man had fallen for my Roxy.

"*Well, I can tell you now Danni; that Roxy does have money and she also has a property down in Brighton, but please do not let her know I have said anything to you about this, because she is a very proud gay man who I know will tell you herself when she is ready. And you do make me laugh when sometimes you refer to Roxy as him, and sometimes as her.*" I asked, knowing coming to the realisation, that he had indeed fallen for her; and I was not going to persuade him otherwise.

"*Thank you Miss Ruby, my lips are sealed; and yes it must seem strange. It is a slip of the tongue sometimes, but whether I call Roxy she or he, it will always be Roxy. Guess that is what you get when your boyfriend is a drag queen, and most the time is a girl. She/he has certainly changed my life; and made me look upon the gay scene differently.*" He replied, as he laughed a few times at the he/she scenario.

I placed my hand on his thigh, as I reached towards him to give him a much needed hug. As he slowly turned to me, I accidently slipped and placed a kiss on his lips, as I then placed my hand further up his thigh and managed to feel just the beginning of his bulge.

"*Miss Ruby, what are you doing?*" He asked
"*I am sorry Danni; I do not know what come over me dear.*" I replied, not knowing why I had grabbed hold of him.

217

"Please stop Miss Ruby, I am with Roxy and I cannot do this. You are my friend, my very dear friend…" He told me, as I quickly interrupted him

"I am sorry Danni; I am so sorry. I did not mean to embarrass you, let alone embarrass myself. Please forgive me." I told him, now realizing that it was a big mistake on my behalf.

I am not sure if he thought I was making a pass at him, but my intentions were to see if Roxy really was, who he wanted; and to see if he could avoid temptations from another. He then left, as he had only just popped in on the off chance before going to the office.

About an hour later, Roxy turned up, and she came right over to me, where she gave me a kiss on the cheek.

I knew then that Danni had not said anything, because I know Roxy would not have kept it to herself, as she would have asked me to explain. She may have been a quiet person, but she would not put up with any crap.

I then looked at her and hoped she had had a good day, when I then told her 'long time, no see.' We sat down and had a cuppa, as I asked her what had been happening in Roxy's world.

Then Roxy told me what Danni had asked her.

"Go for it girl, you will never get anywhere in life if you keep putting yourself on the back burner. You can see that Danni is madly in love with you." I told her, knowing that I was just a sad jealous old cow; and that I could not take Danni's love from her, as his mind was truly made up.

Roxy then told me that she was scared; but knew that she felt she had a safe place with me and Johnny.

"*Life is full of choices dear, and only we can make those choices. We cannot expect people to make them for us, as we are solely responsible. Besides life would be pretty boring if we all did the same things. Think of it as a new adventure dear.*" I said, thinking that maybe I should take my own advice.

 I then told her that Danni had been in the bar regular before she moved here; and all the boys stared and tried to get off with him, as he seemed to have started something growing in their loins. And try as they may, he never took anyone home, as he always stayed either with Johnny or me.
"*You only get one life in this world dearie, don't waste it. If you have a gut feeling; chances are those feelings are true, and it is telling you something.*" I said, now feeling like her mother, instead of sister.

We went back into the bar, as Roxy made a call to Danni to come and pick her up. Shortly afterwards they both left the bar as Danni had come into the bar to collect her. That evening Roxy came over to me, and now she was very excited, as she told me that she would be moving in with Danni in his Victoria apartment.

"*Better start calling you Duchess I think my dear, now that you have gone up in the world.*" I said, as I then hugged her and told her that I was pleased for them both, as I also grabbed hold of Danni's hand and congratulated him.

That week she started to empty her room of her things, and I looked at Johnny and told him that our little bird is flying the nest. Johnny told me that she will be fine, as she still comes in the bar, and we still see her almost nightly. Once she had left our home, the place seemed so quiet without her. I kept looking at the door to see if she was coming back from an evening out, as I expected her to just text and say she is on her way back.

Yes, it was really very quiet in my home without her, which was a bit of a blessing as Johnny left me alone that week, as he could see I was feeling a little bit lost, which I must admit was a blessing in disguise.

I then played on it for a while, because I knew now that Roxy was out of the way, it would not stop Johnny from trying to rekindle the bedroom idea, as he would at some point make a play for sexual advances now that it was the two of us again.

A few weeks later it was the launch of Suzie's show, and we were given VIP seats. I sat there in the middle of Danni and Johnny in anticipation, just waiting for Roxy to make her debut entrance, as I wondered if she would carry it off. When the lights had gone down, and the music began; first out was Roxy. She was nervous at first, but like her first performance at the Rainbow; her nerves left her when she walked down the runway.

We could not get over how stunning she looked in her outfits, and how the make-up artist had done a tremendous job on her; as we all had to look twice just to see that it was her, but by the time she got to the end of the runway we knew it was; when she gave a bit of attitude in her runway walk. She was an absolute success, and Suzie could not have been any happier with her as we saw her hugging our Roxy; and then taking her finale walk with her arm under Roxy, before Roxy then got into line with the other girls.

When the show had finished, they all had one last walk as the audience went wild for Suzie, giving her a standing ovation. Roxy then came over to us once she had changed and introduced us to some of the girls, some who seemed to be rather smitten with Danni.

We spent a few hours there, as cameras began flashing, and reporters swamped Roxy and Suzie. Then one girl ruffled Roxy's feathers and Roxy put her in her place. Danni, Johnny and I could not contain ourselves, so with my arm under theirs I pulled them away so we could leave Roxy to it; and so we could contain our laughter.

I was so proud of Roxy holding her own, because I did wonder at times as she hated hecklers; and left most of them for me to sort out. I just thought if I had done anything to make this girl a star, it was the fact she had listened to me when I encountered hecklers; and she used it to her best advantage.

I knew then that our shows would become less and less, as she now took on the fashion world, followed by her television appearances. I did not mind, as it meant no travelling up and down the country living out of a suitcase. I was really pleased for her; and pleased in everything she had achieved as she shared it with Johnny and me, always letting me know that she would not have achieved anything if it were not for us.

It was a few days before I saw Roxy and Danni again; and I think that was because she really let rip at one of the models; and she felt guilty afterwards because she brought Danni into the equation. In all the time I knew Roxy, I knew she would not use tactics like that, and understood why she sometimes felt the way she did.

I then brushed it off as I knew Roxy would fill me in at some point, so I just let my hair down for once whilst at the bar; and as a result, that evening I had a little bit too much to drink that I gave in to Johnny; and into his alluring ways of seduction towards me.

When we got home, I noticed he was in the bedroom getting undressed; and just seeing him in his nice tight boxers with a bulge I had not seen in a while, sent strange urges through my body as I had a moment of relapse. As he was reaching over the bed to fold his trousers, I went behind him and placed my hands over his chest.

"You startled me then Ruby, is everything alright sweetie?" He asked.

"Yes Johnny, just want to give my man a hug." I replied.

As he was still bent over, I had my body arched over his, as my hands went underneath him, where I began playing with his chest, gently caressing his chest as I began to pull on his now very hard nipples. This was making him very horny, so I moved one hand inside his boxers, and began rubbing his cock and balls. I felt that he was very moist now, so I got my other hand from his nipples and put it to the side where I removed his pants to his ankles. I asked him to step out of them and then

222

told him to spread his legs wide. He made no hesitation in spreading his legs, and I removed my dress as I then sat on my knees and placed my head in between his ass, licking his hairy ass crease, and gently fingering him. Now with his hands on the bed, and his legs wide open; he offered himself to me without pulling away.
I then stood up as I pulled my cock from out of my panties; and placed it by Johnny's now wet hole.
He flinched a little bit, before getting very excited.

"Oh, wow yes… yes sweetie, take your Johnny's hot ass." He said, rather excited.

I then gently pushed my cock into Johnny's ass, before he took all of me. Holding onto his hips I gently pulled him onto my girly cock, as I held him there for a little bit, stroking his back and reaching under his chest following his body down to his cock in which I held in my hands. He was now oozing precum, which had wet my hands, so I slapped him hard on the ass as I told him to turn over, so that I could see his face.
I once again got his legs wide open, and then slipped my cock into his ass. Each time I pushed into him; he shot a little bit of cum over his tummy. I told him to get a hold of his cock and start playing with it for me, as he began jerking on his cock as I thrust into him, holding onto his legs as I pushed deeper and deeper into his hot ass, as Johnny was entwined in excited indulgences.
The moment was becoming too intense, and I could no longer hold on as I began to shake, as I told him that I was going to shoot my load. This made him become more intense, as at the same time I lost control and filled

his ass with my juices, he shot his own load all over his tummy and face, even going to the extent that he shot over his head towards the other side of the floor. He then just pulled me onto him as he told me he loved me and that he did not know what he had done to deserve that.

We just lay there for a few more minutes, as Johnny got up and did the same to me as he got me on all fours.

That evening we made love until the very early hours of the morning, until we both were just too tired.

Even the third time that Johnny got erect again, we were just so tired that we fell asleep.

Over the coming weeks, Johnny and I seemed to get back into our stride where we made love every night, then just as quick as it started it dropped off as I again went to a dark place; and began feeling guilty.

I just thought that I really needed to go and see Dr Brian; so, I told Johnny I was going to go and see him, as I am sure the medication is fucking with me. In the morning I made an appointment to see the doctor, and it was made for the following week.

That week I just concentrated on the bar with Johnny, as I put on the Thursday talent show, and of course made sure my weekend acts were going to be there.

It was now the day of my appointment, and I was a little nervous to say the least, as it had been a while since I had seen Brian. I got to his offices and only had to wait twenty minutes when he came out and called me over.

We went into his consultation room, where he asked me how I had been, as it had been quite some time since we had met last. I explained to him all that had been going on, and how I seem to be getting lots of mood swings. He just told me that this is normal, and some of it is the medication; as he checked I was on the right dosage, and then dropped the bombshell.

"*This will be our last meeting together Ruby, as I am moving to Oxfordshire.*" He told me.
"*Oh no, what shall I do for a consultation now then if you are leaving?*" I asked
"*I have put you in the hands of a very nice young doctor, his name is Dr Chris Siddal. He has all your notes, and as soon as he has caught up with what is happening with regards you and your treatment, you will hear from him in due course.*" He explained, being rather short with me.
"*I will miss you Brian, I will miss you very much.*" I replied, as I had a lump in my throat, and a feeling of abandonment.
I just got up and was about to walk out the room, when he called me back. He then proceeded to lock the door behind him as he then came over to me. He told me how beautiful I was becoming, and if he could get out of it he would. He then told me that his wife had taken a position as governor in an all girl's school, so he had to go as he could not manage the journey all the time from Oxford to London; and this would be the best option to keep the peace. He then grabbed hold of me as he kissed me, undoing his zip as he removed his cock, as he then pulled me towards him and grabbed my hand, making sure I got a handful of what he was offering me.
I do not know what made me do the next thing, but as he pushed my head to go down on his now erect cock, I pulled back off him and just walked out of the room. I did not want it to end like that, and I was certainly not

going to have him fuck me because he felt guilty because he was leaving.

I felt betrayed and abandoned, and just had to leave his office. I had again got myself into a little rut of not talking, wondering what was it that I was doing wrong, whilst all the time trying to concentrate on my shows, and my relationship.

Brian really did fuck me up that day, the day that he told me he was leaving; and I do not think he knew just how much I had fallen for him. I hoped he was going to commute from Oxford; and that we could still see each other, or that he would split up with his wife and ask me to be his girl, I felt as much for Brian as Roxy did for Danni; and my world began to collapse.

A few more months had passed by; and Roxy came in all excited as she was flashing her hand about.

"Omg Roxy you have finally done it, how long has it been now... eight months? It is about time though I must admit, come here darling I am so proud of you, where is the lucky man?" I said, happy for her, but then had a sense of sadness, because I was still stuck in a rut, in a rut in which it was that of Johnny's world.

Roxy then told me that Danni was with Johnny down in the bar, when I continued to tell her that I needed to get on with the show; and introduce Dixie, when after doing so, I would go over and see them both.

"Ok honey, and Ruby we really need to talk. I am worried about you honey, you have not been yourself for

ages now and I can't help think if it is something that I have done." She said, knowing I did have to talk to someone, but was not sure if Roxy was the right person. "*No, it is not you dearie; it's just me, this wreck of a sad old drag queen.*" I replied.

"*Well, you can stop that right now honey, for one you are not a sad old drag queen, a wreck maybe but never a sad old drag queen.*" Roxy said,

"*You say the loveliest things honey, love you* too." I replied, with a look of swallowing a bitter pill. Then telling her that I would visit her on Wednesday, as Johnny would be with the suppliers.

We had a great night of celebrations, and as everyone left, I said to Roxy that I would see her Wednesday as promised. She then reminded me that it would be sooner that that, as she was on early shifts, and that it would be Monday that she would see me next.

"*Oh God yeah you are.*" I replied, as I called myself a dizzy cow and threw a beermat at her, as I followed her to the door.

"*You do look simply gorgeous dear; I am beginning to worry about you.*" I said to her

"*Worry about me* why?" Roxy replied.

"*Because you are developing into a very attractive lady, I have to look twice to see if it is you, you are becoming more feminine and stunningly beautiful by the day.*" I told her

"*Thank you honey, so are you, you are also changing you are like a phoenix coming out of the drag world and coming into your own world.*" Roxy said.

227

"Thank you dear, you are a sweet dear girl and a true friend." I replied, as Johnny shouted over to us, as he told us two soppy women to give it a rest, before everyone reaches for their handkerchiefs. Then calling out that work still needed to be done. Roxy and I then just looked at Johnny, and gave him a dirty look, but not in a nasty way.

That morning I just decided that things are changing within our circle, yet I am still stuck in the same place I was all those years ago. I thought it is now about time things happened with Ruby and Johnny, as I had put things off for far too long; and put others before Johnny and myself. I still recall the conversation I had with Totty, about the up and coming Gran Canaria. I had no problem with the Spanish language, and it would be nice to have a new start away from London.
That night we closed the bar early, as we decided not to have any lock in; and we got a cab and went home.
As Johnny poured himself a scotch, he asked if I wanted vodka; to which I told him a glass of wine would be nicer. Johnny brought the drinks in to the lounge, where he then relaxed on the couch. I sat close to him as I said.

"You know Johnny, everyone seems to be enjoying their lives now and moving on; and maybe we should do the same."
"What do you mean Ruby?" Johnny asked.
"Well, Roxy has settled with Danni, Ellie knows how to run the bar, and sometimes I feel like we are spare parts. Why not sell up and move to the Canaries? Let's start a new life Johnny, I think it is time to say goodbye to

London." I replied, as I looked him in the eyes, with that warm sad puppy dog look.

"*You really would do that Ruby? Do you really want to move to the Canaries?*" He said, in a discerning manner.

"*It's a thought Johnny, a new scene and a new life. I could sell the apartments; and we buy a house and rental apartments; and you could sell your bar to Ellie and get a bar out there.*" I told him, putting everything in place, which I knew would be not only a new adventure, but also, it could give us a better way of life.

"*It's a lot to think about Ruby, a hell of a lot; that we really must be sure.*" He said, not being that convinced it would work.

"*Then let us think about it Johnny, please do not just excuse* it. Please at least say that you will consider the idea." I replied, as I had now got the thought deep in my mind; and where I told myself that this was best for the two of us.

"*Yes, I will consider the idea Ruby.*" He answered.

Having had that conversation with Johnny, I felt as if I had got somewhere with his thinking, so I placed my hand over his chest, as I snuggled up to him, then proceeded by placing a kiss on his lips. He placed his arms around my waist, as I slowly unbuttoned his shirt, my eyes looking at him straight on as I made sexual advances towards him. He did not complain as I undone his shirt, and when I then removed it, I got to my knees and then began touching him over his crotch, as things began to slowly stir. It was not long before he was rock hard, so I undone his belt, and proceeded to undo his zip, as I then told him to lift up so I could remove his trousers. Now staring me in the face was a bulge that was popping out of his pants, so I placed my mouth over his cock which was still in his pants as he took a deep intake of breath. Slowly I placed my hands under his ass as I removed his pants; and caught the full extent of his rather large wet bulge. With pre cum glistening from the end, I reached down and placed my mouth over his cock, as I gently caressed his balls.

"Oh Ruby, that is absolutely fantastic, you are blowing my mind sweetie." He said, now all hot and excited.

He did not overdo it, as he knew I would stop at the drop of a hat if he asked for too much. He just lay there as he let me work my magic. With him half off the couch, and legs wide open I continued sucking his thick cock, as I gently pulled on his balls, smelling his cologne and manly body. I then stood up as I dropped my skirt, revealing my panties and stockings.
Like Roxy, I loved Basques and girdles, but I was more the vintage girl who wore vintage 40s and 50s, as well as the fully fashioned stockings. Seeing me now naked as I removed my jacket, Johnny just stood up to attention even more.
I then straddled him as I pulled my panties to one side, letting Johnny have a taste of my horny ass. I placed it there for a minute, as I reached down and kissed him on the lips. My breasts dangling over his hairy chest, as I slowly placed him inside me.

"Oh... fuck Ruby; that is so nice sweetie. Oh yes it feels good." He said as he began to moan.

I took him deep inside me as I straddled his legs, riding him slowly at first, before clenching and riding a bit faster. He warned me a few times that he was ready to cum, but he would not let go until I gave him the nod. After twenty minutes of riding him and stopping just before he could not hold on anymore, as I looked at him with a devilish smile. Now feeling hot and to put him out of his misery, I told him to grab my waist as I rode him for the last time. He held my waist tightly pushing deeper inside me, as I felt his legs beginning to quiver. I knew he was now very close, so I told him to fill me up with his entire load; in which he could not stop, as he thrust himself deeper into me, holding onto my waist raising me up and lowering me onto him.

He then collapsed over me, as he shot his final load deep inside my ass; holding onto me as he got his breath back. I stayed there for a while until he went limp, then climbed off him as I went to the bathroom to clean up. Johnny shortly followed me into the bedroom, where again we made love for the second time.

"*You are amazing Ruby; I love you so much sweetie.*" He said, as he wished me goodnight.
"*Love you* too." I replied, as I turned over with Johnny's arm around me as we fell asleep.

As planned by Roxy, I decided to go and give her a visit, as I thought it was long overdue. I really did feel I had to speak to her, and I knew she was never judgemental, because she did not have a nasty bone in her body, unless of course it was during one of her shows, where she would bitch somebody in the audience, if they tried to get the better of her. I had never ever heard Roxy talk about anyone in a nasty way, unless of course it was in defensive mode because someone questioned who she is. No, I knew I could go to her and tell her how I really felt, without having the finger of judgement cast.

So off I trotted to Roxy's and once I had arrived, I let myself in through the security entrance, and used my keys which she had given me. When I arrived at her front door, I never just walked in, I would always ring the doorbell and then let myself in; that is unless someone beat me to it.

When I walked in through the front door, to my surprise, Philip was there doing her cleaning when he wished me a good afternoon, so I gave him a kiss and said the same back to him.

When he left, we started chatting with ease.

"This has been a long-time coming honey." Roxy said.
"I needed time on my own; and had to think how to approach the situation." I replied, now wondering where I start.
"Christ Ruby, you sound as if either someone has died, or I am being fired. Sometimes honey, it is just best to come out with things and not think too much; and say them as they are meant to be spoken. Never worry about what others may think, as it only causes you more pain." Roxy said.
"You are my dear friend Roxy; and I think I know how you will react, but I am not 100% sure. I do not want to hurt your feelings." I told her.

232

"Just tell me honey, come on we are big girls. Just let it out." Roxy replied, as I took a sip of my coffee, then placed the cup down and as I placed my hand into hers. *"I know you know me as Ruby Passion, and you think of me as a drag queen like yourself, but the truth could not be further away. I am Transgender or Transsexual Roxy; I have been all of my life. I knew I was born in the wrong body from the age of five or six."* I said as Roxy interrupted

"Yes and!" Roxy said, sitting upright as she held her cup like a queen, and looked at me in her caring way.

"I don't know Roxy, I have been living a gay life for the sake of my relationship with Johnny; and I have continued to be Ruby; much to Johnny not liking it 24/7, as it has been my way of being true to myself. I never ever liked all of the drag make-up, the over the top look as I still felt male. What was inside me never was able to come out because of the predominant drag queen I had become. Since as early as I can remember I knew I never wanted to be a boy, that I never felt right in my body, that something was wrong, but I could not explain why. I then embraced the gay scene and I thought that this was who I really was, but I was still lost, as I felt trapped in this hideous body. I thought it was my hormones, or my upbringing, and a denial, for fighting whether I was gay or not." I said, now beginning to have tears in my eyes. Roxy then looked at me and said.

"Honey all I will say to you is this. We are many cultures in the many gardens that we create, as we fight to be recognised. At the end of the day, we still have to be true to ourselves."

I could not believe how well Roxy was taking things, but deep down I knew she would see it my way; and help me in any way she could. I then looked at her and told her, that what she had just said, was absolutely beautiful, however, life is not that simple. I told her that we live in a fucking awful world where we are spat at and ridiculed, looked upon as freaks and yet I was no different to anyone else.

"One day honey, one day we will all be free to be who we are. Sadly, we are bound by the corruption of the government, and the ignorance of this world. But one day we will stand equal amongst men. We are all very different people honey; with choices we all have to make. We are truly unique to each other; and we have many gardens to explore, and if this is one of your gardens Ruby; then you need to be you and let yourself blossom."

I started to well up as I replied.

"Fuck me Roxy, you should be a politician, you could be the first tranny prime Minister."

We then just laughed with each other, as we spoke a little more about everything and nothing. Roxy may have been a young queen, but she certainly had her head firmly on her shoulders, and she never ever judged anyone. I knew I had done right in telling her, and her approach to the situation made me realise just what a friend I had in her.

I did not want to give too much of my sex life away, as it was personal to me, so I never told her all of the times that Johnny and I made out, where he had my girly cock, neither did I let her know about my affair with the doctor. I just let her know that Johnny was a gay man, who wanted me to be a guy, instead of being Ruby 24/7.

It was my business with regards other matters; and it had nothing to do with them, as that was a part of my life in which I always kept to myself. I had a very enjoyable conversation with Roxy, and for a dizzy drag queen she definitely had her head screwed on.

Time seemed to fly past, and Christmas was once again upon us. We had cabaret on almost every night of December, and my private party was becoming even bigger, that it was now suggested that Johnny gets on with the stage, so that it can collapse and be stored within itself, as well as now having the stairs from the dressing room come directly onto the stage.

It would give us more room to get a few more tables in, and we knew more tables meant more money.

We had arranged with Danni and Roxy; that we would be at theirs Christmas day, as they would come to us Boxing Day, then we would be at theirs New Year's Eve, and they would be with us New Year's Day.

We had decided to open the bar New Year's Eve from around 11am to 3pm, and then not again until 8pm to midnight. As it was a private only function, we decided that it would be tickets only; and only ticket holders were invited, as we did not want any waif and strays or even drunken layabouts bombarding us. Dixie was going to help get the bar sorted with the layout of the food with some of the bar staff. We took off all the expensive spirits and overstocked with the cheaper stuff, as the tickets were £25 a person and this included cabaret, food

235

and free drinks all night including lager and bitter.

We did have a notice made of what was free, as well as to make sure it was printed on the back of the tickets, because being in the trade, we knew that people would still try it on. Other items that were not on the list, they would have to pay for in full of its charge, as we would not sell it cheaper just because it is Christmas.

So, our Christmas was all sorted…

The fun part was going into the city to buy the presents. We decided to give Danni and Roxy their presents, when they came to over to us in London Bridge; and the rest we took over with us for the other guests.

We knew Roxy liked her fake fur, so we brought her a lovely winter coat with a fake fur trim, and some perfume. Danni got the usual, which was cologne, silk ties and double pack of designer shirts; and the rest were just little gifts.

Roxy and I worked hard that month, doing our shows only locally. And we made sure that we did not do a show Christmas Eve, except for bringing the acts on to the stage; and we made sure the bar closed at 12.30am, so we could have a little bit of Christmas to ourselves. Christmas morning, I had the bar open at 10am until 1pm and my now lovely Dixie opened up for us, then it was on to Danni's and Roxy's. Danni had pre booked Marcus to come and collect us, which I thought was really nice, as cabs were charging triple their usual fee. We arrived not long after Rik, when we made our way to the apartment. Danni and Roxy had a stunning 12 foot Nordic pine Christmas tree, decorated beautifully in white and gold decorations, with no expense spared. She was never one for those tacky ceiling arrangements, but did go all out on her tree, as well as a beautiful Nordic pine garland which lay over the marble fireplace. Looking over at the dining room she had another tree in the corner, which was a little smaller just with lights on it, and the table was done in the same theme as her big tree, bringing everything together as the perfectionist she was.

It really was absolutely stunning…

I just thought that she will have to make do with a 6ft one I purchased from Woolworths, as Christmas was difficult for me not having my real family around me, well I mean my birth family.

We had a glass of champagne waiting for us, as we began to mingle; and what was nice to see was Roxy was able to mingle instead of being hostess as Danni and his father took the reins.

Roxy never left anyone out as she came and spoke to us all, and she looked stunning in her red dress. But to be honest I could never fault Roxy, as from the very first time I saw her as a lady, she wore the finest of clothes and could pull anything off. Only thing that surprised me is that she did all of the cooking herself, where if I was having such a lot of guests, I would have definitely got the caterers in.

Having all taken a glass of something, we mingled with everyone until it was time to be seated. Danni made the announcement that we should now take our places, so it was into the dining room we go, where the table was set for a banquet, with all the glasses and cutlery.

I also thought what was nice, was that Roxy let Danni and Rik sit at the head the table. We were seated by Rik, as we got on with him and I was told by Roxy they made the seating plans that way, because we were the only ones Rik really knew.

I was also surprised that they had invited Pip, as he was only the cleaner and our barman, but I guess each to their own as I often said. We were then introduced to Danni's business partner Steve and his wife. I slightly remembered that he was in the property development business, which could come in handy with our project for modernisation, as I know Johnny had used him before.

So, everyone was seated, and then Danni stood up once he and his father had charged our glasses with champagne.

"I would just like to thank you all for coming to this, our first Christmas party. You are all very special too us, and we would like to thank you for making our first Christmas a memorable one. So, speaking for Roxy and myself, I would like you to raise your glasses and wish you all a Merry Christmas." He said, as he acknowledged each and every one of us, and spoke so eloquently, with that soft sexy European voice.

We all raised our glasses and toasted their first Christmas, then shortly afterwards his father stood up and made an announcement.

"To special friends, I would just like to say how happy I am to be in such lovely company today. It beats a quiet room in Knightsbridge. I would like to thank Danni and Roxy for inviting me to this wonderful dinner; and would like to congratulate them on a marvellous presentation." He said, as Danni pointed to Roxy saying all her doing.

"It is nice when special people come together and celebrate as friends; and as one family. So, without going on too much, I would just like to raise my glass and toast Danni and Roxy." He continued to say.

Again, we all raised our glasses as we had a drink and a little natter. Then Roxy got up to go into the kitchen where she brought out the starter. It was a fresh salmon parcel with king prawn in a light garlic and cheese mouse. Ellie had avocado and melon with a Greek dip, as she so loved her healthy Greek dips; and it came with a slice of ciabatta bread. It all went down a storm, as everyone tucked in and never left a drop on their plates. Once we had finished our starters, we had a few minutes whilst Danni and Rik cleared the table, as Roxy went into the kitchen with them.

Next thing Danni came out with a beautiful piece of pork already sliced, as Rik came out with a piece of beef already sliced. Danni then made sure we were all fully charged with drink, offering us now either champagne or our choice drink. Most went for their choice drink, as Ellie, Roxy Mary and I stayed with champagne.

Rik then came out with the biggest turkey I had ever seen, I just thought it could have fed the whole of London. It was a beautiful golden brown, which glistened in the light; and took up most of the room on the platter, as again I was surprised that they made plates that big.

What also shocked me is that they had three meats, I would have easily been happy with just the turkey, but if I remember rightly, Roxy did ask people what their preference was, and rightly so she was making sure she had enough of everything for everyone.

Rik was about to place the turkey by Danni, when Danni told him to place it by himself as he would like him to do the honours. You could see that they were very traditional, and I saw that glimpse of Danni, that became like a very excited boy.

Just then in came Roxy with Ellie's plate, as she said.

"Here you are honey, this is especially for you."

"What's this aunty Roxy?" She asked.

"It's your Christmas dinner Ellie." She answered

"But it is chicken aunty Roxy, and I do not eat meat anymore." Ellie replied

"It is not ordinary chicken Ellie; it is special, because it is vegetarian chicken." Roxy then said

"Vegetarian chicken; Aunty Roxy?" Ellie answered, rather puzzled

"Yes honey, unlike other chickens this one is special as it is corn fed." Roxy then replied

Well… everyone was in hysterics, as we could not help but burst into laughter, with Pip nearly choking on his lager, and Mary and I nearly piddling ourselves. Even Rik, Steve and Sammy could not pull a straight face if they were paid to do so. There was only Johnny and Danni, who were seen to show that they were serious, as they held their laughter back.

Johnny put his hand to his head as if to say, 'oh no you poor thing.' And Danni could just see the look of disappointment as she had worked so hard, even though he had a little smile.

Next thing we knew was Roxy had turned around, and gracefully walked out of the dining room defeated, when

Danni then got up and ran after her.

After about ten minutes she came back in with a nut roast, that I had left for her a few days ago mentioning it was for Ellie. She went over to Ellie and we heard her whisper in her ear that she was so sorry.

Dinner soon got back on track, with Rik carving the turkey as our plates were passed over, as well as serving ourselves to the other meats and vegetables. Again, we all chatted as well as bringing up the vegetarian chicken which eventually Roxy did see the funny side, in which we said it was nice to see that she still had a dizzy side to herself.

Once she started to laugh, she often composed herself as she ate her dinner having little outbursts of giggles.

I think the nicest of all the dinner, was Roxy put her differences aside; and you saw her passion for Danni and his father's culture. She surprised all of us with her cooking skills, but none were more surprised than Danni and Rik when she made a traditional Norwegian dish, much to the amazement of Rik, with Danni being like a little boy, poking his finger in the dessert now and then.

That was the day I think Rik embraced her, as she thought not only of her English heritage with producing a traditional Christmas pudding; but also, that of her partner's heritage, by making his traditional pudding; which was such a lovely treat.

When everything was put away, we all sat down on the two large couches, as the men stood up chatting.

It was then present exchange, and Danni and Roxy had not spared anything.

They had given Ellie a holiday for two on a European river cruise, as that is what she loved to do in her spare

241

time, going up and down the Thames, or spend time with her friends on the Broads; and it was in an executive suite with spending money.

Pip and Sammy were given a two-week holiday in Sitges, all-inclusive with spending money. Steve and Mary were given a box at the theatre for two shows plus a meal at the famous Dorchester. Johnny was given some cologne; clothes and a beautiful omega watch which looked very expensive. And then they surprised Rik, as they both handed him his gifts, as they had gifted Rik some sculpture and painting from his native land.

My presents were the ones that gave me the biggest shock, so much so that I could not stop crying.

Upon opening my presents, I found two boxes within one larger box. When I opened the box, I found it to be a diamond and ruby bracelet; and in the other box, was the matching necklace and earrings. I just stopped dead in my tracks as the tears ran down my face. I made my way over to Danni and hugged him so tightly that I nearly took his breath away; and I then hugged Roxy, as I was telling her that the jewellery was so beautiful.

The final gift came from Rik.

He offered Danni an envelope and being very puzzled, he called Roxy to his side. He told Roxy to open the envelope; and as she did there was another envelope in which she offered it to him.

Well… the look on his face was a picture.

"OMG dad, Roxy look." He said, now like a very excited young boy.

"Oh, my pap's, you shouldn't have." Roxy replied, as her eyes lit up with the surprise of the gift.

"I know how close you two are to Johnny and Ruby, so I thought this was ideal." Rik replied
"Ruby, Johnny; come and have a look at what we all have been given." Roxy said.

She was very excited as Danni hugged her, and then went over to his father to give him a man hug.
It was a holiday to Lake Como in a private villa overlooking the lake.
Roxy then ran up to Rik and just held him telling him how thankful she was as she just hugged him.
We then looked at him and thanked him and could not believe that he thought of me and Johnny.
After all of the hugging, we stayed a little bit longer as we all waited our turn for Marcus to take us home. I was slightly concerned, as I thought it was unfair that he had to drive, as it was not much of a Christmas for him, but I was assured that they never did eat as early as us, as they are late eaters.
Once we got home, I just fell to the sofa, as I was well and truly stuffed, and then just admired my presents.
No one has ever brought me diamonds, let alone diamond and rubies. They were absolutely stunning, and I put them away as these would be for best. I could see that Johnny too was overwhelmed with his presents, especially his watch. It was such a lovely classy silver watch, and it made him look even more expensive when he wore his suit. I again felt guilty, as they had far stretched what we could have afforded, but I know it was not done maliciously, by giving their status of money.
Roxy had a very king heart; and she did not give her

money away lightly or foolishly, so I appreciated what she had gifted to us.

We got Boxing Day out of the way, and both Danni and Roxy were overjoyed with their gifts.

I had never seen Roxy's face light up so much with her coat, and she tried it on straight away giving us a catwalk presentation.

I have to admit it looked very nice on her, and even Danni commented how beautiful it was.

I was so glad to get Christmas and New Year out of the way, as that was my worse time of the year, even though this one was different and I felt a part of a family, it still did not take away my pain for my own family.

I only ever had a card and gift vouchers from my brother, and I felt he was all I had, but was grateful that I did have him.

So yes, as we got Christmas and New Year out of the way; and began putting the bar back to its normal self, as we finally packed away all the decorations ready for next year, which then made the house and the bar look a little empty and bare.

Roxy had become very successful; and I often wondered why I did not take up the offers that were given me all those years ago. Then another part of me was not bothered, as I had money, and although it was Johnny's bar, I still had my Wednesday after hour sessions; and really did not want the limelight that she had.

I was content with what I had, and just needed to save up a little harder to make my life a lot better.

Just then as I was upstairs sorting out the following month's cabaret, as I worked a month in advance to make sure all nights are covered.

Tuesdays were now becoming a very busy night, instead of a quiet one with the introduction of student night. We had quite a lot of beer and lager to use before the new batch, so we introduced a 2 for 1 deal. It cleared the stock room ready for our new stock, and everyone seemed to enjoy themselves, especially Johnny as it meant more money in the till. Johnny then came upstairs, and with a look of surprise he asked me to come downstairs. I asked him what all the fuss was about, as I knew I was not expecting anyone to call. Johnny then looked at me, and he then said.

"*Hi sweetie, there is a young man downstairs asking for you.*"
"*Oh, I am intrigued, who is it?*" I asked
"*His said his name is Marty; and that he is your brother. He asked for Tony, and then he corrected himself.*" He explained.
"*Marty, Johnny it's my brother.*" I replied, very excited as I ran down the stairs.

As I go to the bar, there standing at the end of the bar was this tall slender man. He had short cropped hair; and was clean shaven. I just looked at him and shouted Marty, as I then ran up to him.

"*What are you doing here Marty, why did you not phone me?*" I said, as I gave him such a big hug.
"*I wanted to surprise you; it has been a very long time Tony. Sorry I mean Ruby.*" He replied.

I did not mind that he called me Tony, as there was only Johnny in the bar, as we had not long opened.

"Johnny, could you please bring some drinks over, and I will have a stiff one. I need it." I asked.

Johnny asked Marty what he would like to drink, and he told him that he would have a lager. Then as Johnny brought the drinks over, I introduced Johnny to my brother Marty.

"Nice to meet you Marty, I have been told a lot about you; especially the tricks you used to play as children towards your sisters." Johnny said.
"Oh. We had a great time as kids, always were the practical jokers, although Ruby was the quiet one and needed pushing." He replied.
"Well… I had best let you get on, and Ruby if it gets too crowded you may as well go upstairs." Johnny said.
"Oh Marty, where have you been?" I asked, holding on to him for dear life.
"Just keeping my head down, concentrating on my exams etc." He replied.

I then went on to ask all about home, about mom and dad, and what he was doing. I went on to ask if the family hated me because I wanted to become Ruby; and I did feel they have not wanted anything to do with me because of this.

"I do not care what you do with your life Ruby, so long as you do not hurt me or push me away. You have

always been there for me; and you never ever forgot me when it was my birthday or Christmas. I will always be your brother, but it will take a bit of time for me to get used to calling you my sister." He said with a little laugh, that had been an age since I last heard. His laugh alone always got us to smile, as it was so hilarious.

"*I don't care dear, so long as I have you in my life.*" I said, as I put my hand under his arm whilst in the royal box.

"*There is no reason why I should not be in your life, you are my family Ruby.*" He replied.

We then just sat for a few minutes, as I brushed the stubbiness of his hair through my fingers. With his hair being cut so short, I could not believe how much like dad he looked. He looked at me, and as he gave me a gentle peck on the cheek he said.

"*I cried so much when you left home, as I was left all on my own Ruby. Mom and dad just told me to forget about you, when they then told me that you were queer; and that I should well forget you and your kind; and I did not know what they meant with their strange words that also sounded like nasty words. I thought I had done something wrong Ruby, and that it was because of me that you left home. I cried for months wishing you would come back home, as mother would constantly remind me that you are living a perverse life, and one in which I should forget as it was ungodly.*" He said, as he had tears running down his face, whilst I could not contain myself.

"*I never left you Marty; I had to leave because of my lifestyle. I could not stay at home, as mother was so*

247

against the way I am. And I am not queer, I just feel trapped in the body I was born with Marty. And let me also say, that queer, faggot, shirt lifter are all nasty names that uneducated bigoted people use, which are hurtful to our community" I said, without going into too much detail, because it brought back hurtful memories. *"Well… I could not give a damn Ruby; and I hated mom and dad for years because you went away. I do not care what people say about you, I am grown up now and I can make up my own mind. I still love you so much Ruby; and my love for you will never change. I can honestly say that I have never used such words towards others, as I agree with you how hurtful those words are."* He cried, now with his head on my shoulder.

"Marty don't blame mom and dad dear; they are old school where this is not so openly discussed as it is so unheard of. They are not to blame; it is just one of those things Marty." I said, holding his head on my chest.

"I really could not understand why they said those things Ruby, and I never knew what she was on about at times when I was growing up. And Ruby I have a secret too, because when I was at school and I was about thirteen, I kissed a guy. I also sucked his dick, and even let him fuck me. I only did it a few times, and I decided that it was not for me; and I did not want to go down that road. I have a girlfriend now, and I am going into the army soon. I just want to make sure that you are ok, and I want to write to you if you will let me." He said, as he continued to tell me about what had been said all those years ago.

"Of course, I will let you Marty, and fancy you dipping your finger in the forbidden fruit. You know what they say; you need to try it to see if you like it. I am glad you

248

have a girlfriend, and so proud of you going into the forces." I replied.

"My girlfriend wants to meet you, but at moment she is studying hard at university; as she wants to be a lawyer, so it will be a few months' time." He said, now standing proud.

"That's really nice Marty, I also wish mom and dad would come and see me." I told him, holding onto his hand tightly.

"Give them time Ruby. Mom has only just got used to the fact she thinks your gay, and I know she will come around in time." He said, as he believed they would come round, although I thought it very unlikely.

I kept my mouth shut from there, as I was not going down the road of gay or transgender; and I felt it was not his fault for my parent's ignorance.

I was just so happy that my little brother was in the bar with me; and we were finally talking to each other, after so many lonely years without having him by my side.

We sat there a further two hours before he left, enjoying our chat and also seeing Marty getting chatty with Johnny as they spoke about men things.

When he left, he looked at me and told me he loved me very much, he then looked at Johnny as he said.

"You have a good un there Johnny; please look after her for me as she is special."

"Will do Marty, you take care too." He replied.

Well, what was beginning to turn out to be a boring day, had started with the biggest surprise that anyone could have given me. I loved getting his letters, and I wrote to him often; but to have him actually come into the bar to find me was more than my dreams could have imagined. Johnny and I spoke for a while, as I then told him I am going back upstairs to finish off. Johnny asked if I wanted a drink, and I told him that I would make a pot of tea in my dressing room. I made my way back upstairs and got side-tracked thinking back to my wonderful surprise.

A few days had passed, and life began to get back too normal for me. I was still buzzing from Marty's visit, and often had a few little smiles appear.

As I had the day to myself, I decided to go and see Kitty, as it had been a few months since I last saw her. I got a cab to her venue, and then as I rang the buzzer, I was let into the reception area of her club. There was a young lady on the front desk who greeted me, and I just asked if Kitty was in as it was Ruby.

She picked up her phone and pressed a button which rang, and soon Kitty picked up and told her to send me down the hall. She had really modernised the place lovely, as before it looked like a seedy old dungeon, but now there were rooms down the hallway all with their own personal name on them.

Towards the bottom of the hallway and then to the left was her office; followed by some more rooms.

Kitty came out of her office and shouted for me to come in as she emphasised on the darling, which was her signature word she called everyone. I entered her office which was done out very nicely; and looked more like a boudoir than an office. We had a bit of a catch up when she just came out with it. She asked me if I would like to earn five hundred pounds for four hour's work. I was taken back, as I asked her what I had to do to earn that sort of money. She looked at me through her rimmed glasses, and then told me that I do not have to worry, as not selling myself. That of her girls needs some help with two clients that are about to arrive; and that they had been let down by one of her girls. Still being on my guard, I asked her what it is that I have to do. She looked at me and smiled, as she told me that I would be with Mistress Sasha, that she is a pre-op, and she is taking the role of The Headmistress today. She had two clients and needs a prefect, so would I be interested. I just said sure, why not, as I do not have anything to lose; and that I do not have to be at the bar till five that evening. She got on to her phone, and pressed a buzzer, in which this girl answered. She was asked to come to the office, where shortly there was a knock on the door.

"*Ah, Mistress Sasha, this is Miss Ruby, she has offered to help you out for a little while, if it is alright with you my darling.*" She asked.
"*Yes, Madam Kitty that would be lovely.*" She replied.

Mistress Sasha, then explained to me, what I would have to do. She told me that there is a prefect's uniform in the costume department, and that I should go down and get my size. I then had to come to the Headmistress's office, which was three doors down from Madam Kitty's office. So, having gone and got a uniform from the costume department, I then made my way down to the headmistress's room. I just stood there and took a deep breath; when I thought 'what the fuck are you doing Ruby?' I then composed myself, and then I knocked on the door; where Sasha then briefed me again on what I would be doing, fully explaining that I would not partake in sexual intercourse.

She then went on to say that her client is of high office, and his name is Judge Bellows.

I looked at her in horror, as I then asked.

"OMG, do you mean Judge David Bellows?"
"Yes love, why do you know him?" She asked
"Yes, Mistress Sasha, he comes to my elite parties that I hold at the Rainbow." I replied, now concerned at the fact he could blow my cover.

"Oh, well we had best improvise; if you do not want to be recognised, can you alter your voice?" She asked
"Yes, I can do that." I replied.

With that, I went into a small room joining her room, and got out of my clothes. Sasha saw my tits, as I bent down to tidy my clothes and hang them up.

"Pre-op or Post-op love?" She asked
"Pre-op Mistress Sasha." I replied
"Call me Sasha; the clients are not here yet." She said, in such a lovely relaxing voice.

I explained to her that if I kept in character then I would not make a slip up when the clients arrived; in which she was so appreciating for what I said. Then the phone buzzed, and I heard reception tell her that her clients had arrived. I was now getting nervous, but Sasha reminded me that she would not be using my name.

I had to wait in the little room where I had changed, as

her clients could not know I was there just yet.

So patiently I waited as I heard the door open, and Sasha say.

"*Right you two, you have been very naughty boys I am told.*"

"*Yes headmistress, we are sorry.*" Came the reply.

"*And who do I have here? You what is your name?*" She asked.

I then heard David say his name as David Bellows and the other guy say that he was James Wyatt.

"*Right James, I have a naughty boy hat for you and a blindfold. Put them on and go and stand in the corner, NOW.*" She said, getting into character.

"*Yes Headmistress.*" He said, as he waited for her instructions.

"*And you David, I have been told you will not write out your lines. Do you think you have special treatment not to do as you're told?*" She said, very sternly.

"*No Headmistress, I am sorry Headmistress.*" He replied

"*I have a blindfold for you too David; and I want you to remove your trousers and pants.*" She ordered, as strangely, even I was a little scared of her.

"*Yes headmistress.*" He replied.

The next thing I heard made me jump right out of my skin, as I thought I was going to die there and then.

At the top of her voice, she yelled.

"*Prefect, Senior Prefect; come here at once.*"

253

As silly as it sounded, I was fuckin scared to death; because she was so good at her job and in character, that it sounded so bloody real. She looked at me as I walked in, and noticed I was shaking slightly; and then she looked at me and smiled, then as a gesture moved her hand up and down as to take a deep breath as she had a little smile.

"Senior prefect, we have two naughty boys here, what do you think I should do with them?" She asked.
Having no idea what she was on about or what I should say, she pointed to a cane. And in a softer voice than normal I replied.

"I think that is punishable by having a stroke of the cane headmistress."
"I think you are right senior prefect." She replied
"David, I want you to bend over my desk, and raise your shirt. You need to be punished." She again said sternly.

Now I was scared, and I now knew why. She had such a power over you, just by the tone of her voice. She then proceeded to give David the cane, but not that hard so it drew blood or seriously marked him. She knew he was married, so for precaution there was always a fine linen cloth over his ass. She gave him six strokes of the cane, which was hard enough to feel without leaving marks.
I just could not believe my eyes, and then thought how sexy this was. Just then James murmured something, and Sasha flared up.

"I beg your pardon young man, what did you say? Do you think you are better than I am?" Sasha asked
"No headmistress, I am sorry headmistress." He said slightly nervous.
"What did you say young man?" She again asked.
"I am sorry headmistress; I just said I hope I do not get caned." He replied.
"HOW DARE YOU." She said very strictly.

She then ordered him to place his hands on the wall, as he still stood facing it; she then looked at me and, smiled as she said.

"Senior Prefect. I want you to remove that naughty boy's trousers and pants."
"Yes headmistress." I said in a girly voice.

I am sure David cottoned on, as he was just about to turn his head when Sasha noticed.

"Excuse me; is there something over there which is of concern to you David?"
"No headmistress." He replied, turning to face her.
"Then do not look over there, as it does not concern you. Senior prefect, continue." She replied, smiling and giving me a wink of her eye.

I started to undo James's trousers and as I undone his belt, and then his zip his trousers dropped to the floor. I thought that was easy, as he was not wearing any underwear. I then looked at Sasha with a smile on my face, when she then looked at me as she said.

"Have you done that senior prefect?"
"I am afraid he is not wearing any underwear
headmistress." I replied
"You dirty boy, how dare you come to school with no
underwear." She said, now with a bigger grin on her face.

She then looked at me and then began to say.
"Senior prefect, remove his trousers and his shoes, then
you, you naughty boy, I want you to bend down whilst
still facing the wall."

As he did that, she then ordered me to slap his ass with
one of the slippers she had on her desk. I began slapping
him when she told me to slap him harder as he was such
a naughty boy, as she then sat on a chair and got David
to lie over her knees as she slapped his ass.
This went on for a good while, as they were both
thoroughly chastised. I could see that they were both
rock hard and oozing precum, and I was so tempted to
get on my knees and suck James's cock as it was a
lovely size, and very thick. I stayed in my position,
slapping his ass with the slipper and rubbing his ass
cheeks afterwards to take away the stinging.
Sasha had really got into character, and whilst she was
slapping David's ass; I noticing his hard cock hitting her
now and then. She then looked at me and pointed to
David's cock as well as James', as Sasha mimed to me if
I wanted to have a bit of fun.
I could not believe my ears; and jumped at the idea.
I then waited for Sasha to tell James to turn around still
standing up. She then got David up and told him to lie on

her desk. Now as he was fully naked, she got on the desk and straddled him as she took his cock into her ass.

She then looked at me and told me that she thought I should take the naughty boy's cock and do something with it. I did not refuse her, as I then spoke the words 'yes headmistress.' I then got to my knees, as I held his cock in my hand. He had thick black pubes, and a hairy chest which followed his body to his navel and then the famous line to his gorgeous cut cock.

He was about eight inches big, and very thick that I struggled at times. He tasted very sweet as I started taking him into my mouth, much to his delight.

I felt every inch of his cock swell as I had him inside my hot mouth, and he moaned with delight.

For someone who was told there would be no sexual contact, I was so pleased that there was because I had fallen in love when I saw this young man.

After a further ten minutes of sucking this guy, Sasha looked at me as she whispered to me if I wanted to have him fuck me. I just looked to her, and with lustful excitement I just nodded that I would; as it seemed ages since I had been intimate; and this was work after all.

For fuck sake I was so worked up, that I could not say no., so she ordered me to take James, and move to the chair that was now at the side near the changing room.

She then told James that as a reward for his punishment he could now fuck the senior prefect.

As I got myself on the chair, I removed my uniform, and had James just pull my panties over my ass. He then gently placed his cock by my ass crack as he held onto my hips, and gradually pushed inch by inch as he got his wet cock deeper inside me, as he noticed I had breasts, which sent him crazy with lust, as he pushed that daddy cock home. I could not believe that I had this gorgeous handsome guy wanting me, a handsome guy with a large cock, and it was much thicker than Johnny's; and I made sure I was not going to waste any of it.

I got him deep inside me and this young stud made love to me until he shot his load inside me, withdrawing as he still shot over my ass; at the same time, Sasha was milking David to completion, as he could not stop moaning with passion and shaking as his legs now trembled. I thought it was then going to be my turn to return the favour, but Sasha looked at me and mimed no, as I still had two more sessions with her other clients.

I can tell you as I left Kitty's I could barely walk, as I had never been fucked by so many large cocks in my life, then I thought, I am really happy with Johnny's cock; because at least I don't feel I have been fucked by Big Ben.

I had a wonderful afternoon, and apart from picking up five hundred pounds, I had sex with five lovely men, and not one of them was allowed to have my girly cock.

Three months had passed, and in those few months I had done a few solo shows, as well as Roxy and I having once again working the London scene together.

I began telling her that I was again thinking of coming out of show business as I wanted to concentrate on other things, and I knew she was busy with runway, television as well as cabaret. She never ever complained or caused reason to argue; although she did a few times say it was a shame, as she loved working with me, but our lives were really on two very different paths.

She then came around this one day and had lunch with

me, as we discussed the holiday. I looked in my diary, and also had Johnny's diary on the lamp table in the corner; and noticed that we had three weeks free, in around three months' time. I would just need to shuffle around a few bookings; and needed to confirm Dixie and Felicia could cover for me.

I could see that Johnny had nothing in his diary except for the wholesalers, so I just phoned Johnny to check, and I was given the all clear. Roxy was so excited, and once she left, she phoned the owners of the villa and confirmed the date. This was not a villa that you would have found in a high street travel agent we were lucky, as it was a friend of Rik's, who only hired it out to their business friends, so we were lucky to get the date confirmed. We made sure we had our passports up to date, and of course only thing we needed to get was travel insurance which we did with our banks.

Upon arriving at Gatwick, I was expecting a noisy flight with kids screaming and goodness knows what, but much to my surprise, we never went into the departure lounge. Instead, we went into the VIP lounge, where Roxy then said we are going on holiday in luxury.

We had a private jet waiting for us, they just need to perform the security checks as well as to check us in, and we could then relax in the VIP suite until everything is sorted. There was even champagne waiting for us, as well as a lovely young lady who looked after us.

Once our plane was ready, we waited for the limo to take us across the tarmac to our plane, and as our bags had been loaded, we just casually walked on, as we were greeted by both the captain and a steward.

I just thought I could get used to this, as this was definitely the luxury lifestyle, I think suited me.

Danni and Roxy pulled out all the stops; and this took me back to when Danni used to come out for a meal with Johnny and me, and everything had to be spot on.

This was just a glimmer of that, as once again I got an insight to Danni and Roxy's world, as they made sure we were as comfortable as we could be.

I thought that this is the life, no noisy kids in the departure lounge or on the plane, our own private steward who made sure we had the best in food and not the rubbish the airlines seem to offer.

I felt that I really was living the high life.

We chatted throughout the flight, as we were made to feel very special, but I knew I could never afford this in a month of Sundays, so relished in the moment.

The boys let us sit near the windows, as we were sat there in the nice executive leather seats and no getting cramp in your legs.

There was the latest in entertainment with a movie system and a bar, as well as a luxury bathroom and gorgeous leather couches for relaxation. The journey was wonderful, and as soon as we got over the Alps, we were a little snow blind for looking out too long, but knew we were nearing our destination. I thought we would have landed at the main airport which would have been in Milan but instead we flew into a private airport near Bellagio; and had a limousine to the villa.

Once we arrived at our destination, we just stood there in amazement to take in this wonderful scenery and amazing villa. We were greeted by the owners, who recognised Danni, and he was given the keys where they asked us to enjoy our stay. I just thought three weeks of absolute heaven, even the thought of being here with Johnny raised hopes, as I thought this is the proper setting to get all romantic and loved up; as it had been pretty dismal lately.

I could not fault the villa, and once inside you really did feel you were rich and famous; and I was a fussy cow when it came to cleanliness. Something new to me, but not so to Danni and we knew he was swimming in it, however, he was never one to throw it in your face.

There was a beautiful large open plan diner and kitchen, a bathroom that was out of this world with mirrors and drapes, and a bath that could easily fit six with a double sliding door that over-looked the gardens and lake.

The bedrooms took my breath away which were utterly gorgeous and within the highest standard if Italian décor, with your own patio away from the others.

Our bedroom was massive, boasting a super-king side four poster bed with your own couches and entertainment system. It was more like a suite than a bedroom, and it had an en suite to die for, so you did not have to use the bathroom if you wanted privacy.

The patio was also to die for with beautiful gardens and a view of the lake from every angle. Just towards the end of the gardens were a few shady areas for seating as well as picnics on the lawn, with a beautiful Italian stone wall overlooking the best views of Lake Como.

It was so very romantic; and I did wonder if it would like a spark towards Johnny, to be the Johnny I once knew. After we had put our things down and took in all the views, we just collapsed on the couches as the boys began to take over. There was already champagne in the large double fridge, and Danni brought it over to us, as Johnny made himself a scotch and bourbon for Danni. The drinks cabinet was full of everything you could imagine, and we did not have to pay for it as it was all included, much to the delight of not having to go to the supermarket.

That day we just relaxed in the villa, sitting by the pool as I put on my bikini. Roxy had taken a quick shower and had got out of her clothes where she stayed as Bobby, just so she could relax a little. And it was that, which separated the two us, because I was dressed as a girl all the time, where Roxy had her days as Bobby.

We drank and sunbathed that day, ending up with a beautiful meal cooked by the boys that evening.

Then after some more conversation, with a dig at Roxy's Christmas dinner, we retired and went to bed.

That morning, I got up to the smell of freshly baked croissants, with the usual eggs and bacon, toast and marmalade. I noticed Johnny was already up as he was helping Danni in the kitchen, whilst Roxy was sitting on the couch reading one of her fashion magazines.

The boys suggested we go into the local town, which was just a short walk away, and we could just get our bearings, and maybe stop for a bit of lunch, so Roxy and I agreed as we then sat down to eat breakfast.

As soon as everything had been put away, we just chilled out for an hour by the pool, where Johnny and Danni were playing around together; and where the occasional splash of water would come over to us; much to the annoyance of Roxy bless her, who just wanted to sunbathe and put her face in her fashion magazines.

I was sure I noticed Danni and Johnny embrace each

other, as I looked over and they had their arms around one another; as it seemed that they were embracing one another. And I could have sworn they were kissing, but I think it was just the reflection, as next minute I had a wet ball thrown at me, as Danni got out of the pool with a cup full of water chasing Roxy around the pool.

Well, they were like little children, but it was so nice seeing them that it brought my childish instincts back as I threw the ball to Johnny and told him I would get him back. With that, he reached out of the pool and grabbed the bottom of the sun lounger, where he began to pull it into the pool.

Scream, well anyone would think I was being murdered. Just as I got my legs to the floor it was too late, Johnny had pulled me into the pool, and I went straight under. Next thing I knew Johnny was behind me as I hit him and dunked his head under the water.

We just stood there for a while as I wiped my eyes only to see Danni had now picked up Roxy; her legs kicking franticly and her screaming becoming unbearable in that high pitched girly tone, but which was so funny as we both heard her screaming to Danni, saying NO.

It was too late, as Danni got to the pool and just threw her in. Well, god did she scream, shouting that it was freezing, and she would get her own back.

As she got up, she swam towards me and Johnny and said.

"Let's get him Ruby, Johnny, get out of the pool and give us a hand. Ruby, I will go first and pretend to make up to him and be all lovey dovey, and then you too just pretend you are going to lie down; then grab him."

"Oh, and what are you three plotting together?" He replied
"Nothing Danni, I am just asking if my eyes are not too bloodshot, as the water was too cold; and I had my eyes open." She told him.

Roxy got out of the pool, and began shaking, as if to say she was freezing. Danni quickly grabbed a towel for her, as he wrapped it around her; and held her tight gently kissing her on the lips. Johnny then looked at me, and suggested we go and have a sit down and a drink, as he got the lounger out of the pool and pushed it out of harm's way. We then got out of the pool and made our way to the patio table, to have a drink of orange. Just then Roxy gave us the nod, and she removed herself from Danni as she started to pat herself down.
With Danni's back towards us, Johnny just grabbed him across the top half of his body so he couldn't move his arms, as I then grabbed one of his legs as Roxy rushed to get the other one.

"You crafty buggers," Danni said.

As we got to the edge of the pool, we all threw him in, only to find he had managed to grab Roxy's arm and pull her back into the pool. Again, she screamed as she disappeared under the water, and as we could not see her, we thought she may have bumped her head.
Next thing, we heard Danni say.

"What the hell!"

Roxy got up and threw his swimming trunks out of the pool, whilst we got a glimpse of Danni's ass as he dived under the water. When he came up for air, Roxy had moved; and once Danni got his bearings, he wiped his eyes and looked over to Roxy.

"*You little minx Roxy, you just wait.*" He said, as he swam over to her.
Next thing we heard was Roxy screaming for us to help her, but it was too late as Danni had also removed her swimming trunks too, where she turned around to him and told him to hold her as she was slightly embarrassed. Johnny just looked.

"*Oh well, who gives a shit.*" He said.

As he turned around to face me, looking at me asking me if I was going to go for it. Johnny removed his trunks and jumped into the pool, as Roxy was unaware of what he had done, until she looked at me and saw that I had them in my hand, where she began laughing; and when Johnny got out of the pool to dive in, she covered up her eyes, but not before getting a glimpse of Johnny's cute ass. Then I just removed my bikini top and jumped in as I made my way over to Johnny.
Roxy and I began having a little play with splashing water at them as they did the same back to us, as well as play with the beach ball. Then we just stayed there a while as Danni and Johnny had their backs by the wall of the pool; and Roxy and I were held tightly by them both. We began chatting and laughing before making our way out of the pool. Roxy and Danni got out first; and it was

the first time I had seen Danni's cute bubble butt ass, as it looked so nice and firm, but unlike Roxy, I was not afraid to look at his body, after all I had already seen his erect cock when I walked in on them in the dressing room; and from what I saw he was indeed a very fit and well-endowed young man.

Roxy put her beach towel around her, as she opened Danni's towel for him where he was then embraced by Roxy as she wrapped it around him. Johnny shortly followed after we had a little chat about how funny everything was; and that I would have taken my bikini bottoms off but did not want them to see me fully naked. Once Danni and Roxy were out the way, we climbed out of the pool and we just went into the lounge where Danni made coffee as I sat next to Roxy, before heading back to our bedrooms to get changed ready to go into the village to see what it was like.

I chose a nice green gypsy skirt with a silk top and Johnny put on long shorts with sandals. Going into the lounge we saw Danni also dressed in shorts and walking boots, as Roxy had the loveliest pair of linen trousers, and short blouse.

"Oh Roxy, I love your trousers, where on earth did you get them from." I asked.

"You will not laugh at me will you Ruby; because these are the cheapest, but most comfortable pair of ladies' trousers I have ever brought." She replied.

"Course I will not laugh at you; you silly cow. I think they are gorgeous." I replied

"I got them from Littlewoods in Oxford Street, just down the road from Harvey Nicks." She replied.

"Oh, I know where you mean, I have been meaning to go in there for some time but never quite managed it. I am definitely going there to see if they have any more and they are lovely." I replied, surprised that she was shopping at a cheap department store.

Then the boys did their usual thing by saying girls and shopping, bad combination. I picked up my bag, which was more like a beach bag than a handbag; and Roxy being Roxy had a lovely leather handbag which complimented her outfit. We then walked towards the town as I noticed Roxy had gone for a pair of three-inch club heel shoes, and I thought that was sensible of her, as it was not always practical to wear stiletto's all the time. I had on a nice pair of flat sandals, as I could not be doing with heels unless it was to dine out.

Arm in arm the four of us strolled into the town looking at all the nice shops along the way, before finally stopping for some lunch in one of the local restaurants. At first, we could not understand the menu as it was in Italian, but the boys helped us out by describing what the dishes were. We also thought that this was much nicer than the usual holiday we had, as neither of us liked the beer bellied drunken English men, with their flirtatious tarty women, who gave us normal Brits a bad name. Don't get me wrong, as not all Brits were loud mouthed drunken idiots, as we knew a few who much preferred not to be in the resorts where they were.

It was more the fact we had done package deals; and had seen the affect that some of the rowdy Brits had given us as a culture of drunken idiots, so it was nice to go to a local restaurant or bar; and show them that not all Brits were loud mouthed drunken souls.

Much to our surprise Johnny ordered lunch for us; and like Danni when we were in the French restaurant, Johnny spoke fluent Italian and ordered. Danni was about to order, when Johnny just put his hand on his and asked if he would mind, which I thought was a lovely gesture. Danni sat back and let Johnny be the leading man as he then held onto Roxy's hand and took in the view of the town.

We ate our lunch as people looked over, staring and smiling, and also waving towards us as they also nodded their head in acceptance. Johnny just said they most likely think we are film stars or something like that, as we have two beautiful ladies with us, plus the fact it helps speaking the language as they most likely thought were Italians.

We just smiled and said Si Signor.

We had a lovely afternoon as we saw locals and tourists, and were treated like we were royalty, before leaving and just doing one last shop, as Roxy and I needed a nice hat to shield us from the sun. Then we walked back to the villa, which was a struggle after we had eaten and consumed a few glasses of wine.

As we had finished chatting, in the evening we decided on a BBQ; and the boys did us proud. As time was then getting on, we all retired for the evening, as I know Johnny and Danni had mentioned a drive out to the foothills of the Alps, as he knew of a few finer restaurants in which he thought we would enjoy, especially with the stunning views over towards Liechtenstein and Austria.

We bid each other goodnight and made our way to our bedrooms, where I just lay on the bed as I felt the cool breeze come into the room. As we could not hear Danni and Roxy, we knew that they could not hear us, besides they were on the other wing of the villa. I then got up, just as Johnny got out of the shower and made my way to the balcony. Johnny walked out stark naked with just a bottle of bubbly in his hand, as he sat down next to me and poured me a glass.

"No Johnny, stand up and tantalise me with the bottle of champagne." I said, now in a very horny mood.

"Oh, you mean like sexy role play?" He replied

"Just sell it to me Johnny, be sexy and seductive." I told him.

He got up off the bed and just standing into bathroom doorway, leaning into it as his feet pressed against the other side of the door. With the bottle in his hand, he started moving it over his body, working in towards his cock that now seemed to be coming alive. Looking at me very masculine and very sexy, he dropped a bit of champagne onto his chest and with his other hand, he rubbed it over his body still seducing me with his eyes. He then reached onto the floor where he had left his glass, as he picked the glass up, he filled it with champagne. With his cock very hard, he placed the bottle on the floor between his legs, as he then tried to get his cock into the glass, but his cock was too big to fit into the glass. He sat on the floor with the bottle between his knees as he looked at me; and then poured the glass slowly over himself.

I just thought that he was so fuckin hot, and as he called

me over with his finger, I got on all fours and slowly crept over towards him. I began licking the champagne off his chest, as I moved down to his tummy and to his cock. He then lifted me up so he could embrace me, when he then just kissed me on the neck and whispered into my ear.

"Let's go to bed sweetie, there is more champagne to play around with. I love you so much, let me please make love to you."

He then stood up, and as he lowered his hand for me to grab, he picked me up and carried me to the bed.
We made love till the very early hours of the morning.
The boys looked after us over those three weeks, by ordering our food for us when we were out, taking it in turns to order and sometimes ordering together, as they both sounded very sexy speaking Italian.
We cooked breakfast; and we had lots of fun in the pool, still with Roxy being shy and modest about skinny dipping and not being able to look at Johnny's cock.
Danni, however, was not as shy as Roxy, as many times he stood at the end of the pool staring at us, flashing his cock at us just like a cheeky young man. It did not stop there, because when he just chilled and stood by the balustrade with his ass poking out at us, he looked like he was a model that was posing for a very sexy photo shoot; and I had to admit that there were times that even looking at him, he made my loins twitch, which in turn made me take Johnny's hand and place it into my panties.
Danni had also hired a boat for us, so that we could go on the lake, where we had a waiter who prepared our

food as we just lazed in the sun, whilst the boys were given a chance to steer the boat.

Yes, that was the best three weeks I had had in many a year, and Johnny and I seemed to be back on track again as we made love almost every night, as I let Johnny take control of me and remain being the man, with me only once fucking his ass.

The flight home was just as comfortable as the one over, but even after a wonderful three weeks, I did miss my own bed. As often with my mood swings, I again became a little guilty and went on a little bit of a depressive slump, just using the excuse that the holiday was so refreshing I was not looking forward to going back to London, but deep down inside I could not have been happier. Oh yes, the holiday was wonderful, but as silly as it does sound, I missed my own bed and some proper English food.

A few days after getting back; and being back to the run of the mill with the bar and bookings, I had a text from my brother asking if I wanted to do lunch.

I was excited and immediately I text back to accept the offer of lunch, which we then arranged for the following Monday. I was rather excited, but also scared as I did not want to make any problems with his girlfriend.

I got that week out of the way, and as usual I was now pleased that the weekend was finally over, as I was now getting a little tired of doing cabaret.

Monday soon arrived, and I told Johnny that I would not be in the bar that morning as I was going to see Marty, which he knew I just wanted to remind him.

And then, off to Leicester square I went in a cab.

We went into a lovely little Italian restaurant, where

upon arriving Marty saw me and stood up, as he hugged me like it was the first time.

"Ruby this is Alison; Alison this is my sister Ruby." He said, as she let go of his arm to shake my hand.
"Hello Ruby, I have been told so much about you; it is a pleasure to finally meet you." She replied
"Likewise… dear, Marty has told me so much about you, and I have been dreading this day, but also very happy about it also." I replied, now giving her a hug.
"Why dreading it Ruby, I have not dreaded it." She said, as she had a cautious look on her face.
"I think it is just nerves Alison, just nerves." I replied.

I sat down when the attendant came over who offered us menus, I just asked for a pot of tea to start with, as Marty and Alison ordered coffee. We then began to chat, where I found out that Alison was going to go into law; and specialise in the criminal side of things. Marty told me that he is just about to take his army exams to see if he will be accepted as an officer. And then Alison looked at me and politely said.

"I think you are very brave Ruby; brave for taking the road you are taking. It is something I could not do it, and I have no idea how you keep up with it; and keep yourself looking so beautiful."
"So, you know about the gender issue?" I asked, wondering if she knew where I was with it now, as things had changed since I was back at home with Marty and my parents.

"Yes Ruby, Marty filled me in a while back so not as to cause embarrassment. It is not for me to judge you, or anyone else come to think of it. You have to be who you feel you are; and it is only your concern that should matter. Forget about all the ignorant rude people, life was made for living Ruby, and you need to live your life how you feel is best for you." She replied, as I warmed to this young lady.

"Told you she was amazing did I not Ruby. This lady had changed my whole world; and I would not know what to do without her." Marty replied, now feeling very proud.

"She certainly is Marty; you have found yourself a real diamond there." I told him.

"Alison has also met dad, and although he has given her some good advice with him being a barrister kind of talk, she thinks he is too old fashioned." Marty spoke

"Isn't that the truth Marty? I answered, knowing just how my dad prides himself on his career as a barrister.

"Well at the end of the day Ruby, what you do with your life is up to you and no one else. It is your choice how you live your life and should not be of any concern to anyone else." She told me, now putting me totally at ease.

"You are lovely Alison, thank you for being so understanding." I replied.

I put my hand on her hand and thanked her, and then she suggested we pick something to eat, as she could chat with me for ages. We all chose our meal as we continued to chat, and at the end of our lunch I felt relieved and thrilled. I kissed her on the cheek, and hugged my brother, as they waited until I had got into the cab. Alison then suggested that we should go out one day and go shopping, do some girly things which I thought was so lovely of her, because it was not said in a condescending manner, but more the fact it came from her heart which showed me what a nice person she was. We all waved to each other, as I made my way to the Rainbow. I then received a message from Roxy on my mobile phone, saying not to forget that she was on the Molly Parks Live show tonight on BBC2; and to watch to see if she was ok.

I must admit I had totally forgot as I was thinking about meeting Marty and Alison, and now that I had met her, I could not believe how lovely she was. I knew my brother had good taste, but he really did win the heart of a diamond.

Having got to the Rainbow, I told Johnny all about my afternoon, and took the picture out of my bag that she had given me showing them both together. He then also reminded me of Roxy's television appearance, and he told me he has made sure the screen would be put up. We had a large screen television placed on the stage, which stayed there until we had a show, and then it was placed back into the ceiling out of the way.

Johnny really was very clever when it came to things like that. As for me, I was lucky if I could change a plug. We both left the pub, as we let Ellie take over, and then went home to change; and then get back to the bar before her live appearance.

We did not know how big an impact that show would have had on her, and we knew she was becoming well known for her outbursts and telling it as it was; but I do feel that it was that show that changed her life.

The show was going on air about 10pm, and the bar was

packed with her followers, as well as the locals and our regulars. There was no room left, much to Johnny's pleasure as it meant a full cash register.

As she came on set, we all jeered, as she looked so nervous and quite angelic. Molly then asked her a few questions about her sexuality, and the impact her modelling and runway career has had on her, which went really nice and smooth.

That was until the member of the church kept making little remarks towards her. We could all see Roxy look at him, and then give him daggers before turning back to Molly.

"He had best be careful, because she will not stand for and crap; our Roxy will explode." Johnny said.

That was short lived, as the father started to quote passages from the bible. That was it, he had lit her fuse. She went for him as she told him being gay was not perverse; and attacked the father for being corrupt. The father then again ranted about homosexuality being a sin in the eyes of god; and each time he said something which offended her, you could see her getting wound up. Half the bar was encouraging her to fucking hit the twat, whilst I held onto to Johnny and kept saying 'keep calm dear; don't let him get to you.' With one of her outbursts, we all stood up when she got in his face, when she then told him that religion was a question of faith and not a question of sexuality. We heard the audience jeer too, as Molly seemed to calm her down just enough for her to sit down and regain her posture.

After another conversation with Molly, she also asked

the father something in which again he used the bible as a weapon. Again, our Roxy went mad, as we could see she was fuming when she started swearing.

The ending of her next outburst saying that there was only one person with rights to judge her was nailed to a cross nearly two thousand years ago, and she could not see any marks on his fucking hands and feet, again sent the bar wild as they started screaming and yelling in support of her comment, which also made them laugh. Again, she was like a rocket who had hit its target, as she went for him. Then when the father had another go, she gave just as good as she got; but what stuck in our minds is Molly trying to calm her down, yet they still let the show run. It was what the father said to Roxy next which was the final straw; as Roxy would give this man of the cloth, one last blow in support of our community.

I could see this was getting a bit too much, even though our Roxy was putting up a marvellous fight. I got hold of Johnny and told him to phone Danni right away, as I thought she needed some support, and he could phone her as soon as she had finished her interview, because prior to her television appearance he had asked us to record the show.

Johnny picked up the phone and rang him, whilst still in the bar amongst the cheers from the crowded bar.

Then it kicked off again, Roxy calling the church hypocrites, and that politics and religion will destroy this world. It was shortly after this outburst that the father said the taboo word. He used the word 'your kind' which always got up Roxy's nose.

"The thing is… your kind want your fingers in too many pies." The father said.

Then I noticed that stare. It was just the same as if a heckler had tried to get to her. So, in reply she looked at him and replied.

"Oh really? And it is you and your kind, who have their fingers in too many choir boys."

We all began to jeer and applause her but what came next really surprised us. With Roxy still standing up, she reached for her handbag, and removed a magazine article from her bag, which had a frontpage photograph of this father being accused of child abuse, and the church covering it up. She put the article in full view of the camera, then reached for her glass of water throwing it over him, as she then made the sign of the cross and said.

"Bless you father, now fuck off."

After that explosive performance there were lots of commotion on set, as well as the audience going mad. The bar stood up and were in a fit of hysterics, as they shouted good for you girl; and go get him Roxy, applauding her and shouting so loud I was sure she would have heard them all the way from Newcastle. We never saw Roxy for five days, as she lay low for a while in Hove until everything had blown over. We had our fair share of the paparazzi waiting outside of the bar, just to see if they could get a glimpse of Roxy, and much to the excitement of our locals, interviewing

277

them about what they thought about Roxy's performance, where they spoke in favour of her argument towards the church and their perverse ways. Danni kept us informed, and told us she was in a right state, as she was sure she had blown it for our community with her outburst she had made.

We told Danni to tell her that she has a lot of support, and everyone cannot wait to see her again.

After five days she arrived in the bar after her other television interview which was not live. Danni had let us know the schedule all along, and we decided to put on a little celebratory spread for her. Once she arrived, she got a standing ovation as she made the sign of the cross, and the bar followed suit.

That was the talk of the bar for many a week to come, and after time Roxy got used to it and began to get back to herself.

The months soon started to pass by, as I got to see my brother every few weeks. Alison was doing very well in her chosen career and was ready to take her finals, and then instead of being in training she would have accomplished her status as barrister. Everything was moving quickly, and yet it seemed like I was still stuck in limbo. My private parties had taken off very well, and I was earning in the region of five grand a party, not counting what Johnny took behind the bar. I was also advised by the judge that Alison was making good progress, and she had a lot of passion in her job, and he could see her being very successful. This made me feel so much better, as although Alison and I spoke a lot, she also studied hard and never spoke much about her job.

I now began winding down the cabaret, only doing a few

shows here and there, as I let Dixie take up a lot of the reins by giving her more of my shows in the bar.

I began seeing the new doctor, but he was a little full of himself and thought he was god's gift which used to piss me off, and often he would make me feel worse than I was before I went into his office.

A few times he got the sharp end of my tongue, as I too could be as fiery as Roxy when I wanted to be; and I would not let any young doctor get the better of me; no matter how many fucking letters he had after his name. Johnny had given more control over to Ellie, as she became assistant manager, and as Dixie had shown promise and moved through the ranks, I let her compare more and more, giving me a lot of free time to just sit in the royal box and enjoy myself.

Dixie always knew, though that if I was not at the bar, Roxy was always top dog at the Rainbow; even though I knew Roxy was not one for doing it alone as she was happy at playing the team member.

After yet another year, it was now the beginning of 1983, and after all what had been going on, I made my mind up that I cannot live this life anymore. I decided that it would be this year that I would be going to have transgender reassignment. I had my last luncheon with my brother, as he had passed with straight A's and was accepted as an officer. He held me so much that day, as we were crying in each other's arms, much to the surprise of the restaurant. He told me that it was about time and that I had lived in Johnny world more than my own, and if Johnny loved me, then he would follow me. When I got to the bar, I stayed with Johnny for a while and then told him that when we get home, we needed to have a serious talk. He just looked at me and asked if everything was ok, when I just told him that we will talk when we get home.

That evening when we got home, he did his usual and went into the kitchen to get us a drink, only this time he brought me a vodka and coke, and it looked like he had a triple scotch on the rocks.

I composed myself as Johnny sat down and then I began.

"I am so sorry Johnny, but I have since made up my mind that I am going to go ahead with transgender reassignment. I can no longer live like this as I am living a lie."

"What about me Ruby, I really don't want you to do this. I want back the Ruby I fell in love with all those years ago." He replied, shocked at what I had just spoke about.

"I am not that person Johnny; she was just a girl trapped in a situation that was not hers to control. You knew when you met me, I wanted to go all the way." I told him

"Ruby I can handle you having tits and a cock, but what happens to me when you change, please reconsider Ruby, what am I going to do? I love you so much sweetie, please think it over." Johnny said begging me

"Then let me go Johnny. If you cannot be with me then go and find someone else." I answered

"You know I can't do that Ruby; you are my life." He replied, starting to get upset

"Then stay with me Johnny. I have made up my mind Johnny and I have all the necessary paperwork and contacts; and I am going ahead with transformation in six months' time. I have to do this Johnny, or I know I

will end up taking my own life. I cannot do this anymore please understand me." I said, adamant that I would not back down

"*I am not happy with it Ruby.*" He replied

"*And I am not happy with this situation Johnny, I have done all I can with the gay life; and it is not me. I got side-tracked and my attentions went off what I wanted from the very beginning. You are either with me or against me.*" I said, giving him the option of walking away

"*You know I love you Ruby, I always have; and I will follow you anywhere. We have got too much together Ruby that I cannot be without you.*" He said as he began to cry

"*Oh Johnny, my dearest Johnny, then please be with me Johnny. For once think of me and come into my world, you never know you may like it. I am still the same person Johnny; it is just the gender will change. I am not a gay man, but I am still the same Ruby.*" I said, now realising I must be destroying his world, with me wanted to be true to myself, but I could not back down. I had to be true to me; and true to who I really want to be; and I knew there would be hurt somewhere down the line.

"*There is nothing I can do is there, Ruby; I am not going to be able to persuade you otherwise?*" He replied

"*No Johnny I must do this before it is too late for me, and I want to be able to at least have a happy life.*" I again said

"*Are you not happy then Ruby? I give you everything I can and always will.*" He replied, feeling deflated

"*You know what I mean Johnny; don't make an issue out of it. You always said you would stay with me and if not as a partner as a friend. What ever happened to that? I am having my surgery done in 6 months' time in Brighton end of conversation."* I said, as I dismissed him I then left the lounge and made my way to bed.

Johnny never came to bed that night, and for once I did not feel guilty, because I was no longer backing down. This was the first time I knew I was right in what I wanted, that I no longer wanted the gay life, I wanted my own life. I have always lived as others should tell me, and I always put myself last. Now it was my turn to live, and I did not care who I hurt. I had to be me and no longer hurt myself.

That morning, I woke up and Johnny had already left. His part of the bed had not been slept in, and I can only guess he had slept on the couch.

I had to go into the bar as I needed to sort out the cabaret for the weekend following. As I got there, Johnny said hello; and then told me he had some other news which may take my mind off last night. I then had another shock as Danni had told Johnny and me that he and Roxy were getting married, and would they help sort out the wedding with him. They had already chosen to have a ceremony in Holland, and then come back to London and have a party here at the Rainbow, for those who could not attend the Holland venue. It did not change my mind at all, and I told Johnny it wouldn't, so I then waited for Roxy to turn up so I could get her input.

Well, Roxy was like a very excited girl, who came around and had a list of people for the wedding. She had already got her dress which was a beautiful 1940's liquid silk satin leaf motif vintage wedding gown in white; and I just thought how she had out done me again, as I thought Johnny would have asked me to marry him. But as usual, Roxy seemed to always pull one quicker than I could; and again out of my heart felt words, she still managed to upstage me.

Danni had booked two suites at the Hilton International for three days, as well as the bridal suite for one night. After they had finished in London they were going back to Holland, before flying over to Italy to their favourite villa in Lake Como.

I was overjoyed for them, but a part of me was hurting as I just thought these two have only been together a few years and already they are getting married, where I have been waiting for Johnny to propose for the last twelve years, and the realisation of that cut like a knife.

When Roxy turned up, I greeted her with a kiss; and then she handed me her list.

"Bloody hell Roxy, there is five hundred names on here, which is far too many." I told her, thinking she was doing her usual, which was wearing her heart on her sleeve; and inviting people who had no relevance to be there.

"I just wrote everyone I could think of; and thought you may help me get a decent number." She replied

"Well, I can see you have invited everyone you know including those who you have only ever said hello to. I think we need to sort the important from the not so important dear." I replied, thinking that this should not be my job, as she should have got things sorted first. There was no need for such a list, but she was foolhardy at times, always trying to please everyone.

"Thank you, Ruby, you know me, I have not got a clue when it comes to these things." She replied
"Well, Danni has asked Johnny and me to help, so you just think of your dress and the rings. Let us sort out the rest for you so you do not have to worry." I told her.

We then looked at the list, and from five hundred I managed to lower it to three hundred, and when Roxy had left, I took a further one hundred names off, as I thought she only needed those of importance. I had her colour scheme, which was her favourite white and cream, so I told her I would sort out the other dresses and for her now to worry about a thing. She was really grateful, and it was then that I thought I will arrange my operation for after her wedding, as it would be pointless doing it before, because I would be in no condition to go sorting things as I would need rest.   She was getting married at the beginning of August; and I would then arrange my surgery for the end of August beginning of September.

It was a struggle, but it kept me busy, what with the florist, as well as the caterers my end, as Danni sorted everything out in Holland. Ellie and I were bridesmaids, but I was told by Johnny and Danni, that under no circumstances should I let Roxy know that Jake and Sophie were going to be a special treat.

So many times, Roxy and I had the conversation regarding Jake and Sophie; she got upset over the fact they would not be able to make the wedding; and I did want to tell her otherwise, but I knew she would be overjoyed on her big day with having it as a surprise. Not only did we have the wedding to think about, but also Roxy's birthday was two weeks before her big day. We were told not to worry about her birthday and just concentrate on the wedding. This was proving to be a very busy month, on the Roxy and Ruby calendar.

By the end of June, we had got everything in place, so I was able to rest for a while and concentrate on myself. I could have killed Roxy for this; as it seemed like she was trying to upstage me, but I soon let it pass because I was hard skinned and knew it was only a matter of a few weeks after the wedding that I could concentrate on me. I had also had my meeting with Dr Russell Harrison Britain's top transgender surgeon in Brighton at his clinic, and as I was a private patient, he rushed me through. So, after I had sorted Roxy and Danni out, I then was able to confirm that my operation would still be going ahead.

For a month solid I phoned the hospital and surgeon in Brighton, just to make sure every was still scheduled to run. As a special gift for helping out with the wedding; Danni paid for us to stay at the Grand Hotel in Brighton, in one of their suites, as well as have Marcus drive us down and pick us back up when I was ready. I was not going to say no, as I did do a lot for their wedding preparations; and if truth be known, both Danni and Roxy owed me a lot for what I had done for them. Everything was put into place, and everything was beginning to fall just nicely, with no further hiccups.

It was such a very busy month, what with the wedding on the 5th August in Holland, 6th August in London, her birthday, and then my surgery booked for the 30th August, that there were times I nearly gave up, as this was from pure exhaustion. I just did not know how I got the energy to carry on, apart from thinking to myself, that when this was all over, then it was time for me; and no one was going to ruin it.

It was finally time for Danni and Roxy's big day. We arrived at the Hilton International two days before the wedding, where Danni and Johnny had made sure the arrangements were in order. The girls were booked into the Rembrandt suite room 120a, whilst the boys were booked into the Van Gogh suite, directly above us in room 220a.

Roxy was not much into hen nights, as we had done so many in our cabaret years. She just wanted a nice meal with us all, before the big day. That night when we began to retire, Danni stopped off at our floor as he sat with Roxy on the couch by the elevator.

I think this was pre wedding jitters…

After about twenty minutes I came out of the suite, and told Roxy there was a coffee waiting for her; and looked at Danni pointing to the lift and telling him it is best he left and this bride to be needs her beauty sleep.

Roxy blew a kiss to him, as he stood in the elevator holding the button so doors would not close. I then waved to Danni as Roxy and I went into our suite to relax before the morning; and then I shut the door keeping Danni away from her. Then Roxy and I then sat down together and had coffee, as poor Ellie was completely shattered and went to bed as Roxy and I chatted till 3am. She chatted about her meeting Danni, and how things have gone well for her, then she said that none of this would have happened if she did not meet me, which I was happy that she still thought it was because of me and Johnny that the two of them got together, so I was happy for a bit of recognition.

We then got on to the subject of gay and transgender, and she told me that she also thought a few times as whether or not she should go down the same road as I was, as a lot of girls have told her she looks gorgeous as a woman, as did I. I then just asked her if she has ever thought that she was in the wrong body; and did she ever think that her sexual organs were an abomination and she felt like cutting them off herself? Did she ever get suicidal because of not being able to be true to herself? She said no to all of my questions, so I told her that I could understand how she felt towards her sexuality, because she was a gay man and most likely had never had those thoughts like I did, because she had lots of times as Bobby, where I was always Ruby.

I then looked her in the eye and told her that she was a gay man who likes to dress as a woman. That she had made a career out of it; and has become famous in doing so. That she says that she dressed up as a girl, when she was a little boy; and that she had a second character that is female, but never once did she ever say that she wanted to be a woman from birth. Therefore, I told her to be happy as a gay man, with a female character. That she was NOT transgender, so not to let it worry her, because any questions about her gender, should never arise. For her to consider going down the same road as me; and for the sake of people who think she looks good as a woman, is the wrong path for her to take. That she should make use of her beauty as Roxy; and embrace her status as a gay man, because she would indeed have the best of both worlds. I then told her not to fuck it up, by making the biggest mistake of her life, because it is something that cannot be reversed. That she should stop listening to other people; and instead listen to herself; and to be true to herself as a gay man.

Roxy thanked me for my kind words; and put to rest that she was indeed a gay man who loved to dress as a girl. That she considered herself to be bi gender, because of her two characters; and she assured me that she never had any inkling to ever wanting to change sex.

She told me that there would always be conflicting issues on that subject, because Bobby would never allow Roxy to transgend and be fully female; and Roxy would never allow Bobby to be predominately male.

For her to be able to survive in her Roxy world, she needed both of her characters, which to me after another glass of vodka seemed to make sense.

I got up early that morning, only having a few hours' sleep; and at around 8am I got Ellie to take some breakfast into Roxy, as she should be getting up herself shortly. She still had a bit of a hangover as I was putting Drambuie in her coffee before we went to bed.

She wanted to go back to bed but we insisted she couldn't as we had a lot to do, but I did give her a few minutes to wake up. Her hairdresser would be here shortly, and as she used her own hair she had to be up, as it was not as though she could get away with a wig.

However, we got through the morning without a hitch. Ellie then called out to Roxy to start to get ready because it was now12.15, so with that she went to the bedroom to get ready.

After a short while of not hearing anything, I decided to go to her bedroom to see what was happening, where she

288

seemed a little upset as she told me that she wished her parents were with her and how she yearned for them to have said they loved her as Roxy. That just reminded me of my family, but at least I had my brother. I told her so long as she was happy with herself that was all that mattered. She threw her arms around me, I looked at her and told her that it was show time. Then I went back into the sitting room, as we waited for her to finish; and then started to get ourselves ready.

We went through formalities, something old something new, but when it got to the colour blue, she had forgot her garter and she began to panic. I told her not to worry and I then phoned Johnny. Johnny came rushing to the room, and he had a blue dickie bow, as he always carried a spare, so Ruby got a bit of thread and made sure it was fixed to my thigh. And then she told Johnny not to let Danni know how she looked. Just at that point the doorbell began to ring, where I told Roxy to go into the bedroom just in case, whilst I opened the door.

Shortly after opening the door, I called out to Roxy.

I then went into the bedroom and told Roxy that she really did need to go to the lounge.

This was one of our first surprises of the day.

All of a sudden, the children ran into her bedroom, as Roxy got the surprise of her life; because there running into her bedroom, was her little Jake and Sophie.

They ran up to her, as she had saw them and got to her knees, as the children began telling her what had happened and that they were on a plane all to themselves. Roxy came into the lounge with the children and sorted some orange juice for them.

She really loved those children, and you could see it

from the moment they were in her company; because you could also see, that the children also loved her just as much. Roxy looked at me and told me thank you, but her second surprise was already in the lounge, and as she looked up; standing by the couch was a man in a white uniform.

It was her father, and we were so pleased that we managed to get him to come to the wedding.

I was just about to introduce him, when she cried out dad and ran into his arms. Then as I was in charge and we were running at a tight schedule, I told everyone we need to go otherwise we will hold everyone up.

We finally arrived at the function suite, and Roxy had both her father and Johnny to walk her down the aisle, which I thought was still nice of her to include Johnny, as he was the first one, that she originally chose. Just before we got to where Danni was standing, Johnny came by me and with his arm held open I placed mine through it and we made our way to our positions.

The room was decorated beautifully with flowers along the aisle as well as two large pedestals either side of the desk. Staying with tradition, and much to Roxy's surprise, Danni had obtained two desk flags of their family's coat of arms, rather than a traditional flag of their country which I thought was very regal.

After the ceremony which only lasted twenty-five minutes, we made our way out of the wedding hall, as we were directed to the banqueting suite.

Danni and Roxy had gone upstairs, as I believe now they were going to the bridal suite to chill out until all the guests had been seated.

It was like walking into a grand palace, and this was

definitely the way to live, as this is how I would like my wedding to be, if I ever get married and not stay like an old maid that I am becoming.

Through the ceremony I welled up a few times, still thinking that this was my dream wedding; and just like Roxy, she had beaten me to it. I was still waiting for Johnny to pop the question, but now our relationship was flawed; and I could not ever dream that this would happen to me. After the ushers got us all seated, which took around forty minutes, which in the meantime we were given refreshments; and then sat in our designated seated area.

I felt very proud as Roxy placed us at the top table with them, so knew she still classed us as family.

Then the master of ceremonies entered the room; and made the announcement that Danni and Roxy Svenningsen were about to enter the room.

She walked in with Danni, and they were both beaming. Once they sat down, she kissed both her fathers on the cheek, as she then came up to Johnny, Ellie and me and did the same, by kissing us on the cheek. The little ones could not sit still and ran over to them, as Roxy sat Jake on her lap, and Danni had Sophie. You could see that both the little ones, were very happy at seeing Danni and Roxy; that they were never far from their sight.

With Danni running around the ballroom with them, as he played just like a little boy himself. Then Roxy, being the mature one, as she danced with them both; and made them feel as special as she always said they were.

Roxy definitely had the mothering instinct, as a few times she had to calm Danni down, what with his childish antics. However, it soon made her laugh, as

Danni too got Roxy to see the funny side.

Yes, Danni was a little boy when he was around his brother and sister, but Roxy never held it against him as she knew he had missed them so much.

You could see from the party that a lot of the guests were wondering if they were theirs, as the children did have a resemblance to Danni. But also, Roxy had a special way with them just like that of a mother, as if they got hurt, they seemed to run to her for a cuddle

Both fathers made a speech, as Johnny then made his speech as requested by Danni. Johnny decided to talk about the first time he had met both Danni and Roxy, about how close they have become to him and me, and about family and that they were indeed our family. He made some silly jokes, as well as telling the Christmas story, which got a few laughs; then asked us all to toast the happy couple. We all sat down and began our wedding feast. The little ones were typical little ones, going from Danni and Roxy, to Rik and Roxy's dad, and then coming over to Johnny and me. They were not naughty however, just very inquisitive and restless; and I think being shown some attention was what they needed, because it sounded like their mother did not give them any. They were just children, who loved to be around everyone that day; but most of all, to be in the presence of their dear Roxy and Danni.

After the meal, the waiters and waitresses took away the food, as they then opened the doors of the banqueting suite to show the band and the very large dance floor, well, ballroom actually. The first song was played, which was a waltz, and I did not know Roxy could dance. She picked up the train of her dress, as Danni took her by the hand; and they began to dance. It was elegant and was a piece that would grace any television dance show. The little ones again got restless, and ran up to them, and in a Danni and Roxy fashion they picked them up and continued to dance with the little ones in their arms. When they took hold of the little ones, everyone could see just how much they were loved, and it was no wonder people would have thought they were a complete family. Roxy really did have such lovely mothering instincts, and looking at Jake and Sophie, reminded me again of Marty and myself growing up; and how it should have really been. I knew then, just how special Roxy and Danni were, as they beamed happiness, and these children… well if you could put a price on Danni and Roxy's love for these children, they would be the wealthiest children in the world.

Watching Danni and Roxy dance together, was like watching Cinderella dance with her prince which brought a tear to my eye; and for once in my life and but for a split second, I was slightly jealous of her.

She had the fairy tale wedding, a wealthy handsome husband who loved her as her equal; and two young children who looked upon her as a mother, as well as two fathers who doted on her. She also had status within the celebrity world; and wealth of her own, but most importantly she lived her life just the way she wanted too; and she could not give a damn about what people; or the tabloids said about her.

I remember one conversation we had, where she told me if she ever believed everything the tabloids wrote about her, then she would be in a mental institute because it would have got the better of her, with all the lies that the press wrote about celebrities, just to sell their newspapers, and I had to agree with her on that.

Yes, I may have had a moment of jealousy, but I knew that my time was coming; and it would not be long before I became that butterfly, that I had waited so long to become.

When the music had stopped, there were older style dances from the band, as in turn with the men asking Roxy for their hand, as Danni also was given the same treatment by us females.

I too had my dance with Danni, as I wished him lots of happiness, whispering this into his ear as we danced. Danni also wishing me all the best for my future, and that they would always be there for Johnny and me. Next thing I had someone tugging at my dress, and as I turned around, Jake was standing there with his arms held up. I picked him up and started to dance with him, as I played with him and tickled him on his tummy.

He kept saying no Aunty Ruby, as he placed his arms around my neck and kissed me, telling me that he too loved me, just as Sophie ran up to Danni. I then wished if ever I could have had children, then I would have wanted them to turn out as lovely as Jake and Sophie, as not only were they well behaved, they were both as cute as a button. Towards the end of the evening the celebrities had left; and there was only Danni, Roxy, me and Johnny left just having one last drink. Rik had taken the children upstairs to bed, Roxy had persuaded her father to stay the night, and then we all decided to call it a night. We had enjoyed the band, as well as the disco; and the food was out of this world, so finally we decided that it was time that we all retired.

The next day we headed back to London where Johnny and I put on a spread, which was brought around to the guests, as we also had a night of cabaret.

Apart from our drag all-stars, I managed to get a few up and coming pop stars, who had been on top of the pops. We had a lock in, as this was a private party, so I had no worries from public. I managed to cram all the drag queens into one dressing room, as most of the food was in Roxy's dressing room; and her costumes were placed and locked in the little dressing room down the hallway. Danni and Roxy stayed with us till about 4am, with just a few selected guests; and the show went as planned with no hiccups, and I was so pleased when it was all over as it was then my time at last.

All of their presents were locked away, as we said goodbye to the happy couple, as they parted to go on their honeymoon. I decided to leave the bar in the state it was, and I had asked Adam to come in early the next day, as I needed him to help me tidy up.

Adam was a lovely barman, I never had any reason to ever shout at him or ask him to do anything as he was always on his game, unlike some of the other boys, catching a crafty few minutes, where they fooled around with each other. Then I just thought I can now concentrate on me, on Ruby. I wished that Roxy had arranged her wedding a little later than she did, as I really needed her support. I could not talk to Johnny as he went into quiet mode; and I felt Roxy was the only one who truly understood.

Felicia and Kitty were fine to talk too, but I just felt it was Roxy who had that understanding I was looking for without trying to patronise me.

A few weeks had since passed, and now the time had come for me to get ready and pack for my big day. I was just waiting for Roxy to come over as she had since come back from her honeymoon; and I knew she was eager to tell me all about it. Johnny and I was going to give her the agenda for the next few weeks, as we would explain what we would need from her as in running the Rainbow. We knew she was competent; it was just me really as I was one who liked things to run smoothly and have all the t's crossed and I's dotted as it was how I had done things from the start.

She was coming to the apartment in London Bridge as Ellie had already taken over the running of the bar a little bit more, which took the pressure off Johnny, so he could concentrate on me. I did get the feeling though, that Johnny would have been happier just staying in the bar rather than be with me through my transition.

Just then the buzzer rang; and I let Roxy in; and as I got to the door, she was already standing there so I invited her in. I hugged her tightly, and I was a little bit emotional as I told her to come in and make her way to the lounge. Johnny too hugged and kissed her, as he then asked her if she wanted a drink. She asked for a coffee, which was another reason why I thought she was hypo, as she drank so much coffee; and then Johnny asked if I wanted a pot of tea, which was silly reason, because I never gave up any opportunity to have a pot of tea. I was never one for a tea bag in a cup, it had to always be in a china pot. As we sat down, she asked me if I was having second thoughts, as in less than four days; I would finally have my wish come true. I looked at her, and then told her that it was just pre-op jitters. She asked me if I was ready for that long haul to Thailand, as it was quite a journey to take. Speaking as if she knew from experience, but then again, she had flown to America a few times, so I guess she knew a little. I then told her that I had changed my mind with regards my schedule, as I had decided to pay extra by going private; and would now be having my surgery in Brighton, with Britain's leading surgeon, as it saves on the hassle of such a long flight. She looked at me, and then asked me why on earth did I not say anything, when I explained to her that it was her day. It was her wedding day; and I did not want to mention it, besides I was still in two minds as whether Thailand or England; but decided to pay an extra twenty grand so I could stay in this country and not worry about taking long haul. Again, she told me that I should have mentioned it, then offering us her apartment in Hove, so I could recover in peace and quiet. I did not want to be owed such a thing with Roxy, because although she never held it against you, there were times she did have a sarcastic streak; and I did not want that to happen. I looked at her and told her that it was ok, and then just came out with it, and I did not care about the consequences, as I was getting a little tired of her droning on. She was all over the place with her wedding; and then telling me all about her honeymoon, that I was sure she had forgotten, that in a few days' time I was having surgery, but still, it seemed to be all about her.

"No dear, Danni has sorted it out. I thought he may have told you. He has booked us into the Grand in Brighton, for two weeks whilst I can prepare for surgery, and then

relax after surgery; before I get my paperwork to be able to fly. Johnny and I are going to France for a further two weeks so I can have a well-earned rest." I told her
"*No Ruby, Danni did not tell me; but like you say I was all over the place with the wedding; and thought you and Johnny did an amazing job. I still cannot believe you got my dad and the little ones. I really cannot thank you enough. But enough of that, you have to let me know everything that is going on and if you need me, I will come down to see you.*" Roxy replied
"*It will be ok; I just need to relax, or I will become a nervous* wreck. So dear, let's get on with the running of the bar." I told her, knowing that she was the last person I wanted at the hospital, or even when I was recovering.

We explained that she would not have to pay any wages, as Johnny would sort all that out as it only needed to be electronic transfer, and she would only need to bank the money from the takings. I also told her that she did not have to worry about the cabaret, as everyone had confirmed and all she needed to do was to take their fee out of the till; and she must get them to sign the contracts. We then sat and had a catch up, as Johnny looked after us, then shortly after she got up and wished me the best and she would see us later.
I told her that if we were not in the bar later, not to worry as I most likely would be packing and making sure I have all that I need. Then just as I was tidying up and sorting a few things out, I noticed she had her hand on Johnny arm as they were talking. I just left them too it, as I went into the bedroom to go over my check list again.

So, the day came where it was time to travel to Brighton, and right on cue the buzzer rang, and Marcus announced that he was downstairs waiting. Johnny brought the luggage down as I just had my vanity case to carry.

I did not want anyone to see me off as I knew I would have an emotional breakdown; and thought Roxy may try and talk me out of it if she saw me upset.

I just told myself, that I have not spent thirty grand out for nothing; and wild horses would not change my mind. I know I could have got it done for about ten grand on the NHS, but I would have had to wait another couple of years, and I had the money so decided I would go private.

We headed for the car as Marcus greeted us, as he held the door open and told us he would put the bags in the boot. We then drove off as I looked forward to getting to Brighton where I could chill out for a while.

Just over an hour and a half later we turned up at the Grand Hotel, and we were greeted by the concierge who got us a bell boy to help with our luggage. Marcus told us to be safe and wished me all the best, as he then put the bags in the hands of the bell boy, when he then drove off. We made our way to reception where Johnny announced who we were; and we were given our room keys to the suite, which over looked the beach.

Johnny and I had a comfortable few days, going out for a meal in the lanes, as well as eating in the hotels finest restaurant. Then the night before I was going to check into the clinic, I just lay there as I let my mind wonder over my past. Johnny was very quiet not saying anything, just sitting there holding my hand.

Sunday then came around, and my nerves went into overdrive. I checked into the clinic where I had Russell visit me and with a nurse escorted me to my room.

The clinic did not look like a clinic from the outside; it just looked like a large private house. It was surrounded by countryside, with a view overlooking Brighton through to Peacehaven; and had beautiful gardens that were immaculate.

My room was a large double and I was fortunate to have sea views with views along the downs. I was made comfortable as Dr Russell came in a few times to see me. Johnny stayed with me for a few hours as I then told him to go back to the hotel. I was then told that my surgery would be at 10am the following morning, and he could come back then to see me before I went to the theatre.

That morning I was woken up at 6am for an enema, as I had to be thoroughly clean before surgery. Then at 7.30 Dr Russell came into my room with two consent forms, one for the clinic and one for me to keep in my records. At 8.30 Johnny turned up as we began chatting, to get my mind off things. Johnny had gracefully accepted defeat, as he was asking if I was alright, still ending with you can still change your mind. Now with the time being 9am, the nurse came in with a wheelchair to take me to theatre on the third floor. Just before I left for theatre, I saw Johnny's head sink as he sat on the bed. The nurse then told him that he could come with me as far as the anaesthetic room, then he would have to return to the family lounge. Johnny followed me to the anaesthetic room, where once I was prepared, I looked at him, as he began stroking my cheek, and then I slowly lost consciousness.

After a successful procedure I began to come around as I drifted in and out of sleep, but the nurses would not fully wake me up. I was finally awoken in the late afternoon, where I noticed I was on an intravenous morphine drip. I did not see too much of Johnny, but I was told he had never left my side once I was brought back to my room. I did hear his voice a few times, but I was so out of it with the contents of the drip.

The next day I had the morphine removed from my arm as they did not want me to get addicted to it, and instead I was given paracetamol and ibuprofen much to my annoyance. I was in discomfort with the vaginal packing to keep my legs open but knew that this would be worth it in the end once the fuckin pain would shift.

I was becoming to come around properly, after the second day of just sleeping everything off; and I got to see Johnny a lot more, even though conversation was at a minimum. I sometimes just wished he would fuck off, as he was not helping the situation, and I just wanted to be left alone.

Four days later I left hospital, as all the packaging and bandages were removed. Once Dr Russell had come to see me, and he was completely satisfied, I was released from the hospital where Johnny took me back to the Grand Hotel.

It was a further week before I went back to the clinic to get my hospital form to say I was fit to fly, so that following Saturday we flew to France for another two weeks, just to get some much needed rest.

We never went out much as I was still very sore, and so I just lay on the couch or bed; and if we did go out Johnny was kind enough to have a wheelchair for me, so that I did not overdo the walking. I had exercises to do, but was told that I could not over exert myself; as for hygiene, I was told not to use soap or perfumes down below in my genital area, and if I needed to shower then it would be best to buy some incontinence pads; just so I do not get the dressings around my vagina wet

I will give Johnny his due, he looked after me a lot in those weeks after surgery, and I just wondered if there was any glimmer of hope, that we could kind of rekindle what we once had all those years ago.

I thought what we had was really too much of an investment to just throw away, because I had since had surgery should not have made a difference as we both have a history. I really did love Johnny, even though I knew deep down inside he was a gay man; and chances of a gay man and transgender woman staying together was very slim. I still hoped he would see that I still loved him; and I hoped that he loved me; and could see it from my position

Our last day in France, Johnny made sure all the bags were packed, as we made our way to the airport for our flight home. Danni was going to meet us in Gatwick at 6pm that evening, as he said he would be in the area. Once we landed and made our way through customs, there was Danni as he waited for us to come through the barriers, where he just held his arms open and he hugged me carefully telling me how nice it was to see me; and he hoped all had gone well. I just told him I was still a little sore, and just wanted my own bed, as you could not beat your own surroundings for the best therapy. He then went over to Johnny and gave him a manly hug as he kissed him on the cheek. We then made our way out of the airport, where Marcus had come around and parked right outside, so I did not have that far to walk.

Johnny and Danni loaded the car, as we made our way back into London, with Marcus making sure it was as comfortable as he could. Danni told me that Roxy had sent her love, and that she would come over tomorrow to come and see me. I just told him that it would be fine and would be nice to see her, although I was dreading it, because I was slowly becoming a little distant from her now, as Danni began asking me how things had gone. I did not go into detail, but I did say it had gone successful; and wish I still had the morphine as some days are better than others.

We finally got home where the boys took the cases upstairs for me whilst Marcus waited downstairs for Danni to finish. Danni came in and spent a further hour with us as he then said he had to go and pick up Roxy; and he hoped to see us real soon. I told him, that I am not even going near the Rainbow for a good few months, as I want total rest from the bar. Danni then gave me a kiss on the cheek as I just collapsed on the couch, whilst Johnny saw him to the door. They stopped in the doorway for a while, as they were still chatting with each other; and then Danni gave Johnny another hug before closing the door. I knew that Johnny was telling Danni that he was not happy, as they whispered and never looked back. It was then that I knew that Johnny would always be a gay man; and that we at some point would part ways. I no longer had what he wanted; and I so wished he would find himself a nice young man, or even a fuck buddy, because he would no longer be interested in me now sexually.

I just chilled out; and began reading all the cards that were on the coffee table; and admiring the many bouquets of flowers I had received. It overwhelmed me, but not as much as when I opened this one card. It was from my mother and she sent me her blessing and wished me a speedy recovery.

That was it, I just broke down as Johnny came running towards me, panicking as I then handed him the card. He comforted me, as I then told him I was off to bed as it had been a very long emotional day. I suggested he sleep in the spare room for a while as I was very sore and fidgety which he did not mind.

That morning he brought me breakfast in bed; and he hoped that I had a comfortable night. I told him I was fidgety and still could not sleep properly so I told him that I was going to ask the doctor for some sleeping pills to help. I got up and just lounged about in a dressing gown, when the buzzer rang and as Johnny answered the door; Roxy came into the lounge and told me it was so good to see me. She could see that I still had some bandages around me; and that I had them changed daily as she saw a box on the floor with extra supplies.

She sat down on the chair next to the couch, where we started to make conversation. I told her that I have to go back to my own doctor if things get any worse, and I was going to get Johnny to ask him to come out and see me as I needed some sleepers.

She just told me that she was there for me, which was nice and refreshing, but to be honest I just wanted to be left alone as I needed a lot of rest. She then mentioned the private parties she had been hosting which I already knew about, and I told her that I did not think it was her type of thing but was pleased that she had kept them going, as it brought a big income into the bar.

I then politely told Johnny to get back to work, as I would be fine on my own; as all I was doing was resting, so there was no need for him to stay around.

With that he arranged with Ellie and Roxy and came up with a schedule as went back to work.

Roxy would pop in on a daily basis after work just to see if I was ok and if I needed anything, which a few times I gave her a list of things to fetch from the chemist.

It had been a few weeks now since my surgery, and I no longer had bandages around my body, which resembled an adult diaper, as I had begun to heal quite nicely, and I was told that I should now let the air help in my recovery to heal. I still had a little bruising, but it was not half as bad as it was a few weeks ago.

Then this one day, Roxy came over, she brought with her a lovely bouquet of flowers and a bottle of champagne ready for when I was back on the drink. I asked her if she wanted to see my surgery to which she agreed, but when I opened my dressing gown, I thought she was going to pass out, as she went all white and unsteady on her feet. I do not know if it was shock, or still seeing the signs of bruising, so we sat down where we again started to chat.

"*How do you feel now Ruby, any regrets?*" She asked, trying to be concerned, as I thought that Danni must have told her what Johnny had said, and therefore she was being sarcastic.

"*None at all Roxy, I should have had this done a long time ago*. I now feel like I am truly me. I now feel 100% woman." I replied, letting her know that I was so glad I had finally transitioned.

"Good for you honey, I am so pleased for you. I am so glad that you have finished your journey, and you can now start your new life properly, just like you have always wanted to do." She answered.

"Thank you Roxy, that means a lot to me." I said as we gently hugged, now knowing she was as false as her second character she talks about.

A few weeks had now passed; and I let Roxy continue with the private parties, as I still wanted them to carry on as if nothing had changed. I was now walking a lot stronger than before with the odd walk to the local shop for milk and bread, making it a little longer walk each day. Then this one day, just as I was settling down to a bit of daytime television the intercom buzzed, so I got up and walked over to see who it was.

"Tony is that you?" A woman's voice spoke

"Tony sorry no one by that name here." I replied, not even thinking about my male name.

"Sorry Ruby, is that you?" She spoke again

"Yes, this is Ruby, who is asking?" I replied

"It is your mother, can I please come in?" She asked.

"My mother, who is this playing practical jokes on me because it is not funny?" I said sarcastically

"Ruby this is your mother, Marty gave me your address. Can I please come up?" she asked.

I could not believe it but knew it had to be her, as not many people would be lame enough to joke like that to me without getting the sharp end of my tongue.

I was quaking in my boots as I let her in, and then

thought shall I phone Johnny to come home or ask for Roxy to see if she will rush over to me.

I thought no, if my mother doesn't like it, then she can fuck off, but then thought why has she come and what was her motive?

Then next thing my doorbell rang.

"*MOTHER.*" I said, very shocked

"*Ruby.*" She replied

"*Please come in mother and take a seat.*" I said, making way for her to come over the threshold

"*Thank you, dearie.*" She answered

"*Please let me take your coat m*other." I asked, thinking that this was going to be very awkward.

"*Thank you Ruby, you have a nice apartment; I am very impressed Ruby. You have impeccable taste.*" Mother said, as she looked at the fine paintings and sculptures that was placed around the lounge,

"*Thank you mother, we try our best.*" I replied, now like a child, waiting for approval.

"*Oh yes, the we scenario. Are you still with Ermm what's his name?*" She asked

"*Johnny mother, his name is Johnny.*" I replied

"*Ah yes, are you still with him?*" She said with her frowning look

"*Yes, mother we are still together, even though it is hard at times.*" I replied, rather softly

"*Well, he must love you if he is still with you.*" She replied, sounding like she still does not approve of my lifestyle.

"*Not sure about that mother, we are more like friends and companions now rather than partners.*" I told her

"Oh, I see, well leave him if it is not working, no good wasting your life." She said, now sitting on the chair *"Let's not talk about him mother, how are things with you, and what about dad?"* I said as I was about to mention my sisters
"Oh, father is ok, busy with court. I have asked him to retire as it is not like we need the money." She replied.

She then asked me if I was ok, and was I eating properly. She began telling me all about Marty; and how well he is doing in the army, and how his girlfriend is now becoming a quite a distinctive member of the bar. I did not let her know I already knew as Marty had already informed me, I just wanted to listen to her for once, and I was like a little girl… very excited about what her mother was talking about.
I then could not help it, as I placed my hands to my face and began to cry. My mother put her hands onto my hands and asked me what I was crying for. I told her that I loved her, that I loved her so much that I could not begin to explain how much I needed her. Then in her soft calming voice, that I always remembered, she told me that she too loved me. That was the very first time I had ever heard my mother say she loved me, and I broke down. Then to my surprise, she told me to just give her time to get used to things, to get used to her little boy becoming a woman, as she had spent most of my absent life getting used to me being gay. That really hurt, as I now became as stern as my mother, when I told her that I was never gay; and it is so hard to explain to someone who has no idea about the LGBT lifestyle. Then mother

being mother, sat upright, and then talking to me just like those times she was angry with me she said.

"You do not have to explain Ruby; I do have a brain dearie, and I have been reading up about your situation at the library. It is just that I thought you were gay; and that you had this successful larger than life drag queen persona to help you hide from who you were, by giving you a much larger ego. Marty also helped me in a lot of things, and now I learnt that you have totally changed it just has to sink in, so I need time. I am here now so together we can learn from each other. You have a lot to tell me Ruby and I have a lot I need to understand dear, besides, I never liked you as a boy, as I despise boys with a passion. I always wanted you to be a girl; and when I saw you dressed up in my clothes, yes, I was horrified, but a part of me inside confirmed my belief that you should have been a girl. But I did not know what to do, because you was a boy; and being a boy, you know it was wrong to dress up in mothers clothes. Now come here let me give you a hug."

I dropped my head into my mother's breast, as for the first time in my entire life; I finally had acceptance from my mother. I finally had her here with me comforting me, and I finally had a mother's love, where I no longer felt alone.

"Do not expect your sisters to come around Ruby, they are too old fashioned; and to be honest, since they had their inheritance your dad and I have never seen them

again, I really do not know where we went wrong with them." She explained, as she knew they would never be as understanding as she was.

"*You gave in to them too quickly that's what the problem was mother. They only wanted you for money, unlike Marty and me who just wanted your love when we could. And what about dad, mother?*" I asked

"*Again, give your father time, but he has assured me that he is going to give you a phone call over the next few days. Knowing your father, it will be Sunday as that's the only day he seems to have to himself now, as it is golf on Friday dearie. I hardly see him myself, I may as well have stayed single.*" she said, as she laughed.

"*I really do love you mother, I always have.*" I told her, now pleased that we had had that conversation everyone dreads.

"*Now do not get upset, I have always loved you too Ruby, I just never knew how much because you were a different child. I pushed you away because of my ignorance about your situation.*" She said, as I now saw her side of things, as it could not be easy to have a child who wants to be a different sex, especially in the era of not many people understanding transgender.

"*Don't blame yourself mother, at least you are here now when I need you the most.*" I told her, as again I hugged her tightly.

"*I am here yes, and I am not letting you go a second time Ruby, we have a lot to talk about.*" She said, as I finally had got my mother back.

I just hugged my mother all afternoon getting up to make tea as I caught up with stories from my childhood, as she asked me about my life since moving home.

When she left, I think I had cried all my tears that I had for the last thirty years, but at last I was finally happy and overwhelmed that I had my mother back.

I waited up until Johnny came home and I told him all about my day. He was so pleased for me and told me that it was now water under the bridge, and I can rebuild all those lost years. I really wanted to hug him and go to bed, but he just kissed me on the cheek and made his way to the spare room.

On that following Sunday my father plucked up the courage and called me, we had a lengthy conversation and I listening to how he felt, he also listened to how I had always felt, but reminded me that I was always in his thoughts; and as the eldest boy, he thought I would have followed him into law. He too told me to give him time, as he too told me that he loved me and that we needed to catch up at some point or other. I was invited around their house next time Marty was over and the four of us could have Sunday dinner like we used to. I just said not quite like it used to, but I knew what he meant.

Several weeks had passed now, and apart from Roxy coming over to visit, my mother came over every few days to bring me provisions and flowers, as we started bonding more and more, and she told me just how much I looked like my aunty May. She came around to calling me her daughter, which for my mother was a very big step, and I knew once she let people know I was her daughter I was accepted. My world was coming together just nicely, having struggled all my life as a boy, I now truly felt I was living my life as I was meant to; and no longer felt I was not wanted and was all alone.

I just thought to myself, it could not get any better than it is right now; apart from Johnny getting down on one knee, and asking me to marry him, but I knew it would never happen. Just like Roxy, I know had a purpose; and my purpose was family. I thought that she no longer needs to gloat and wallow in her family, then telling me that I was part of it. I had finally got back what was so very important to me, my natural family. My birth family, which was all I needed to be who I was.

Next thing I had a phone call; and it was Johnny.

"Ruby, is Roxy there, have you seen Roxy?" Johnny asked

"No Johnny she is not here, why what's the matter, what's happened?" I asked, thinking what drama had she caused now.

"She has walked out on Danni, it's a long story but she thought she had caught Danni in Adam's arms." Johnny replied

"Oh what, what has the dizzy queen done now." I asked

"I am on my way over, Ellie is looking after the bar, and I will explain more." He told me

"Ok see you soon, and what do I do if Roxy turns up here Johnny?" I asked

"Keep her with you; I am on my way, bye." He replied.

When Johnny got home, he explained that Adam had turned up to see Roxy, but she had gone out. I then interrupted, to let him know she had come around earlier, but left just before her mother came around.

Johnny continued to say that Roxy had caught Danni and

312

Adam in an uncompromising position; and got the wrong end of things and just stormed out.

"*She is such a fuckin drama queen Johnny; what next is going to happen?*" I said, now beginning to get a bit tired of Roxy's little dramas.

"*Wouldn't you be the same Ruby, if I had done something like that; and you had walked in and found us in the same position?*" Johnny said.

"*In all of our years together, nothing has happened Johnny; and I am sure it is not going to change now. For the fact I may have walked in on you with another guy would have been a godsend, as I know at times, I wished you would have taken a fuck buddy.*" I replied, telling him in a way that it would not worry me if he did.

"*Oh, charming I must say. Chance would be a fine thing anyway, even though once or twice I did think about straying with one of the bar staff, but then again you would have caught wind of it, because you know I cannot keep anything from you.*" Johnny replied.

I was pleased that Johnny had opened up to me; and strange as it may seem, I really did wish he had gone ahead with his thoughts, because that way, it would have taken away the moments I wished he was not sharing the bed with me. And I would not have classed it as a love triangle, because it was not as though I would have wanted a threesome with the guy, but no Johnny was faithful towards me, much different to how my shady past was like.

After a few days it all came out, and it was when I was at the bar that Adam came in to do his shift, that I asked him to come and see me. He told me that it was all a mistake, and he apologised for not coming into work, as he felt crap from not hearing from Stuart after their argument. He explained that Danni went mad at him, as he looked dirty, that he told him to take a shower. He then got upset, and it was then that Danni just went over to him and hugged him, then Roxy just walked in on them. He cried in his hands, as he told me that nothing had happened between him and Danni; and he would not do that to Roxy as it was not who he was. He told me that he loved Stuart too much, and he did not want to jeopardize anything he had with him.

I just looked at him and told him that everything would be ok, and all we can do now is to wait for Roxy to calm down before it all got sorted, as I continued to tell him that I think she was a bit of a drama queen, as the first thing she should have done, was to ask you outright and not just run off. This seemed to calm Adam down a little, as he again swore to me that nothing had happened, as he was not a person who would go and cheat, let alone sleep with someone's partner behind their back. I believed him, even though I felt the whole truth had not come out. I know Roxy doted on her boys, and she was a little protective towards them, and something did not ring truth to me. Sure, I believed Adam, but somehow something was still amiss. I decided not to continue asking Adam about that day, as he told me nothing happened, so I had to believe him; even with that niggling stab that was going through my body.

A few nights had passed; and Roxy finally called me. She used to annoy me when she did things like this, as she showed she had not a care for anyone else but herself; as she just went silent on you for a few days, with not a peep out of her. When she was ready, she would then surface as though nothing had happened, and did not care for anyone else's concern; whilst she wallowed in her self-pity; and locked herself away.

I am sure deep down inside; it was just to seek attention, just like a drama queen would act. I told her that she had got it all wrong, and put Adam's case forward, and in the process, she let it slip where she was staying; as I then told her that I thought she had acted like a drama queen; and had not looked at the situation properly. After an hour on the phone with her, I called Danni and I let him know where she was, which was a big relief for him as I told him to just go over.

That night I was doing my act, and I noticed she walked into the bar with Danni, where I then waved to her, even though I was still frustrated with her carry on. Johnny went up to her and gave her a kiss on the cheek, as he also shook Danni's hand and then hugged him. Shortly after she entered the bar, I noticed she had managed to get hold of Adam, where they went through to the dressing room. I finished the show, and then made my way to my dressing room; before going into the bar. Roxy then came over to me, and we began chatting. As we were chatting, Danni and Adam came from the direction of the dressing rooms; and Roxy then looked at me, where she then said.

"Oh, that's nice Ruby, the family has made up. I can't believe I acted like I did, but you know what I am like."
"Yes, I do, you drama queen. Well, it's done and dusted now dearie, you got your boys back so that must be a

relief? And you got a posh apartment for a break, so it can't be too bad." I said sarcastically

"*It's nice to see them back, and sorry I disappeared upstairs; I just needed to make sure Adam was ok as he has man trouble.*" She told me, not really caring anymore, as I knew we too would part at some point.

"*Oh, not the dreaded man trouble, what are we going to do? We can't live with them and we can't live without them.*" I said, as I told her she should by now not be as dizzy as she is.

"*That's true, boys will be boys, and if anything, and I mean anything should upset them, they soon come running to Miss Ruby and Miss Roxy.*" Roxy said.

We all sat down and ended up having a nice evening, full of laughter and tears; and lots of drink.

A few more weeks had gone by, and now I was getting a letter a week from Marty. My mother also called me twice a week and I also got to speak to my dad a few times as he soon began calling me Ruby without sounding uncomfortable. It was a further three weeks before Marty called me and told me that he was coming home on leave, and he was very excited. My parents had also contacted me, to make arrangements for that Sunday dinner; that we often spoke about. Johnny stayed at the bar, and he took Ellie out for Sunday dinner; and treated her to a Greek meal. I made my preparations for the afternoon ahead, and just hoped that my dad would accept me in person, as he did on the phone.

I chose my dress wisely as I did not want to go looking tarty, as he would not be impressed. I went for the conservative look; and chose a trouser suit which I thought was far better than a sequin dress, or indeed a mini skirt, as that way I did not have to wear such big heels, and I knew I could be comfortable in a pair of two inch heels. I got myself ready, and Johnny took me to my parents, as he then went to the bar to help Ellie. I knocked on the door, as I did not just want to walk in; and Marty came to answer.

"*Lovely to see you again Ruby, you look absolutely gorgeous; so conservative.*" He said, as he then told me that mom would definitely approve.
"*I did not want to come dressed loud, or even tarty in mom and dad's eyes.*" I replied, winking at him, because he had seen my extended wardrobe.
"*You should be you Ruby and not dress because you think it going to be accepted.*" He said, "*And sod them; and the neighbours come to that, as they peer through their white starched net curtains, thinking that people will bring down the neighbour*hood because they do not adhere to their wishes and beliefs."
"*I know dear, but this is mom and dad; and I agree with the neighbours, as they always have their heads up their arse.*" I replied.

He then took my coat, as he gave me a kiss and told me that mom and dad were in the conservatory. I walked through the lounge and could see that where the dining room was, they had now had the wall knocked down and an extension for the conservatory. It looked absolutely gorgeous.

"*Hello Ruby.*" Mother said.

"*Ruby?*" Dad said, in a quiet manner.

I said hello to them both, as mother got up and gave me a hug, then dad came over and did the same.

Well, I did not know how to react, and mother just looked at me and put her finger to her mouth as to say keep quiet. I sat down on the couch next to Marty, and we all started talking, laughing about things that had happened when we were small, and how things have changed. I decided to tell them about Roxy's Christmas blunder, to which they all laughed, in which it really did break the ice. I began telling them about my life, as I was asked what I had been doing for all of the past years. After a long chat and lots of tears; dad decided to get us to have a group hug. Once we had a group hug, he asked me to come into his study with him. I looked at mom and Marty, and together they looked at me and assured me that everything would be fine, so I left the conservatory, and followed dad to his study.

Father then looked at me and then said.

"*I had only just got used to you being a gay man and a drag queen, and then Marty told me that you wanted to become a woman. I did not know what to do, as you are my eldest son. After a lot of conversations with your brother, and a lot of explanation I could not hold it against you. You have to do with your life what you feel is right for you. Give me time Ruby, please just give me time, just so I can get used to this. If you were gay then I would now be fine with it, as I have now got a few gay men and women who are colleagues.*"

"*I will give you all the time in the world dad; I just hope you are not disappointed in me.*" I asked, hoping that he would approve of me

"*You are not a disappointment Ruby; it is me that's the disappointment as I turned my back on you.*" He replied

"*No dad, you are never a disappointment.*" I told him

"*You are not a disappointment Ruby, because look at what you have achieved. You have two properties, a bar, celebrity status. You had goals and dreams and you went for them.*" He said, as I had tears in my eyes.

"*I just wanted you to be proud of me dad; I love you so much and it hurt when I never heard from you.*" I cried.

"*I am proud of you my dear, so please trust me when I say that. Now, wipe your tears Ruby, I love you too. Come here and give your dad a hug.*" He asked, as he held his arms open for me.

I hugged him like it was the very first time and never wanted to let him go. He held me tight as he patted me on the back; and assured me that everything would be fine. We then went back into the lounge, and then dad opened a bottle of champagne, and for once in my life I was now fully complete. I got my birth family back, and they accepted me as Ruby the more that time went by. Those years of being alone and struggling to survive, of wearing drag make-up to gain success; and the guys I fucked to get where I am now made it worth the while. Sitting at the dinner table now as Ruby, with my brother Marty and my parents, was a dream that I had a very long time ago, wishing that one day we could all be together.

I now knew that dreams really do come true…

That evening, my father dropped me off at the Rainbow where he told me to call him anytime; and to come over to the house when I wanted too. I walked into the bar a different Ruby, as it was no longer the Ruby that had to fight against prejudice anymore, because I now had the one important thing in life. I had my family, and I had my birth family back in my life.

Over the coming months I got the stride back into my step. Johnny and I decided to book our holiday, and this time we were going to go to Gran Canaria, as I wanted to finally check out the island. I had the number of an agent on the island, which Totty had given me; and I gave them a call. I was sent a brochure of villas and apartments that they had for rent and after looking through both Johnny and I rented a villa in Maspalomas, near the golf course. We had arranged our own flights, and then it was a well-deserved shopping spree for new clothes; especially now that I was beginning to lose weight.

Unlike Roxy and Danni, we could not afford a private jet, so had to make do with a normal flight, although we were lucky enough not to book for the school holiday; and it was so nice, that Roxy did not throw the private jet card into the equation, because although she did not realise it, she did use it a lot with regards her status and money; and it did annoy me at times, that it came across as her being nothing more than a snob.

So, the day finally arrived where we made our way to Gatwick Airport, and Danni drove us there as has he had a meeting in Surrey. He then dropped us off and wished us a nice holiday; and asked us to let him know when they arrived safely. We were so pleased to get through customs; and get the flight out of the way as the flight seemed to drag a little that day.

Once we got through customs the other end, we then made our way to the hire car office; and again, Johnny upgraded as the one they offered was not suitable.

We finally got to the villa, which was very quaint, and not like the one we stayed in with Danni and Roxy in Italy, but I knew that this would do, as it was only the two of us this time.

The villa was a lovely and clean; and was just big enough for us. The kitchen was very small, but we were not going to be eating in that much, so it was adequate for just doing breakfast or a quick snack. It was also an open plan lounge diner/kitchen; and although it had a dining table inside, it also had a dining table in the patio area. There were two bedrooms, one being a double and the other being a twin. The double had a patio door, directly going into the closed patio area off the poolside; and then you could walk out of the patio area towards the grounds where it housed a lovely pool.

We dropped off our bags, and then I asked Johnny to take me shopping so that I could get a few provisions. As I could speak Spanish I stayed away from the touristy supermarkets, and we drove to one of the local supermarkets, so with bags in hand, we then made our way back to the villa.

We spent that day just unpacking our bags; and chilling out by the pool with our drinks as we chatted till dusk. Being Spain and having a gay area, we knew that the nightlife did not really start till around 11pm, so we decided to go out then to see what the nightlife was like. As we had been drinking, we decided to get a cab, and we then made our way to the famous Yumbo centre. The atmosphere was fabulous, but it did remind me of Soho but just a lot hotter and cheaper. It was one of those resorts that once you have gone in all the bars, you knew which would be your favourite and you stayed there. The drag was fabulous, and sometimes a little tacky, but no one cared as it was cocktails and cabaret. There were lots of restaurants as well as clothes shopping and the usual perfume and tobacconists, as well as a few tacky gift shops that you often find around resorts such as this. As for being gay, well it was absolutely gay, right in your fuckin face, or as 'Camp as Christmas' as Totty used to say.

Then there was the kissing; I had never seen so many same sex couples kissing on the island. It did not matter if you were gay or lesbian, you were classed an equal; and no one bothered you if they saw you kissing in the street. I did not see one trannie bar, although there were a few trans people at the resort; and like always, we transgender girls had to mingle with the gays and lesbians, although here we were all one community with no hatred. It was then that I had the idea of opening a complex for transgender people, because that way I thought it would be nice for them, to have a hotel of their own, where they did not have to rely on the gay community; and listen to some of the gay men throw rude names towards them.

We spent the next few days travelling around to get a feel for the island, and as well as going into the agents we got the keys from, we looked at what properties they had for sale, both as bars and apartments. We looked in those areas to see what we thought of the area. Johnny fell in love with Playa Del Ingles, and I think that was because it was more gay, than straight or transgender; so he could associate with that.

I liked Maspalomas, although it felt family orientated to me with lots of complexes which were ideally set at coaxing families away from the Yumbo centre; and have them stay in their complex. It was not until we looked around San Agustin, that I felt truly felt comfortable and at ease with who I was. It was my kind of area, Spanish and cosmopolitan and away from the noisy drag scene. I knew I did not want to live on the doorstep of the gay community, as it was an area that did not close until the sun came up in the morning, so to have the discos banging on all night with their loud music was not my scene. On the third day we went to go out, and I told Johnny that for once we should leave our phones at home, as it still felt like we were in London with people calling all of the time.

He agreed; and so we locked our phones in the safe. That day was spent going to a lovely animal park called Palmitos Park. It had lots of animals as well as a dolphin show, but what was nice is that it was away from the crowds, as we seemed to pick a day where it was older people who visited. From there we went back into Maspalomas and found a very quiet Irish bar overlooking the sea.

After having such a lovely day, we went back to the villa and had a few hour's siesta before going out that following evening. Johnny went into the safe to get his

phone, and then made himself a scotch.
Then I heard Johnny's phone bleep like crazy.

"OMG Ruby, come here." He shouted, in complete shock.
"What's the matter Johnny?" I replied, thinking
something had happened to the bar, or to Ellie.
"It's Roxy she has been..." He started to say as I
interrupted him
*"Oh, what has the fuckin bitch done now? Can I not have
five minutes, without the dizzy cow getting up to some
sort of mischief?"*
"If you let me finish Ruby." He replied
*"Finish then, go on. Can't we get away without that
dizzy queen causing drama?"* I said now getting pissed
off
*"You finished??? There has been a commotion in the bar.
Some guys were shouting abuse to people going into the
bar, and as the doorman grabbed hold on one, the other
got inside the bar."* He replied as he got annoyed with
me
"Yes and?" I said, knowing that she had her support
group with her; and there was no need to contact us, as
she knew we wanted a peaceful holiday.
*"AND Ruby, he got hold of Roxy; and there was a scuffle.
They ended up in a fight, and she has been stabbed."* He
said rather worried
*"Fucking hell, send her flowers Johnny. I am not going
back; I am going to have this holiday if it is the last thing
I do Johnny. We both deserve this break Johnny, and
again that bitch Roxy, tries to fuck it up for us."* I replied,
now fuming
"Are you not concerned Ruby?" Johnny asked me

"Yes, I am, and I said send her flowers. I knew she could hold her own. But I think now it is about time we got more door staff. She has people who can be around her, so why are we being told this. Is it her way of ruining our holiday, because she hasn't come, or is it because she wants to be centre of attention again. Johnny, I am getting so fucked off with her. I just want some peace, for Christs sake." I shouted. Seething now at the fact that this holiday seems to be going tits up.

"I agree. Hope she is ok. I will have to call Danni." He replied now very concerned

"Johnny this is why we have to move out of London, as it's becoming unsafe now. Look how relaxed it here, look how free we are. For god sake we forgot to lock the villa up when we went out this afternoon; and I left my purse on the coffee table with all of my credit cards and about five hundred euros inside, and look how safe it is, not trying to tempt fate mind you." I replied, knowing this was a good excuse to bring up the conversation of moving

"True, but we can't think of that right now." He replied

"Oh no I forgot... poor Roxy; poor fuckin Roxy, again stopping me to have a well-deserved holiday." I answered sarcastically, wishing I had never laid eyes on that dizzy bitch.

"No need to be bitchy." Johnny snapped

"Really, then you would say that wouldn't you Johnny?" I replied, as I decided to get myself a vodka and coke.

"You have changed Ruby; I do not know you anymore." Johnny replied, as he sat down on the couch, scrolling through his texts

"I am not getting into an argument; it's supposed to be our fuckin holiday. Like I said send her flowers." I said, as I rushed to pour myself a drink

It seemed to put a strain on things after that, but with much persuasion I did get Johnny to consider moving over here; and told him that I did not want what had happened to Roxy to spoil the holiday.

After a day of stewing over Roxy, and with Johnny phoning Danni and Ellie, we found that Roxy was in hospital, but the guy had not hit a major organ and she would be fine in a few days. Johnny told Ellie to man the bar with Dixie and that we would be home soon.

That evening, to cool the situation down, we went to have a meal in the Yumbo centre; and then hopefully tried to enjoy ourselves without Roxy coming into their conversation as she had been of late.

In my own special way, I really did love Johnny; and I so wished that he would come around to the idea that I am now a complete woman. I knew Johnny was gay and I accepted him being gay, that I wished he accepted my lifestyle, and I often questioned myself about what he favoured the most, that if he wanted cock, then he would leave and find a nice gay boy with whom he could find love again. But for the fact he was still with me, spoke more about us as a couple; and I felt that in time he would come around to me being a transgender woman, and that he would change for me.

Yes, I had seen Brian; and I had often had liaisons with other men, but that was before I had surgery. Now I wanted Johnny, and I wanted Johnny to embrace my femininity, to come into my world just to see if he could like it as I once tried his world.

When me and Johnny were on form however, I looked at him in such a way, that he was mesmerised for a short time. He was captivated by the colour of my sky blue eyes, and the intensity that was in my gaze.

He had often told me, that he never dreamed that he would ever find that kind of intensity in a person; let alone have it affect him the way it had with me, which only told me more, that in time he would come around to my way of thinking.

In our early years, it was easy for us to continue with our flirtatious mannerisms; as we became part of each other's social network, and my friends were his friends; and vice versa. There were never any expectations with Johnny, as I was so at ease with him, even on the occasions, that I allowed him to touch my girly cock.

Whilst Johnny and I finished our meal in the German restaurant, we decided to go to the bar Hollywood.

We had been there before, and had seen the acts that were there which were not just English, but also Spanish acts, both local and from the mainland.

It was whilst we were in the bar, that we spotted another couple, who became very friendly.

They introduced themselves to us as Adrian and Lisa. Adrian was an openly gay man, and his girlfriend was transgender. They both met in their hometown of Blackpool, and at first, they had a gay relationship with each other. When Lisa told him that she was transgender, he supported her throughout her transition to feminisation. Adrian told us that he will always be gay; and that he and Lisa; his wife of five years, will never split up. They both have an open relationship, with Adrian having a part time pretty boy as a boyfriend, and

Lisa having a guy who can satisfy her needs as a woman. I thought it was strange at first, listening to this couple; then it all became clear to me, as I had often told Johnny to find himself a boyfriend.

They also told us that they had a civil ceremony five years ago, when they were guys; and as soon as she transgendered, they just had a blessing as they were saving up for their wedding which was going to take place next year. I could see that both people were still madly in love with each other, and their forwardness to their other partners, was explained as just casual sex with another. Adrian then said; that sometimes Lisa would fuck both of her boys, as well as he and her boyfriend who would engage in anal, whilst she blew the pair of them. Lisa looked at me and then said, that it was not uncommon to see her husband fucking her boyfriend, whilst he is fucking her; and what a turn on it was, as she not only had a husband, she also has a very handsome and sexy lover.

Johnny spoke up and told Adrian, that he did not think he could do that; and he was not sure about wanting another guy, whilst he was still with Ruby. He also told them that he was not sure about the vagina scenario, as he was a gay man who liked trans-girls who still had their cock. It was what helped him identify his gender, as he had always claimed he was a gay man who loved tits and ass, and a nice girly cock.

"Just give it a go Johnny, after all; you have said that you like tits and ass. Just think of Ruby's vagina, as being her front ass. It is all in your mind at the end of the day." Adrian told him.

Johnny said he still did not know; and asked Adrian if he had ever fucked his wife's pussy. He told him that he tried it a few times, but it did not appeal to him, as he could not get fully aroused.

Because Adrian and Lisa had always had an open relationship with each other, it was suggested that they do not play around separately, but instead find another significant other for their sexual desires, because as a couple they were very happy with each other. He then told us that it was not always the case, as sometimes they would get horny, and Lisa would take the dominant role and satisfy her husband, by fucking him with a dildo. Listening to them was making me so hot and flustered, and I knew that something like that would be perfect for us. I also agreed that Johnny should first have a bite at the flower, before dismissing it from his thoughts.

But then as a double standard answer, I then said I was not so sure about us both having other partners, as I still loved Johnny too much.

"It works both ways Ruby, as you could buy yourself a double strap on; so not only do you get to fuck your husband up the ass, you can also fuck your own vagina and enjoy the whole experience. Fuck me, when Lisa puts on that strap on, and takes my ass, whilst I am sucking and rimming her boyfriend, gets me off so quickly. And a few times her boyfriend has fucked me, whilst she has fucked him. At the end of the day it is just sex, because we would never so it with anyone other than our proposed boyfriends; and they know they are

safe, because of just that." He explained, now with his hand up Lisa's skirt.

We spent another few hour's in the bar, before making our way back to our villa; where we then bid goodnight to Adrian and Lisa, where we arranged to meet up with them again the following night. Johnny hailed a cab, as we waved to our new friends; and then Johnny asked the cab driver to take us home.

On the journey home, I began thinking about what Adrian had been saying, and so I placed my hand onto Johnny's thigh. He was shocked at first, and then slowly came around as I then moved my hand over his crotch, where I began stroking his cock which by now was coming alive. Just a short while after we had got into the cab, we had arrived at the villa; and Johnny now had a massive hard on. I paid the cab driver as we both slipped out of the cab a little worse for wear, but extremely horny. Fumbling with the keys, I dropped them on the floor; and as I knelt down to pick them up, my face brushed against Johnny's bulge where I just said I am going to blow you later big boy.

By now Johnny had got his keys, and he opened the security gate. As I was a little drunk, more than Johnny, I was leaning against the gate when Johnny opened it, and therefore I ended up falling with my ass facing the stars. Johnny just laughed at me, and then with his hand he stroked my ass, and told me that he was going to have that later too. He then helped me off the floor, as we proceeded into the garden.

Now standing by the patio door, as Johnny was behind me, I just held onto him as I placed my hand over his

cock; and then purred like a cat as I told him I was going to suck him dry. Johnny then placed his arms onto the patio doors, as he began kissing me, as he then said.
"*I want you so bad Ruby; so bad that I could rip your clothes off here and have you butt naked before me.*"
"*Really Johnny; and why is that*?" I replied, as I then placed my hands onto his ass, and pulled him closer to me, feeling his throbbing cock press firmly towards my vagina.
"*Because you are making it very hard for me to be a gentleman Ruby*." He said, as he whispered into her ear.
"*You're so God damn sexy Johnny; I am sure you are going to get me into trouble one day.*" I said to him, as the moon silhouetted behind his tall masculine frame.
I so wanted Johnny badly, as it had been ages, since the two of us had been this intimate.
"*I never asked you to be a gentleman Johnny; just be yourself and make love to me, that's all I ask of you.*" I told him, as I fluttered my eyes at him, and grabbed hold of his tie.

Johnny then kissed me, as he now turned me around; and as my back pressed firmly into his tummy. He then placed his hands firmly onto my breasts, as his now thick bulge, pressed firmly into the crease of my ass, from his growing passion that was noticeably stirring.

"*Be careful what you ask for, R*uby." He whispered into my ear, as he began to tease his tongue over my ear lobe.

I then looked behind me, as I placed my hands into the front of Johnny's boxers, grabbing hold of his moist throbbing bulge, as I began to rub it gently. Johnny was now nibbling on my ear and neck, as he squeezed my breasts gently, telling me to work his cock like I used to. Looking behind me again, I released Johnny's cock from his boxers, and then saw the look of lust on his face. What I saw, reminded me of our earlier days, and it made me want to see more of this lustful man that I so loved. I had surprised myself, that I too had begun to tingle as my inner thighs had become moist with the excitement, as I was sure I was going to orgasm; in which the surgeon said, it would take a while, but I would get certain sensations down there.

I gently slid a finger into my vagina; and felt that I too had become very wet. I noticed that Johnny had looked at me briefly, as he then unzipped my dress, so that it dropped to the floor by the patio doors, revealing to him my basque and stockings. I swooned as his fingers swirled around my now very hard nipples, as I became very aroused. I then opened my legs a little more, as I reached behind me and placed Johnny's throbbing cock underneath my ass towards my vagina.

Johnny then stopped for a second, and then slowly moved so that his hard wet cock was pressing against my ass. I did not mind at this point, as my breasts were rock hard, and my fingers very moist from playing with my vagina. Johnny oozed precum which flooded my ass; making it easier for him to guide it into me. He then inserted his thick cock inside my ass, as I closed my eyes and gasped, as he filled me to the brim with his 7inch cock. Thrusting in and out, like a piston working on overdrive, occasionally slipping right out of my ass; and brushing his wet cock against my now soaked vagina.

Johnny again thrust himself deep inside me, as I placed two fingers into my wet vagina. I then closed my eyes involuntary, as I was now about to orgasm. With my eyes closed, and I then wondered if Johnny knew how close I really was.

"You are so hot Ruby, and your sweat tastes delicious." He said, as he began panting heavier.

I then felt his teeth against my neck, as I pushed myself further into Johnny. Now Johnny was unable to control himself as he began to quiver, as he came close to orgasm, filling me up with his hot manly juices.
When he had finished, and he thrust one last time making sure I had every drop of his cock, Johnny began kissing my neck and playing with my breasts once again. He soon began to get aroused, as his cock began to swell up inside my ass. I then fell backwards into his arms, as Johnny wrapped himself around me. I did not mind that he had penetrated and cum in my ass, but I so wanted him to take my vagina, as I had always dreamed of being taken like a real woman, and who best to do this, was my partner Johnny, in which I knew he needed time.

"Do you want to go again Johnny? Do you want to play a little bit more?" I asked him, as I removed his cock from my ass; and turned around to face him.
"Sure, I do Ruby, look at me, you drive me crazy." He replied, as he pointed to his throbbing cock.

My heart began to pound, as my self-control just snapped, as I kissed him hard, and almost yanked his cock off in the process of jerking him off. Johnny told me that if I did not slow down, that he would cum there and then with my pounding of his cock.

"Johnny; you are not going to have to wait long; because I think I will cum too soon." I said, as I quickly fell to my knees; and placed his wet cock into my mouth. *"What are you doing? Oh my God Ruby; that's fucking great sweetie."* He replied, as he pushed himself further into me; holding onto my head to steady his cock. *"Oh God Johnny, I cannot believe we are doing this; as it has been so long."* I replied, I told him as I then stood up and led him to the bedroom.

When Johnny brought his throbbing erection back to my mouth, my eyes grew wider; as my breathing became slightly ragged, as he guided his cock into me. Seeing how much I was dribbling precum from the moistness around my mouth, Johnny thrust a little harder, sinking his cock deeper into me as I slightly gagged from the force. I then decided to change position, as I lay on the bed and opened my legs slightly allowing Johnny to slide in between me. Feeling my moist body under his, I placed Johnny's cock next to my vagina; and again, Johnny thrust hard, sinking his wet cock deep inside me. Johnny firstly shut his eyes, as he began to whimper in surrender as he then began fucking me on the bed like the real woman I had become, and without question. My hands were now gripping his shoulders tightly, as we both found our rhythm, and were soon kissing each other deeply, as he continued to enter my pussy like he was a dab hand at fucking a woman. I had already been on the edge of cumming again, as I felt the heat of my orgasm

boiling in my tummy. I then moved slightly, as I placed my hands onto Johnny's shoulders; pushing him further down my body, until he reached my wet pussy.
"Come on Johnny, fuck me, fuck me hard with your tongue baby, and let me see you cum over me. Come on Johnny, lick my pussy dear." I told him, now on the edge or orgasm.

Johnny then just froze, as he began shaking. He then looked at me as he was as white as a sheet.

"Ruby I can't, I can't do it sweetie. You are now a woman and I so long for cock, I can't go near your woman's bits, I am so sorry. I am so sorry Ruby, please forgive me." He said, as he then got up and left the bedroom.

I was furious, as I was on the verge of orgasm; and now I was just cast aside. I thought he was ok, because he did at least penetrate my pussy a few times, so why all of a sudden would you freeze? I picked up the pillow next to me; and then threw it at him as I called him all the names under the sun, telling him to fuck off and go and get one of the many boys looking for cock in the bars.
Johnny did not come to bed that night, as I heard him cry in the next room. I did not go into him because past events made me understand that he needed to be alone, as it brought memories of the times, that I froze on him, so a part of me understood, but not fully as her had fucked my pussy more than once the night before.
I knew that he had to get used to the idea that I was now a woman; and I did give him plenty of opportunity to

take a boyfriend, so that he got what he needed which was cock. Even meeting up with Adrian and Lisa over the next few days did not help, as we tried a few times on that last week to make out, but again he froze when it came to touching my pussy, so we just gave up as I thought maybe I should find myself a straight guy, as I needed to be satisfied.

Well, another two weeks out the way, and again the drama from Roxy disrupted any break I could have wished for, as she came up time and time again in conversation; even to the point of Johnny wishing I was like her when we tried to make out; but I had to keep telling him I was not a guy anymore. Even in the bedroom, Roxy somehow became involved with us, and it was at those times, that I wished I had never laid eyes on her, as I constantly had to tell Johnny that I was not Roxy, that I was Ruby; and if he wants a cock in a frock then maybe he should go with one of the trannies, as I was getting so pissed off with him by now.

It was now back to London and back to sorting out the bar, but I soon got back into the swing of things with my laborious routine, whilst Johnny kept in touch with Danni and he kept us up to date with Roxy's condition. I then arranged to meet up with my mother and father, as I needed to speak to them about moving away; and how would they feel about it, after we had only just found each other again. I was also preparing for another show at the Rainbow, as the act I had booked cancelled at the last minute; and my back up acts were busy working; so, it was now left to me to take their spot.

By now Johnny had interviewed people for the door job and he decided to get another guy, and with Ellie's suggestion he also employed a female for the girls that came into the bar. I decided to do an old show, as it had been a long time since I went back to the beginning.

I was halfway through my show, and then I saw Danni enter the bar with Roxy following behind. I did notice that the crowd began to stir when she came through the doors, as they went to the side of the bar to get their drinks. I looked at her and pointed for her to go to the dressing room, and once she had been given a hug from Johnny and Ellie, she then disappeared behind the curtain. I then went into my last but one number, and then when I finished, I asked the DJ to put the main lights on and take off the spots.

It was then that I addressed the audience to what had happened with regards to the bar, and why we needed extra security as it was not just a matter of people bringing their own drinks to the bar and not paying for ours, but also got onto the incident with Roxy.

I then stood still on stage and looked at the audience, where I then said.

"Ladies and gentlemen, let us not ignore the fact that if you piss off a drag queen, you will get bitch slapped; and I hear Miss Roxy Garcia can give a good left hook. So, ladies and gentlemen, after her kerfuffle in the Rainbow brawl I give to you Roxy Garcia."

As she walked on the stage the crowd whistled and jeered, and as she gave me a kiss on the cheek, I offered her the mic where she then said.

"Thank you all for your kind support, with the flowers and cards. It is nice to have such a big family think of you in that way. I am sure you know the old saying 'can't keep a good bitch down' well no fuckin gay basher will get the better of me or my community. I am not one for violence; but let them come here and try to kick the fuck out of us; you will not win for I will always stand tall amongst my community. And with that I would like to sing a classic song by Elton John, titled the bitch is back."

Somehow, I knew she would choose that song as we could often read each other's minds, so I made sure the DJ had the track ready. I then left the stage as I got changed for my last number; and knowing that they were coming into the bar I downloaded the last track for us to finish off together. At the end of the show, we both had a standing ovation, and I let Roxy take the light with what she had done. She had lots of well-wishers coming up to see her and then laugh about her fighting as she looked more like a pocket rocket than a fighter. However, looking at her proved me right, as again, Roxy was centre of attention, where she liked to be.

Over the coming weeks I had conversation after bloody conversation with Johnny about moving away, and I told him that I am definitely putting both the apartment and the basement flat on the market. I also told him that I am going to see my family in a few days' time; as I needed to let them know what my plans were, and I have already arranged a visit. We argued again, as he was asking if he did not go then where would he live; and so, I told him to buy the basement flat.

It was a few weeks of ups and downs with Johnny; but my mind was made up about leaving England.

Finally, Johnny gave in as he made an offer to Ellie to buy the bar, where she jumped at the offer.

I went to see my mom and dad who gave me their blessing; and they told me once I am settled that they would come over and visit often, as dad had now decided to take semi-retirement.

It was now March of 1989, and Roxy and I decided to do one last tour which our agent sorted very quickly.

We had three months to sort out our tapes and costumes, as we were going to have a six month tour, starting with the Rainbow and ending back there Christmas week, giving us Christmas Eve and Christmas day to ourselves. Our agent and promoters did us proud by organising this so quickly, because no sooner had we discussed it, that we were packed and heading up north. It was just the living out of a suitcase; and actually, spending six months alone with Roxy that I was worried about.

I just kept thinking what would she do, would I get drama tantrums, and how am I going to cope with her without Danni.

Six months had since passed, and I got through it without any hiccups. Roxy was fine; and kept herself to herself by going to bed early after each show.

I just thought fuck her I am going back to the bar.

I will admit it felt great, as I was often given compliments by some of the gay and bisexual guys. When I let them know I was now a fully transgendered woman, most of the gay boys dispersed. I think this was because they no longer felt they could suck off a drag queen, as there was no cock to suck. I did, however, have one or two bisexual guys still hang around; and who were intrigued at the thought of being with a transsexual. As to them they were typical men, thinking they were with a man who was now a woman. It is kind of how they preceded their own sexuality of accepting they were not quite gay, as they wanted to still be with a woman, but had the inkling of wanting to be with a man who looked like a woman and not like a man.

I had this one guy who was Mediterranean follow me around from most of the venues up north. I can be honest enough to say that there were a few times I would go back to his room, where the sex between us was absolutely great. Roxy had since gone to bed; and so, I quietly left my room hoping not to disturb her as I walked by. I made my way back down to the club; and it was not long before this guy came and sat next to me. Before long he enticed me onto the dancefloor; and we were dancing like we were the only once in the club.

His aroma, as I placed my hand by his smooth neck was intoxicating. He looked at me and said that I was by far the hottest woman he had ever picked up, and actually he thought I was one of the hottest transgender women, that he had ever seen in real life.

He then placed his lips onto my neck, and just held them there as he inhaled, leaving a warm sensation on my now hot neck. I then moved closer to him, as I offered him my neck, where he gave me small but sensuous kisses around my neck and leading to my exposed shoulder.

My hand became daring, as I reached for his zipper, where I invaded the entrance of his now bulging jeans. My fingers slowly inserting themselves into his underwear, as I found his stiff throbbing cock, feeling its thickness and then rubbing it backwards and forwards, just to justify its length. It was then that he whispered into my ear to take him to my room, as we were being watched by a small group of guys, who seemed to be getting off with us being so intimate towards each other. I grabbed him by the hand and escorted him off the dancefloor before we got arrested; and with his zipper still open; and just the tip of his cock peering through his jeans, we made our way to my room.

When we got through the door, I told him to keep the noise down, as I had a friend who was sleeping next door; and so, I grabbed onto his ass and with my hands he pulled me closer to him. His cock, though still in his pants, soon found its way out as I undone his top button and let his jeans fall to the floor. With his cock now fully exposed, and my dress now laying on the floor besides me, he rubbed his cock against the underside of my pussy, as he slid his tongue deep into my mouth.

I moaned slightly as he inserted his fingers into my pussy, so I slid my hand towards the top of his leg, as I reached for his cock and enjoyed what was in my hand. This guy had to be at least ten inches if not more, and I could not believe what I was doing. My nipples were so rock hard, that he ended up gently biting them, sending me into an uncontrollable frenzy, when a part of me told me that I should not be doing this; and I should tell him to get the hell out of here, but the other part of me could not help but to be submissive to this stud.

My hands then moved from his shaft down to his balls, where I cupped my hands to receive them. I bent down slightly; and with my hand I just raised his cock and balls to my face and licked the tip of his cock a little. I then put the head of his cock back into my mouth where I twirled it around my tongue, making him squirm as my tongue slid over his helmet. He then lifted me up as he moved his fingers back into my pussy, that was now moist with the excitement of what we were doing. He then told me that he will soon cum, and that he does not how long he can hold on, so he guided his ginormous cock into my awaiting pussy. He pumped himself up and down in my pussy, as he nestled his face into my breasts, his hands holding onto my ass as he thrust himself deeper into me, until he reached the moment of climax. With his head stuck firmly between my breasts, he shouted that he was going to cum; and at the time he ejaculated, he brought me to orgasm with just as much intensity. He then got dressed and just left without saying goodbye. It was then that I knew I had to get myself a straight or bi guy as a lover.

Yes, finally we had now finished the tour, and our very last show was where it all began. I was grateful the shows were over, but I truly missed my man friend, who helped me pass the lonely evenings, with him looking after me as a man should do.

Back at the Rainbow…

I got to the bar early, as over the next few days Felicia was coming over to see me, as I was going to give her first choice on my costumes; and what she did not want I was going to give to Dixie. I was all over the place that day, and once Roxy came into the bar, I felt a little bit better. We chatted for a while, and then it was time to get ready for the show; when I thought that I had really given her a bad time as of late, and it was not her fault. I also had to think of me, and I knew Roxy could only ever see the side of a gay man; because she did not truly understand what it is like being transgender.

She has a good heart, but I still felt she only had the mentality to understand her own gender, as she would never embrace the life of a transgender woman, so therefore somethings I could not talk to her about, because they went way above her station. I just sat on the chair as I looked in the mirror; and started to apply my make-up; thinking to myself that I am so glad that this is the last show.

Once I had finished, I looked at my reflection and just said.

"Well, my dear Ruby Passion, what the fuck do you look like? This is so not the true Ruby anymore, but I thank you for giving me some of the best times of my life. I will miss you Ruby Passion, and I will do you proud tonight."

The show then began, and everything was going well. I asked Roxy to take the lead role, as I just wanted to take a back seat; in which she did the Rainbow and me proud. Then I was all set for my last number and as I was waiting in the wings for the very last number to begin, Roxy was on stage and she had just finished her number when she went into a little bit of banter.

"I see they have let in royalty tonight folks. I can see you have got dolled up special tonight love. You shouldn't

*have bothered its only Ruby and me... What... what...
you even had special hair do's... Oh I see... Where have
you drag queens come from?* She asked
"*What. What... Dover... I am surprised you were not
stopped by passport control to see if you were hiding
stowaways in your beehives.*" She said as the audience
went wild.

I then managed to have one last vodka, when I pulled the
curtain back slightly to see Roxy picking on a couple
who looked like it was a 60s revival they were going to,
could not tell if they were drag queens or not as they
looked convincing.
She then started again as they spoke to her.

"*What... speak up honey... Oh you are going to a 60s
party afterwards, that explains it... Do I want to go? No
honey, I got a wooden leg, and if you get me on the
dancefloor doing all that spinning around, chances are
you will screw me to the floor.*"

I heard the crowd go wild, and then I just saw Roxy
wave her hand as to simmer the audience down.

"*Ladies and gentlemen, well it had come to the end of
another show, of another era. Foxy ladies started their
career on this stage, and tonight we finish out show here.
The stage that has given you all a wonderful exceptional
person; and it has been a pleasure to be her understudy,
and her friend. Now for the very last time at the Rainbow,
ladies and gentlemen I give to you my other partner in
crime. The one and only Miss Ruby Passion.*"

I then waited for the intro of the song and then walked out to a tremendous applause and a standing ovation. I was overwhelmed with how the crowd reacted; and felt very honoured that I had such a following, and had such love from them. They had to start the song twice because I could not compose myself. Then on the third time as the crowd began to quieten down, Roxy and I closed the show. Again, when it had finished, the crowd jeered and applauded, again giving us a standing ovation, where all of a sudden two of the bar staff came to the stage with the biggest of bouquets for me and Roxy. I just thanked them, and as I could not speak, I looked to Roxy and just said.

"I got to get out of here dear."

I then left the stage with Roxy, as the bastard DJ called us back three more times. On the third time I looked at him as to say no more. That was finally the end of Foxy Ladies, and a part of me was so very relieved. I placed my flowers in the dressing room, and then Roxy came into me and asked if I was alright. I was in tears, and with that she came over to me and put her arms around me and then congratulated me on the show, and then said.

"It just proves that your followers love you Ruby, you are going to be truly missed. You are a Rainbow legend, always remember that."

I could not explain why all the tears, but a big part of me knew that it was because I had held onto that life for

such a long time, it was like losing a big part of you.
I did enjoy my times on the stage, as I had flashbacks
from the very beginning of my career, and then with
Roxy, until this final last one tonight.

I was saying goodbye to my old life, as I now had my
new one to live, as now I did not have to hide behind the
mask, that once nurtured me, as I could be true to myself
now. I just looked at Roxy and told her I need a few
minutes before going to meet the crowd. Roxy gave me
another hug and told me that she would see me when I
came out. The times had now turned, as Roxy had kind
of become me, as she took the lead on the show, and she
went out to the bar first as they waited for me.

She had come a very long way since her first show, and I
was very proud of her, as I forgot about all the bitchiness,
I had for her. I composed myself, as all of a sudden
Johnny came into the room. He asked if I was ok, and I
told him all was well. I was just about getting into my
dress, when he told me that I did well and that my public
now waits. I walked out of the dressing room to the bar,
and as I got through the curtain.

Danni was at the bar where Johnny stood, with Roxy by
his side, just like we were on Roxy's debut. Then Roxy
announced me again over the mic, and the crowd stood
up in applause. I made my way to every one of them
giving them a hug and telling them thank you for their
support, before going to the royal box where I just sat
and relaxed with people coming up to me, as Roxy took
a backward step and stayed by the bar.

She allowed me to have that one night to myself.

It was now Christmas once again; and this time we had a Christmas away from Danni and Roxy, as Johnny spent Christmas day with Ellie and Di as I went to my parents. My father then dropped me back in the evening as he wished me all the luck in the world on my new venture. We had both been invited to go over to Danni's and Roxy's home, on New Year's Day; and it was there, that I broke the news to her about moving away.

I explained to Roxy, that it is something we both have to do, as I told her that London has lost its appeal, when Roxy was coming up with excuses to make us change our mind, so I looked at her and sarcastically said.

"We are four hours away by plane that's all, and if you are lucky enough to have a private jet, then it's even quicker."

I thought that went down like a lead balloon, as it had upset Roxy to see us be determined to leave the UK. I was not going to back down, and even looking over at Johnny; I gave him a choice. I told him he could still change his mind; and stay in London; or he could move to the Canaries with me. I told him that I would hold no grievances, but I hoped he would pick the latter.

Johnny really surprised me, when he told me that he would move with me; because I thought he would want to stay with Ellie and Danni; and of course, his precious Roxy.

So, it was settled; as we made plans over the coming weeks to start to pack, and to sell things that we would not be taking with us.

Roxy was so quiet, over those first few weeks, which

was not a surprise to me; because it was one situation, in which she did not get her own way. Danni and Johnny helped sort things out with the bar; and helped Ellie with any work she needed doing; and when he invited me out for lunch; he asked me if I was sure that I wanted to relocate. I looked at him and told him, that I indeed wanted to leave London, as the appeal of the big city, and the stage lights were nothing more but a shadow to me now. I wanted to live my life as Ruby, and wanted to go somewhere, where I could feel totally safe with who I was; and not have to look over my shoulder every single minute; because of the homophobes, and those who looked down on us transgender people.

Danni just placed his hand onto mine; and told me that he wished Johnny and me all the best. I thanked him; and told him that he did not have to be a stranger, as it was only a few hours away by plane; and this time I spoke from my heart, unlike the way I spoke to Roxy.

"You have been through a lot Ruby; it is about time you found yourself a bit of happiness. I will not lie, I will be sorry to see you go, but I know that you must live your life the way that you intended. If London no longer holds your heart, then you must find a place that will embrace you." He said, as his words warmed me to the core.

I told him that it was a new life, and a new beginning; and at the end of the day, if it does not work, then I always have a chance on coming back. I knew I had to give it a shot, because if I did not, I knew I would only kick myself later as I grew older; and would become bitter about it. I was so glad that Danni understood, and was grateful for his words; because for once they made me realize I was doing the right thing, and not being a silly queen like Roxy.

It was the summer of 1990 when we left, and I could not get through the barriers quick enough as I could not stand seeing all of them crying. I gave each and every one a hug and then walked through the barriers without waving. I just thought to myself finally, finally I can live my life now, and for once I am not going to regret it. We rented a property for six months, until the sale of my apartment and basement flat went through and was all above board. I asked my father to keep an eye on my properties; and I was told that he stayed there until the sale of them. A month later the money was in my account, so I could now look for something suitable for what I wanted. I decided that I wanted to look for an apartment or villa, with holiday apartments also in the grounds; but still having that bit of privacy. Johnny managed to find a bar, and it was only a couple of weeks before he opened it and he started trading. It was not big enough for cabaret, but he did make sure there was food available, just as much as drink, as he needed the extra revenue.

It was a further six months before I found the apartments that I was looking for, which I was successful with my offer; although it took a long time to get there.

We had rented longer than I wanted to, but finally there was a villa with six rental apartments on the grounds which had become available. I phoned the agent straight away and managed to get a viewing within seconds.

The villa was in very good shape, but all six apartments

needed re-decorating; and luckily for me it only meant a fresh lick of paint; so, I knew I had a bargain.

The furniture would last a few more years, and I was still a dab hand with a sewing machine so I could recover the couches and I had planned to make new bed throws.

I did not like the yellow and orange that seemed to be the Canaries colour, so I was going for white and blue which I felt was a lot crisper and bright; and gave that Mediterranean feel about the property; but as advised by the agent, I left the outside walls of the property white.

Just then Johnny rang me and told me to stay where I was as he was on his way over. He had panic in his voice; and I could not for the likes of me imagine what had happened. I hated it when he did that, as the decent thing would be to give you some sort of clue.

Around twenty minutes later he turned up and parked the car, then nearly taking the door off its hinges he said.

"Ruby, there's been an accident."

"Where, who?" I replied

"It's Danni." He replied, as I cut him short

"Oh God, what has Roxy been up to now. That girl is going to be the death of me. Can't they function on their own, without giving me grief all the time?"

"No Ruby, its Danni. He has been in a horrific car accident. He is fighting for his life in hospital." He said, now getting rather upset.

"Oh my God Johnny, what can we do?" I asked, as I began to panic

"I think we should go over there to see him, I think we need to give him and Roxy support." He replied, now shaking

"*I cannot go Johnny, I got the decorators in, and I cannot leave them on their own.*" I said sternly

"*Could you not delay it Ruby?*" He asked

"*No Johnny I cannot, I have got the decorators in, and I have got a travel company coming to visit me next week to take photographs of one of the properties to put into their brochure; so, I cannot cancel. You will have to go Johnny; I cannot leave the business.*" I told him

"*Oh, I see, you can't leave the business, but I can leave the bar.*" He said rather annoyed

"*Well, you got bar staff, and English ones at that. I am sure you can let one of them look after the bar for you; besides you have done so before when we went out for the night Johnny.*" I told him, knowing that I could not delay the contractors anymore, even though I knew I should go and see Danni, because he had done nothing wrong towards me.

"*Or you could look after the bar for me; and wait until Chris and Antonio come back from Egypt, as I am sure they will look after the bar.*" He said, still trying to get me to fly over to the UK with him.

"*Yes ok, I will look after the bar, and I will ask them if they can take over when they arrive, but I will need you to message them.*" I said, just to get him off my case.

"*And will you come over Ruby? I am sure Roxy would really appreciate your support.*" He asked, almost begging me to go over with him.

"*I will try Johnny; I will have to see how far the decorators get; and see about the bar. Let me see what I can do first.*" I told him, not really wanting to face Roxy, as my life had changed so much now, as I had now become who I wanted, and I did not want the dramas of Roxy interfering with my life.

Johnny then drove to the airport, to see about getting a flight. I was in total shock, and it had not sunk in that Danni was as bad as they had said. I just thought maybe Roxy has overreacted again, as she was such a dizzy queen, and thought until I get a message back from Johnny, I would have to tone it down and not worry too much. I was certain it was not that serious, and Roxy had over thought the situation. Maybe it was just a nasty bump or something in the car and not as exaggerated as mentioned.

After about an hour and a half, Johnny got back and told me he had to wait four days for a flight, as he could not get any earlier ones without staying at the airport every day as a standby passenger; and although he would have done that, he wanted to make sure he had a guaranteed seat. Those four days, Johnny was constantly phoning Ellie as Roxy had her phone switched off and no one could get hold of her for any details. His phone was never silent with Stuart, Ellie and Paul contacting him constantly, whilst Johnny kept letting them know that he will be over as quick as he could.

When it was the day of his flight, I wished him a safe flight, and told him to give Roxy my kindest regards.

I drove him to the airport that morning, and then rushed back as the decorators were going to be finishing off two more apartments. I did as Johnny said, by taking an hour away from my business, as I went to his bar and opened up for him. Once one of the boys turned up, I told him that he was going to have to run the bar on his own, and could he call the other barman to come in and help, as I then explained to them that Johnny had rushed to England because of his friend being involved in a road accident. I told them that I would come over later that evening and I would take over, as I told them I did need their help as I could not do both jobs all by myself.

I guess I was fortunate that Johnny had good staff, because without them, one of the businesses would have to close; and it was certainly not going to be mine.

Then this one morning that I opened up, I did the usual thing by putting out the tables as I greeted Felipe; who was the chef and who made the breakfasts before then going to his other job in San Agustin; and then I began to sort a few things out for Johnny's bar.

After about an hour I settled down to a bacon and egg sandwich offered to me by the chef as requested, and it was the best breakfast sandwich I had ever tasted.

I just thought you cannot beat a bit of Danish bacon; and I am so grateful you can buy it on the island. It was then that I thought that maybe I should ask him if he would like to work for me, as I was ok with cooking breakfasts, and my cleaner and part time kitchen help Marianne was ok, but I did need someone who knew what they were doing. I also wanted a Spanish chef, as in my complex I did offer to my guests both English and continental breakfasts. As I settled down to my bacon and egg sandwich, and the usual mooch through the English papers this figure stood before me.

"*Excuse me but are you open?*" This male voice said.
"*Yes dear, sit down and someone will be with you soon.*" I replied, as I looked over towards Felipe.

The guy then sat down as the Felipe made his way over to him to see what he wanted, as the other guy was only just setting up the bar. It was not until he spoke a little bit more that I seemed to recognise his voice from my past somewhere, then I just brushed it aside for a moment. Again, this guy began to speak to Felipe, when I started to have flashbacks. I looked up and to my shock I recognised this guy, a guy that I had not seen for such a long time.

"Brian, what are you doing here?" I asked
"Hello Ruby, I thought it was you." He replied, as he looked at me and smiled.
"What are you doing here? Where is the wife? Are you on holiday?" I asked.
"So many questions, you never change Ruby. I am here on my own, as I needed a holiday." He told me, looking almost like the Brian I used to know, but with a few bags under his eyes, that were not there before.
"On your own Brian?" I asked
"Yes Ruby, me and the wife divorced; and I have moved out of the house. I went to find you in London but found out, that you had since moved out of the country. I then went to one of the parties that Roxy held and managed to get Paul to one side; and cutting a long story short he told me that you and Johnny moved here." He said, now looking at me as my memories came flooding back of our times together.
"Blimey Brian, I never thought that you would have ever divorced, your marriage seemed perfect to me.
What happened?" I asked

"*It just did not work out Ruby. She was given another position in yet another private school and wanted me to move with her. This time I put my foot down and told* her *I was not moving anymore. We had a big argument, and after so many months of fighting, I called it a day as it was interfering with my work.*" He explained

"*I am so sorry Brian, it cannot have been easy, and I can relate to the arguments as I have had my share too with Johnny.*" I told him, as I sat down next to him.

"*Ah yes Johnny, where is Johnny now Ruby?*" He asked, as he had a bit of a mischievous boyish look about him

"*Have you not heard? Danni has been in a road accident, and Johnny has gone over to see what's going on; and to give Roxy any support that she needs.*" I replied

"*I did not know Ruby; I have been here for two weeks now; and it has taken me this long to pick up the courage to come into the bar. I saw Johnny a few times, but I was at that bar next door keeping a low profile, hoping I would get a glimpse of you.*" He answered, sorry to hear the news that I had been given.

"*I do not really come onto the scene here Brian; I do not like the gay scene. I have my own business in the next town as I have a villa and rental apartments. I prefer it over there as it is quieter, and I have more of a life with the locals and being a part of their community than a gay community. I have lived on the gay community for so long to be accepted, where here I can mingle as a local without having to be classed as gay or tranny.*" I told him.

"*I am impressed Ruby; you are really living your dream; and I am very proud of you. Something told me a long time ago when I first saw you, that you would make more of your life than any woman I had ever seen. There was just something about you Ruby, so congratulations are in order."* He replied.

We then got into conversation, as I then told him to come back with me to my apartments, as the other bar staff will be here soon and I do not want any questions from them, as the other one who works here, Tom, is a really nosey queen as he sticks his nose into everyone's business. We then agreed that as soon as they turned up, he would act as a customer so not as to get them thinking too much; and then he pointed to another bar in which he said he would go to that bar and wait for me.
An hour later the Tom turned up and I had one drink with both Tom and Craig as I then handed the keys over to the head barman Craig. I then said my goodbyes to the three of them, as I then went out of view and met up with Brian in one of the restaurants on the higher level of the Yumbo centre. Brian then told me that he only had another week on the island, and he would have to go back to England, as he still had things to sort out. Just then I had a text come through and it was Johnny, so I looked at the text and began to cry.

"What's the matter Ruby?" Brian asked
"It's Danni, oh Brian its Danni; he has died." I cried.
"Oh, Ruby I am so sorry to hear that, come here." He replied, trying to comfort me.

I rested my head into his shoulder as he comforted me from my tears, I told him that I cannot go over to England as I was looking after the bar, and I still had my business; and unlike Johnny I could not leave my business to be run by anyone because I did not have anyone I could trust.

That night we went out together, and when we walked along the seafront hand in hand; and I just thought that this was all my dreams in one coming true for me at last. I have a guy who wants me to be me, and with the sad news of Danni, he comforted me and kept me close to him making sure I was alright without being selfish and pushing for anything more. Somehow, I knew there was a reason for me to stay behind, but I never would have assumed that it was because of Brian being here.

The last time I spoke to Brian, he was leaving London ready to relocate to Oxford with his wife. I just knew as I had a gut feeling that I should stay behind; and it was not a feeling that told me it was because of our business's; it was that gut feeling you get when something out of your control is going to happen.

I had told Johnny to stay with Roxy, and that I would look after the business and the bar. I told him that when he was ready to come back to bring Roxy with him, as I was sure she could have done with the break.

At first, I thought he was going to tell me that he and Roxy were not coming over; and that he was going to stay with her a little longer, but alas it was nothing of that nature. However, I did often feel a little guilty by not dropping everything; and going over to England with Johnny. But I also felt that Danni and Roxy had become a little distant towards me as phone calls were not as regular as they used to be, and news was either by a letter now and then as Roxy was too busy with gallivanting to America every few months.

She was living her life as she wanted, with no thought to those who put her where she was. It had been such a long time since I saw them both, and I often would have welcomed that phone call from Roxy; but nothing ever came of it, so I guess it is true what they say when they say out of sight out of mind.

I still mourned for Danni however, but I had to do it in my own way; and I needed to do it away from all of the people we knew back in England.

The closeness that we all once had was no longer that close anymore, as I had got on and built a life for myself, and it was much different to the life I had in England. Brian really comforted me that night, as he listening to me whilst I waffled on about Danni and Roxy and how we had somehow drifted apart. How I was sorry for her loss, as Danni was a very special guy; and I really did have to think about my life now as no one else had considered my feelings. They just expected me to up sticks and travel and be a part of the crowd once more, with no thought about my business, or how the news had affected me.

No Roxy had her fair share of shoulders to lean on, she did not need mine, besides, she would be coming back with Johnny for a week or so after the funeral; and I could then give her my shoulder away from everyone else looking over and wanting to know what is going on. When Brian and I had finished our meal, I told him that I was just going to check on the bar, before I thought about heading back home. The boys had done a marvellous job, and so I took the takings out of the safe and then left the bar letting them know I would be back the next day, as I also knew they were competent enough

to lock the bar up without me looking over them.
It did not seem to be much of a busy night, as most of
the holiday makers were over the road at the cabaret bar.
I then told the boys, that if they wanted, they could go
and enjoy the rest of the night, even though they said
they did not mind working a little longer. I advised them
that I thought it best too close and I would inform
Johnny that they had worked their hours so no money
would be deducted from their wage, but it was up to
them as I did not mind them going home a little earlier
than normal. As I got to my car Brian asked me if I was
alright, in which I told him I was fine just a little sad
about Danni. He then told me that he had best get back
to his hotel, and if I needed anything, that he insisted that
I must call him. I drove Brian to his hotel which was
only a short distant away, and as we arrived, I just
looked at him and asked him to stay with me that night.
He looked at me with a happy, yet strange look, as he
asked me if I was sure, as he was brushing my hair out of
my eyes. I told him that I was sure; and that I did not
want to be alone. Then asked him to go and grab some
clothes; and then come back and stay with me overnight.
Brian then placed his head into the car as he gave me a
kiss on the cheek, as he told me he would not be too long.
I waited about fifteen minutes when Brian came back
with a small holdall.

"Are you sure about this Ruby?" He asked
*"Yes, Brian I am sure, now put your bag in the back and
let's go home."* I replied.

I then drove us back to the villa; and was glad that I would be having company for the evening. Brian and I sat up most of the night talking, as he told me that he was glad I had invited him back as he was so worried about me. That evening was finished off with a nice bottle of chilled champagne, as we chatted contently. Brian had come to respect me and respect me as the woman I always was, and he never attempted to force himself upon me, instead when it was time to retire to bed, he asked me where the guest room was.

That proved to me, that this was the man I wanted to spend the rest of my life with. I now realised that I no longer loved Johnny the way I used to; and I felt we were both living a lie for the sake of each other.

I thought to myself that when Roxy comes over with him, I will get her to go out as much as she can, so I do not have to listen to her whine and drone on. When she has spent a few weeks relaxing, and it is time for her to go home, then and only then will I confront Johnny about breaking up. I thought that it was finally the time to put an end to the charade that we had both been living, as I knew Johnny also deserved to live a life in which he would be happy; and there were plenty of boys on the island who would snap him up, as I too had seen how his young manager had been looking at him; and it was not as a manager owner situation.

His bar manager, and head barman Craig, had eyes for Johnny, and for once I was not going to step in his way and try and save something in which I knew was over. Through the week, I only went into Playa Del Ingles just to see if the boys were ok, and as there were no problems, I left them to it as I went about my own business. I was a little bit of a daydreamer as I went into my own world, reminiscing about the times I had spent with Danni, looking back at the funny moments that had occurred as well as how he listened to me; and how he made me feel good about myself. I would often just walk down to the beach, sit in one of the many café/restaurants and look out towards the distant horizon, as Danni engulfed my thoughts as they made me smile, and also brought a tear or two to my face.

I was also pleased that Brian was on the island, as I meant I could chat with someone who did not know the history in detail about my Rainbow family; and spoke to me without being prejudicial on the matter.

Brian listened and he helped me through my bad times, still without trying to force the issue of whether we would be intimate or not.

Brian and I were getting closer and closer, as we also had those special walks along the seafront, walking together hand in hand with a gentle kiss here and there. The decorators had since finished my apartments, and the agents had taken the photographs ready for next year's season. It was much better now to just lock up and not worry if you were going to be broken into, which made it more of a nicer evening when Brian and I went out into Maspalomas town or into San Agustin.

I remember from the time we lived briefly in Maspalomas that there was a lovely Irish restaurant that Johnny and I frequented, so it made a change to go there as well as to stay local in my own town of San Agustin. Brian had let me know his intentions clearly, as he was now hoping that we would start dating as he told me that he had never forgotten about me.

Just on the off chance, he was hoping that I would say yes, because by now he had already struck up an interview in the local hospital; and that they had since offered him a job. He was now waiting on me, to see where we stood before going ahead with his proposal, as he told me that it would be pointless working on the island if there was no chance with me and him getting together as a couple, as his main reason for coming over to the island was to do just that.

I just told him that he should still go ahead with his job proposal, despite what my answer would be, as this island was in need of outstanding surgeons such as himself. I then told him that I needed to have that long talk with Johnny, and to explain to him how I now felt with regards the two of us. He told me that he would consider it over the next few days, as he would have to go back to England to sort out formalities and to give notice, as well as trying to find somewhere here on the island to live until he could find his own property in which he could settle. I then let him know about the agency that offered me the villa in Maspalomas; and thought that maybe they would have something for him nearer the hospital.

So, with that sorted we enjoyed that last week together, going out for meals, walking along the promenade, and even getting silly and loved up by walking on the beach and taking a quick paddle in the sea. It felt as though all of Brian's efforts to woo me, were working, as my heart skipped a beat each time we were together.

That last week with Brian, he gained my respect as never once did he try anything on with me or make me feel uncomfortable. After a few nights sleeping in the guest room, I invited Brian to spend the rest of the nights with me in my bedroom.

That first night he shared my bed, he only cuddled up with me making sure that I was ok and not to upset over events that had arose with Danni. For once it felt nice having someone hold me and like everything about me; and although I would have jumped at the offer to have him make love to me, I also knew that I could really wait for him without spoiling it by having sex.

I wanted to be wooed and to be romanced, as I did not think a quick night of intimacy was right. I wanted to do things properly; and in time I would tell Johnny.

I just wanted to make sure this was indeed the right thing to do; and that it was right for both Brian and me. I just wanted to make sure he was really the right one, as again I was not too fussed, as I knew I could have any man on that island. I wanted to get to know Brian all over again, and I wanted him to get to know me because I was not the Ruby, he once knew all those years ago.

I was not looking forward to him going back to England, and when that day came, I was so unhappy.

He kept telling me he would be back in six months' time, and that he would text me every day. When I saw him go through the barriers, I just wanted to run after him but then turned around as I sent him a text telling him to hurry up and come back.

I had only been back a few hours, when Johnny text me to let me know that he was coming back to Gran Canaria in the next day or two; and that he would be bringing Roxy with him, as he felt she should not be on her own. I was not too concerned, as I was now on a high and I knew she would only be here for a week or two, so I text him back to let Johnny know that would be fine and that I would make the spare room up for her.

How wrong could I have been?

No, it was not one week, it was not even two weeks, as by now it was coming up to nearly two months and I was beginning to get really fucked off with her.

The first week or two was nice as we spent some time together, but I also got her out of the villa as I did not want her moping around all the time, as it was starting to bring me down, as she continuously cried when we approached the subject of Danni. I just thought that she should hurry up and get over him, because life was for the living and not the dead, as she stayed in bed some mornings until 11am, and some days hardly said a word to me. Then this one day, I just could not take it anymore, and the inevitable happened. Roxy and I had our first argument, which to be honest was a long time coming, I can tell you.

"I thought that you said it was really nice to see me Ruby." Roxy said

"Yes, Roxy it is nice to see you, I thought you were only coming for a week or so, not fuckin move in." I told her

"I have not moved in Ruby; I am still in mourning can you not understand that?" She replied

"Danni has gone Roxy, now get over it." I said, snapping at her in the process.

"What has happened to you Ruby, you never used to be like this?" She replied, looking like a little girl, with a frown on her, as though she had been told off.

"I am not the Ruby you knew all those years ago, I have changed Roxy." I replied

364

"*You can say that again Ruby.*" She said rather bitchy
"*If you don't like it Roxy then fuck off. In fact, Roxy why don't you fuck off to the bar and be with Johnny; because I know you fancy him, because I am not daft, I have seen you looking at him with those seductive eyes of yours, eyeing him up and down from the very first time you laid eyes on him.*" I scowled
"*I really don't know you anymore Ruby. If you did not want me here, you only have to say. As for Johnny he has been a big support to me, as have my other boys and he is a friend, he is family Ruby, how can you say such hurtful things? I do not know where you got that information from, but it is so wrong, and no you are not daft, you are just an evil queen who has gone crazy.*"
She said, as her argumentative streak flooded through her veins
"*Yeah, right Roxy. And you and your boys, still the same old Roxy acting like the queen bee, trying to be something you're not. It would not surprise me if you had not been fucking them also. You and your boys, I think it is about time you wound your neck in Roxy.*" I replied, showing her that I still had that streak about me too
"*You have turned nasty Ruby; those pills have cooked your brain.*" She said as she looked at me dirty
"*Look Roxy I have a friend coming over and he doesn't like gay people, so why don't you disappear for a few hours. Johnny is a nothing but a worthless gay man, we have not had sex for ages as he wants me to take it up the ass, which I no longer do because I am not a gay man. I don't love him anymore Roxy; so, take the bastard off my hands for Christ's sake. He is a pathetic*

gay man like a lot of you people are, and I have found myself a real man now who is going to be a top surgeon here on the island. So, fuck off to the bar please Roxy and let me get on with my life with Brian." I shouted back to her

"*You…you, fuckin bitch Ruby, does Johnny know about this, have you told Johnny?*" She said, now rather mad, as I slapped her across the face

"*No not yet, I will tell him in my own time and it's no fuckin concern of yours. As for the bitch remark, yeah don't ever forget it Roxy. It was this bitch that put you where you are Roxy, never forget that. Now do me a favour and fuck off.*" I cursed, as I made my way to the bedroom.

Next thing I knew was the door had slammed, and when I went back into the lounge Roxy had gone.
I really was expecting all hell to break loose now, especially as I had now told Roxy about Brian; and I knew she would not keep that juicy information to herself. I was totally wrong however, Roxy never did tell Johnny; and after that argument Roxy gave me my space, to the point we never spoke again.
Whenever Johnny went to work, she would get herself dressed and then go out, with no words exchanged between us. There was definitely an atmosphere now what with the argument that was really long overdue, but I only told her a few home truths.
After a few more days Roxy decided to go back to England, and I could not have been happier. This was going to be the only one argument that Roxy would not have won; and in reality, I really did not give a damn

about her. I know she was not all innocent, and it really would not have surprised me if she was not carrying on with her so-called boys; and then I thought about the situation with Adam and Danni; and as much as I loved Danni, I actually wondered how much of it was true, and was it just a smoke screen they put up to stop me knowing their shady goings on with one another.

No Roxy had lost this argument; and for once it proved that she was not invincible.

On the day she left, I just wished her a safe flight, as I told Johnny to drive carefully. She looked at me with ice cold eyes as she just said to me goodbye, as she then turned her back on me and got into the car, where she then waited for Johnny.

Johnny asked me if I wanted to come along, and I just told him that I had said my goodbyes, and I do not like farewells at airports. He gave me a kiss on the cheek; as I saw Roxy look at me as though she had eaten a sour apple; and then proceeded to give me daggers.

Then they just left, as Johnny took charge of her cases and they drove off, as I thought to myself, even to the end she thinks she is better than anyone else, as she sits in the car waiting for Johnny to put her cases in the boot, when the idle bitch could have put them in the car herself.

I was so relieved when she had gone as I had my home back; and I was fed up of going down memory lane with her, as she spoke about Danni, and the things we all used to do. I no longer wanted to hear about that part of my life, as I knew that it was our past memories that make our future dreams come true. I wanted to live in the future, and not reminisce about the past, as I wanted to forget all about it, so yes, I was over the moon when Roxy finally put her ass into gear and flew back home. I just thought to myself, all that money she has, and she is still acts like a dumb blonde. I thought she would have at least tried to get a personality transplant.

Then there was my Johnny, how he made me want to throw up as he followed her around like a little lap dog on heat, but part of him still tugged at me as strangely enough I still loved the man. He had been my boyfriend and stayed with me for all those years; and it was hard at times as I thought about if I was doing the right thing.

Another year went by, and Johnny had now moved into the spare room. He worked very late at the bar most evenings now and when he got in, he used to wake me up, so I then suggested that he goes into the west wing of the villa as it would be better.

Over the coming months we just decided that it was best, and although sometimes there was that little sparkle with Johnny, it never amounted to anything as he always went for my ass and left my tits and pussy alone. Brian had complications in England and his move was delayed by a year, but I was so glad when I had that special text, that told me he was coming over that following April, as only seeing for a weekend on a monthly basis was not doing us any good as we clearly wanted to be together.

They had sold the house and he had given her a settlement, in which she was happy with. He had given notice at the health centre and hospital back in England; and decided he would have a few month's break before starting work at the local hospital. The hospital had kept him on record; and told him that once he was ready to move his job would still be there for him; and for him not to worry as they understood the hassle relocating can have when you come up against unforeseen obstacles; and I just could not wait for him to arrive, that I am sure I nearly let it slip a few times when having a chat with Johnny.

In those months I waited for Brian to move to the island, I had a surprise visit from my family. I had a phone call the night before to let me know what flight they would be on. Luckily, I had enough room in the villa to accommodate them, and I was so very excited as it had been a few years since I had seen them. I could not wait to see my brother, as again it had been such a long time. He continued to write to me and phone me when he could, and he told me that he and Alison were planning on getting married real soon. I told Johnny about my family coming over, and he suggested he had one of the apartments because of him coming back late from the bar. I just told him that it would be fine, as I hardly saw him anyway.

The first few days of my family being there, we spent it looking around the island. My father could not believe how well I looked, and how well I had done for myself with my home and business. I told them that they would most likely not see Johnny as he goes out at around 6am to help Felipe get the breakfasts ready at the bar, and I do not see him again until very early the following morning as he often works twenty hours a day, apart from coming in for a siesta.

My father thought it was a strange set up, but knew how relaxed the people were, and how life was different here on the island as they have been to Spain many times before. But they still thought that Johnny would have made more of an effort; after all it was not as though they visited me all the time. I just apologised; and told them that they may see him at some point, but not to hold it against him as he was a very hard worker and a very proud businessman. It was then suggested that we all go out for a meal sometime; and that we should go to Johnny's bar and invite him along. I just played it by ear, as I really had no plans to go into the Yumbo centre just to ask Johnny to come out, but I knew our paths would cross at some point of my family visiting.

My mother wanted to visit the Yumbo centre, as she had been told that they have lovely restaurants and shops there too, so we arranged to go there the following day. It was not until the third night of them being here that we decided to go out for a meal. My dad asked me if Johnny would be coming along, where I just told him that he had the bar to look after, and he did not want to get in the way, as he knew how much I had missed my family that he thought it would be nice for us to spend it together.

My mother and father were not one for the noisy gay scene, so we stayed away from the bar and clubs and instead we decided that we would walk over the road, to one of the local Canarian bars, which gave us a feeling of the community spirit, rather than a lot of drunken gay men making a fool out of themselves.

Mom and dad had already seen the outrageous sights of the gay bars, with men half-dressed and of course kissing like there was no tomorrow, as well as seeing some girls from the transgender community as well as mistaking drag queens as transgender, so it was a bit of an eye opener at first.

I got myself ready and once I had come out of the bedroom, my brothers jaw just dropped as he told me I was stunning. I wore a beautiful white flowing cocktail dress, with the jewellery that Danni had brought me that first Christmas we were all together. And I had a pair of beige four inch heels which matched my handbag.

We did not need to order a cab, as we were only going over the road; and then after we had had a drink or too, we were going to walk down to the seafront and then go into one of my favourite Spanish restaurants.

The usual foot crew were there along the way, as they tried getting you in to their bars, but we just brushed them away as we made our way to 'Los Canarios.'

As soon as we got there, it was the usual hustle and bustle as this was a local's restaurant; so I just stopped and said.

"Hola, es Alejandra equi Senior?"
"Ah Alejandro, Si Senora." He said, as he showed us to a table.

Just then Alejandro came out to greet me, as he had done so many times before. We started speaking in Spanish right away, as I then introduced him to my parents and my brother. He then told me to get up and he offered us one of the bigger tables on the balcony, which is usually only used for family, so I was very happy indeed.

We had a clear view of the sea and the people walking along the promenade; and as the Spanish men are very much gentlemen, he held the chair out for my mother, as my brother did the same for me.

This was more luxurious than the regular dining area as

the seating area was beautiful wooden tables with matching chairs that were padded. Downstairs were glass tables and cold chairs. I asked everyone what they wanted and then I looked at Alejandro to grab his attention.

"Hola Alejandro. Pedria I favour pedr una Martini y limonada, una gran Cerveza, una gran Whiskey, y un gran Vodka and coca cola. Ademas de una botella de vino tinto y blanco. Gracias."

My mother and father just looked at me and my dad said.

"When did you learn to speak Spanish Ruby?"
"At school dad, you did not think I wasted a good education, did you?" I replied
"Not at all Ruby, I am just shocked at how fluent you are, and I am very proud of you." He replied
"What did you order Ruby?" Mom asked.

I told her that I just ordered a martini and lemonade for her, a pint of lager for Marty, a double scotch for dad and a vodka and coke for me, plus, a bottle of white and red for the table.
My dad then said that he knew I would not be a worry here in Spain, as he knew I could get by. He told me that they had also thought about moving over to Spain once he retired, and I suggested he come here to the Canaries. Both mother and father said they would consider it, and just then Marty started to get up to his childish antics like he used to when we were young. Mother looked at

the two of us and started to laugh, and this was the first time I had ever seen her laugh in so many years.

Dad was getting a little merry, as he was getting used to the Canaries double shots, and Marty and I were beginning to laugh at him, especially when mother told him to tone it down because of him getting slightly too tiddly, as he began asking if he would make a good drag queen, as he saw a few scurry past, as they hailed a cab to go into Playa del Ingles. Mom and dad were going on about our childhood and for once I was glad to hear it, and not because I wanted to hear about Tony, but how girly I was and how Marty and I were such little devils, even though I told my mom that it was Marty who egged me on. We were all laughing over those stories, and a few hours later mother suggested she take dad home as he was getting a little loud again. It did make Marty and I laugh, as we had never seen dad drunk before or even act so silly come to that; and we laughed at mother, when she began putting him in his place.

Marty then looked at me and said.

"Do you fancy going for a drink Ruby?"
"I would like that Marty; do you want to go to the Yumbo centre?" I asked him
"The gay centre you mean Ruby?" He replied
"Yes, do you want to go there?" I asked again.
"Not my scene Ruby, let's go to a nice quiet bar and talk, I noticed there was an English bar just down the road if you're up to it?" He told me.

We told mother that we were going to stay out for a while, and mother just asked Marty if he would help her get dad home. I told him to go ahead as I would stay here and wait for him, and I would have a word with Alejandro and apologise, as dad couldn't take his Spanish drink that well.

Thirty minutes later Marty got back to the restaurant and after I gave the staff a kiss and a big tip I left with my arm under Marty's where we went to the English bar.

I had a lovely evening just catching up with Marty as he asked how things were with Johnny.

"Are you happy Ruby?" He asked, now being that concerning brother in which I had missed.

"No Marty? I just put up with it." I replied

"Why Ruby, we all deserve to be happy. What's wrong between you and Johnny?" He asked again

"There is nothing there anymore Marty. The love went a long time ago, and we hardly see each other now. On the few times that he got a little bit fresh with me it was just the old Johnny. He wanted me to take it up the ass, and I am not like that anymore." I explained as I had a tear in my eye

"You have to say something Ruby; you cannot live like this anymore. You have gone through so much to become who you are and still you are unhappy. I am sorry if I am being a nasty, but you need to tell him to fuck off. You are not gay, and he needs to find a gay dude." He explained, knowing that either Johnny needed to change, or I had to end the relationship.

"I have a secret Marty, and I am going out of my mind as I have not told anyone." I told him

"*Oh, you have a secret, since when?*" He asked, now with his eyebrows raised, as he tapped me on the arm as he asked me to spill the beans.

"*I have met someone else. And I am hoping it is going to take off, but I am not sure.*" I told him, relieved that I had finally told someone, who would not judge me.

"*Why are you not sure Ruby?*" Marty asked

"*Because I have history with Johnny, and I just want to be loved. I do not want a gay relationship, but I do want a relationship Johnny before I get too fuckin old to do anything.*" I told him

"*Ruby again you are still living in Johnny's world, it is clear it is not working. To be fair to you and to Johnny you really must tell him Ruby. How many times do I have to tell you to think of yourself? You always put others first. Now fuck them Ruby and live your own life. Do you want me to have a word with Johnny, because I will tell him to fuck off?*" He said getting annoyed

"*No Marty I know I have to do it, sometimes it is hard letting go of the past, especially when you are unsure of the future.*" I told him

"*You have done it before Ruby, you went from Tony too Ruby and that is one of the biggest steps you could ever take.*" He said as he whispered in my ear.

"*I know Marty, but I am s*cared." I replied

"*So, who is this other person Ruby?*" he asked

"*His name is Brian, he was my doctor in London, and he knows all about Ruby. He is moving over here as he has got a job at the local hospital as a surgeon.*" I explained.

"*Go for it Ruby, a doctor eh, if he makes you happy Ruby, go for it. You cannot keep living like you are now. I knew there was something wrong when we got to the villa. Just do it Ruby, be happy.*" He told me.

I just got hold of him and gave him the biggest hug I could; and knew that I had to move on. I needed to go forward and finally get rid of a past, that I still have tried to hold onto more for comfort sake rather than for my sake. I had to choose from a life of unhappiness, and a life of the gay scene I so long had turned my back on; or a life with a man who saw me as a woman; and wanted to be with me. There was not much of a debate, and so I decided I must do this, as I now had a CHOICE, and one I knew would be the right move.
So, my family left the island after having a wonderful holiday; and I told them not to leave it so long next time; and I too would come over to England and visit them.
I did not want to let mother and father know about Brian just yet, as I still needed to make sure that we were right together; but I was sure I had to end it with Johnny no matter what.
A few more months had gone by, and again I very rarely saw Johnny. He hardly came into the villa; and stayed in one of the apartments until I had them booked.
Brian had since moved back to the island, and I was so glad that I had someone to talk to. Again, we continued with getting to know each other, and our relationship was blooming. We often went for meals just outside where I lived, as he had by now purchased an apartment by the hospital in which he worked which lucky for us both was in San Agustin.
After a further six months I knew that I had to do it as the time was right, I knew that I really had to tell Johnny

that we were through as it was hurting me and getting in the way of what I could have, and who I could be happy with. I was now 100% sure that Brian and I were on the right track, as he even brought up marriage and kids a few times. I knew that I was doing the right thing, and after texting my brother, he called me a few days later because he was concerned about me; and after such a lengthy chat I was never more certain about things as I was now. I now had that chance of happiness with a man, a possible husband, and children in which we said we would adopt. I had money, and a business, and with Brian being one of the leading surgeons at the hospital; that now I also had respect and status alongside Brian. I felt I could finally live my dream and it was a week later that whilst I was plucking up the courage to tell Johnny that I think we need to talk, when it was him who surprised me.

"I think we need to talk Ruby; things are not as they should be. We have not made love in about a year; and you have become distant with me. You no longer come into the bar, and I have no idea what is going on in that mixed up head of yours." Johnny said
"Yes, we do need to talk. It just is not working. We have not made love Johnny because I have tried with you, and you just want my god damn ass, and will not make love to me as a woman." I said, as I was interrupted
"Because I am gay and don't want." He replied, as I cut him off
"I have not finished Johnny, you asked me a question so let me answer. You will not make love to me as a woman, so I no longer offer you sex. I do not come into the bar,

because that is a part of my life; that I no longer want to be a part of. I am fed up of the fucking dizzy drag queens, the camp gay guys and the whole lot of you. I am a woman and do not want that in my life." I replied sarcastically

"You have really changed Ruby; I do not know who you are anymore. You get me to leave London to set up here, you get me to buy a bar in which you want nothing to do with it, and you live a life of a real woman, when you were born a man. Ruby you pretend to be something you are not; and hide away from your past. You chose this life Ruby not me." He said, now becoming rather angry, as his temper flared.

"I chose nothing Johnny. If you did not want to come here, then you should have ended it a long time ago. And you're your information, being inside a man's body was not a choice Johnny." I said, as I began to get annoyed with him.

"You always had a choice Ruby. You used your cock because you had a choice. You fucked my ass because you had a choice. You dressed as Ruby because you had a choice. And you lived a gay life because you had a choice, so don't play that fuckin card with me." He yelled.

"Oh, give it a rest Johnny; I did that to get on with my life; to make life more bearable. And yes, that was a choice, but you, you pathetic man, being born in the wrong body was never a choice, how many more times do I have to spell it out?" I replied

"Then if that is the case, you should have finished with me a long time ago, instead of leading me on." He told me, trying to make me feel guilty.

"I never led you on you bastard, I had to live my life to the best of my ability, and it was not for me living a lie like I had to for so many years. Being transgender is not a choice Johnny it was never a choice; it is a birth defect and one I had no control over. If you ever had heart problems; then you would have been given heart surgery. If you ever had lung problems; then you would have been given a lung transplant. If your kidneys fail, then they would have been replaced. But if you are transgender, they say it is all in your fucking mind." I said, now rather pissed off with him.

"You do have a choice, you always have a choice Ruby, and now you choose to make excuses Ruby." Johnny said.

"No, YOU have a choice Johnny. You can choose whether to be gay bisexual or straight. You can choose whether to stay with me as a woman, or you can make the choice to fuck off and find a gay boy." I shouted

"I still love you Ruby, I just do not like what you have become." He replied

"NO Johnny, you love my ass; and I am not taking it anymore. I want to be made love to like the woman I am, and not for what I used to be. For thirty years you have butt fucked my ass and it has got to change; and if you don't like it you can fuck off." I cursed

"I wanted you to stay like Roxy, Ruby. But you never ever thought how I was feeling, or what I was going through when you wanted to become a woman." He told me, now bringing that bitch of a Roxy into the argument.

"Oh, you had to bring her name into it didn't you. I am not like Roxy, as Roxy is a man in drag; and I have always been a woman. I did cabaret to survive to save up and pay for surgery. I sold my apartment to get a new

life and a new start, as I was fucked off with the old life. It would not surprise me if you were fucking Roxy behind my back, when she came over here; as she was always at the bar with you." I yelled, now hitting him where I knew it hurt.

"*That is so cruel Ruby. Roxy and I never got it on, she was my best mate's girlfriend and wife. It was you who made her come over to the bar, as you did not want to spend any time with her making her feel uncomfortable. But come to think of it, yes, it would have been fantastic to be with her, because she was and always will be a better man and woman than you ever were.*" He replied, now letting me know just how much he thought of me.

"*You, fuckin bastard Johnny. Yeah, she was Danni's boyfriend and wife, but it did not stop you eyeing her up all the time. I bet as soon as Danni died, you were pleased because you could have your chance with her. I would not surprise me if you were fucking her before and after the funeral.*" I told him now very angry

"*You fucking wicked bitch Ruby, she is supposed to be your friend. How can you be so fucking bitchy and say that?*" He shouted at me

"*Because I can, and she is no fucking friend of mine Johnny. She never calls me anymore, and she lives in her own little world. She is a gay man, and I am a woman, we are two different people.*" I told him

"*You are really something Ruby, where did all this hate come from?*" Johnny asked

"*She swans around in her designer clothes and diamond jewellery, thinking she is lady muck, when she is nothing but a gay man who made quite a lot of money from her dead partner. If it was not for me, she would not be where she is today, and do I get a thank you? No, I fucking don't.*" I replied in a rage.

"*It's all about you isn't it Ruby? You're fucking jealous of her. You could have had exactly the same as she had, but you got wrapped up in your own little selfish world.*" He said, turning words against me.

"*She was all Danni; and never me, now Fuck off Johnny and leave me alone.*" I replied.

"*Oh my God Ruby you are jealous of Roxy. You are jealous with what she had with Danni, and why as you said they are gay.*" He said, as I now had had enough.

"*FUCK OFF and leave me alone Johnny, it's over I have had enough. Pack your fucking bags and get out of my home.*" I said as I stormed out of the lounge.

Johnny then grabbed a few things and just left, as I heard him slam the door behind him. I gave him a week to get his things out of my house, or I would put them all in the trash. It seemed very quiet without Johnny being there, but as strange as it seemed; he was not really there anyway as he slept in the spare room. I just sat down and gathered my thoughts; and questioned if I had done the right thing. Reality then kicked in, and I knew I had done the right thing, as Johnny and I had not been intimate, in such a long time. I was now Ruby, and not the Ruby I was all those years ago. I just thought I have finally done it; I have finally got rid of my past, so I can now concentrate on my future. I then went over to the drink's cabinet, and poured myself a very large vodka, as I picked up my phone and text Brian to see how he was. About an hour later Brian texted me back to let me know he is going to be busy most the week as he would be in surgery. He hoped I was ok, and he let me know that he loved me and he would text me every night after he had finished at the hospital.

I then messaged Brian back, to let him know that I had thrown Johnny out; but that his things were still in the villa. Brian just let me know that he was there for me; and was pleased that I had gone through with what I intended; and that he was sorry that he could not be with me due to work.

I knew if I asked him to come over and stay, he would have done, but I also knew he would have much preferred that Johnny was truly out of the way.

I knew Brian was busy and this did not worry me, as I too had a lot of things to do around the villa, and with the apartments; that it kept my mind of things throughout the day. Brian was my rock, as through the evenings, or when he was not working; he would text me to see if things were alright, and then ask if he could phone me.

A week later, Johnny text me to say he was coming for his things, so I made sure I was out; telling him to be gone when I came back. I just text him back letting him know that I would not be there, so he was free to get his things without any confrontation, as I no longer wanted to argue.

I went for a walk to the beach, as my guests were all out for the day, so I did not need to do anything.

The guests did not need laundry until the next day, and my maid would turn the beds around anyway, so I had no need to stay in the villa. I did not want any confrontation with Johnny, as I had had my fill of arguments; so, I just left the villa to go to the beach. I stopped for a little bit of lunch, as I admired the views

just down the road from my apartment in San Agustin.
I walked the long peaceful and beautiful walk of the
promenade of Playa San Agustin, relaxing along the way
as I was offered a chair in the restaurants that joined the
sunny promenade.

After about two hours I had a text from Johnny saying
goodbye, and he hoped I sorted my twisted head out; and
he thought I would have had the decency to have been in
when he dropped the keys off. I just ignored him and
returned to the villa, as the gardener arrived to cut the
lawns to the rental apartments. I know it made me look
like a bitch, but there was nothing further to do or say.
The relationship was over; and I was no longer the
person that Johnny wanted me to be. I had come a long
way; and I had not paid all of that money, only to be
called a lesser person than Roxy. I was who I had always
wanted to be; and I should have known a long time ago
that Johnny was not in my future plans, because he was
gay; and gay men and Trans women do not mix sexually.
Johnny had taken all of his things; and left the keys to
the villa and apartment on the coffee table with a note.
I then picked up my phone and text Brian to let him
know that it is finally over, that Johnny has left and
taken all of his things; so, there was no chance of him
returning. He then texted me back asking if I was ok, to
which I replied I was fine and felt a lot better now that
Johnny had moved out.

I then had another text saying that he was on his way.
I moved over to the double doors overlooking the pool,
and just took a deep breath.

I had a double vodka and coke in my hand, as I admired
my home as I finally let go of my past. I then decided

that I was going to take a shower, as the day's heat and then excitement had got the better of me.

Whilst I was in the shower, I could not get the thoughts of Brian out of my mind; and in doing so I began to touch myself. Every time I touched myself in my special place, I thought of Brian more and wondered if he would accept me as a woman, or like Johnny would he be disappointed that I no longer had a cock as he had once tasted what my girly cock had. As the shower gel fell downwards towards my breasts, towards my vagina, I let my fingers slide over my pubic hair, the warmth of the water and the aroma of the shower gel aroused me even more, as it filled the room with its intoxication.

The wild rose and raspberry shower gel; filled my nostrils with its intense fragrance, as I envisaged Brian taking my flower for the very first time.

I then got out of the shower and dried myself off carefully, as I tried not to arouse myself again until Brian had arrived. I sat down on the bed, as I picked out a few trinkets from my jewellery box, then floating towards my dresser I picked out my newest of basque's.

It was about another thirty minutes when Brian turned up, as I heard the car pull onto the drive and heard the sound of the alarm being set. I stood up quickly, when I thought what on earth is he doing here so early, as I looked at my clock and realized it was now 6.30pm and thought how stupid it would look to him, if he walked in only to find that I was still in manner of attire that was purposely ready to go to bed.

I quickly fastened my basque; and fastened my stockings as I slipped into a little black number that I knew was always a winner. I then proceeded towards the front door,

where I smiled at him and said, '*Hi Brian.*'
I could not ignore the fact that he was still incredibly handsome; and still had a cute smile as he had already noticed when I gave him the once over as I checked him up and down.
By this time Brian had noticed I had been crying; and then he removed his hands from behind his back; and presented me with a large bouquet of roses which took me by surprise. Brian then reached up to me and gave me a kiss on my cheek, as he then said.

"*A beautiful woman like you; deserves beautiful flowers. Now Ruby, my sweet Ruby; it is over with now. You can finally live your life and not have to worry anymore. Come here Ruby, come here baby.*"

I then smiled at him, as I saw his eyes cast over my body, as I also saw something else begin to stir as I looked towards his loins, again looking at each other, I moved back into the hallway and asked Brian to come on in, as he kicked the door behind him so that it closed with a deafening bang. When we both got into the lounge, I began to arrange the roses into my best vase; and at that point Brian walked over to me and began to kiss me on the neck. I groaned, as I then backed up onto Brian, as I felt his throbbing erection touch me in the base of my ass.

"*So, you are in the mood to play already Brian? I can feel something sticking in my ass, you horny devil.*" I told him, as I teased him more by sliding my ass over his bulge.

"I certainly do Ruby. Do you know how long I have waited for this moment? I may be 50 Ruby; but I have the stamina of that of an 18 year old. I have waited all my life for you, and to be in this position without fear of interruption." He replied, now nibbling on my ear. *"Then enough talking, take me to bed Brian."* I told him, as I moved the vase to one side.

I took hold of Brian's hand, and led him towards the bedroom. I then began to walk over to him; and then just stood there as Brian came over to me with lustful looks. He stood behind me; and began to kiss my neck; as his hands touched my arms, where he gently stroked them. With my head tilted to one side, I offered him my neck fully as again he kissed and nibbled at my exposed neck and ear lobe.

Brian unzipped my dress and he let it slip off me as I stepped out of it, revealing to him my tightly fitted basque which pushed my breasts up towards him; as he placed his hands carefully over my body savouring every moment, as he found a way with his tongue that got me all hot and bothered. I then was led to the bed, where Brian told me to relax. He then knelt on the bed, as he undone his belt and zip letting them fall to the floor before he climbed onto the bed; now revealing his very large bulging package through his nice tight black boxers, where he then straddled me. He lay on top of me, as we both kissed one another as I began removing his tie and shirt.   This was the first time in a long time that I was able to fully admire my Brian, and not worry about anyone or anything that would spoil the moment. Standing six feet tall, and now having short cropped brown blonde hair, with a now average middle aged body with just the smallest of love handles, my eyes followed the shape of his body that I found I could now fully appreciate his large endowment of a ten-inch cock, nestled in the finest of a mousey brown blonde pubic hair. As we kissed each other, both our aromas filled the room, as the rose and raspberry, mingled with the sweet smell of his Armani cologne. Then being seduced by the intoxicating aroma of his cologne Brian then flipped me over onto my tummy, as he got behind me. Now being placed into the doggy position, Brian rubbed his hands over my back, as he gently kissed me, as his erection kept banging against my ass. I then reached behind me, and began to touch Brian's wet throbbing cock, as I urged him to take me. Thinking that Brian was going to fuck me up the ass, I raised myself slightly to accommodate him; but to my surprise, he positioned himself in between my legs, as he guided himself into my wet pussy. He slowly entered me, filling me up with his thick throbbing cock until I had taken all of him deep inside me.

I then slowly raised myself, still with Brian deep inside my pussy so that my moist back was pressing into his moist tummy. Brian then began kissing my neck as he caressed my breasts, squeezing my nipples until they were excitingly hard as he fucked me harder.

Moments later his body became as hard as rock, as he tensed himself up, and drove his cock deeper into me, as he exploded and filled me with his hot sticky juices. Then with a cry of pleasure, he loosened his grip for a moment; and then flipped me around so that my legs were now over his shoulders and my pussy was underneath him. He then thrust his dripping cock deeper into my pussy, as we both suddenly convulsed out of control. With both of us coming to orgasm at the same time and without hesitation, he wrapped his hands around his dripping erection, as he squeezed it harder, as I watched him still cumming over my pussy and tummy.

"Fuck me Brian; I have never known you to be like that. You are far better than any 18 year old, as I think you are positively a porn star. I have never seen anyone cum as much as you, let alone orgasm twice in a short time." I told him, as he still continued to shoot his juices over my pussy and tummy.
"Do you want to go again; because I can assure you, there is a lot more where that came from Ruby." He replied, with a big smile on his face.
"I sure do Brian; I have waited for you all my life to make love to me as a woman; not I no longer have to wait. I am all yours Brian, I am all yours." I told him, as he then lay back on top of me and kissed me on the neck and lips.

Again, we made love with each other, as his third orgasm, although it took longer it still triggered my own climax at the same level of intensity as his. I watched him fill me up and cum over my tummy, as he then let me straddle him; and he could see himself fucking his Ruby as he always dreamed, he would.
At the end of the third session, we were both pretty wacked with pleasure as every muscle in our bodies tensed up, until it subsided and again, we managed to compose ourselves and get out breath back. I then got up

off my Brian, and as I was looking for my dressing-gown I said to him.

"I have been waiting so long for this Brian; and I never dreamt in a million years, it would ever happen to me."
"So have I Ruby, I wanted you when I first saw you on the island. I wanted you so bad, but I was afraid in case you had either squared it up with Johnny; or you were happily married with another." He replied
"We have all the time in the world now Brian; and I will never let you go again." I told him.

As he got up, he looked at me and said.

"Miss Ruby, I want to make love to you like we were meant to; and I will never let you go."
"Brian, it is no longer Miss Ruby, please just call me Ruby as those days have long gone. I am not the same Ruby that you met all those years ago Brian, this is the real me now; and so we can clear a few things up, please remember that it is you who is the man, as I am all woman." I told him, now dismissing my previous life.
"Ok Ruby, I will remember that, now come on let's go out and eat." He told me, as the sexual workout had given him an appetite.

We both got dressed, and Brian hailed a cab to take us into town. There we ate at the finest restaurant, as we drank champagne like it was going out of fashion.
I just thought to myself at last my dreams have come true. I too have money in the bank, and a business, and a partner who is a surgeon. I am now living the high life, and it hasn't come quick enough, as all of this should

have happened a long time ago.

I did not miss Johnny, and I did not miss Roxy and all of her dramas, I was now happy with who I was. I was very happy that after so many agonising years, I had finally got my man; and that he was himself happy that we had rekindled what we once started back in the seventies.

I was also pleased that I finally had my family back, as I too felt as blessed as I could be.

All of those years I spent beating myself up, had finally paid dividend as everything came together just as I believed it would, although I never thought there would be casualties in the game of love.

I knew Johnny would go back to his sister Ellie; and somehow, I knew he would be alright, so I made a promise to myself that I would never speak his name again, as I removed all photographs of him and placed them in a trunk in the bedroom.

We stayed at that restaurant most of the night, as between us we must have spent a fortune. We got to know the owners and we made sure that there was champagne on the table so that their family could also join in with our celebrating. I then looked at Brian; and told him I think we should go back home. Brian said that he liked the sound of that, as this time when the word home was mentioned, he also knew that he was safe from confrontation. The owner called us a cab, and he told the driver that he would pay the fare, so we said our goodbyes and we headed back home.

When we got to the villa, I offered the keys to Brian, and he opened the doors. He looked at me, and then he picked me up as he carried me into the bedroom. As he placed me down on the bed, he got onto the end of it and slowly crept further up the bed as he kissed my ankles, then my knees, until he got to my mouth. With his body arched over mine, again he placed a kiss on my lips and then began kissing my breasts. With my legs now slightly apart, Brian then entered me as I gasped and told him that I loved him, now having him enter my vagina and not my ass, looking into his eyes as he looked at me and began fucking me gentle and not the usual roughness that he used to be. With him now inside me, he arched his body as he told me that he loved me too, as he made love to me yet again as a woman he so long desired. Everything had finally come together at last, as I felt complete as were making love, and for the first time I now felt all woman as Brian made love to me all through the night.

The next morning, I was woken up by Brian who had prepared breakfast and told me it was time to get up. I put on a dressing gown and tied my hair up, as I made my way to the dining area. I sat down as I had a mouthful of orange juice, as Brian brought over breakfast. Brian sat down next to me, and before we ate, he picked up his glass and raised it towards me, as I did the same when he then said.

"To the two of us Ruby; to a new life together, to a new beginning together; and to the most beautiful woman in the world."

"To us Brian; to our new life together, and to a new beginning; and to the most gorgeous man in the world."
I replied, as we looked over towards the beach and sea.

391

I then told him that he needs to give notice on his apartment, and he should move in with me as soon as he can. Brian was so humble, as he asked me if I really meant it. I assured him that I really meant it, and that I also did not want him to give up his job just yet.

He smiled at me and told me that he loved his job at the hospital, and he was not ready to retire himself just yet. He did however help me out with my business, and we had many special nights out together; then a casual walk along the prom as we headed back home.

It was a further two years before my parents moved out to the island, and with their previous visits they soon began to get on so well with Brian, that they soon started to call him son. Brian helped my parents find a suitable villa themselves, which overlooked the sea, and wit as only a short distance from where we were.

My mother helped out with my apartments, as dad helped me out when I needed some decorating doing, or some quick DIY jobs that I knew he could do quicker than the Canarian's.

On my afternoon off, when all the work and chores had been done, I would be seen shopping with my mother, as we both went for lunch in San Agustin, whilst dad and Brian would go golfing when he was not in surgery.

Mother and father had soon got their own circle of friends, from a few ex-pats who were in and around our quaint town of San Agustin. They also got to know a few of the traders, who had shops in the Yumbo centre; and often you could see mother stop and chat to them, before we headed off to do our usual things

But for sure, every Sunday we would stay traditional and we have a roast dinner; as that was one thing that my parents could never change about their new lifestyle, as they believed that Sundays were all about a roast dinner, and about bringing the family together.

'We all feel that we must make a change
to better ourselves…
and it is not for people to judge us.
For they should try and understand who we are
and accept us for the choices we make.'

©P W Matthews 2015

L - #0110 - 250321 - C0 - 210/148/21 - PB - DID3051966